HER DESERT KNIGHT

BY
JENNIFER LEWIS

Published in Great Britain 2014
by Mills & Boon, an imprint of Harlequin (UK) Limited,
Eton House, 18-24 Paradise Road, Richmond, Surrey, TW9 1SR

© 2014 Jennifer Lewis

ISBN: 978-0-263-91484-9

51-1114

Harlequin (UK) Limited's policy is to use papers that are natural, renewable and recyclable products and made from wood grown in sustainable forests. The logging and manufacturing processes conform to the legal environmental regulations of the country of origin.

Printed and bound in Spain
by CPI, Barcelona

Jennifer Lewis has been dreaming up stories for as long as she can remember and is thrilled to be able to share them with readers. She has lived on both sides of the Atlantic and worked in media and the arts before she grew bold enough to put pen to paper. She would love to hear from readers at jen@jenlewis.com. Visit her website at www.jenlewis.com.

For my sister Annabel

ACKNOWLEDGMENTS:

Many thanks to the readers who asked me for more stories about the Al Mansur brothers and fired my imagination to write them. Also thanks to my agent Andrea and the many people who read and improved those stories, especially my editors Demetria Lucas (book one), Diana Ventimiglia (book two), Charles Griemsman (book three).

One

Going to her favorite bookshop in Salalah was like stepping back into a chapter of *Arabian Nights*. To get there,
Dani had to walk through the local souk, past the piles
of carrots and cabbages, the crates of dates and figs,
winding her way through knots of old men wearing their
long dishdashas and turbans just as they must have done
a thousand years ago.

Then there was the store itself. The double doorway
of time-scarred wood was studded with big metal rivets,
like the entrance to a castle. Only a small section opened,
and she had to step over the bottom part of the door into
the smoky darkness of the shop. The smoke was incense,
eternally smoldering away in an antique brass burner
that hung in one corner, mingled with pipe smoke from
the elderly store owner's long, carved pipe. He sat in the
corner, poring over the pages of a thick, leather-bound
tome, as if he maintained the shop purely for his own
reading pleasure. It was entirely possible that the store
was a front of some kind, since there rarely seemed to
be any customers, but that didn't diminish Dani's enjoyment of its calming atmosphere.

The books were piled on the floor like the oranges
in the stalls outside. Fiction, poetry, treatises on mari-
time navigation, advice on the training of the camel: all

were in Arabic and nearly all were at least fifty years old
and bound in leather, darkened by the passage of many
greasy fingers over their smooth, welcoming surfaces.
She'd found several gems here, and always entered the
shop with a prickle of anticipation, like someone setting
out on a journey where anything could happen.

Today, as she stepped over the threshold and filled
her lungs with the fragrant air, she noticed an unfamiliar visitor in the picturesque gloom of the interior. The
light from one tiny, high window cast its diffuse glow
over the tall, broad-shouldered figure of a young man.

Dani stiffened. She didn't like the idea of a man in her
djinn-enchanted realm of magic books. She didn't like
men anywhere at all, lately, but she gave the shop owner a
pass as he was quiet and kind and gave her big discounts.

She resolved to slip past the stranger on her way to the
stack she'd started to investigate yesterday: a new pile
of well-thumbed poetry books the shop owner had pur-
chased at a bazaar in Muscat. She'd almost bought one
yesterday, and she'd resolved overnight that today she
wasn't leaving without it.

The interloper was incongruously dressed in Western
clothing—jeans and a white shirt, to be exact—with ex-
pensive-looking leather loafers on his feet. She eyed him
suspiciously as she walked past, then regretted it when
he glanced up. Dark blue eyes ringed by jet-black lashes
peered right into hers. He surveyed her down the length
of an aristocratic nose, and the hint of a smile tugged at
his wide, arrogant-looking mouth. A younger, stupider
Dani might have thought he was "cute," but she was not
so foolish now. She braced herself in case he had the
nerve to speak to her.

But he didn't. Slightly deflated, and kicking herself
for thinking that anyone would want to speak to her at

all, she headed for her familiar pile of books. Only to discover that the one she wanted was missing. She checked the stack twice. Then the piles on either side of it. In the dim, smoky atmosphere, it wasn't easy to read the faded spines, the gold-leaf embossing worn off by countless eager hands. Maybe she'd missed it.

Or maybe he was reading it.

She glanced over her shoulder, then jerked her head back when she discovered that the strange man was staring right at her. Alarm shot through her. Had he been watching her the whole time? Or had he just turned around at the exact same moment she had? She was annoyed to find her heart pounding beneath the navy fabric of her traditional garb.

"Are you looking for this book?" His low, velvety male voice made her jump, and she cursed herself for being so on edge.

He held out the book she'd been searching for. A 1930s edition of *Majnun Layla* by Persian poet Nizami Ganjavi, with a faded green leather binding and elaborate gold tooling.

"You speak English." The first words out of her mouth took her by surprise. She'd intended to say yes, but her brain short-circuited. She hadn't heard anyone speak English since she'd come back here from New Jersey three months ago. She'd begun to wonder if she'd ever use her hard-won language skills again.

He frowned and smiled at the same time. "Yes. I didn't even realize I was speaking English. I guess I've spent too much time in the States lately. Or maybe my gut instinct told me you speak it, too."

"I lived in the U.S. for a few years myself." She felt flustered. His movie-star looks were disconcerting, but she tried not to judge a book by its cover. She cleared

her throat. "And yes, I mean, that is the book I was looking for."

"What a shame. I was about to buy it." He still spoke
in English. His features and coloring looked Omani, but
his Western clothing and ocean-colored gaze gave him
a hint of exoticism. "You were here first." She shrugged,
and tried to look as if she didn't care.

"I think not. If you knew it was here and were looking
for it, clearly you were here first." Amusement danced in
his unusual blue eyes. "Have you read it?"

"Oh, yes. It's a classic. I've read it several times."

"What's it about?"

"It's a tragic love story." How could he not know that?
Maybe he didn't even read Arabic. He had a strange accent. British, maybe.

"Sometimes I think all love stories are tragic. Does
anyone really live happily ever after?"

"I don't know. My own experience hasn't been very
encouraging." As soon as she spoke she was shocked at
herself. She'd resolved to keep her private torments secret.

"Mine, either." He smiled slightly. "Maybe that's why
we like to read a tragic love story where everyone dies in
the end, so our own disastrous efforts seem less awful by
comparison." The light in his eyes was kind, not mock-
ing. "Did you come back here to get away from someone?"

"I did." She swallowed. "My husband—ex-husband.
I hope I never see him again." She probably shouldn't
reveal so much to a total stranger. Divorce was rare and
rather scandalous in Oman.

"Me, too." His warm smile relaxed her. "I live in the
States myself but I come to Oman whenever I need to
step off the carousel and feel some firm ground beneath

my feet. It's always reassuring how little has changed here while I've been gone."

"I found that alarming when I first came back. If it wasn't for the cars and cell phones we could still be in the Dark Ages. My dad and brothers don't like me leaving the house without a male relative to escort me. What a joke! After I lived in America for nearly nine years."

He smiled. "The culture shock can be jarring. I've been living in L.A. for the last four years. It's nice to meet someone else who's in the same predicament. Would you like to go down the road for a coffee?"

She froze. A man asking you out for coffee was a proposition. "I don't think so."

"Why not? Do you think your father and brothers would disapprove?"

"I'm sure they would." Her heart pounded beneath her conservative dress. Some mad reckless part of her wanted to go with him and drink that coffee. Luckily she managed to wrestle the urge under control.

"Let me at least buy you this book." He turned and headed for the shop owner. She'd forgotten all about him, ensconced in his own world in the farthest corner of the store. He showed no sign of having heard their conversation.

She wanted to protest and insist on buying the book herself, but by the time she pulled herself together the store owner was already wrapping it in brown paper and it would have been awkward. She didn't want to make a fuss.

"Thank you." She accepted the package with a pinched smile. "Perhaps I should buy you a coffee to thank you for your generous present." The book wasn't cheap. And if she were paying, it wasn't a date, right? She was twenty-seven years old. Hardly a blushing girl. She could share a coffee with a fellow English speaker to pass a dull afternoon. Her pulse accelerated as she waited for his response, torn between hoping he'd say yes, and praying that he'd say no.

"That would be very kind of you." His gaze wasn't very wolfish. He couldn't help being so handsome. Women probably misinterpreted his perfectly ordinary gestures of friendliness out of wishful thinking. She wasn't so foolish.

They stepped out into the fierce afternoon sun and walked down a long block to a row of modern shops, including a fairly new café. It had hip westernized décor, which was strangely reassuring and made her feel less like she was about to commit a massive social faux pas.

He pulled out her chair and she settled herself into it, arranging her traditional dress. Then she realized that she didn't even know his name. She glanced about, wanting to make sure no one could overhear her. The attendant was gathering menus by the bar, far enough away to be out of earshot. "I'm Daniyah…." She hesitated, her ex-husband's last name—McKay—on the tip of her tongue. She suddenly decided not to use it anymore. But using her father's last name, Hassan, which she'd given up when she married against his will, didn't feel right either. "But you can call me Dani."

"Quasar." He didn't say his surname, either. Maybe it was better that way. They were casual acquaintances, nothing more. And he was even more fearfully good-looking in real daylight, with a strong jaw and tousled hair that added to his rakish appearance.

She glanced away quickly. Her blood heated just looking at this man. "I'll have a coffee with milk."

He ordered, in expert Arabic, without looking at the

menu. "Me, too. Though I suppose we should be drinking it black, with some dates, now that we're back in Oman."

She laughed. There was something about the way he said it that made her feel like his coconspirator. "It's terrible. I find myself longing for a burrito or a foot-long sub."

"Are you going back to America soon?"

His question took her by surprise. "I don't know. I'm not sure what I'm doing." It was a relief to be honest. Maybe because he was a stranger, she felt she could let down her mask a little. "I came here in a hurry and now I seem to be becalmed."

"Becalmed?" He tilted his head and surveyed her with those striking gray-blue eyes.

"It's an old-fashioned term for a ship that's stuck out at sea because there's no wind to fill her sails." Maybe Quasar was the wind she'd been waiting for? This afternoon was already the most excitement she'd had since her arrival three months ago.

"So you need a bracing gust to set you on your way again."

"Something like that." She let the gleam in his eyes light a little spark of…something in her chest. The way he looked at her suggested that he found her attractive. Was that even possible? People used to tell her she was pretty, but her ex made her feel like the ugliest loser in the world. Right now she felt odd and frumpy in the loose dress and pants she'd worn to look modest and tasteful, but Quasar didn't even seem to notice it. He related to her as easily as if she were in her familiar jeans and T-shirt. "Why are you here?" she asked.

"Visiting my brother and his family. And trying to reconnect with my culture. I don't want to stay away too long and have my roots shrivel away." His wry grin was disarming. Just looking at him, seeing the way his white shirt and jeans showed off a powerful physique, was stirring feelings she'd almost forgotten existed.

"If you want to reconnect with your roots, you should wear a dishdasha." She could barely picture him in the long, white traditional garment, with its knotted sash and ornamental dagger at the waist.

He raised a brow. "Do you think I'd look better in one?" He was flirting.

She shrugged. "No. I'm only wearing this because I don't want to scandalize my family. I've done that enough already."

Curiosity flared in his gaze, as she'd predicted. "You don't look like the type to cause a scandal."

"Then I guess my disguise is working. I'm trying to fit in and fly under the radar."

"You're too beautiful to ever do that." He spoke softly, so the waiter couldn't hear him, but his words shocked her. She blinked at his bold flattery.

"Even traditional clothing allows your face to show," he said. "You'd have to hide that to go unnoticed."

"Or just never leave the house, which is what my father would prefer. He has no idea I'm out here right now. He thinks I'm at home writing poetry in my childhood bedroom. I'm twenty-seven and divorced, for crying out loud, and I have to sneak around like a naughty teenager."

Quasar laughed and looked as if he were going to say something, but just then the waiter brought their coffees. Dani watched Quasar's sensual mouth as he sipped his drink and she cursed the shimmer of heat that flared under her voluminous clothing.

"I think you are ready for that breeze to catch your sails," he said at last.

"I don't know what I'm ready for, to be totally honest. My divorce just became final."

He lifted his coffee cup. "Congratulations."

She giggled. "That sounds so wrong, but it does feel like something to celebrate."

"We all make mistakes. I'm thirty-one and I've never been married. That has to be a mistake of some kind. At least that's what my two happily married brothers keep insisting."

"They think you should find someone and settle down?"

"Absolutely. In fact I'm not sure they'll let me leave Oman until I'm legally wed."

She laughed. Since his brothers would not be likely to encourage him to marry a divorcée, this put them on a "friends only" footing that was rather reassuring. She could admire him without worrying that anything could come of it. But sadness trickled through her at the realization that she was damaged goods, and safely off-limits. "How do you feel about the idea?"

"Petrified." He looked rueful. "If I was cut out for marriage, I'd probably have plunged into it by now."

"You just haven't met the right person yet."

"That's what they keep telling me."

"It's better to wait for the right person than to have to extricate yourself after you've chosen the wrong one." He must have no shortage of women trailing after him. In fact two girls had sat down at a table near them and she could see them glancing over and whispering to each other.

Then again, maybe they were whispering about her. She didn't know how much had gotten out about her… situation. When she'd first arrived she assumed that no one would remember her or care what she'd been doing, but she'd forgotten what a small town Salalah could be, at least when it came to gossip.

She stiffened, and sipped her coffee. "What kind of business are you in?"

"Any kind of business that grabs my attention." His gaze stayed riveted on her face. The way he stared at her was disconcerting. She wasn't used to it. "I love to jump into a new field and be one of the first to stake out unknown territory."

"You make it sound like mountain climbing."

"Sometimes it is. Three-dimensional printing technology was my most recent fascination. Printers that can render a solid object. It's going to revolutionize manufacturing. Just imagine, you could design and print out a new pair of shoes right in your own home."

"That sounds fun."

"The technology is even being used to print human tissue for operations like skin grafts."

"Very cool."

"That's what I thought, so I invested in a start-up and helped them develop the technology. I just sold my share."

"Why? It sounds like a fascinating industry."

"I was ready to move on. Try something new."

"You're restless."

"Always."

So that's why he wasn't married. He got bored easily, then moved on to someone new and more exciting.

"What do you do?" He leaned close enough that she imagined she could smell his scent. But she couldn't. The aroma of coffee was too strong. Why was she thinking about the way he smelled? She must be attracted to him. That would explain the quickening of her pulse and the way she was growing warm all over.

This was breaking news. She didn't think she'd ever be attracted to a man again. At least that part of her was still alive, not that it was likely to do her much good.

His eyes glittered with amusement and for a frightening second she wondered if he could read her mind. "Is your occupation a secret? Do you work for the CIA?"

Her face heated. She'd been so busy noticing her brain's reaction to him that she'd forgotten he asked a question. "I'm an art historian, and most recently worked at Princeton. The ancient Near East is my area of expertise."

"Am I right in guessing that Oman counts as the Near East?"

She nodded. "It's a large area, and was the seat of many great civilizations."

"Mesopotamia, Sumer, the ziggurats at Ur-Nammu." Tiny smile lines formed at the corners of his wide, sensual mouth.

"Most people think of ancient Egypt."

"Do I sound like a show-off?"

"A little." She fought a smile. His arrogance and confidence had an effortless quality that was oddly appealing. "But I won't hold it against you."

"Thanks. You should see the museum my brother's put together. He built a hotel on the site of an old Silk Road city."

"That sounds like an art historian's nightmare."

"You'd like it! There wasn't much left, just a few stumps of walls out in the middle of an old oil field, and he's recreated it as a luxury retreat, preserving as much as possible of the original."

"Your whole family sounds rather unusual."

He laughed. "Maybe we are. We all march to our own beat. The archaeologists who excavated the site found some pottery and small figurines. You might find them interesting."

"I'm sure I would. Do you know what era they're from?"

"No clue. Maybe we can visit the place together. It's only a short drive outside Salalah. We could go tomorrow."

She froze. There was no way she could go for a drive anywhere with a total stranger. Even a seemingly handsome, charming and educated one. She didn't really know anything about him. For all she knew, he could be making everything up. And besides, her father and brothers would forbid it. "I can't."

"Maybe another time, then. Let me give you my phone number."

She glanced at the two girls at the nearby table. Their dark eyes were still darting to her and her companion. They'd be sure to notice. But what harm could come of it if she never called him?

Her heart pounded while she watched him write the number in an assured hand on the back of the blue paper napkin. "I'm staying at my brother's hotel here in Salalah. It's right on the beach. Where do you live?"

She swallowed. This was getting dangerously personal. "Not far." No one knew she was here, which was by design. "I really should be getting back." She shoved the napkin into her pocket.

"I'll walk you home."

"Oh, no. There's no need. You stay here and relax." She put down some cash to pay for the coffee. He thrust it back to her with a shocked expression, and she decided—once again—to avoid a scene by accepting his hospitality. "Thanks for the coffee." He rose when she did and for a split second she had an insane thought he might try to kiss her. Her whole body braced as adrenaline rushed through her. Then he thrust out his hand and she shook it. "And thanks for the book."

"Call me. I'd like to go see the artifacts with you."

She picked up her new book, then turned and walked out of the café as fast as she could. Most likely the tension and excitement was all in her head—and her body—but she couldn't be sure. Either way, it was exhilarating and she felt more alive than she had in months. Years, even. And all because of a man she had no business even talking to.

She walked home quickly. Her dad wouldn't get home for a while but she wanted to arrive before her brothers came back from their respective schools. Her younger brother, Khalid, usually came straight home to do his homework, but her older brother, Jalil, often stayed late in the technical college library to pore over the designs for his latest engineering project. She liked to make them a snack before they returned, but today she wouldn't have time. In fact she barely had time to put her new book in her bedroom and shove the napkin with Quasar's number into a drawer before the front door opened and Khalid crashed in and flung his book bag down in the hallway before heading into the kitchen.

"I took a nap," she fibbed, as her brother's eyes scanned the empty kitchen counters. Maybe they were growing too dependent on her. She didn't plan to be here forever.

"A nap? In the middle of the day? You're going soft."

What would he say if she revealed that she'd let a strange man buy her a book—and a coffee? He'd probably question her sanity.

She read her new book for a while before she heard her father's distinctive rap on the door. Even though the door was open he liked someone to let him in. She pulled back the latch, forcing a bright smile. "Hello, Father." She kissed his cheek. As usual he brushed it off as if she were a fly. "How was your day?"

"Same as usual." His gruff voice and glum expression rarely softened. "Too many fools in this business. Always looking for new cheaper ways to do things that have worked just fine for decades." An engineer, he was often irritated by new technologies and methods. He asked her brother about his schoolwork, as usual. He never asked her about her day, which was a plus today since she couldn't have said anything truthful about it.

"Help Faizal prepare an excellent supper tonight, dear." Faizal was the cook who came over to make dinner every night. Her father fixed his beady gaze on her. "A friend of mine will be joining us." He looked her up and down in a way that made her stomach muscles clench.

"That's great. Is he a friend from work?"

"Not from the firm, no. He's a supplier. Rivets and nuts." He squinted at her for a moment. "Wear a color that suits your complexion more."

She glanced down at the navy blue she'd worn all day. "Why?"

"That blue is rather draining on you. Something brighter would be more attractive."

Dani stood speechless. This was the first time her father had expressed an opinion on her clothes. Was he planning to set her up with his friend? She wanted to ask but didn't dare.

She'd assumed he saw her as such a social pariah that it wouldn't be worth the bother of trying to marry her off again. Maybe he'd grown tired of having her under his roof and hoped to find someone who would take her off his hands. She hurried to her room, wondering if she could find an even less flattering color to wear.

Quasar hadn't thought she looked washed out in the blue. The way he'd looked at her had made her feel as if she'd been glowing like a spring flower. His daring gaze made her feel desirable—and it made her feel desire. The memory of it made her blood hum.

Alone in her room she let herself dream about him for a moment. What would it be like to accompany him to his brother's hotel/museum or whatever it was? People had said her ex-husband was good-looking—she'd thought so herself until she grew to understand his true character—but he had nothing on Quasar's dramatic features and playful charm.

Of course, the man she'd just met was undoubtedly used to women drooling over him. He was probably shocked that she refused his suggestion that they meet again. If she were in America, without traditional rules to consider, would she have said yes?

No. She had to be honest. She wouldn't have accepted an invitation from a strange man who gave every impression of being a playboy dilettante of the worst kind. Let him go charm someone else into making a fool of herself with him. Dani Hassan wasn't making any more mistakes in the man department.

Changing into a dark forest-green dress with silver edging, she went back to the kitchen to help the cook prepare a traditional chicken dish with rice and vegetables. She wasn't sure how the elderly Faizal felt about her assistance—Dani suspected he'd just as soon she butt out and leave him to his business—but joining him in the kitchen gave her an activity to look forward to, when there was precious little to do around the house all day.

She arranged the meal in the dining room, on the carpeted floor, Omani style, with more attention to detail than usual—artfully folded napkins, the prettier glasses—and waited with grim curiosity for her father's "friend" to arrive. When he finally did, she hung back and waited in her room with headphones on, pretending to listen to music, until her brothers had been introduced and one of them was sent for her. The sight of her prospective beau made her heart sink.

"Daniyah, I'm delighted to introduce you to Mr. Samir Al Kabisi." He was at least sixty, with thinning gray hair combed over a freckled scalp and a bulbous nose like a misshapen potato. His eyes were yellowish and his teeth crooked as he spoke the traditional greeting.

He didn't extend his hand, so she bowed her head and attempted a smile. Did her dad seriously consider this man a potential partner for her? He must have a very low opinion of her worth.

On the other hand, maybe she had too high an opinion of herself. She didn't know this man at all. He could be perfectly nice and here she was judging him entirely on his looks—or lack of them. Wouldn't a kind and sensible man with a homely appearance be better than a gorgeous and dashing jerk?

She'd prefer the company of a good book.

"Do come in and have some coffee." She kept her smile fixed while she served the fragrant hot drink in the ornate brass urn they kept for visitors. Her father engaged their guest in riveting conversation about the nuts and rivets industry, and he responded with brief comments in the rasp of a heavy smoker.

Dani wished she could go hide in her room. They stumbled through dinner with innocuous conversation about the city and a recent burst of new construction. After dinner her father leaned forward and pinned her with his gaze. "Mr. Al Kabisi was widowed seven years ago."

"I'm so sorry for your loss." Uh-oh. Seemed like her father was finally getting to the point.

"He's mourned his wife for many years but I've persuaded him that perhaps it is time to set the shroud of grief aside."

Dani swallowed.

"Boys, come out into the garden with me for a few minutes." Her brothers looked perplexed for a moment, especially Khalid, who probably wanted to go play with his Xbox, but they got with the program and followed her dad out of the room.

Alone in the room with this man more than twice her age, Dani had no idea what to say. He stood and cleared his throat. "I see no shame in a woman divorcing a man who is cruel to her."

Her heart clenched. He must know her humiliating story. "That's kind of you." Now what was she supposed to say? She did see considerable shame in marrying a man old enough to be her father, whom she had less than nothing in common with, out of desperation. And she had no intention of doing so.

"I own my own business and my house. My three sons live and work in Muscat with their families, so I am all alone here. My income is—"

A desperate need to interrupt his sales pitch overcame her and she rose to her feet. "You're very kind but I really don't think—"

He rose, too, with considerable difficulty since they were sitting on the floor. His eyes bulged. "I am still potent." His fetid breath stung her nostrils. "So have no fear that you will be neglected."

Her dinner churned in her stomach. "I'm not ready to marry again. It's too soon. I'm still…recovering." She'd be in permanent recovery if this were the kind of prospect available to her.

At that exact moment she resolved to throw caution to the wind and take Quasar up on his invitation.

Two

Quasar emerged from the warm water of the pool with chlorine-blurred eyes. Sun shone on the sandstone surfaces of the elegant hotel buildings, and a light breeze ruffled the rows of majestic palm trees.

"Your phone's ringing," Celia, his brother Salim's wife, called from beside the pool, where she was relaxing with Sara, the wife of his brother Elan. They'd just eaten a leisurely poolside breakfast and were planning a day of relaxation on the nearby beach. Quasar was soaking wet and bouncing his three-year-old niece, Hannah, on his shoulders. "I doubt it's anything important. I'm taking a break from business."

"Throw me!" Little Hannah could yell surprisingly loud for such a small human.

"I can't. You can't swim." She'd watched him tossing her cousin and was desperate to join in the fun. He ducked down and almost dunked her, then rose up fast, making her scream.

"You're so good with kids. You should have some." Sara sipped her nonalcoholic cocktail. She was pregnant with her third child.

"Nonsense. I just need to spend more time with you guys. I think this is the first time we've all been together

since Salim's wedding. I'm not going to let that happen
again."

Salim and Celia lived in Salalah, with their children
Kira and Basia. This hotel was the headquarters for his
chain of luxurious resorts throughout the region. Elan
and Sara lived in Nevada, where they ran their thriving
fuel exploration business while raising Hannah and their
son, Ben. Quasar was usually jetting around cooking up
projects and it was rare for them all to make the time to
relax. For the last decade he'd been so busy starting businesses and partying hard that he hadn't had time to get
bored. Now he was beginning to think he'd missed out
on something. Something big.

He didn't even have a permanent address right now.
He'd sold his L.A. penthouse for a profit too good to refuse, and his worldly goods were in a storage unit near
Hollywood. He'd recently bought a farmhouse in the hills
near Salalah, but it had needed months of renovation so
he'd barely spent any time there.

"It's ringing again." Celia peered at his phone, which
sat on the table next to her. "Same number. Want me to
get it for you?"

"Okay."

She picked up his phone. "Quasar's phone. Celia
speaking." Then she frowned. "They hung up." She lifted
a brow. "I hope I didn't scare off one of your girlfriends."

He swung his niece around until she shrieked loud
enough to pierce his eardrums. "I don't have any girlfriends." Then he froze.

Dani.

What if she'd decided to call him, and now a woman
answered his phone? "Let's go dry you off, kid." He carried his niece to the steps and climbed out, dripping onto

the sandstone tiles. He dried his hands on his towel and snatched up his phone.

Celia leaned toward Sara. "I think he does have a girl-friend or two that he's worried about."

He didn't recognize the number, but it looked local. He called it, and listened while it rang.

"Hello?" a shy, thin voice answered.

"This is Quasar. You just called my phone." He didn't want to say her name in case it wasn't her. He'd made that mistake before.

"Hi. It's Dani." She hesitated, possibly wondering about the woman who'd answered his phone.

"I'm so glad you called." He walked along the edge of the pool, away from his sisters-in-law. He could feel their eyes on him. "I was hoping you would. That was my sister-in-law Celia who answered."

"Oh." She sounded relieved. "I'd like to go see the museum pieces with you, if you're still interested."

"Absolutely. Is this afternoon good?" He didn't want to wait and take a chance that she'd change her mind.

"Okay."

"Excellent. If you give me your address, I'll come pick you up."

She told him that she preferred to meet him outside the vegetable stalls at the end of the street with the café. Apparently she didn't want him coming to her house. And she had to be home by four, at the latest. It was all starting to sound intriguingly cloak-and-dagger.

"Sure, I'll be there at noon." His blood pumped a little faster at the prospect of seeing her again. He wondered if she'd wear the elegant traditional attire she'd had on yesterday, or something more Western. He was curious about her figure. He could already tell she was slim, but he had no idea about the cut of her hips, the shape of her legs, or the curve of her bosom. There was something to be said for that kind of mystery.

Still, he promised himself that he wasn't going to make even the slightest hint of a move on her unless she showed signs of strong interest. He was a guest here in Oman and although he didn't remember too much about the local customs, he knew that toying with a woman's affections was a total no-no.

Unfortunately that didn't dampen his enthusiasm one bit.

"Did I hear you say that you're meeting someone this afternoon?" Sara asked. She was smoothing sunblock on her arm. "I thought we were doing a barbecue on the beach."

"Something came up." He tried not to reveal his excitement.

His willowy sister-in-law Celia tilted her head. "Is she very beautiful?"

"How do you know it's not a dull business meeting?" He rubbed himself with the towel.

"The look in your eyes." She smiled, but raised one of her slender brows, too. "Those dangerous blue eyes where a woman is likely to drown in passion."

"I suspect most women are better swimmers than you think." He swatted six-year-old Ben with a towel as he ran by. "And as it happens I'm taking her to see the restored oasis that you created." Celia had first come to Oman as the landscape designer for the project. "She's a historian specializing in this region so I think she'll be interested in the artifacts you found."

"I bet she will. Something tells me you don't want to turn this into a family expedition where we all meet her."

He smiled. "Not yet. I only just met her myself. I don't want to scare her off."

"Very sensible. Though maybe she should be a little scared. The press coverage from your latest shenanigans hasn't even died down yet. Laura was creating a stir on Twitter this morning talking about her broken heart."

Ouch. Meeting Dani had shoved his most recent girlfriend out of his mind. Unfortunately she was still in a lot of other people's minds since she was a well-known actress with a talent for self-promotion. "I promise I didn't really break her heart. She broke it all by herself. She's one of those people who are in love with an impossible ideal of love. I don't think anyone could make her happy."

"In love with love?" Celia laughed.

Sara wandered over and sat down next to Celia on one of the elegant cushioned chaises that surrounded the pool. The shade of a nearby palm tree kept the sun off her face as she settled in. "Who's in love?"

"Everyone's in love with Quasar. It's very trying for him."

Sara shrugged and pulled off her T-shirt to reveal a turquoise bikini. "Not me. I'm still in love with Elan."

Quasar draped his towel over the back of a chair and flexed his shoulders until they cracked. "And so you should be. He's much more reliable than me." His stolid, workaholic brother had hired Sara as his secretary and was suitably appalled when he fell in love with her.

"Nor me. I still love Salim." Celia said it while looking at her husband, his oldest brother, who, incongruously dressed in a dark gray pinstripe suit, had just walked up to her and kissed her on the cheek.

Quasar watched in mock amazement. "We can tell. I never would have thought I'd see the mighty Salim indulge in public displays of affection."

"The right woman can transform any one of us. Most likely when we least expect it." Salim spoke with the quiet assurance of a prophet, his arms draped around his beautiful wife's neck. "Even you."

Quasar laughed. "Don't be so sure."

"He has a date this afternoon," Celia said into her husband's ear.

Salim straightened up. "Tell me she's kidding."

"It's nothing to worry about. We both spoke English so we struck up a conversation."

"Where?" Salim's dark, penetrating eyes narrowed. Quasar drew himself taller under their accusing stare.

"A local bookshop."

Salim stared at him while Elan jogged up, looking muscular and athletic as usual. "Quasar is the only man I know who can go out to buy a book and come back with a woman. Even in Oman."

"I hardly came back with her in my pocket. She was interesting, that's all. I have no intention of indulging in anything but conversation with her."

Elan laughed. "I'm sure you've said that before."

"Have a little faith in me." Quasar grabbed Kira, Salim and Celia's oldest, around the waist and swung her up onto his shoulders. "Kira has faith in me, don't you?"

"What's faith?" Kira lisped both words, looking confused.

"When you believe in something without having actual proof."

Kira stared at him for a moment. "Like a fairy."

"Yes. Like a fairy."

Kira pushed her lip out. "I don't believe in fairies."

Quasar couldn't help laughing as he set her down. "Thanks for nothing."

Salim crossed his arms, looking sensible and invincible as ever in his suit. "Well said, Kira. An Al Mansur prefers some empirical evidence." His stern features softened. "Would you like to come help Daddy in the office? I have some papers that need coloring in."

"Yes please!"

Quasar stared after Salim and Kira, shaking his head, as his *über*-serious older brother walked off, hand in hand with the little girl he hadn't even known existed until she was two.

"I've never seen Salim so happy. Nor you, Elan."

"We've shared our secrets, brother. It's all about finding the right woman."

"And managing not to fire her or drive her away." Sara winked.

Quasar thought for a moment. "There's a theme here. You and Celia were both working for my brothers. Maybe I need to hire someone," he teased.

Sara cocked her head. "And get her pregnant by mistake. Don't forget that happened to both of us, as well."

"At least that's one thing I can't be accused of."

"Yet," said Celia, smoothing sunblock onto her long legs with a wry smile. "Be careful. Obviously Al Mansur men are very potent."

"Like I said, we're just going to talk. She's an Omani. There's no question of us getting naked without elaborate negotiations involving goats and camels."

"That's a relief, then." Celia leaned toward him and whispered. "Still, take a condom with you."

"Sister, you shock me."

She patted his arm. "Just speaking from experience."

Dani arrived at the fruit-and-vegetable market a full ten minutes before noon. She didn't want to take a chance of getting held up and missing their meeting. She busied herself looking over the stalls full of fragrant limes, garlic and bright piles of carrots. Young children darted around their mother's legs, making a game of tagging each other with their blue plastic shopping bags. She was trying to look busy testing the freshness of oranges at a citrus stall when something told her to look up.

Her gaze fell on Quasar, striding along the dusty street, chin high, gaze fixed intently on her. Dressed in white linen pants and shirt, he looked as cool and fresh as a tall glass of water.

She braced herself, hoping he wouldn't draw attention to them by calling out her name. She put down the orange and walked to meet him, keeping her gaze averted.

Luckily he was discreet. "Good afternoon," he said quietly. Her eyes wandered to his lips, and imagined them kissing her hello. Which mercifully didn't happen.

"Good afternoon. Almost afternoon. We're both early." Her heart fluttered with excitement, which was silly since she barely knew this man. The sun had kissed his skin a shade darker since yesterday, making his incongruous blue eyes shine even brighter. Even white teeth glittered in his wolfish smile. He looked like trouble. If she had any sense she'd make up an excuse and run for home right now.

But she didn't.

"My car is parked around the corner." He seemed as if he were about to thread his arm through hers, or put his hand at her waist, but he hesitated, aware of the conservative local customs. The unmade gesture ratcheted up the tension between them. Her body hummed with both the desire to be touched and the fear of it. She walked beside him self-consciously as he led her to a silver Mercedes, already covered in a fine film of inevitable dust, and opened the passenger door for her. "I'm so glad you're coming out to the resort. I haven't been there since my brother Salim's wedding."

"I bet it was spectacular."

"Oh, it was. Salim doesn't do anything by halves."

"I bet you don't, either." She snuck a glance at his bold profile as he pulled out onto the road.

"I do tend to throw myself into things."

"Until you grow bored with them." She regretted the words as soon as she'd said them. It sounded like she was scolding him. "I'm sorry. I shouldn't have said that."

"Except that you're right." He shone those fierce blue eyes on her. "I have been accused of having a short attention span. I prefer to think that there are just so many things to do that I can only devote so much time to each one."

No doubt he felt the same way about women. He could never pursue a proper relationship with her since she was a divorcée and wouldn't meet his obviously demanding brothers' criteria for wife material. On the other hand, he might have no qualms about having an affair with her. She had to be careful to resist his charms.

They drove through a cultivated grove of date palms, then out of the city into the desert. She snuck furtive glances at him while he drove, taking in the sharp cut of his aristocratic features, and the sensual curve of his mouth. Resisting his charms might take some doing and she'd better take the resisting seriously since her heart was still in repair mode from her one and only serious relationship. The last thing she needed was to get it bruised or broken again by this man.

She resolved to keep her eyes focused out the window. The desert landscape was hypnotically minimalist, with its subtle colors and bold blue sky. The fog-shrouded mountains rose up ahead of them, and the landscape changed dramatically as they drove up into the lush green oasis of plant and bird life that made Salalah a tourist destination during the annual rainy season. Right now it was June, dry and sunny, in between the spring rains and the summer downpours that got underway in July.

Quasar kept the conversation rolling with no apparent effort. They chattered about the lifestyle differences between Oman and America, and the bond deepened between them as they agreed that it was hard to move from one country to the other without severe culture shock.

"So you haven't really lived in Oman at all."

"I haven't lived here permanently since my mom died. My dad packed Elan and me off to boarding school overseas. I was young enough to adapt easily. I never really looked back."

"You didn't miss your family."

"I didn't miss my father. He was very strict and kind of mean. I guess I'm not the type to get hung up looking for Daddy's approval. I made friends and moved on."

"And you've been moving on ever since."

He turned to her. "You think my nomadic lifestyle is the result of childhood psychological trauma?" He sounded serious, but she saw a twinkle in his eye.

She shrugged. "I don't know." She wondered what depths lay beneath his cocky exterior. Was there a wounded little boy craving approval and love? "Where is home for you?"

He shot her a glance with those piercing blue eyes. "Good question. Until recently it was L.A., but I just sold my condo there. Right now the only place I own is a house out in the desert here. I don't know if I'd call it home since I just had it renovated, but I bought it as a place to put down some roots and reconnect with my heritage, so maybe I'm heading in the right direction."

"Or the wrong direction." She laughed. "Do you really think Oman is your home now, or are you more comfortable in the United States? I feel more of a stranger here these days than I did in New Jersey. Moving around the world hasn't made my life easier."

"How did you end up in America when your family is still here?"

"My story's not so different from yours. I was sent to live with my aunt in New Jersey when my mother died. The idea was that I would go to college there then come back and work in my father's engineering firm while pursuing a suitable husband. I don't think it occurred to my father that I could just switch majors and stay there."

"Did he mind?"

"He went ballistic when I told him I wasn't coming back to Oman. It took me a long time to pluck up the courage to admit that I'd majored in art history instead of engineering. Since I paid the bill myself with an inheritance from my mom he didn't find out until it was too late."

She saw a smile tilt the edge of Quasar's mouth. "So you're a bit of a rebel."

"Only a very tiny bit."

"I wonder." He gave her a mysterious look.

She had been a rebel in choosing to chart her own course in life. The fact that she'd been blown right off it and ended up back here again made her wonder about her choices. She planned on sticking closer to the straight and narrow from now on. A degree in engineering certainly would present a lot more employment opportunities than her currently useless art history Ph.D.

"We're nearly there. It's called Saliyah, after my sister-in-law Celia, who designed the grounds and ensnared the heart of my brother Salim."

"That's so romantic." They turned on to a side road in

the desert. Spreading date palms cropped up to line the desolate road and cast lush shade over its dusty surface.

She gasped at the sight of a large animal underneath a nearby tree. "Look, a camel."

Quasar laughed. "Salim's always complaining about them. They eat his expensive landscaping. I figure he should just consider them part of the scenery and worth supporting. This place has been attracting a lot of visitors from overseas and they eat that stuff up."

The road led up to a high mud-brick wall with an elaborately carved arch. They entered and drove around a large circular fountain, where moving water sparkled like diamonds in the hot midday sun. Quasar helped her out of the car and it was whisked away by a valet while she blinked and adjusted to the bright light. They walked across a smooth courtyard of inlaid sandstone into a shady lobby that looked like the throne room of an ancient palace. Colorful mosaics covered the walls and lush seating arrangements were clustered around impressive botanical specimens. The guests were an interesting mix of glamorous Omanis and other Arabs, their traditional garb accented with Chanel sunglasses and Fendi handbags, and chic Europeans showing a lot of carefully suntanned skin. Waiters served coffee and dates, and the scent of rose petals filled the air.

"Would you like some coffee, or do you want to get right to the good stuff?"

She glanced about, feeling awkward and out of place. She didn't belong here among these stylish and confident members of the international elite. "I'd like to see the museum."

"I suspected you would." He shot her a smile that made her blood pump faster. "Follow me." She walked across the elegant foyer, trying to keep her eyes from tracking the lithe roll of his hips in too obvious a manner.

Sexual magnetism radiated from him like an exotic scent. Women's eyes swiveled to him from all directions, and it was all she could do not to glare at them. As if he were even hers to be jealous about! She felt their critical gaze on her, too. No doubt they wondered what a fine specimen of manhood like Quasar was doing with a mousy nobody like her.

Quasar led her out through a grand arch into a formal garden with a trickling fountain. Romantic-looking couples sat on upholstered sofas, chatting under the shade of the exotic plants. For an instant she imagined sitting there with him, just enjoying the afternoon. But he would hardly romance her in front of the employees at his brother's hotel.

Was he attracted to her? It was hard to imagine that someone like Quasar, whom almost any woman—including the wealthy, beautiful, famous and brilliant—would find desirable, would be interested in her. But if he weren't, why did he invite her here?

Quasar waited for her to pass him when they reached the path to the museum, but she hesitated, uncertain. "This is it." He gestured at the carved wood door, almost hidden by flowering bushes.

Dani peered at the door with a sparkle of excitement in her eyes. Today she wore a traditional Omani getup in a rose shade that brought out the roses in her cheeks and lips. He hadn't noticed yesterday what a mobile and sensual mouth she had. "It's almost as if they didn't want people to discover the treasures inside."

"Maybe they don't. I suspect they're more interested

in selling them expensive massages." He smiled. "Let's see if it's open."

He tried the handle. She played with her headscarf, almost nervous. What was she afraid of? Being alone with him in a cool, darkened room filled with antiques?

Hmm. If she knew his reputation she'd do well to be afraid. But she couldn't know anything about him. They hadn't exchanged last names.

He tried the brass handle and the door creaked open, sending a rush of air-conditioned air toward them.

The room was dimly lit, with spotlights shining down on a few key pieces, mostly ornately carved silver.

She walked right past those to some dull-colored pots displayed on a shelf against the far wall. "These are ancient," she breathed, and she rushed forward to examine the closest one. "Two thousand years old at least. Back when this area was a pit stop along the Silk Road."

The same color as the mud-brick walls, the pottery didn't look that exciting to Quasar. Still, Dani's exuberance was contagious.

"Everything here was found buried beneath the sand at the site. Celia says the oasis was in use for thousands of years."

"Camel trains would come through Salalah before making the long trek up through the desert toward Jerusalem." Dani wheeled around, and headed for a display case filled with silver jewelry. "Look at these pieces. They're exquisite."

He examined the big heavy silver bracelets and necklaces that were large enough to strangle a camel. "I bet they're heavy."

"I bet they're not." She smiled at him. "Some of them are hollow. You could store prayers in them for protection. Look at the carving on this one. It must have taken

the craftsman weeks to make all those intricate designs."
She sighed. "We're too busy these days to make anything
so beautiful."

"How come you don't wear jewelry if you admire it so
much?" He noticed for the first time that her ears were
pierced, but unadorned by earrings.

"You don't wear jewelry when you're trying to disappear." She flashed him a wry smile. "The ladies wearing
these pieces wanted everyone to notice them."

"And to gossip about how rich their daddies or hus-
bands were, I suspect."

"Absolutely." She grinned. "I bet they enjoyed it,
though."

She moved over to a display of colorful clothing.
"These aren't antique."

"Nope. Celia thought it would be a good idea to include them to celebrate our traditional clothing. Hardly
anyone wears such bright colors these days."

"They wanted to stand out against the dusty back-
drop of the desert, like magnificent exotic birds. Maybe
I should start wearing stuff like this myself?" She lifted
a brow.

He laughed. "I can't picture you in something that
loud."

"Me, either." She sighed. "Truth be told, I prefer to
disappear into the scenery. I suppose I always have."

"Even before you were married?" He burned with curiosity to know more about her marriage, but didn't want
to jump the gun and scare her off by asking too much.

She nodded. "I guess I'm a wallflower at heart."

"You could never hide against a wall, even though
your dress today is a similar color to this rosy clay."
He picked up the end of her scarf and felt the soft fabric between thumb and finger. Desire stirred in him as

he imagined lifting more of the fabric to discover what lay beneath.

Her breath quickened and he thought he saw her pupils dilate a little. The attraction between them was definitely mutual. She turned from him and hurried over to a shelf with a display of big brass serving platters. To him they looked like something he could buy in the souk this afternoon if he wanted. She seemed riveted by one of them, though. He moved right behind her, so he could almost feel the heat of her body in the cool air. She peered at the largest dish. "What a pretty scene. It looks like the Dhofar mountains. It's quite unusual to depict something representational in the post-Islamic era—"

She turned to him, that glorious mouth still talking, and he fought an almost unbearable urge to kiss her.

He managed not to, though. Desire raced through him like fire along a line of gasoline and he tried hard to fight it back. *You just met her. You don't know her.*

Heck, that had never stopped him before. The best way to get to know a girl was to become intimate right away. Let the chemistry mingle and see what kind of explosions happened.

Not this girl, though. Dani had been hurt, and he didn't know the details. She was recovering from a bad marriage and the last thing she needed was to be seduced by a roving stranger who was only in town for a couple of weeks.

Well, he didn't know how long he'd be here, but it wouldn't be long. He was just visiting family and trying to figure out what to do next.

And all he wanted to do right now was kiss Dani.

Mercifully she'd moved away, and was examining a series of *khanjar* daggers hanging on the wall. Most of the sheaths were ornately carved silver, but she was bent over the least elaborate one. "This must be camel leather and camel bone. I suppose this is what they all looked like many centuries ago, when people carried them for use, not for ornamentation."

Keep your dagger sheathed, he commanded himself.

"Why are you smiling?"

"I told my brother I wouldn't indulge in anything but conversation with you today. And I was just thinking that you're making it very difficult." He was nothing if not honest.

She looked startled for a moment, then regained her composure. "Why did you tell your brother that?"

"He's worried about me embarking on an unsuitable romance. He doesn't trust my judgment."

"You'd better keep your distance. As an Omani he's not going to approve of me since I'm divorced, so you can go ahead and think of me as off-limits."

"What if that just makes me want you more?"

"Then you're incorrigible."

"You wouldn't be the first to call me that. Actually you might. That's a pretty unusual word. *Impossible* is a more popular choice."

A smile tugged at the edges of her mouth. "An impossible man is the very last thing I need, so I think we can mutually agree to be platonic."

"Speak for yourself."

"I think I just did." She smiled and walked quietly over to a display of large, ornate coffeepots.

Dani wasn't playing hard to get. She *was* hard to get. In fact kissing her might take the same amount of effort required to climb Mount Kilimanjaro. On the other hand, it might well be worth it, and he did enjoy a challenge.

Three

How could a simple glance get her excited? Especially from someone who was an obvious playboy. He wouldn't be this confident and flirtatious if he weren't. He was exactly the kind of man she needed to stay away from. She shouldn't be here at all. And when she looked at her watch, she realized she'd be lucky if she got back home in time. "I really do have to get back to Salalah now." They'd been browsing in the museum for nearly two hours. She'd endured many exciting brushes against him as he leaned over a new oil jar or polished brass mirror to get a closer look. His scent filled her senses like an intoxicating drug. It was lucky he hadn't made a move on her as she wasn't at all sure how she'd react.

Like a junkie, probably.

"Of course. Let's go." He pushed the door open from behind her. "I have to admit that I thought of this stuff as a bunch of old junk last time I was here, but seeing the pieces through your eyes brings them back to life."

Seeing herself through his eyes was bringing her back to life. When Quasar looked at her she almost felt as if he could see right through her billowing traditional attire to her body beneath. Her skin hummed with awareness of his interest in her. The desire racing along her veins shocked her, when she'd been so sure she'd never feel it again.

"I'd love to learn more about the history of the site." She tried to distract herself from the mysterious sensations tingling in her blood. To focus on the unusual townlike layout of the resort, with its central oasis and native plantings.

"You need to talk to my sister-in-law—Celia. I know she did some research in order to plan the landscaping."

Dani swallowed. She couldn't imagine that he'd really introduce her to his family. They'd be bound to disapprove of her.

Quasar led her past the bubbling fountain and back through the spacious, open hotel lobby.

"What a lovely place."

"Very profitable, too, apparently. It got recommended in *Condé Nast Traveler* almost as soon as it opened and it's been booked solid ever since."

"Tourism will be good for the Omani economy. It's important to diversify. The oil won't last forever."

"Too true. I should probably be paying more attention to business opportunities while I'm here. Usually that's foremost on my mind, but I seem to be a little distracted." His flashing glance made something ripple inside her.

A valet had Quasar's car ready before they even reached the main entrance. Quasar opened the door for her himself, a thoughtful gesture that touched her. She told him about her Ph.D. thesis as they sped back across the desert.

"Persian painting, huh? Aren't some of those erotic?"

"Absolutely. Some were even intended as instruction in the art of lovemaking."

"Have you tried following the instructions?"

She laughed. "No. That would not have been my ex-husband's style at all. He didn't like being told what to do." Sex with Gordon had been very wham-bam-thank-you-ma'am. At first she'd enjoyed it anyway for the sheer physical pleasure and the emotional connection she thought she'd felt. Later it had become just another wearing encounter with him that she wanted to avoid.

"I wonder if it's worth attempting."

"If what is?" She'd got lost in unhappy memories about her marriage, staring through the windshield at the bare, brown desert.

"Following the advice in the erotic paintings." He shot a dangerous glance that made her stomach quiver.

"I suppose there's only one way to find out." She lifted a brow.

"Is that an invitation?" She saw that smile tug at his mouth.

"Not even slightly." Her body begged to differ. In fact he had quite literally brought her dormant libido back to life. She didn't think she'd ever be attracted to a man again after the depressing downward spiral of her only serious relationship. For two years now she'd felt nothing, until Quasar had looked at her in that bookshop. As they talked, she'd sensed her body literally switching back on, like an electrical circuit that had been disconnected for a while and was now plugged back in so current could flow through it. Right now it was flowing to all kinds of nooks and crannies she'd all but forgotten.

She watched his long, elegant fingers resting on the wheel, and wondered what they'd feel like on her skin. Good thing she was too sensible to find out. Her reputation was already in tatters and she certainly wasn't going to rush headlong into another unsuitable relationship. A glance at the dashboard clock made her nervous. "Will we really be back by four?"

She felt the car surge forward as he accelerated. "If it can be done, I'll do it."

"Let me guess, that's your personal motto."

He flashed those slate-blue eyes at her. "You're not so far wrong. Lately I've been thinking it might be time for me to slow down, though. There may be some things I can leave undone."

Like seducing me. "You plan to become more selective as you mature."

"Exactly. At this point I think I should focus on only the very best."

"Business opportunities?"

He took his eyes off the road again and kept them on hers for far too long. After an agonizing interval that heated her blood almost to the boiling point, she glanced nervously out the windshield, half afraid they'd driven right off the narrow strip of tarmac.

"Among other things." When he finally looked back at the long, empty road—not a moment too soon—her heart was pounding and her lips parted. The effect he had on her was a little frightening.

"But how do you know something is the very best until you try it?" She wanted to fill the air with conversation. Right now the thoughts in her brain and the sensations in her body were making her very uncomfortable.

"I have a lifetime of experience. Enough to be something of a connoisseur." He spoke softly, and glanced at her quickly this time. Just long enough to convince her that he was completely serious.

She believed him. The desert swept past, and they climbed into the lush mountains again. She let out a breath she didn't realize she'd been holding. "I can't believe how beautiful it is up here. This is the first time

I've come to the mountains in years. My dad and brothers have no interest in nature."

"Let's come back tomorrow." He said it casually, and didn't even look at her. "I'll bring some binoculars and we can look for birds."

No. Just say no. You can't do this. Going out with a strange man a second time—or would it be the third, if she counted that cup of coffee?—would confirm that they were having some kind of…relationship. She wouldn't call it an affair since there was nothing sensual or romantic about it, except in her mind.

Her mouth wouldn't form the simple rejection. If she said no she'd probably never see Quasar again. That would be very sensible but the prospect was too depressing to contemplate. There'd be nothing but dull days at home, cooking the same familiar dinners, tidying her bare room, broken up with occasional walks to the bookshop and the fruit stalls. Possibly a frighteningly unattractive suitor would take pity on her from time to time. Since she didn't have any kind of promising escape plan, who knew how long that might go on for? "Okay."

He turned to her with an expression of surprise.

"You thought I'd say no."

"I did."

She loved that he didn't lie. "Apparently I'm more reckless than you thought."

"I like that in a woman." His wicked grin hinted at trouble to come. And strangely enough, she was starting to look forward to it.

The next morning she dressed in jeans and a T-shirt. Considering she'd worn little else for all her years in the United States, it was odd how daring it felt to don them. When she returned, her father had told her she should wear conservative clothing and conduct herself like an Omani woman, and—grateful for the chance to stay here—she'd obeyed. They were only clothes, right? She quickly adapted to covering her arms and legs, and her hair—the way she'd been taught as a child.

But dressing in Western clothing again was liberating and felt right. She did don a cover-up and headscarf before Quasar showed up, but she shed them in the car with relief and enjoyed Quasar's admiring gaze on her body-hugging jeans and T-shirt.

Driving up into the lush green mountains with a handsome man, Dani felt a sense that anything was possible, something she hadn't experienced since her college days. They parked and walked along a wooded trail as thick with leaves and scents and life as any trail in the New Jersey woodlands. It amazed her that during this season, paradise existed right here in her arid homeland. In a way it proved that anything was possible—anywhere—with a little rain and mist to break up the relentless heat and sun that scorched most of Oman into a virtual wasteland.

"A steppe eagle." Quasar stopped and grabbed her arm. He pointed high in a tree where a magnificent bird looked posed, as if it sat on an ancient Egyptian frieze. "It's seen something."

The bird stayed frozen for a few moments, then dropped like a rock toward land, before swooping up on broad, flapping wings with some small creature in its mouth.

"It caught its prey. What a magnificent sight." Dani peered after it as it perched on a branch nearby. "Though I can't help but feel bad for the animal that's about to be eaten."

"Eat or be eaten." Quasar's grip on her arm had softened into a sort of caress. "It's the way of the world."

His touch heated her skin. She was usually the one being eaten. "Do you really believe that? Isn't there any middle ground?"

He looked amused. "I suppose so. I haven't explored it myself."

"Since I can't imagine you being eaten, then I assume you're used to being the one doing the devouring."

He laughed. "Too right. I used to keep a falcon for hunting. Trained it myself. I'd spend hours out here tracking prey with it when I was a kid." She shrank a little from his touch. His admitted predatory attitude should make her wary. "But don't be afraid. I won't eat you."

"No?" She looked up into his face. His dark blue eyes were soft, curious.

"No." The high midday sun illuminated his aristocratic features. Of course he wouldn't be interested in devouring her. Obviously she'd been out of circulation too long to think that a man as magnificent and confident as Quasar would be interested in her.

"Maybe just a tiny bite." His wide, sensual mouth hitched slightly. Something strange was happening in her belly. It was the way he looked at her, like he held her in his grasp. She couldn't look away. His face was moving closer, his sparkling eyes still fixed right on hers. She could smell his musky, masculine scent. Any minute now she'd feel the roughness of his skin....

His lips met hers in a rush, like the eagle falling on its prey. Far from diving for cover, her mouth rose to his and melded with it. Sensation crashed over her. She was dimly aware of their natural surroundings—the wind in the trees, animals scurrying nearby—and of his hands resting warmly at her waist, but her whole being focused on the kiss and the powerful and intense effect it created in her body. Heat flooded her core, spreading out to her limbs, squeezing the breath from her lungs as she gave herself over to the sensation. She'd never experienced a kiss like this. Chemistry, was it? Or was it that she'd never kissed a man as gorgeous and dashing as Quasar. Either way the effect was overwhelming.

She had no idea how long they kissed, but when they finally pulled apart and she opened her eyes, she found herself blinking against now-unaccustomed daylight. "Oh, dear." The words spilled out. The intense sensations pouring through her had sparked her to life in a way that seemed dangerously familiar. She hadn't felt this way since the early days of her marriage, when she was so sure that love could solve any problem, if she could just find a way.

She'd been wrong.

Quasar gave an amused frown. "'Oh, dear?' That's not the effect I intended."

She sucked in a breath, fighting the urge to fan herself. "It's just that I haven't…I'm not used to…I didn't think…" She didn't know what she was trying to say. Had she really come here to watch the birds? She was old enough to know better than to accompany a gorgeous man into the wilderness if she couldn't keep her wits about her.

Her heart fluttered in her chest, the emotions that she thought she'd abandoned back in the States scaring her. Her conviction that from now on she'd live a sensible life, free of passion and drama, had all but deserted her. Right now she wanted nothing more than to kiss Quasar again.

Which was a terrible idea. He was only here for a couple of weeks, tops. He'd made no further mention of introducing her to his family. For him this was just a diverting vacation fling. If she could enter into this with that spirit it would be fine, but she couldn't. "We should go."

* * *

Quasar felt his smile fade. Just moments ago Dani had been one with him, lost in a delicious and enthralling kiss. Now she shrank from him, her muscles stiffening. "I didn't mean to alarm you. That was a sensational kiss but I'll behave myself from now on if you prefer."

The countryside hummed with life that echoed in his body. A soft breeze tossed Dani's hair and arousal kissed her cheeks with pink. The secluded natural setting, high up above the world, was the perfect place for a little impromptu lovemaking.

But something told him that wasn't going to happen.

Dani's lips had tightened into a white line. "I need to get home."

What had changed? She'd warmed to the kiss instantly, and enjoyed it as much as he. She was giving back as much as he gave the entire time. They'd kissed for a full three or four minutes! Part of him wanted to seize her in his arms and kiss her again, so they could jump right back into that world of passion.

But he could tell that would be a terrible idea. "What's the matter?"

She shook her head, blinked. She inhaled as if to speak, then didn't.

"Is it that we don't know each other well enough?"

"Yes." She spoke fast, obviously glad of a way to respond. "But it's not just that."

"We can get to know each other slowly." He took her hand and squeezed it. It felt cold, and tightened in his grasp.

"We can't. You're leaving soon."

"Not that soon." He'd be here for at least two weeks. On the other hand, maybe that was no time at all to her. He wasn't too sure of Omani dating customs. It was probably customary for them to glance at each other across the stalls of a souk for nine months before a single word was exchanged.

But she was wearing jeans and a khaki T-shirt and looked like an American today. Even the lush green hillside with its winding, rocky trails looked like somewhere in the Ozarks. He didn't care where they were. All he knew was that he needed to keep her here. If he drove her home now he'd never see her again. "Let's climb higher so we can look down on the eagles. Maybe we'll even see their nests."

"I don't think that's a good idea." Her dark eyes wide, she looked so confused he just wanted to take her in his arms.

"Of course it is. We're grown adults and we can do anything we set our minds to." He scanned the horizon, hoping for an impressive eagle, or at least some rare sparrow to distract her with.

"I don't know what came over me. I haven't kissed anyone since…since…"

"Your marriage?"

She nodded. A furrow formed between her elegant brows. "I didn't think I'd ever want to kiss someone again."

He smiled. "And then you did."

He heard her inhale. "It was a mistake."

"I should take that as an insult." Her whole body was so tense he could tell she was deadly serious, but still he wanted to lighten the mood.

"It's not you, it's me."

"You're a lovely woman. You're single, or at least so you've told me. What's wrong with you enjoying a kiss?"

"I am single." She looked shocked that he'd called that

into question. "And believe me, I am not looking to get into a relationship ever again."

He wanted to quip that she'd found the right man for that—relationships were not his strong point—but he restrained himself. "Just because it didn't work out with one man, doesn't mean you shouldn't ever enjoy romance again."

"Yes, it does." She hugged herself as a breeze ruffled the trees. "Can we leave now?" Her eyes implored him.

"I guess we could start walking back toward the car." It was a good twenty minutes away. Hopefully he could win her around by then. "Why are you so afraid of another relationship?"

She walked ahead of him. "Being part of a couple turned me into someone else."

"How?" He walked faster to catch up with her.

"I lost myself. I became the person he shaped me into. The weak and useless person he despised." He saw her shoulders shiver.

"You didn't become that person. He just made you feel that way. Was he abusive?"

"Not physically. He never hit me." Her voice was very quiet. "He didn't do much at all. I became a victim so easily. I gave up my career, gave up my friends, stopped doing everything I enjoyed and turned into the nobody he wanted to hate." Gravel scattered at her feet as she hurried along the loose surface of the trail, over tree roots and around rocks. At this rate they'd be back at the car in less than ten minutes.

"He sounds like a jackass."

She stopped and turned around. "Yes. He was a jackass. I can see that now, but at the time I thought it was me. I lost all perspective on my own life. You can see how I don't want to get myself into a situation like that again."

"You won't. You just had the bad luck to give your heart, and your trust, to someone who didn't deserve it. Most men aren't anything like that."

"Aren't they?" A pained expression flickered across her face. "My father thinks I'm a fool."

"Then you need to get away from him, too."

"I can't. I have no job and very little money. The divorce lawyers took almost everything I had left, which wasn't much. We didn't have any assets to split and I didn't want alimony as it would have given my ex-husband a hold over me when I needed a complete break. With my—as both my father and ex-husband pointed out—useless career, I'm not likely to make money anytime soon." Tears rose in her eyes. "I guess I planned my life like a fairy tale, where I'd live my dreams surrounded by art and love. I was stupid."

She turned and started walking again, batting branches away from her face, descending the trail so fast he worried she'd slip on the loose gravel.

Quasar's chest swelled with pity. Which annoyed him. She didn't want pity. He hurried after her. "You had a job at Princeton. That's the epitome of success."

"And I gave it up because it interfered with me being home to vacuum the carpets. Obviously I didn't deserve it."

He grabbed her arm. "What kind of pity party is this? You need to turn your life around, not whine about it."

She'd stiffened at his grip, and now she tried to tug her arm away. Then a sob emerged from her throat, like the sound a wounded animal would make. "I know. I know! I hate myself."

Remorse clutched at his heart. Had he added to her sorrows by insulting her like the men who'd tried to crush her? "I didn't mean to hurt you. I'm just upset to see an intelligent and capable—and very beautiful—woman selling herself so short. You have an amazing amount of potential and you should tap into it."

Her eyes were bright with tears. "I know I do. I don't know what's wrong with me."

"Nothing's wrong with you." He'd softened his grip on her arm, but didn't let go. He couldn't shake the feeling that she'd run away if he did. "You need to believe that. And a good start would be to look around at the incredible beauty surrounding us and let yourself appreciate it for a moment."

She blinked, and a small tear rolled quietly down her cheek. She looked up and he saw the sky reflected in her gaze. A dark shape darted across her pupil: the flickering outline of a bird high above. He turned and watched a kestrel circling over them. "Careful," he whispered. "Don't show any weakness or he might come eat us."

A smile tugged at her sad mouth. "We'd be awfully big bites."

"And I'll protect you with my bare hands." He lifted the one that wasn't holding her upper arm.

"You have very capable hands for a businessman."

"I play sports."

"Oh." She glanced at his body. A flash of awareness jumped inside him. He hoped she felt it, too.

"So I'm fit enough to protect you."

"I guess that's reassuring." The smile now reached to her eyes. "And you're right. It is stunning here. I mustn't let myself get wrapped up in fear again. I'm trying to get away from that."

"Good. Because before that happened I think you were enjoying our kiss."

She looked up at the bird again. "I was." Her lip

quivered slightly. "Too much. I enjoyed kissing my ex-husband at first, too."

"I'm not him." He let go of her arm gently. She didn't run off. That was a start.

"I know you're not." She fixed her eyes on him. "It's just that I was so in love. It started with attraction and quickly spiraled into me giving him my entire life. I don't trust myself to be sensible."

"I don't trust myself to be sensible, either, very often." He was more inclined to plunge in headfirst and deal with the fallout later. "Sometimes you have to take a leap of faith. Don't lose the part of you that feels, or that cares. That's what makes us human." He couldn't stand that she thought shutting herself off from experience was the best way to protect herself from pain.

Even if she might have a point, especially where he was concerned. He didn't exactly have the best track record when it came to long-term loving relationships. "Look at the view from here." They'd reached a bend in the road and a gap in the trees revealed a clear view down to a river sparkling in a valley below them. "Isn't it amazing to see a river running here so close to the vast barren desert?"

"This whole mountain range seems to rise up out of nowhere. I guess it shows you that life can flourish in surprising places."

"And joy can flourish in unexpected places, too."

She turned sharply to look at him. "You're a flirt."

"Either that or I'm speaking the truth."

"Or both." She laughed. "I think you're very easy to take at face value."

"Good. Would you like to walk down toward the river? There's a path here—look." A narrow trail between the trees zigzagged across the hillside.

"Why not?" The sparkle was back in her eyes. "In fact, I'll lead the way." The kestrel spiraled overhead as she proceeded—gingerly—down the gravelly path toward the sparkling water in the wadi below. He enjoyed the view of her body in the fitted jeans that showed off her athletic-looking curves. The mystery of her traditional clothing had its own allure, but he preferred the what-you-see-is-what-you-get simplicity of Western clothing. Maybe mystery wasn't his thing. His hands itched to run themselves over her lithe body, but he counseled himself to take it slow. *Take your time. It will be worth it.* The last thing he wanted was to add to her burden of grief and regret. When they parted, he wanted to leave her smiling.

His own thoughts jolted him, and he almost slipped on the loose ground. Why was he thinking about their parting already? In business he always had an exit strategy in mind. Was he the same in relationships, even though he'd never admitted it to himself?

Something felt different this time, though. What were his intentions with Dani? She was quieter and gentler than the kind of women he usually dated, and that made him take their whole new relationship more seriously. He knew everything that happened between them would mean a lot to her, and that made it important to him, too. Already he felt a connection to her far deeper than such a short acquaintance would normally produce. He wanted to make her happy.

"Almost there!" She flashed him a brilliant smile that made his breath catch in his lungs. In moments like this he could see Dani shake off the shroud of fear and transform back into the vibrant young woman she was supposed to be. Her exhilaration was catching and he bounded down the last few yards like a clumsy gazelle, arriving on the pebbled shoreline at the same tizme she did.

"I wonder if the water is cold." He crouched and dipped his fingers in it. "Yes. It must be spring water."

She let her fingers play in the water. "In the old days there were underground channels that carried water hundreds of miles through the desert—all the way to the cities—without evaporating."

"Proves that in some ways our ancestors were more advanced than we are. Today that kind of pipeline is usually filled with oil."

"One day something else will replace the oil. A few centuries ago the frankincense trade was the beating heart of this area. You still see the trees dotting the landscape. Some of them are hundreds of years old, maybe even thousands. They tap them for the sap, which dries into hard chunks of frankincense. People still burn it for the aroma, though it isn't worth more than gold anymore."

"Value is always relative." Quasar splashed water on his face and neck. "Anyone in business will tell you that. Can't knock the oil, though. It made my family wealthy, though they've since branched out. Is your father in the oil industry?"

"He used to be. Right now he's employed by the latest building boom. He does pretty well but for some reason he's always complaining. I think he feels he should be a millionaire by now. He's never satisfied. He's griping about supporting me again. I wish I could find a job."

"Have you looked?"

"Here in Salalah?" She laughed. "I haven't. I've just assumed there's nothing in my field."

"Don't give up before you even try." He splashed a little water at her. She shrieked and splashed him back. Suddenly they were engaged in an all-out splash war that left them both drenched and breathless—and kissing again.

Four

Dani's clothes had almost dried by the time she unlocked the back door to the house and snuck in, hoping no one had noticed Quasar's car on their street. He could hardly drop her off at the market damp and disheveled, so she had to take the risk.

"Where have you been?" She almost jumped out of her skin at the sound of Khalid's voice.

"Why are you home from school so early?"

He stood in the hallway looking gangly and awkward in his too-small school uniform. At fifteen, he was going through a teenage growth spurt and had shot up about three inches just since she'd been home. "Our algebra teacher is having surgery. They let us go home. Why are your jeans wet at the bottom?" His eyes traveled back up to meet hers. "And why are you wearing jeans at all. I thought Dad told you to dress traditionally."

"I'm a grown-up. I can dress how I want." She attempted to sweep past him but the hallway was narrow and their elbows bumped.

"Hmm. Sounds like you were doing something you're not supposed to."

"I know. Walking around without a male relative. It's a shame you weren't here or I could have taken you with me to the dry cleaner."

"How did you get wet at the dry cleaner?" He was following her down the hallway.

"I stepped in a ditch. Someone must have just emptied water in it." The lie made her flesh creep a little. It was pathetic that she couldn't even tell her own younger brother that she'd spent the afternoon in the mountains. He'd probably be interested in hearing about the steppe eagle they saw, but she knew her father would freak out and possibly never leave her unattended again if he knew she'd been out in a car with a strange man. There was no way she could tell the truth.

Which was ridiculous. "Are you going to follow me into the shower?"

"Why are you taking a shower in the middle of the afternoon?" Her brother's question grated on her nerves. He wasn't a bad kid. She'd been trying to get to know him since she'd been back here, since the age difference between them meant they'd never been especially close. He'd only been about six when she'd gone off to the United States for college. He was very by-the-book, though. The kind of person who'd never be able to sleep at night if his homework wasn't done and his teeth not brushed. He was not someone she'd dare confide in.

"I'm hot. It's always hot here in Oman, but I guess I'm not used to it anymore."

"What's it like living in America? I bet it's pretty cool."

His wistful voice made her turn. Leaning against the wall he looked much less like an inquisitor and more like a curious fifteen-year-old. "It is pretty cool. The food takes some getting used to but there's stuff going on all day and night and more places to go than you can imagine."

"Do you think Dad would let me go there for college? He let you go."

She sighed. "I don't know." He probably wouldn't be willing to risk another of his offspring going astray. She hadn't exactly stuck with the program. "Wait until the dust has settled. I think he's still stirred up about me being back here with my life in shambles. He doesn't think America is a very good influence."

"Do you think it's a bad influence?"

She frowned. "No. It's big, though, and confusing. You have to be careful or you can just…get lost." She'd lost herself, giving her heart and soul to a man who could never be happy.

At least now she could see that the fault lay with him. It had taken some time to gain that perspective. And even now she wondered what she could have done differently. What she could do differently in the future so she didn't screw up again.

Quasar was different. Excitement flickered in her heart at the thought of him. Khalid walked back down the hall toward his own room, and she sagged with relief. She'd been afraid to even let Quasar cross her mind until her brother had taken his keen eyes off her. She worried about what he might see—a telltale sparkle in her eyes, a giveaway flush in her cheek. Even thinking about him produced a physical reaction. It was startling and disturbing.

She closed the door of her room behind her and glanced down at the wet cuffs of her jeans. She'd better hope Khalid didn't mention anything to her father. And if he did she'd better have a good story. A glance in the mirror showed that her face was tanned from their afternoon in the sun. She unwound her headscarf and let her hair fall down her back. A memory assaulted her of

Quasar's fingers raking through the long strands, of his hand pressing against the base of her skull as they kissed, so deep and long that she could barely breathe.

Quasar.

Fear mingled with the excitement flooding her veins at the memory of him. What was she doing? She'd let him kiss her. Worse yet, she'd kissed him back. Her lips buzzed at the memory. She'd told him things that she'd never told anyone else: her shame at letting her ex-husband strip away her self-confidence; her fear that she was worthless, unemployable and a disappointment to everyone.

And he was nothing but encouraging. And interested. She had to admit that that alone did a lot to boost her confidence. She smiled at her reflection in the bathroom mirror before she turned on the shower. Her ex-husband had made her feel like no man would ever want anything to do with her. Quasar had already proved him wrong.

But what did he want from her? They'd already kissed and the chemistry was palpable.

Next stop was sex. With no promises.

She'd have to be completely insane to even consider it. Every time she saw him, he occupied more of her brain space, more room in her heart. Of course it was encouraging that her heart was actually beating again, especially when he was nearby, but she didn't want it to get broken, and since she was still in a fragile state that might happen quite easily.

Quasar was a freewheeling, fun-loving guy who moved on when he got bored. Which could be next week.

The chilly water made her gasp. She needed to cool herself off. Quasar was a fun companion. An exhilarating break from routine. He was not her future, and she'd better remember that.

* * *

Sometimes when people asked too many questions it was easiest to stay silent.

Quasar's brothers and their families were all sitting around one of the hotel's private dining rooms, enjoying a lavish dinner. So far he'd managed to avoid revealing anything other than his excursion into the mountains. In the absence of further details they assumed he went alone with a sporting objective.

"Quasar all alone with the kestrels." Elan broke off a piece of bread. "You're giving me flashbacks to when you were a kid and you trained that bird to hunt for you. I think you're channeling your inner Omani again."

"Nothing wrong with that." Quasar shot his brother a smile. "And the views from the mountainside are pretty impressive."

"I am pleased that you're enjoying what Oman has to offer." Salim raised his glass. "You can help promote our country in America."

"I don't think you need any help. Isn't the hotel at capacity?" Quasar helped himself to some more rice.

"I have plans for a new hotel just north of here."

"On the beach? Or out in the desert like Saliyah?"

"Right on the shore, waves lapping at your toes. It's a property I've been saving for the right application. Celia's been dying to plan the landscape ever since I showed it to her."

Celia leaned against her husband. It was obvious she loved working with him. "It's going to be so lush. Not that you'd know it to look at the place now. I don't think there's a single plant growing there. Just some old torn fishing nets and driftwood." She rubbed her hands together with pretend glee. "But I love a challenge."

"Celia, I get that Salim keeps you busy creating oases

in the desert, but don't you sometimes want to take other jobs?" Quasar was curious about how this whole work/romance thing worked.

"I do. I was in Mexico City last month working on a corporate headquarters there."

"And the kids stayed at home with Salim?" Quasar topped off his sister-in-law's glass of lemonade.

Celia nodded. "Of course—we have plenty of help here at the hotel. And sometimes they all come with me. It's nice now that the kids are young enough that they don't have to miss school."

Elan still worked with his wife, Sara, too, though now they were business partners, not boss and assistant. Quasar couldn't imagine how you could spend all day *and* all night with someone. Didn't they ever get tired of each other? That must be what true love was like.

Most likely he wasn't capable of it. He was better suited to brief affairs. Intense journeys of exploration and enjoyment that ended while everything was still fabulous. He couldn't wait to continue his voyage into the intriguing world of Dani. Her passion was so unexpected and he suspected he'd just bumped the tip of the iceberg. It was time to take her to his private getaway in the foothills of the mountains. He'd be staying there right now if Salim hadn't convinced him to stay at the hotel to spend more time with Elan and Sara while they were visiting. He hadn't even stopped by since he'd been here.

A waiter brought a round of coffees and a plate of dates. The children were excused from the table and started to run around it like maniacs, which made everyone laugh.

Quasar had formed a plan. "Have you guys been out to my house lately? I had a decorator fix it up for me and she sent me pictures, but I haven't seen what Celia did with the landscape yet. You've all kept me so busy I haven't had a chance to visit."

"There were twelve frankincense trees on the property," said Celia. "They hadn't been tapped in years and we did it ourselves. I'm going to send you some of the finished product for Christmas."

"Does that mean I'm not invited here for Christmas?" He pretended to look sad. He did feel a little weird about the acknowledgment that he'd soon be gone. He didn't want to leave. Not without Dani.

The thought struck him like a slap. He'd been on a total of three dates with her. Something about her had captivated him. He couldn't even explain what it was. Yes, she was lovely. She was sweet. Her vulnerability coaxed out of him a nurturing side he hadn't previously realized he had.

And then there was the attraction between them. Powerful, insistent, a chemical brew that made him want to kiss her and hold her and make passionate love to her. And for that, he needed peace and privacy and a chance to get the place prepared to entertain her.

"I want to spend some time at my house tomorrow. You know, get a feel for it. There's no sense in owning a house if I never go there."

"I'm surprised you went to the mountains today and didn't even visit it."

"I planned to but didn't have time." And didn't want to scare the life out of Dani. An unplanned kiss in the wilderness was one thing. Luring her into his lair without scaring her off would take some delicacy.

"Before you become a hermit, Quasar, I want you to know that Sara and I have been hard at work searching for the perfect woman for you." Celia bit into an olive. "Do you remember her sister, Erin?"

"Of course I do." A bubbly, pretty girl with a young daughter, Erin had been at both of his brothers' weddings.

"Her latest boyfriend has turned out to be just as much of a loser as the last two." Sara took a sip of her lemonade. "So we've determined that she needs some help in the matchmaking department. We thought it might be interesting to set you guys up. It's a slight snag that she lives in Wisconsin and you live in…where do you live these days, anyway?"

"To be determined." He smiled. "I'm a free agent ready to move where the action takes me."

"Perfect. We'll have to get you guys together. There's a school break coming up in two weeks. I'll see if we can get her and Erin and her son on a flight out here."

Quasar stiffened. "I don't know, Sara. I'm not really ready for a new relationship. I want to take some time, to figure some things out." With Dani. The last thing he needed was to be set up with someone when there was no way he could be interested in her. He didn't want to hurt Erin's feelings, either. She sounded like she'd had enough of that already.

"It can't hurt to meet her, can it?"

"It might, if we meet at the wrong time and end up blowing it." He shrugged.

"I suppose you're right. It's probably better to wait until you're ready. I notice you haven't mentioned that woman you met at the bookshop. I assume she very sensibly brushed you off."

He felt a sheepish expression pass over his face. How could he keep such a big secret from his own family? All of these people wanted the best for him. Why was he so reluctant to tell them what was happening with Dani? "Actually, she was with me today."

"Ah." Salim didn't look surprised. Or pleased. Sara and Celia smiled at each other. Elan kept a poker face.

"I'll have to bring her over to meet you all soon. Her name's Dani, short for Daniyah."

"That's a pretty name. I don't think I've heard it before," said Sara.

"My lawyer was filling my ears with gossip about Daniyah Hassan the other day." Salim frowned and put his coffee cup down sharply. "It's not her, is it?"

"I don't know her last name. Isn't that funny? I'm not sure I told her mine, either."

"Well, you should have. That might have put a stop to this before it even started." Salim's expression was grim.

"Why?"

"Did she just come back from the States after a failed marriage?"

Quasar sat up. "Yes. How did you know?"

"Salalah maybe be a big city by Omani standards, but it's a small town by anyone else's. We all know each other's business."

"Isn't Mohammed Hassan the guy who sued you over that waterfront property?" Elan sipped his coffee.

"Yes. That's her father." Salim stared at Quasar. "Twelve years in the courts. That's why my lawyer's keeping tabs on the family. I don't know Daniyah personally, but her father is like a pit bull. The case still isn't resolved. Though it will be before we break ground next year. Count on it."

"Why don't you resolve it amicably?"

Salim blew out a breath. "That land is ours. Our father paid three thousand rials for it in 1976. I have the paperwork to prove it."

"Then what's the problem?"

"Old Hassan insists that his father, who sold the land,

was sick and under duress and was badgered into selling it. He claims the handshake contract is null and void, and he wants the land back." Salim crossed his arms. "Not going to happen."

"I'm guessing the land is worth a lot more now?"

Salim snorted. "Add three zeros and you're still not close. Hey, the old man needed the cash and he made a deal. I'm sure we'd all be wealthy as kings if we could renegotiate some of the bargains we made at the wrong time. Besides, it's not like he's starving. Hassan is one of the best-known engineers in the country, and he has two intelligent sons. Some people should learn to count their blessings."

"Dani's not involved in any of that. I doubt she's even aware of it. She's here to regroup after her bad marriage."

"And you're helping her out with that?" Elan crossed his arms.

"Out of the frying pan, into the fire…" Sara whispered with a wink.

"You do realize that here in Oman you basically need to marry a woman in order to kiss her." Salim leaned back in his chair, arms still crossed. "You can't carry on like you're back in L.A. Especially not with the divorced daughter of a man who's battling us in court."

Quasar regretted mentioning Dani. "We're just getting to know each other. There's nothing to even be discreet about."

"Good. Then you can break it off and no one will know." Salim arched a brow.

"Salim, you should understand from personal experience that it's not always so easy to break off an unsuitable relationship." His wife's eyes twinkled with humor. "You dumped me twice and still ended up married to me."

"That was different." His gaze, so filled with love,

made Quasar want to shake his head over the transformation of his stolid brother. "We loved each other. Quasar can hardly be in love with a woman he met two days ago."

"Three days." Quasar ate a sticky date.

"Not that you're counting." Sara winked. "Are you falling in love with her already?"

"All I know is that I enjoy her company and I want to spend more time with her." He couldn't explain the powerful feelings she brought out in him. He wanted to protect her, nurture her, make her smile. He wanted to chat with her about little things and see her eyes light up.

"I heard a rumor that her husband was abusive. She may be psychologically damaged." Salim regarded his brother coolly.

"It's true about her husband. He sounds like an ass. There's nothing wrong with Dani, though, except that she's a little wary."

"As well she might be with a lothario like you on the prowl." Elan grinned.

"She doesn't know anything about me."

Sara laughed. "Believe me, women can tell a ladies' man. You're far too good-looking for your own good, for one thing."

"But you still want to set me up with your sister?"

"I know you're a good man at heart. You just need the right woman to steady you."

"And Daniyah Hassan is not that woman," growled Salim. "A divorced woman can have a hard time finding her way in our traditional society. If word gets out that she's had an affair?" He shrugged. "Do the right thing and let her be."

"I can't believe you're worried about her reputation if her father is your sworn enemy."

"Are we the Three Musketeers? I don't have sworn enemies. I have business rivals. And her father doesn't even qualify as one. He's a mere…insect buzzing in my ear."

Quasar laughed. "Then what I do with his daughter doesn't really matter, does it?"

"The Al Mansur family has a reputation to protect."

"You work on your reputation as a ruthless and brilliant hotelier, and I'll tend to my own as an international playboy." Might as well make light of the situation. Attempts at genuine discussion were getting him nowhere. "Now, isn't it about time for me to read the kids a bedtime story?" He raised his voice so the children, who were still running around the table at full tilt, could hear him.

"Yes, Uncle Quaz! Please do!" The resulting flurry of activity was just the distraction he needed. Quasar vowed never to mention his love life to his family again. He also decided not to mention the dispute over the land to Dani. It was sure to spook her and it really had nothing to do with them. When the time was right he'd approach her father and find a solution that would make everyone happy. In the meantime, all that mattered was making Dani happy.

"It's not that far away, only thirty minutes or so. It's in the foothills."

Dani held the phone away from her ear as if removing the source of Quasar's voice would reduce its powerful effect over her. Every cell in her body yearned to say yes. She could picture the mischief sparkling in his dark blue eyes, see the arrogant and sexy cut of his cheekbones, imagine the sunlight dancing in his tousled hair.

She wanted to bury her face in his shirt and inhale the rich masculine scent of him.

"I can't."

"Of course you can." Quasar obviously wasn't the

type to take no for an answer. "I can pick you up at your house. Or any clandestine location you prefer. I'll have you back by four."

"My youngest brother was home when I arrived today. He noticed my jeans were wet. I can't take any more chances." She'd been cursing herself ever since. She was listening at the door in a panic when her father came home, wondering if Khalid would say something and expose her to inquisition-style questioning. She had no business whatsoever disappearing for another tryst with Quasar.

"Are you trying to tell me that you'll never see me again?"

Her heart seized. Is that what she meant? It seemed too awful to imagine.

"Because if that's what you think, you're dead wrong. I haven't achieved the success I've found in business by giving up easily."

She wanted to laugh. She found his persistence sexy and appealing. But then there was the other side of the story. "You freely admitted that you quickly grow bored and move on. I can't afford a casual affair. My emotions are too fragile and if that wasn't enough, my reputation is in tatters already and I can't risk it getting any worse."

"Your reputation will be as safe as the sultan's treasure. Besides, you might find the place interesting. It's an old farmhouse. I have no idea how old but possibly a thousand years or more. There are twelve frankincense trees on the property. It's a window into an earlier time."

She hesitated. History was an intoxicating drug to her. A thousand-year-old farmhouse *and* Quasar? Hard to resist. "That does sound rather intriguing."

"Ten o'clock, then. At your house?"

"No! The neighbors might see." She wanted to go,

though. How could she resist? "I'll be at the market again." The neighbors might see her there but somehow it seemed less likely. Her temperature rose at the prospect of meeting Quasar again. It was embarrassing how her resolve flew right out the window at the mere sound of his voice.

Much as it had when she'd first fallen for Gordon, against the protests of her girlfriends that he was too old for her, and too possessive. She'd been so sure of her heart. Only to watch it be trampled and left bloodless and empty.

Quasar had already hung up. Probably he was on to his next activity of the evening, barely thinking about her at all. And she faced another sleepless night of fitful dreams mixed with colorful fears and scary anticipation.

As usual the drive sped by. Quasar was so easy to talk to. He knew so many things and had been to so many places but never made her feel inadequate by comparison.

"We'll have to go to Angkor Wat together. Some of the temples seem to grow organically out of the jungle, like they really are holy and mystical creations." He talked with such conviction she could almost see them heading for the airport, ready to explore the ancient ruins of Cambodia, or Peru, or someplace she'd never even heard of.

They drove into the green-cloaked mountains, along a winding road that seemed to go on forever. High, heavy vegetation on both sides hid the outside world and made her feel as if they were driving in an alternate universe, where the dry deserts and bustle of Salalah didn't even exist.

The road finally petered out and they drove across an expanse of grass toward a building unlike any she'd seen in Oman. "Are we really in Oman?"

He laughed. "I'm pretty sure of it."

"But your house has a pitched roof. It looks like something you'd see in New Jersey!"

"It's much rainier here than the rest of the country. That's why it's green. I suppose the old farmers figured they needed a pitched roof to keep the rain out of their houses."

The stone walls had been left unplastered and had an intriguingly ancient appearance. The house was on a sloped hillside, and the frankincense trees formed an orderly rectangle on the higher side of the slope. She could easily picture sheep grazing under their scraggly branches, on the rich grassy hillside that looked like it belonged in Ireland, not Oman. "This place is so well-hidden I'm amazed you even found it."

"I spent a weekend walking in the mountains two years ago, and I stumbled across it. It was empty and falling down so I looked into the ownership. The old man who lived here had died and his family were in Muscat and didn't know what to do with the place, so I bought it from them. I love it here. It's the perfect escape from the real world."

He reached a tall wooden door, studded with nails, and punched a code into the keypad nearby. The lock clicked and he pushed the door open. "Electronic servants are so much more discreet than the human kind." He paused in the doorway and kissed her softly on the lips. Her breath hitched and a shiver of awareness passed through her.

All alone.

In private.

With a man who stirred her senses in a way she'd never dreamed possible.

The door clicked shut behind her and Quasar held her hand as they walked across a dimly lit interior room, decorated with embroidered hangings. Unlike the unadorned exterior, the inside had been renovated into a comfortable blend of minimalism and luxury. The walls were plastered smooth and the stone floor scrubbed and honed to shiny perfection. Striking pieces of contemporary furniture added pops of rich color, and eye-catching modern art ornamented the walls. The space was eclectic, warm and filled with personality and exuberance, much like its handsome owner.

Her palm warmed against his and excitement trickled along her nerves. She had a feeling he was leading her to the bedroom and the idea scared and enthralled her in equal parts.

He opened an arched door into a large, octagonal room with embroidered curtains draped over the windows, filtering the midday sun. A wide, low bed, strewn with pillows like a lovers' playground, filled the middle of the room.

She was right. And this was so wrong. But as he held her hand, she could imagine the feel of other parts of his body—his muscled chest, his sturdy thighs, his strong arms—pressed against her and the siren call of desire echoed through her.

"I'm so glad you're here with me." Quasar's soft voice was a balm to her nerves. He turned to face her and fixed those tempting blue eyes on her. An invitation to pleasure. "We won't be interrupted."

"Except by my conscience." She tried to smile.

"You're not doing anything wrong."

"Not yet. But I have a feeling I'm about to."

"It all depends on your definition of wrong. Enjoying a peaceful afternoon in the mountains with a good friend is very right, in my opinion."

"Am I really a good friend after such a short acquaintance?"

"Indubitably."

The strange word made her laugh. How did he manage to get her so relaxed? Today he wore white linen pants, rather wrinkled, and a white shirt with the collar thrown open to reveal his tanned neck. It wasn't fair for him to be so ridiculously good-looking. How could any girl resist him? They probably couldn't, so at least she wouldn't be alone in throwing caution to the wind and engaging in an illicit affair.

"I haven't had sex in…in…" She felt as if she should warn him that she wasn't some princess of delights who'd know how to acrobatically leap through twelve different positions without missing a beat. She couldn't even remember the last time she'd enjoyed sex. Her ex-husband had struggled to stay aroused enough to please her. At first she hadn't minded. Sex wasn't everything. She was a virgin when she met him so she didn't know any different and expected that things would improve with time.

Oh, how wrong she'd been.

"Good."

"Why good?"

"Because you're starting all over again, fresh and new."

"Like a virgin?" She laughed, thinking of the Madonna song.

His dark blue eyes sparkled. "Exactly."

Five

Was it possible to forget the past, or at least leave it behind? Dani reached for Quasar's shirt collar with a renewed sense of optimism. She actually wanted to undress him. She'd wondered late at night what his body looked like naked, and now was her chance to find out.

His eyes rested on her mouth as she undid the first two buttons of his shirt, her fingers trembling against his hot skin. Tanned by the sun, and hard with muscle, his chest outstripped her fantasies.

And now his hands were on the buttons of her navy blouse. His long fingers deftly pulled the tiny buttons from their holes, and she hesitated as she saw the bright white of her bra exposed. Unsure of what his eyes would do to her, she didn't dare look up at him. Instead she busied herself with the remaining buttons on his shirt, trying to keep her breathing steady as she traced the line of buttons down to the waistband of his pants.

"Stop." He took her wrist gently, which was a relief as she wasn't sure what to do when she got to his pants. "And kiss me."

Their kiss melted away the tension building inside her. Quasar's embrace wrapped her in soothing warmth. She loved that he wasn't trying to rush her into anything. Her body ached with need, and the feeling was as confusing as it was exciting. Even by American standards she hadn't known him very long. She could easily postpone this until another time—or indefinitely—and make a show of touring around the house and looking at the old books.

But she didn't want to. She wanted to see Quasar's naked body, and feel it pressed against hers. The desire alone felt so rebellious and freeing after the way she'd shut herself down—been shut down—to the point where she'd forgotten what pleasure really was. Now it lapped at her from all directions.

Her fingers found their way to the button of his pants, and undid it. He was hard, aroused as she was, and as she lowered the zipper, it thrilled her to know how much he desired her. He'd unbuttoned her blouse and now lowered his head to her bra, licking her nipples through the thin fabric.

Her hips bucked at the rich sensation pouring through her. She shoved her fingers into his silky hair and gasped at the sensation. Then he undid her bra and suckled her bare nipple until she shuddered with arousal.

She'd never wanted anyone so much. Maybe it was the years of pent-up longing, or maybe it was just Quasar, but she wanted to make love to him so badly she could taste it. "You have a gorgeous body." She'd lowered his pants down his legs to discover that they were as muscled and powerful as his torso.

"Me? You're the one with the gorgeous body." He'd already removed her shirt, and now he unzipped her pants and eased them down over her thighs. "Look at that hourglass waist. And a man could lose himself in between these luscious thighs." He crouched and buried his head between them, suddenly flicking his tongue in her most private place and making her gasp. When he licked again, she let out a tiny high-pitched noise that might have been embarrassing if she were with anyone but Quasar.

"Oh, my." She didn't know what else to say. She clung to his shoulders, enjoying the tensed muscle under her fingertips. Arousal rushed through her, leaving her breathless. Every inch of her was alive with sensation. Quasar's tongue flicked back and forth, sending little shudders along her legs.

"Lie on the bed," he commanded softly.

She obeyed, her body almost limp with desire. She eased herself up onto the soft covers and let herself relax. Quasar bent over her, kissing her body, stroking her, and licking her most sensitive flesh until she could barely stand it. "I want to feel you inside me," she whispered. She couldn't remember ever wanting anything more intensely.

"It would be my pleasure." His low murmur was the sexiest thing she'd ever heard. She could hardly believe it was her lying here on this bed, writhing with delight. Even being naked with Quasar felt completely natural. The warm air kissed her skin and the soft, diffused light was gentle on her dilated pupils.

He rolled on a condom, then eased his strong body on top of hers and entered her very gently. He looked right into her eyes at the moment of penetration in a way that said, *I'm here with you right now and nothing else matters.*

Arms wrapped around his back, she welcomed him into her and gave herself over to the strange and wonderful sensations flooding her body. He filled her, making her gasp and moan with pleasure. It seemed impossible that just a few days ago she'd been alone, sure she'd never feel a man's arms around her again. In fact she hadn't wanted a man anywhere near her. She'd grown afraid of masculine energy and its demands. She preferred the safe solitude of her bedroom and the comfort of quiet loneliness.

Meeting Quasar had changed everything. He had been so sweet to her from the moment they met. Kind and encouraging, nonjudgmental, supportive… He was like a fantasy come to life—in the form of a breathtaking man with boundless confidence and the world at his feet. And now here he was, making love to her with all the power and passion he possessed and driving her into a realm of intense bliss.

"Oh, Dani." His voice rasped in her neck. "You're doing something to me. I'm losing control, I…I…" He climaxed with a dramatic shudder and, breathing hard, clung to her. "I don't know what happened." His arms wrapped around her, holding her close. "I meant to last longer but…" His words trailed off into her hair.

"It was perfect," she murmured, wanting to reassure him. And it was. She'd climaxed so powerfully that her muscles must have gripped him and driven him over the edge, whether he was ready or not. The thought made her want to laugh. That she had so much control over such a powerful and commanding man was funny and made her feel sexy. "I've never had an orgasm like that in my life," she admitted.

"Good." He heaved a sigh. "Me neither." He laughed, letting his head fall next to hers. "I don't know what you're doing to me, Dani, but everything's different. It's just so…different."

She laughed.

"See, you're making me inarticulate with passion. Usually I'm a quick-witted charmer, but around you I just…" He pressed his cheek to hers for a second, and she enjoyed the masculine roughness of his skin. He kissed her firmly, then softly, then firmly again on the mouth. He was still inside her, and she felt him throb, and her own sex respond. It made her smile. She couldn't remember that ever happening before. Her body was having a conversation with his body, an intimate conversation that had nothing to do with their brains, or her fears, or anything other than the sensations and emotions they created together.

"I'm not too articulate at the best of times, but I have no words to describe how I'm feeling, either." She stroked his hair and nuzzled his cheek. His skin smelled fabulous, rich and musky, with a hint of fragrance like some ancient incense. "Except that I feel very, very good."

"I'm so glad. You deserve to feel wonderful. Your lover should make you feel cherished and special and beautiful, and it pains me that you've ever felt otherwise."

"You're making up for it right now." She smiled, and kissed his nose.

"Good. From the sounds of it I have a lot of making up to do, but I'm up to the task."

"I have no doubt about that."

"I promise you I'm a skilled lover, when I'm not overcome by unexpected and intense feelings." His dark gaze met hers, and she enjoyed the sparkle in his eyes.

"I'm glad I was able to overwhelm you. I'd think an experienced lover could get jaded and bored easily." Pride tickled her that Quasar was so excited that he literally couldn't contain himself. Who'd have thought that little Dani—as her ex had derisively referred to her—could have that effect on a man?

Quasar eased out of her and she watched as he walked to the adjoining bathroom. His body was magnificent, sculpted like a bronze statue, and he strode with the lithe confidence that characterized everything he did.

Part of her couldn't believe her luck to be here with him right now.

The rest of her wondered how she'd hold up when it was all over.

When he was wrapped around her it was easy to forget that her time with Quasar was limited. Everything felt so effortless and perfect she was tempted to assume it would go on forever.

But there was no forever. Everything in human existence had its time limits and her time with Quasar would be a few more weeks at the most. She tried to tell herself it was freeing to know that the relationship had a sell-by date and she didn't have to worry about it turning sour like her marriage. Still, she'd miss him.

"Why so serious?" His silhouette filled the bathroom door. She hadn't noticed him watching her.

"I know I should make the most of our time together, but I can't help thinking about the future."

He frowned, and she regretted her frank confession. "It's better to live in the moment."

She felt his comment like a stab to the chest. He was right, of course. All the philosophers pretty much agreed on that point. Happiness was in the present moment. Everything else was just an idea or a memory. "I'm going to miss you when you're gone." Her whispered words hung in the air.

It was pretty amazing that she was still confident enough to admit her true feelings. But that was the cool thing about Quasar. She knew she could say anything and nothing bad would happen. Her ex had been so touchy that she had to carefully vet every phrase that came out of her mouth to make sure it wouldn't get under his thin skin and make him fly off the handle.

"I'm going to miss you, too. I'll miss you tonight when

you're alone in your bed in your father's house, and I'm alone in my bed in my brother's grand hotel. It does seem a crime that we can't be together." His eyes brightened. "Why don't you come stay with me?"

She stared. To him it was a simple practical consideration—*I won't miss you if we're together*—and he'd come up with a practical solution.

That wasn't practical at all.

At least not if she wanted to preserve what little was left of her reputation. Ending a bad marriage was embarrassing but not utterly fatal to her future prospects. Openly engaging in a sexual affair with a man she wasn't married to, in full view of his family and the whole world, would be almost up there with hanging a red light outside her window.

"I mean it. My brothers are both married to Americans. They're not old-fashioned. They'll understand."

"I can't. I intend to live in Salalah for the time being so I have to abide by the customs or I'll quickly become a pariah. I swear some people already cross the road when they see me coming. I've committed a multitude of sins in their eyes by running off to America and marrying Mr. Wrong."

Quasar sighed. "I suppose you're right. Still, wouldn't it be wonderful for us to spend the whole night together?"

Or the rest of our lives? The stray thought popped into her mind and she quickly banished it.

He stroked her cheek softly. "Are you sure you can't think of an excuse to stay over?"

His persistence amused her. "I'm not that clever."

"Usually I am, but you've disarmed me so much that I'm not on top of my game." His mischievous gaze made her smile. He leaned forward and murmured in her ear.

"So I think we'd better make love again and see if I can get my sanity back."

Desire tickled her insides as his low voice stirred her senses. "That sounds like a good idea."

"At least I still have some good ideas left." He trailed a finger along her torso, tracing a line between her breasts, and down over her belly, which twitched as he passed it. "And some condoms."

She giggled. The prospect of feeling him inside her again was ridiculously exciting. She felt like a kid about to unwrap a bar of her favorite candy. If someone had told her a week ago that she'd be gazing at the naked thighs of the most gorgeous man she'd ever met, she would have laughed in that person's face. If someone had told her she'd ever even be excited by the prospect of sex with a man again she'd have expressed some doubt. Just a few days had transformed her from a wary, shy recluse into a sensual woman ready to risk her heart for a few brief moments of pleasure.

Her heart could handle it. It must be steel-plated by now after all she'd been through in the last few years. As long as the affair was secret and no one else knew about it, she could deal with her private pain when it was over.

Quasar lay on the bed next to her, and she ran her hand over the hard muscle of his thigh, letting desire rise inside her like flood water. Already he was erect again, ready for her. She watched his taut belly contract as she lowered her lips and licked him. He uttered a low groan when she took him in her mouth, and again she loved the power she had over him—power she intended to use only for pleasure, never to hurt him. She enjoyed feeling him grow harder still as she pleasured him with her tongue, then she eased herself up and trailed kisses over his flat stomach with its sprinkling of rough, dark hair.

Her ex had a hard time maintaining an erection and coaxing it back from the dead had become a tiresome chore she dreaded. This was clearly not an issue with Quasar. After he'd rolled on the condom, she climbed over him, and eased herself down on top of him slowly, reveling in each delicious moment of sensation as he filled her.

Her ex hadn't liked her to go on top. He liked to be in command of everything and probably didn't want her to think her pleasure was hers for the taking. Quasar's broad smile and blissfully closed eyes showed her that she was welcome to enjoy him however she liked. She smiled as she moved her hips, and rich, intense waves of pleasure started to roll inside her. "This feels so good," she murmured. It was wonderful to choose the rhythm, and control the motion, with their mutual pleasure as her only goal.

"It feels even better for me," he rasped. His fingers stroked her skin, gently rubbing her nipples and driving her even wilder with excitement.

Already her breathing came in ragged gasps and it was hard to form thoughts. Something inside her took over and she found herself quickening the movements as powerful feelings washed through her. When he climaxed with her, moving inside her as her muscles gripped him, the intensity of the sensations made her cry out. She felt so close to him at that moment, with nothing between them, no worries or anxieties or hang-ups, just a shared burst of joy bringing them together.

How could this be wrong if it felt so good and didn't hurt anybody? She collapsed gently on top of him and his strong arms closed around her back, holding her close. His chest rose and fell beneath her and emotion welled inside her. In his embrace she felt so supported and cared for and cherished, just as he'd said she should. Which was silly, since they really didn't even know each other that well. There was a connection between them that neither of them could fully understand or articulate, but it was there all the same.

She wrapped her arms around him and buried her face in his neck. She wished she could stay here forever, pampered by his affection and his simple enjoyment of her company.

"That was something else, Dani." His gruff voice and the gentle way he stroked her hair almost undid her. Their bodies seemed to fit so perfectly together, still throbbing and pulsing with enjoyment even as they lay quietly in each other's arms.

"You're something else." She wasn't telling him anything he didn't already know, and that was okay. She didn't even mind being one in a long stream of eager women. Why not? It was the most pleasure she'd ever experienced during sex; she'd probably never know anything like it again. "And I'm very glad you interrupted my reading that day."

"Me, too. It pains me to say this but it's almost time for you to leave."

"Already? I feel like we just got here." A glance at her watch revealed that he was right. How had three hours flown by so fast? And how sweet of him to keep an eye on the time for her when he could have ignored it in the pursuit of his own pleasure. "I really wish I could stay, but we both know I can't."

"Can you come back tomorrow?"

She smiled, her face still pressed to his neck. "I'd love to."

The next day they could hardly wait until the drive was over before they peeled off each other's clothes and made steamy, passionate love again. The attraction between them was so intense it threatened to singe their flesh. Dani had never known such powerful desire. It undid her inhibitions and let her revel in pure enjoyment for its own sake. Afterward, they wrapped themselves in luxurious silk robes from the bedroom closet, and unpacked a lunch Quasar had brought from the hotel. They were in a room that had been remodeled into an open kitchen and living-room area. The ancient pale stone walls contrasted with the light-filled modern spaces, and stained-glass lanterns sprinkled glittering jewels of color over the walls and ceiling.

"Goodness, look at this salad. It must have twenty different things in it." There were lush slices of fruit, nuts, fresh greens—everything looked as if it had been picked that morning.

"Salim scours the world for the most creative chefs and makes them an offer they can't refuse."

"It must take some convincing to get them to come to Salalah. I bet most of them have never heard of it."

"Money talks." Quasar grinned and spooned helpings of the salad he'd brought into beautifully painted earthenware bowls.

"Not to everyone."

"Sooner or later, most people will listen to it. That's my experience, anyway."

"That's a very mercenary view of the world." She poured them both a glass of fresh limeade with fragrant mint leaves.

"True. What do you think motivates people?" His gaze contained a challenge. She resolved to rise to it.

"I think most people want to be happy. I know I do."

"To a certain extent I agree." He stretched out on one of the sofas, dish of salad balanced on his knee. "The problem is that no one really knows what makes them happy. They rarely even know when they are happy. They just notice when they're not."

"And they decide that a few more zeros on the end of their bank account balance will make them feel better?"

"Pretty much." He winked.

It was hard to counter, since she wasn't motivated by money at all. She'd been lucky enough never to have to worry about where her next meal was coming from. Family loyalty might come with obligations, but they were amply paid back by the security her family offered when she needed it most.

On the other hand, was she happy?

She looked at the gorgeous man seated on the sofa next to her, contentedly munching on the exotic salad. Right now, the answer was unequivocally yes. She was happy. She knew it wouldn't last forever, or even for much longer, but right now she was in bliss.

"I'd like to meet your father."

"What?" She almost dropped her fork.

"It's not right for us to keep meeting in secret. We're in Oman and we should abide by Omani custom."

She swallowed hard. "I don't think that's a good idea."

"Why not?"

He won't like you. And with good reason, since you've tempted me into an illicit affair. "You're only here for a short time. There's no point."

"Of course there is. We don't have to tell him we're having sex, but at the very least he should know we're friends."

"But we're not friends." *We're a lot more than that. Or much less.* She wasn't quite sure. Her stomach had shriveled into a tiny knot. Her feelings of blissful happiness were evaporating into the air-conditioned atmosphere as she faced the true nature of their relationship head-on.

Quasar still looked relaxed and at ease, sipping his limeade. "Don't worry, I'll charm him."

"He's not really susceptible to charm. He's an engineer. He's all about structure and substance." *He'll want to know when the wedding is.* She couldn't say that. She'd rather die. A pleasure-seeking international playboy like Quasar would not be marrying her in this lifetime. Even in the throes of passion she wasn't delusional enough to think that.

"Trust me."

She shook her head. "Trust *me*. It's not a good idea. Besides, I don't like being told what to do. That's what my ex-husband specialized in, remember?" She was proud of herself for speaking her thoughts. She didn't need a man to run her life and tell her what was appropriate. Not that she was pleased with herself for sneaking about, but under the circumstances it seemed like the only approach that protected both her feelings and her reputation. Quasar cared about her feelings because he wanted to please her, and her father cared about her reputation as a matter of family honor, but neither of them really had much reason to worry about the big picture.

"I don't want to tell you what to do, but I don't like this sneaking around. It doesn't sit well with me. We have nothing to be ashamed of."

"You just admitted there was no reason to tell him that we had sex." She noticed how he called it having sex, not making love. "So it's not like you wouldn't be hiding something anyway. It will be easier for me if he never knows about us."

"I've spoiled your appetite for this delicious food." He looked ruefully at the fork now sitting idle on her plate.

"I'm sorry. I'll drop the subject. If you want me to be your secret lover I'll try to go along with it."

She managed a smile. "I bet this isn't your first secret affair."

"I cannot tell a lie. I'm no stranger to subterfuge. I think I'm getting too old for it, though. I'd rather have everything aboveboard."

"Sometimes that's just not possible. Besides, you're thirty-one. That's not old."

"I'm a mature man and you're a mature women and we should be able to enjoy each other's company openly."

"In America, maybe, but not in Oman." Things would be so different if they were in New Jersey, or California. On the other hand, if they were, Quasar would probably be spending the afternoon with a glamorous starlet or a sexy businesswoman, and would never have noticed her. She didn't exactly have men pursuing her everywhere. Her cousin said it was because she gave off energy that said, *Stay away!* Her ex had been persistent enough to break through her reserve. Then he'd been persistent enough to steamroll right over her and empty her life of anything but him. She didn't know how to have a normal relationship. Her affair with Quasar was anything but normal but maybe it could be if the circumstances were different.

If they weren't in Oman.

If Quasar were an ordinary man.

If she were an optimistic, confident woman who still believed in love and happily-ever-afters.

But none of those things were true so she had to make the best of where they were right now. She picked up her fork and tried for an encouraging smile. "I appreciate you wanting to meet my father. It really is sweet of you. It just isn't a good idea."

"I'll bow to your superior wisdom on the topic. You've lived in Oman a lot longer than I have." He didn't look mad, or even put out. Probably it didn't matter much to him either way and he'd just made the suggestion to please her. Which was sweet.

She forked some salad into her mouth and let the sweetness of orange and mango spread over her tongue. She needed to live in the moment. To be happy while the opportunity presented itself.

Which shouldn't be hard given the circumstances. Diffuse sunlight poured through the lattice screens on the arched windows, pooling in luxurious patterns on the marble floor. Quasar's slate-blue eyes sparkled with the passion and excitement that she'd put there. In bed he'd been making love to her with a look of rapture on his face. Who wouldn't be happy in her place?

It wasn't as if she were falling in love with him. Now that would be stupid. She wasn't stupid. They'd enjoy each other's company, then they'd go their separate ways. There was no danger of getting in over her head. In the meantime she just needed to keep her head, and protect her heart.

"I can see you're not hungry, beautiful." Quasar put down his plate and knelt at her feet. He kissed her fingertips, then her lips, and desire flared through her, banishing her doubts and worries. "Shall we go back to the bedroom?"

She placed her plate on an inlaid wood table. Feeling was so much easier than thinking. Right now all she wanted to do was press her naked body against Quasar's and lose herself in his touch. "Absolutely."

Six

"I'm telling you, leave well enough alone. Her father hates our whole family." Elan reined in his horse, who was blowing hard. They'd trailered two horses, borrowed from a close friend, and headed out to the mountains to let off some steam. They were up on a high slope with a view of Salalah partially visible through the trees.

Quasar leaned back in his saddle on his gray mare, who was puffing and blowing from the effort of the ascent up the mountain. "But I can reason with him, make a deal that will win him over. I'm famous for negotiating my way out of tough situations."

"Or into them. Are you going to marry her?" His brother's intense gaze slammed right into him.

"I just met her."

"See? You're just experimenting. Playing around. Seeing what will happen. And I think we both know, based on your history of relationships, what will happen."

Quasar frowned. "You think I'll grow bored with her."

"I don't know her. How could I predict that?" Elan leaned forward to flick a fly off the neck of his sturdy chestnut gelding.

"I want to bring her over so you can all meet her."

"That will tell her that you're serious."

"I am serious!"

"Not by Omani standards. Serious means marriage. Don't lead her on until you know where you're going."

Squinting into the late afternoon sun, they guided their sweating horses down a winding trail on a wooded slope. "How do I know where I'm going if I don't at least get started in the right direction. Did you know right away that you would marry Sara?"

Elan laughed. "Hell, no! I was determined to have nothing to do with her. She was my employee, for crying out loud."

Elan had not only had an affair with his secretary, but he'd also accidentally got her pregnant. "But you ended up in the right place, married to the woman you love."

"Yeah." Elan took a gulp from his canteen. "I learned to stop being the boss and trying to run the show, and let Sara be my partner. So if Dani doesn't want you to meet her father, then don't."

"I see your point."

"You can't charm your way into every situation. Or out of it. Old man Hassan hates our family with a passion that could last for generations. If you can manage not to fall in love with his daughter you'd probably be doing both of you a favor." Elan's familiar piercing stare caught him off guard again. "You're not in love with her already, are you?"

"Me?" Why couldn't he stop thinking about her? Wanting to be with her? Wanting to tell everyone about her? Was that love?

Probably not. Nevertheless, it was likely some possessive male thing that would still get him into trouble.

"Because if you're in love with her then it's a different story."

Their horses were happy to reach level ground. Elan launched into a spirited description of the newest Arab mare on his ranch back in Nevada. "Women aren't like mares, little brother." Elan pulled up his horse and stared at him again. "They don't like being told what to do. They need to make up their own minds."

"I suppose you're right." Of course he didn't love Dani. He barely knew her. They had great chemistry, no doubt. Unbelievable sex, hell yes. Interesting conversation, for sure. Enjoyable companionship, yes indeed. But love? He didn't even know what that was.

"Then don't approach her father. If you do, he'll think you're serious. And if you don't love her, you're not serious. Shall we gallop on this flat land?"

"Sure." His mind whirred with confusion as he urged his horse faster, until the gray mane was flying in his face. Why were matters of the heart so much more complicated than corporate affairs? Since coming to Oman he'd already come up with three viable new business plans, each of which excited him equally. On the other hand, there was only one woman on his mind.

"Race you there!" Elan called back, pointing to a lone frankincense tree in the desert.

Whipped on by his own competitive instincts, Quasar charged forward until they were neck and neck, their powerful horses speeding across the desert, hooves tapping out a quiet drumbeat on the sandy soil. Pursuing Dani was all wrong. He didn't want to hurt her again after what she'd suffered in her marriage.

When his horse passed Elan's, Quasar let out a yell into the desert air. A whoop of triumph that also contained a howl of frustration at the situation he found himself in with Dani. The sex they shared was insane. He could talk to her about anything. He craved her company when he wasn't with her. And everyone, including her, thought he should stay away from her.

So why did he want to ignore them all and take matters into his own hands?

"Good news, my darling." Dani's father arrived home that evening in an uncharacteristically festive mood. She didn't remember ever hearing him call her *darling* before. It struck a note of alarm in her heart.

"What, Dad?" She took his briefcase and put it in its place under the hall table.

"Samir Al Kabisi came to my office today." He was beaming. Dani froze. This was the man who'd told her he was still potent so her needs would not go unmet. "He made a generous offer for your hand in marriage and you'll be happy to hear that I accepted."

"What?" She knew the custom of *mahr*, in which the husband offered a certain sum of money to his bride. It was a tenet of Islam intended to protect women by making sure they had money of their own in case they needed it. But these days it was customary for the man to make his offer of marriage to the woman herself, not her father, wasn't it? And how could her father possibly accept without asking her? Her heart pounded and her breathing grew unsteady. "I'm not marrying him."

"Don't be foolish, Dani." Her father's cheerful expression had barely altered. "It's an excellent offer and he's a good man. He owns his own firm and could comfortably retire tomorrow if he wanted. He's the chief supplier of nuts and rivets in the gulf region."

"But I'm not in love with him." Her voice was shaky. She knew her father couldn't make her marry this man, but her refusal was bound to cause a rift between them.

"Love grows. It's a silly modern fashion to try to fall in love before you're committed."

"I'll never love him. He's too old. I'd make him unhappy as well as myself."

Her father's expression darkened. "Daniyah, I've been very indulgent with you since your unfortunate return home. You tried to do everything your own way once, and the results were disastrous."

She didn't deny it.

"Now it's time for you to listen to the wisdom of your father and an older generation, when life was simpler and people were happier."

She couldn't argue and say that her parents' marriage wasn't happy. She suspected it wasn't but since her mother wasn't alive to agree with her, she could only speculate. "I'm not opposed to marrying again, but it needs to be someone I can grow to have feelings for."

"Samir is a kind man. He hosts a party at the orphanage every year during the *Eid* holiday."

"I'm sure he's lovely, but those aren't the kinds of feelings I'm talking about. We're both adults here. If I'm to share a bed with my husband I must have some attraction to him."

Her unruly brain conjured an image of Quasar next to her in bed, languid, his tanned, muscled body against the white sheets, eyes shining in semidarkness.

"Daniyah, I'm shocked at you. Discretion is an essential quality in a woman."

"I have to speak the truth. I've survived one bad marriage and I'm not willing to take a chance on another. You'll have to tell Mr. Al Kabisi that I refused his kind offer, or I'll go tell him myself."

Her father clucked his tongue, his good humor utterly gone. "A father does not expect to endure the burden of his daughter returning home in middle age."

Stung by humiliation, Dani drew herself up. "I'm hardly middle-aged. I'll find a job."

"As an art historian?" He snorted. "You should have studied something sensible, as I always encouraged you to. You could have been an engineer, or a chemist, or even an architect, but no, you had to study something foolish and whimsical with no career prospects, almost as if you intended only to be a rich man's wife."

Tears stung her eyes. "Art is my passion."

"Fishing was my passion, when I was a child. I did not, however, choose to become a fisherman. If I were still inclined to pursue it, I'd fish simply as a hobby."

She had to admit his words made sense. She'd been so blinded by the cheerful attitude that everyone should follow their bliss, which had prevailed at the small New Jersey university she'd attended. "You're right. But I'll find something. I'll work in a shop."

He looked doubtful. "At least take the night and think it over. You'll be very comfortable with Samir. He has a spacious house only a few streets away and he drives a Mercedes."

"I won't change my mind," she whispered. "I have a headache. I'm going to go lie down." She'd skip dinner and help herself to something later when everyone else had gone to bed. She couldn't face sitting around with three male Hassans looking skeptically at her every move.

Not for the first time she reflected that maybe she should have stayed in New Jersey, where at least she wouldn't have elderly suitors shoved down her throat. But how? New Jersey was very expensive. She had no job and no place to live, and she could hardly return to live with her aunt, who had four daughters and now considered her to be a bad influence. Her self-esteem had been shattered by her ex-husband and she no longer believed herself capable of supporting herself and living independently. At the time she'd seen no other option than to run home with her tail between her legs.

Now that she'd had the time and distance to regain some perspective, she could see that coming home actually left her in a worse position. Her employment prospects were dimmer than ever, and she had another domineering male to answer to.

In her bedroom she lay on her soft bed and gazed up at the high ceiling with its ornately carved wood beams. This house she'd grown up in was grand by Omani standards. She'd always been well provided for and treated like a princess, at least by her indulgent and warm mother. She'd seen little of the world outside the filigree wooden shutters and had imagined it to be a brilliant and exciting place similar to the one she saw on American television shows. In college she often felt like the star of an upbeat sitcom where anything was possible. When her future husband, Gordon, had arrived on the scene, she'd assumed she was the heroine of a romance being swept off her feet by his insistent pursuit.

As her marriage progressed she'd realized she might be starring in a future episode of *Law & Order* instead. As her husband's psychological abuse ratcheted up slowly into verbal abuse, and he began to pound his fists on the table or the wall, she knew she'd be next to feel his wrath and she'd finally come to her senses.

Hot tears leaked from her eyes as she reflected on all the foolish dreams she'd had. And now Quasar had come into her life as if to mock her with the kind of romance and passion she couldn't really hope to enjoy, at least not for more than a few stolen sessions.

Noise from outside her room made her jerk her head

up from the pillow. She heard raised male voices, and one in particular made her breath catch in her throat.

She could almost swear that was Quasar's voice.

Dani climbed off the bed and hurried to her bedroom door. The house was one story, centered around a hall-way, and if she opened her door the men would likely see her. The voices seemed to be coming from the direction of the front door.

"I know exactly who you are," her father was shout-ing. "Your whole family has played a part in the plot to deprive my heirs of their birthright."

What? Dani pressed her ear to the door. Now she was desperate to hear the other voice. It couldn't be Quasar, could it?

"Mr. Hassan, I come with nothing but the utmost re-spect for you. You may not be aware that I have lived in the States for many years and have little to no involve-ment in my family's affairs. I certainly have played no part in the lawsuit between our families."

Dani's chest rose and fell rapidly. It did sound like Quasar. But it couldn't be, because she'd explicitly told him not to come here. And if it was Quasar, they'd be talking about her. And they weren't. She had no idea what they were talking about.

She frowned and turned back toward her bed. Ob-viously she was losing her mind if she thought some random man who came to the door must be her lover. When she wasn't with him, thoughts of him haunted her day and night. His image always seemed to hover at the edges of her consciousness, taunting her until she could see him again. He'd talked her into letting him pick her up at the house tomorrow. He'd convinced her that re-peatedly meeting out in public was getting too risky and it was wise to mix things up a little, so she'd given him her address.

Her chest—and other parts of her—tingled with excitement at the prospect of seeing him again and spending another languid afternoon in their remote and luxurious love nest.

But what on earth was going on in the foyer?

"I curse the name of Al Mansur and I will never let one of those sons of dogs anywhere near my daughter!"

Dani froze; the word *daughter* struck fear into her heart.

"I'm not here as a representative of my family or anyone else. I come simply as a man of honor seeking your approval to meet and talk with her."

Now she was sure that the voice was Quasar's.

She crept back to the door, blood pounding in her head, and pressed her ear to it. Oh, how she wished there was a keyhole to peer through!

"My daughter is spoken for. A man has just today asked for her hand in marriage, and I have accepted his offer."

"Surely Dani must have a say in the matter." Quasar sounded shocked. As well he might. She hadn't mentioned her father's plans to him. "She's an adult woman, not a young girl who doesn't know her own mind."

"She's made up her own mind in the past and it proved to be a bad idea. She understands that I have only her best interests at heart."

Dani could stand it no longer. She tugged open her bedroom door and stepped out into the hallway. "What are you doing here?" she heard herself ask Quasar. She stood, staring at him. He looked oddly regal in traditional Omani attire—it was the first time she'd seen him in it—but she was furious with him for going against her wishes.

"You are a respectable Omani woman, and I am a respectable Omani man, and it is customary for me to meet your father and ask permission to court you."

"Permission is *not* granted!" growled Dani's father. "And I do not give you permission to place your accursed feet in my house. What do you have to say for yourself, Daniyah? Have you encouraged the attentions of this reprobate?"

She swallowed. "I…"

"She has done nothing whatsoever to encourage my attentions. I simply noticed that we both share a taste for books, and a brief discussion suggested that we have some interests in common. I would like to get to know your daughter better." Quasar turned his gaze to Dani, and those deep blue eyes seemed to hold her in a trance.

"I didn't ask you." Her father scowled at Quasar. Then he turned his attention to her. "Daniyah, have you spoken with this man?" She'd never seen her father so angry. His eyebrows stood on end like little furry animals, and his lips had grown white.

"Yes, Father. I have spoken with him." If he had any idea what else she'd done with him, he'd probably have a heart attack on the spot. She couldn't think of anything to say that wouldn't either incriminate her or enmesh her in a lie she'd later regret.

"Your daughter's conduct has been unimpeachable."

Dani stood rooted to the spot. That was a very subjective view of her conduct, which by any traditional standards was shocking in the extreme.

"If you don't leave my house right now, I'll call the police."

"Sir, let me beseech you. I'm happy to simply exchange a few words with your daughter here in your house, under your watchful eye."

Quasar seemed totally unfazed by her father's apoplectic rage. If anything she thought she saw a twinkle of humor in his eye. Which, under the circumstances, really ticked her off. He'd taken no personal risk coming here. If her father hated him, who cared? He was going back to the States and would soon forget the whole affair.

She, on the other hand, would have to live with the repercussions of this ill-starred visit for the rest of her life. "You really should leave." She found herself speaking coolly, looking directly at Quasar. How could he have totally disregarded her wishes? She'd told him not to come. Who did he think he was?

"If Daniyah wishes for me to leave, I shall leave." He swept a bow in her direction. The chivalrous gesture would have excited her if she weren't almost as angry as her father. Quasar nodded to the older man and apologized for alarming him, muttered a traditional goodbye and left, striding confidently in his long white dishdasha.

Dani wanted to sag with relief as he disappeared out of sight, leaving the front door open to the gathering dusk. Instead, her instincts told her to turn and run.

Her father calmly and quietly closed the door. "What is the meaning of this, Daniyah? You are not in Hackysack."

"It's Hackensack."

"I don't care what it's called. You are in Salalah now. You can't strike up a conversation with any Tom, Dick or Harry who happens to stroll past you in a shop! You must have encouraged him to give him the confidence to come knock on my front door. Do you have any idea who this man is?"

She shook her head mutely. She didn't, really. It was hard to believe she'd never even asked his last name. It hadn't been relevant. And maybe she hadn't wanted to know. It would have made their relationship seem more real, and then it would hurt more when it turned out to be a dreamlike interlude, as she knew it ultimately would.

"Quasar Al Mansur is the youngest son of Hakim Al Mansur."

The name sounded vaguely familiar. She'd never paid much attention to local society gossip but she suspected he was some kind of oil-rich sheikh.

"Hakim is mercifully no longer on this earth, but his sons continue to refuse to recognize our family's ownership of the old Fabriz property. They tricked my father into selling it for a few thousand rials when it was simply a mediocre fishing spot. Now it's worth millions as prime waterfront investment property, and they're maintaining that the pathetic deal he was forced into is valid."

"If it was his father's doing, Quasar probably wasn't involved at all." After she'd spoken she realized she sounded as if she were defending him. Her best course was to pretend she barely even recognized him.

"I've had a lawsuit pending against the Al Mansur family in one form or another since the eighties. I haven't won yet, but I haven't lost, either. Salim Al Mansur has been itching to build one of his accursed hotels on that property for years, but he hasn't been able to because the title is clouded by my lawsuit." A look of satisfaction crossed his face for a moment. "It's only a matter of time until my rights are legally recognized and the property is returned to our family. Your brothers deserve to reap the riches that can be sown there, not those grabbing Al Mansurs, who already have more land and money than they know what to do with."

Dani blinked. She'd known the family was wealthy

and powerful, but it was just her luck that the first man she fell for would be her father's sworn enemy.

She wanted to go back, lie on her bed and continue crying. But that wouldn't solve any problems. "I won't see Quasar behind your back." The resolution was easy to make. He'd deliberately ignored her plea that he not come here. He obviously didn't care about what she thought and had run roughshod over her own thoughts and wishes just like her ex-husband would have. She was done with him.

"But I won't marry Samir Al Kabisi, either." She screwed up her courage. "I'm not ready for marriage again, Father. It's too soon. I'm sure he's a nice man but I'm also sure that any attempt to match me with him would lead to disaster for myself, disappointment for him and further damage to my reputation. I'm sure you don't want that."

"Indeed I do not." His eyebrows were starting to subside a little and color was returning to his pursed lips. He sighed. "Things were so much easier in the old days when a girl listened to her parents."

The next morning Dani woke with a heavy weight in her chest. It was all over. She'd known her affair with Quasar couldn't last forever, but she'd secretly hoped for a couple more weeks of romantic bliss. Last night had put an end to that. She'd promised her father she wouldn't see him in secret, and she meant it.

She'd done an internet search on Quasar's name and the results had been alarming. There were more stories about his love life than his many business triumphs. While she looked at the seemingly endless stream of photos of him, accompanied by an assortment of gorgeous women at movie openings, nightclubs and celebrity parties, it sank in that she really was just another notch on his bedpost.

The day stretched ahead of her like the barren desert. She could do some shopping for food, but even the cleaning was taken care of by a kind older woman who'd been alarmed by Dani's offers of help, probably fearing she'd soon be out of a job.

She resolved to stay under the covers in her bed and read until she regained her equilibrium. After about five minutes, though, she grew restless. She was not going to lie around and wait for life to happen to her. She needed to make it happen, and right now that meant finding a job. Maybe one of her brothers' schools could use an administrator? She decided to visit their offices, and showered and dressed conservatively in a dark green ensemble with that intention. She was arranging her hair when she heard a knock on the door.

She glanced at her watch. It was ten o'clock. The time she'd previously arranged to meet Quasar.

She stood staring at her shocked reflection in the mirror. Could he really have just shown up as if nothing happened?

Another knock, this time more insistent, stirred her to action. If it were Quasar, she had to get him off her doorstep before one of the neighbors saw him. She hurried down the hallway and peered through the peephole. The sight of Quasar's handsome face made her breath catch, as it always did. She braced herself against the effect he had on her and opened the door. "Come in, quick."

Already she was breaking the promise to her father, but it was to prevent further gossip, so hopefully he'd approve.

Quasar stepped over the threshold, his face more serious than usual. "Good morning, Dani."

He bent down to kiss her, but she ducked back, heart thudding. "You shouldn't be here. I told you not to come."

Quasar had the decency to look a little wistful. "I was hoping to make a good impression. I thought if I could talk to your father, he'd see what a nice fellow I am, despite any rumors to the contrary."

She wanted to laugh. Or cry. "And now you can see how wrong you were. I told not to come and you totally ignored me. Did you know he's suing your brother over some piece of land?"

He shrugged. "I did know. I was hoping to find a resolution to that problem as well."

She fought the urge to growl. "You're so arrogant! Charm can't fix everything. In fact it probably can't fix anything at all, ever. I can't believe you knew our families were at odds and you didn't even tell me. I was so clueless and naive I never thought it was important to know your last name. Even I've heard of the Al Mansurs."

"So if I'd told you my name from the get-go you would have run a mile in the opposite direction?"

"Absolutely."

"Then discretion was the better part of valor."

"Hardly. Now my father is furious and doesn't trust me. If he had any idea what we've already done together he might throw me out on the street. I probably deserve it."

By Omani standards she'd been the worst kind of loose woman. At least she wasn't sleeping with a married man, but beyond that the situation had no redeeming features. "You need to leave."

"I came to see your father because I really care about you, Dani." Quasar's gaze fixed on her with the intensity of a laser. "I didn't want to sneak around like we're having some meaningless dalliance. My brothers warned

me that if I came to see him he'd think I meant business."
He frowned. "And I do."

Dani's heart was beating so fast she couldn't think,
let alone speak. Did he mean that he wanted to marry
her? No, he hadn't said that. She cursed herself for even
being foolish enough to think it. "You have to go. The
neighbors might have seen you arrive."

"I'm not leaving unless you come with me." He seized
her hands and held them. Her hands were so cold inside
his. "Don't tell me you don't have feelings for me."

Nameless emotion flared in her chest. "I have feelings all right. I'm angry with you. You deliberately did
something I told you not to."

"Come with me and let's talk about it. At least allow
me that much." His slate-blue gaze implored her.

Common sense warred with much stronger feelings
as he held her hands and kept his eyes locked on hers.
Could she really just make him leave without an explanation? Her heart said no. "Okay, we'll just talk. Nothing
more." If his car was parked outside, she wanted it gone.
"Let me get my shoes."

Once outside the house, she glanced furtively in both
directions and dived for his silver Mercedes. She prayed
no one had seen it. At least it was such a popular car here
in her affluent neighborhood that it didn't say a whole
lot about its owner. She climbed into the passenger seat
and donned a pair of dark glasses that were sitting on the
shelf above the glove compartment. "Quick, drive away
before someone sees us."

"You're making me feel like I'm in a spy movie."

"You'll be in a very different kind of movie if my father discovers that you came here again."

An infuriating smile played around the edges of Quasar's mouth. "Why? What would he do to me?"

"He did threaten to call the police. He'd do it, too. His cousin Ahmed is the chief of police."

"Ouch. I'd better keep my head down, then."

She sank back into her seat as they pulled out on to the main road. She hadn't seen anyone she recognized. On the other hand, she was now heading who-knew-where with Quasar, when she'd sworn to stay away from him.

Adrenaline fired through her. "I can't believe you totally ignored what I told you. You decided to take charge of my life, regardless of what I think. Just like my ex." She stared right at him as she said the last part, daring him to argue with her.

He turned to look at her, and she was gratified to see contrition in his eyes. "I didn't think of it like that. I'm sorry."

"You should be. The last thing I need is another man telling me what to do. Or even worse, not telling me! It was not a pleasant surprise to hear your voice in my hallway." It felt good to voice her feelings. She'd been afraid to do that for so long.

"I thought that if I talked your father around, you'd be happy about it."

"Your confidence is both awe-inspiring and infuriating. Who knows my father better, you or me?"

He shrugged and looked sheepish. "You. I confess I'm not used to waiting around. I prefer to get up and make things happen."

"Typical male."

"I suppose so. Do you think you can forgive me?" Already she saw the twinkle of familiar humor creeping back into his annoyingly seductive gaze.

"No way." She focused her gaze on the windshield. It was dangerous looking at Quasar. He was far too handsome for his own good, or anyone else's.

"What am I going to do with you?"

She decided that his seductive tone was only going to fuel her anger. "Say goodbye to me for good, and drop me home." She snuck a sideways glance at him, just long enough to see if she was immune to his charms.

The answer was no.

He turned to face her again, a mysterious glow in his eyes. "I have a much better idea. Come meet my family."

Seven

Dani's response was immediate and came straight from her gut. "That's a terrible idea."

"I disagree. You'll like them."

"If you meeting my family was an unmitigated disaster, what makes you think me meeting your family will go better?"

"I'm willing to take a chance." Quasar had already steered the car in the direction of the ocean.

"You're obviously more of a risk taker than me. But that's hardly a surprise since you like extreme sports and I like reorganizing my bookshelves. We have almost nothing in common."

"Nonsense. We have something very important."

"Chemistry?"

"Something bigger than that. Call it a life force. Something you can't ignore."

"Says who?" Dani noticed with alarm that they were now driving past the palaces of Salalah's wealthiest citizens.

"Me. And I'm right more often than you'd think."

"Not about love. I did a Google search of your name last night, now that I finally know it." She watched for his reaction and wasn't surprised when a muscle twitched in his cheek. She didn't say more. She was curious to see what his response would be.

"What did you learn about me?"

"That you're known as a fickle maverick entrepreneur in the business world, and that you've dated a large number of beautiful women."

"I can't deny either accusation. I have been fortunate to enjoy the company of some wonderful women." His smile was barely apologetic. "But none of them outshone you."

Pride and embarrassment threatened to heat into a blush. What a flatterer! She shouldn't take his words to heart. "Did you march over and meet their fathers?"

"No. That should prove to you that what I feel for you is different."

They drove through a tall archway with scrolled gates that opened before them. Panic flashed over her. "Wait. You can't just drive in here. I haven't agreed yet."

"Too late. We're here." Salim drove calmly along an avenue of date palms.

"A man who tells me what to do is my worst nightmare." She wiped her now-sweaty palms on her forest-green dress. At least she'd gotten dressed up today. Was he really going to drag her in to meet all his *über*-successful relatives?

"A woman I'm crazy about who tells me never to see her again is my worst nightmare. So at least we're even." He smiled. "Relax. Don't worry about impressing them." He must have seen her fiddling with her scarf. "They're very nice, really."

"Like you?"

"I actually think I'm probably nicer than both of my brothers. They're a little scary, at least when there's business involved. Both of my sisters-in-law are lovely, though. They'll put you at ease."

"Even though they have no idea I'm coming! What if they're busy?"

"They're not. I know they're planning to spend the day relaxing on the beach with the kids. Everyone's on vacation right now."

"I'm not exactly dressed for the beach."

"Don't worry about that. They'll have everything you need in the hotel shop. And don't try to pretend you wouldn't feel comfortable in a swimsuit. I've seen your gorgeous body with my own eyes." The wolfish look he gave her should have sent her fury into overdrive, but instead it had the far more irritating effect of making her aroused.

"What if I don't want to meet your family?" His arrogance was almost unbelievable. This whole escapade was further proof that he was all wrong for her.

Quasar steered the car into a large circular driveway with a spectacular fountain in the middle. She'd heard about this hotel before. It was insanely expensive and very exclusive. It looked like a sultan's palace. Further proof that Quasar Al Mansur was out of her league in every possible way.

As well as being a total jerk.

He parked the car and took her hands in his. "Dani Hassan, I like you very much. Getting to know you better is important to me, and I want you to get to know me better as well. If you then decide that you hate me, I can handle it." That familiar sparkle of amusement lit his eyes. His hands warmed hers and softened the frigid wall of reserve she'd tried to build around herself. "But please do me the honor of meeting my family. It would mean a lot to me."

Her heart swelled when he spoke with such apparent sincerity. Of course this was probably how he'd behaved with all those beautiful women in the gossip column photos. But who was she to think she could resist him any more than they could? If an A-list actress hadn't been able to say no to Quasar, she didn't stand a chance. "Okay."

Before she could gather her thoughts, a bellhop—wearing a uniform the exact same green as her own clothes—opened her door, and she stepped out into the bright sunlight. Quasar immediately rounded the car and threaded his arm though hers, as if hoping to forestall her escape. She glanced around nervously. What if the family felt much more strongly about the land dispute than Quasar, and considered her their enemy?

Even if they were friendly, what if one of her father's associates were here? Or a neighbor? Or almost any ordinary citizen of Salalah who might gossip at the souk about who they saw on Quasar Al Mansur's arm?

She tried to calm herself with the thought that she'd been in the United States since she was a teen so people weren't likely to recognize her. And most of the guests looked foreign, judging from their scanty attire.

"They're probably still having breakfast. That's where they were headed when I left them less than half an hour ago. Things tend to move very slowly when the whole family is gathered together." He led the way into a grand lobby with tall arches and rich mosaics on the walls, and through it to a series of sunlit dining rooms. In the farthest one, a veranda with a view over the beach, she saw a group of people laughing around a large round table. The two blonde women must be his American sisters-in-law. They both glowed with good cheer and the effects of the Omani sunshine. Four children, ranging in age from two to about six, wriggled in seats next to them, finishing the remains of pastries and scrambled eggs. Two tall and handsome men sipped their coffee and looked with calm indulgence over their rather messy offspring.

"I'm so glad you're all gathered in one place." Quasar's deep voice immediately commanded the attention of the group. "I have someone very important for you to meet."

Dani blanched as he said her name, wondering if they'd react with hostility or disdain. Their warm smiles and greetings soon put her at ease, though, as Quasar made his way around the table introducing each one. The taller blonde was Celia, the landscape designer, who was married to his oldest brother, Salim. Her husband looked more than a little forbidding in his dark pinstriped suit, but he made her promise to make herself at home at the hotel. She was relieved that he didn't even mention the lawsuit.

Muscular Elan looked much more casual in jeans and a white T-shirt. He laughed when Quasar apologized for dragging her here, and consoled Dani that the Al Mansur men do need some retraining at first. Elan's wife, Sara, was sweet and welcoming and said that she was just getting to know the vast hotel complex herself and still got lost here sometimes.

A waiter brought two new seats and baskets of fresh pastries and fruit, as well as another pot of coffee, and to her surprise she soon found herself and Quasar making easy conversation with them about life in America versus life in Oman. She relaxed a bit as it became clear they did not consider her to be their enemy simply because of her father's lawsuit.

"Quasar pretends he lives in the States but lately he spends as much time here as he does there," teased Salim. "He even has a house out in the desert because staying at my hotels isn't homey enough for him."

Dani froze. They obviously had no idea she'd seen his house in the desert and tested the firmness of the mattress.

"I like to enjoy the best of both worlds. I come here to relax and unwind and step back to a simpler time. Now if only I could find someone trustworthy enough to look after a falcon for me when I'm in the States, my life would be complete."

"You should have seen him hunting with the falcon he had as a kid." Elan leaned forward and looked warmly at Dani. "He caught and trained it himself and he would spend all day out there in the middle of nowhere in pursuit of some imaginary quarry."

"You'd be surprised how many rabbits we brought home for Mom's cooking pot. All it takes is patience."

"Most people don't have that kind of patience. To look at your life now, I wouldn't have guessed you did, either," said Salim. "I can't believe you just sold another promising business that you could have taken to the next level."

"It was time to move on." Quasar sipped a glass of berry-colored juice.

"See? You're always looking for the next big thing."

Quasar frowned. "Maybe that's what I've been doing wrong lately. Too much rushing, not enough waiting." He looked at Dani and the expression in his eyes made her breath catch. "It's possible that I got off track and now I'm finding my way back. I can be as patient, steady and persistent as the Al Hajar Mountains themselves when I need to be."

She blinked and swallowed, then looked away. Did his whole family know about their relationship? She couldn't believe he was speaking so intimately in front of them. She felt as if he were trying to convince her he could be the kind of reliable, steady man she could count on. On the other hand, maybe he was just talking about falconry.

"Lately Salim's taken up sailing," said Celia. "He said it's both humbling and awe-inspiring learning to work with such powerful forces as the wind and the currents."

"Yes." Salim raised a brow. "I don't think I would have been ready for it if Celia and Kira hadn't already quietly demonstrated to me that the world doesn't revolve around me, I'm simply part of a much bigger picture."

Sarah laughed. "I think the Al Mansur men attract energy like a vortex. You all have to learn to use it wisely."

"And perhaps that is best accomplished with the help of a good woman," said Quasar softly.

Everyone looked surprised, perhaps that he was speaking so frankly in front of Dani. She wasn't sure he'd even mentioned her to them before. She pretended to be busy tugging apart a croissant. Did Quasar really have such strong feelings for her? It was a little intimidating. She hadn't let herself dare to imagine that he might feel anything beyond attraction and lust. They hadn't known each other long enough.

And her father hated the whole Al Mansur family with a fiery passion.

"Dani, is your father Mohammed Hassan?"

She felt her eyes widen at Salim's question. Apparently the time for niceties had passed and he was going to bring up the lawsuit. "Yes."

"Our father paid for that land fair and square," Salim continued. "There's no written contract because…"

"Because my grandfather couldn't read or write." She'd heard the sob stories about an illiterate fisherman being cheated out of his legacy. And his brilliant, self-educated son—her father—devoting his life to getting it back.

"Exactly. But that doesn't invalidate the deal. A handshake was as good as an iron-clad legal document back then. Still is, to men of honor."

She bristled. Was he trying to say her father wasn't a man of honor? He wasn't the warmest person in the world, but he'd worked hard to provide an excellent life for his family. Right now she felt guilty at not always appreciating the sacrifices that must have involved. "I confess I don't know much about the matter except that my father feels very strongly about it."

She glanced at Quasar, wondering what he was thinking. It was quite rude of his brother to bring the matter up. Was he hoping she could convince her father to drop the suit?

"Hardly anyone in Oman could read or write before 1970." Quasar shrugged. "We were still living in much the same way we had in the Middle Ages. Sultan Qaboos started a slow revolution that has created an educated populace and modern infrastructure, but kept the heart of our traditions. I'm pretty sure he would think a handshake contract is binding."

"Why don't you ask him next time you're riding one of his spectacular cavalry horses?" Elan sipped his coffee. "Quasar became buddies with him a few years ago when he sold him a little gray mare he'd trained for tent-pegging. They go riding together around his estate."

"I doubt he'd be interested in a piece of empty coastline. He likes to talk about emerging technologies. I swear I thought he was going to buy that networking software company I sold three years ago."

Dani was speechless. Quasar rode with Sultan Qaboos? She'd seen the sultan in parades and he always seemed like a figure from an ancient myth, not someone you could have a ride and a chat with. More proof that Quasar lived in an elevated realm far above hers.

"Of course the original contract is binding," murmured Salim. "Money changed hands. That in itself is a contract. And although it appears a small sum now it was quite reasonable at the time. It's provoking that this lawsuit is clouding the title when I'm now ready to develop the property."

Dani frowned. Her father's lawsuit was actually preventing the Al Mansurs from going ahead with their plans? A cold shiver ran through her. Was it possible that Quasar had actually brought her here with the ulterior motive of putting pressure on her to get her father to abandon his suit?

Maybe all along he knew who she was and he'd approached her with the explicit aim of winning over her father. That would explain why he came to the house to press his claim on her, even when she'd asked him not to. Her croissant stuck in her throat and she tried hard not to search their faces. Were they all in on some conspiracy against her family?

"Why can't you pay Mr. Hassan enough money to buy his good graces?" Quasar suggested brightly, as if the idea had just occurred to him.

"Don't think I haven't thought of it." Salim sighed. "But I find in business that when you offer an olive branch like that it can be turned against you as proof that your original claim on the property wasn't valid. It's usually better to hold one's course until the storm is over."

Celia caught Dani's eye and shrugged. She looked embarrassed. At least someone was. She couldn't believe they were discussing this right in front of her as if she weren't there. Unless it was part of some plot. Why hadn't Quasar intervened to stop the conversation?

"Are you hoping I can convince him to drop the suit?" She finally spoke up. It was either that or run from the room, and since she'd resolved to take control of her life, speaking up was better.

"Of course not." Quasar looked shocked. "I'm sorry it's even come up. Salim, you're making my guest uncomfortable. I brought her here to meet you all and get to know you and you're stirring up some family feud that has nothing to do with her. I'm so sorry." He looked so genuinely contrite that she almost forgot her ideas that this visit was part of a scheme to end the land dispute.

Almost.

"That's okay. As I said, it has nothing to do with me. I wish my father would drop his lawsuit but I really don't have any influence over him in the matter."

The children had grown restless during the boring adult discussion and were now chasing each other around the table. "I think it's time to hit the beach," said Sara. "I'll grab the towels and sunblock if someone else could bring the sand toys."

"I'm on it," said Elan.

"I'll herd the children," said Salim, with an indulgent smile at them. And just like that they were all headed for the beach. Dani wasn't sure whether she liked being bundled so easily into the family group. Her nerves jumped when Quasar touched her a couple of times as they walked along the elegant allée of date palms that led to the beach. Part of her was excited and flattered to be here, and the rest was terrified that she was in way over her head.

They spent about two hours building a magnificent kneeling camel out of sand, kept damp by an elaborate network of canals hand-dug by Elan and his son, Ben.

When the camel was done, it was solid enough for the children to climb carefully onto its back and "ride."

No further mention was made of her father and his land claim. In fact the conversation centered around education and the dilemmas that the Al Mansur parents were facing regarding the benefits of homeschooling their children so they could travel freely, versus letting them enjoy the social environment of a real school. Both families had decided to travel and homeschool while the children were younger, then worry about where to settle so the kids could enjoy more stable social lives once they were in their teens.

It was refreshing to hear people who thought nothing of living part of their lives in the States and part in Oman. When she'd moved to New Jersey for college her Omani friends had been appalled and swore that she'd never come back. You'd have thought she'd decided to colonize deep space. When she met her husband and settled there, with her father's stern disapproval, she did indeed wonder if she'd ever see Oman and her brothers again. It had taken a lot of courage and humility to come back, and at the time, her departure from the States had seemed final and permanent.

Now she wondered if in fact she could make a life that involved both places. Her expertise seemed to lend itself to that, if she could just find the right niche. She felt invigorated and excited about her future by the time Quasar pointed out that it was time for her to go home.

She was forced to admit, on the drive back, that Quasar's family was both warm and welcoming and that she'd actually enjoyed herself. She'd almost forgotten her fears that they'd brought her there to convince her to win her father over.

Until Quasar brought up the subject. "How much do

you think your father would take to drop his claim on the land?"

"Are you serious?" Her worst fears flared up again.

"Why not? It would solve a lot of problems. He might even start to like me if I can resolve this issue that's been nagging at him for decades."

She snuck a sideways glance at him. Was he interested in her because she could help him solve the land problem, or was he interested in the land problem because it could help him win her?

It was too confusing for her to tackle. "I don't think he'd take money at this point. I think he wants the land back."

"What would he do with it?"

"Sell it on the open market, I suppose. But there's no way to know what it's truly worth until he does that. He says the location is so prime there would be multiple offers for it."

"Salalah has a lot of empty coastline."

Suspicion flickered inside her. "Not in the middle of town."

"You'd be surprised. It may not be worth as much as he thinks."

Her throat tightened. "I have no idea what it's worth and I don't want to get involved." She wanted to get home and away from Quasar before he charmed her into anything else.

"What about one million dollars? American money."

Now she was really getting upset. "I don't know. It's not my land. You'd have to ask him." If this were the real reason for his visit last night it would explain why he didn't care if she wanted him to meet her father or not.

"He says he won't negotiate with an Al Mansur."

"Then you have your answer." She checked her watch.

It was nearly three-thirty and to be safe she needed to be home by four. Her youngest brother often got home from school around that time. Luckily they were already in her neighborhood.

Quasar sighed. "I wish I could convince my brother to just give him the land. Now that you've met Salim you can see that Salalah would have to freeze over before that happened."

She softened. "If Salalah froze over the hotels might not be so popular. Unless he opens a ski resort in the mountains."

Quasar laughed. "I suspect he'd like the way you think." He pulled on to her street and drove up to the front of her house. Then he glanced both ways and drove around to the back entrance. "I can't stand to leave you. I want to spend more time with you."

I want to make love to you. She read the words in his gaze and they echoed in her heart.

Was this part of his charm? A slick gloss over an ulterior motive? Or was Quasar really as smitten with her as she was with him?

"Can I come in, just for a moment?" His soft words scandalized her.

"You've got to be kidding. I promised my father I wouldn't see you again. You've already made me a liar and now you want to trespass in his house?"

"I've been accused of having a different set of morals than most people."

"I don't think that's a good thing." She gathered her bag off the floor. "I have to go."

"Kiss me."

His gaze, hooded, dark and filled with passion, stole her breath and every last ounce of her common sense. Suddenly her lips were on his, kissing him with tenderness. His arms wrapped around her in the cramped space of the car, and his exhilarating male scent filled her senses. The effect he had on her was shocking. Once minute she was normal and sensible, the next…

"I'm desperate to make love to you." He gestured to the house with his head.

"No way. You're crazy."

"Kiss me again, then." He covered her mouth with his before she had a chance to refuse. His hands on her body stirred passion that grew into an ache. He pulled back just enough to look into her eyes. "You know you want to."

"I do, but…" The prospect of making love with Quasar in her own bedroom was terrifying and electrifying at the same time. Her whole body burned to feel his pressed against it. "We'll have to be really quick." Heart pounding, she extricated herself from his embrace and climbed out of the car. She couldn't believe she was about to do this, but apparently that wasn't enough to stop her. It was a crazy foolish risk but somehow that felt right. She'd been tiptoeing quietly through life, putting her own needs and desires last for far too long. Following her instincts felt daring and liberating.

The back door had a key code and she unlocked it and ushered him down the dim hallway past the empty servants' bedrooms. "In here." She ducked into her bedroom and pulled him with her, locking the door behind her. Her familiar bedroom, with its calming lilac walls and floral-patterned bedcover, looked utterly different dominated by the tall and commanding presence of Quasar.

Within seconds they were grabbing at each other's clothes and shucking them off to reveal bare, anxious skin. Dani clutched at him, pressing her chest to his, reveling in the closeness that banished all her doubts about his intentions.

He wanted her. Nothing else.

Quasar kissed her face, her neck, her hands, with worshipful passion. He kissed her thighs, her knees and her ankles. Then, easing her back onto the bed, he licked her sex until she gasped with pleasure.

For an instant she was distracted by the framed picture of her high school class photo, then by the stuffed bear her friend Nala had given her. Things that reminded her there was a real world out there beyond Quasar's intense embrace. Then she forgot again and folded herself into him, watching with joy and impatience as he donned a condom. Welcoming him into her and moving with him on her familiar bedspread, letting sensation and emotion wash over her like a tidal wave she couldn't fight but could only hope to flow with.

They climaxed in a rush of almost unbearable tension and release that made her cry out so loud that Quasar clapped his hand over her mouth and startled her. Eyes gleaming with arousal and amusement, he urged her to be quiet and not give them away.

She watched her own chest rising and falling as if she'd run a marathon. "What have you done to me?"

"Awakened you." He kissed her cheek softly, his eyes closing for just that instant. "You were like the sleeping beauty, sleepwalking through life. Now you're living in the moment."

"Living like a crazy person." The clock on her wall said 3:45 p.m. "My brother Khalid could be home any minute."

"You can tell him I'm the mailman."

She smiled. "He'll know you're not. The real one gives him gum sometimes."

He put on a mock serious expression and pretended to check his pockets even though he was naked. "I don't have gum." He let go of a wistful sigh and stroked a finger along her body. "You're beautiful, and sensual, and affectionate, and I can't get enough of you."

"Sorry to disappoint you yet again but you need to leave *right now*." Half-playful and half-serious, she pushed him off her and reached for her clothes. It was hard to tug them on. Her whole body was trembling with excitement and something akin to shock.

"What if I won't go?" Sprawled across her single bed, he knitted his hands behind his head and pretended to ease farther onto the mattress. "Then what will you do?"

"That's not funny. I hate bossy men, remember?"

He smiled and rolled up and onto his feet. "I'm not really bossy. I'm just..." He seemed to think about it for a moment.

"You're just trouble." She picked up his pants off the floor and threw them at him. "Get dressed and get out of here." Even while she pretended to scold him, excitement at their escapade rippled through her. They were both healthy, consenting adults. Why couldn't they enjoy each other's company?

Quasar pulled his pants on far more slowly than she liked. She tried to bundle his arms into his shirt to hurry him up, but he ended up grabbing her around the waist and kissing her until she wondered if they'd need a second condom.

Then she heard something and froze. Footsteps in the hallway.

Eight

"It must be Khalid." Her heart was jumping around in her chest.

"Why don't you introduce me?"

Dani motioned for Quasar to be silent. "He probably saw you here last night. He certainly heard you. There's no way we can pretend you're just a friend, even if it wasn't totally inappropriate for me to have a male friend come visit me here alone. We have to get you out of here without him seeing you."

"I'll climb out the window." He looked amused by the idea.

"You can't. It has a grating over it. It's locked from the outside and I don't know where the key is."

"That sounds very dangerous in case of a fire."

She motioned again for him to be quiet. Now was not the time to worry about fire safety. He shrugged his shirt on, quickly buttoned it and examined the window. "Will he come in?" He gestured toward the hallway.

"No. But he might wonder why I haven't come out to say hello. I'll have to pretend I was napping and didn't hear him come in." It was hard to speak quietly enough that the sound wouldn't travel into the hallway. "Maybe you should hide behind the door. I'll go distract him with something in the kitchen, and you can dash out the hallway past the servants' quarters."

"It's lucky you don't have any servants." He tucked in his shirt. "I'll sneak out like an experienced diamond thief."

Dani's heart was in her throat as she opened the door with Quasar hidden behind it. If her brother saw her he'd rat her out for sure. He wasn't mean but he was a Goody Two-shoes. She'd been one at his age, too.

"Khalid? Is that you? I fell asleep!" She hurried down the hallway toward the living room. Her brother often threw his bag down in there and lay on the sofa before he started his homework. "Could you help me get the lid off the new olive jar? I've been trying all afternoon." She had to lure him into the kitchen. It was the only room where you couldn't see into the central hallway. She prayed that Quasar would be patient enough to wait.

"Dani! I'm resting. Give me a minute."

"Oh, come on. I'll make your favorite snack. Anything you want."

"Well, in that case…" He eased off the sofa. She held her breath as he glanced in her direction. The hallway was clearly visible behind her. Then he turned toward the kitchen and she followed him, hoping there was an unopened olive jar somewhere.

"What did I do with it?" She made a big show of clattering around in the pantry, trying to make as much noise as possible while straining her ears to hear if Quasar had made his escape. "Oh, here it is. I don't know why it's so stuck. I even put it under hot water. I couldn't get it open." She glanced over Khalid's shoulder as she handed him the jar.

He opened it without a moment's hesitation. At that exact moment the back door clicked shut.

"Did you hear that?" Khalid wheeled around. "It sounded like the door."

She shrugged. "I didn't hear a thing. Thanks so much for opening this. What would you like to eat? I could make *halwa* if you like. Aunt Nadia gave me a new recipe."

"I swear I just heard a car engine start back there. I'm going to check."

She grabbed his sleeve. "Wait, there's a bottle of oil I couldn't open, either. Just do that before you go. And do you want me to make the *halwa?*"

"Sure, *halwa* sounds good. But it takes a long time and I'm pretty starving so I'm going to grab something else while I'm here." He dove into a packet of crackers. By the time she found a bottle of oil and looked impressed while he opened it, she'd quizzed him about his homework and he seemed to have forgotten about the door and the car and was telling her to make sure the *halwa* was sweet enough.

As soon as he returned to the living room she locked the back door and hurried to her bedroom to rearrange the disordered bed. The condom wrapper lay on the floor like a pointing finger of accusation and she quickly crumpled it up and shoved it down into the toe of a boot she didn't wear often.

She sagged onto her bed as waves of guilt and relief crashed over her. Was she completely out of her mind? She'd let Quasar make love to her in her bedroom, only hours after promising her father she wouldn't see him anymore.

He had a frightening amount of power over her. The worst part was that she was so willing to do all the inappropriate things he suggested. Her ex-husband had talked her into doing all kinds of things she didn't want to because he'd pout and whine and make such a fuss if she didn't. It was impossible to imagine Quasar doing that. He'd just smile and shrug and seduce her until she wanted to do it even more than he did.

Her body still tingled and pulsed with the sensations Quasar had created inside her. A quick examination of her face in the mirror showed her lips were pink from kissing and her hair messy. Lucky thing her brother wasn't too observant, and she'd mentioned waking up from a nap. Still, she'd taken a huge risk that her father would discover her affair. He would go ballistic if he found out what she'd been doing. He might even throw her out of the house.

Quasar was making her careless. Reckless. Which was all well and good while he was there and she was having the time of her life, but she'd have to live with herself and what little reputation she had left when he was gone.

Her phone pinged. And she grabbed it out of her bag.

Made it.

She smiled. He hadn't sent her a text before. Of course this was just one more piece of incriminating evidence, like the condom wrapper. She resisted the urge to respond and quickly deleted it. And now she had to go make *halwa* from scratch. At least creating the sticky dessert would keep her busy!

Another ping. I miss you.

Her heart seized. Did he really? She supposed he must or he wouldn't be texting her. She couldn't resist typing back, I miss you, too. She turned off the volume on her phone so her brother wouldn't get curious.

Being apart like this is foolish.

She frowned. What we're doing is foolish.

No, it isn't. I need you.

The tiny words on her screen made her breath catch and she told herself to get a grip. It wasn't as if he'd told her he loved her. Not that she'd even believe it if he did. *I need you, too.* She wanted to type the words. But she didn't. It was much safer to keep her feelings secret.

You have an alarming effect on me. That was less incriminating and no less true.

He responded immediately. The effect is mutual. I can't stop thinking about you.

She glanced over her shoulder. You really shouldn't text me. Someone might see it.

Come to the hotel tomorrow. Ten-thirty?

She paused, and inhaled very slowly. I can't. I have to go see about a job. She'd gotten sidetracked today, but establishing her independence would be the first step to securing her own future. If she made money she could rent her own apartment and see—within reason—whomever she chose. Even Quasar, if he still wanted to.

After that, then. How about two?

Could she? Of course she wanted to. The prospect of going all day without seeing his mischievous smile was grim. But she had to be sensible. I won't have time.

I can't go a whole day without seeing you.

She couldn't help smiling. Sure you can. You've been through many days in life without seeing me. She headed out of her bedroom, and down the hallway to the kitchen.

That was before I met you. Now everything's different.

She bit her lip. She could almost swear he was sincere. Then she remembered the twinkle of humor that always hovered in his slate blue eyes. Was Quasar ever serious about anything?

If you don't agree, I'll come back right now.

Dani frowned. Part of her knew that the humor was still there and he was just teasing. The other part, that had been bullied and ordered around for nearly five years, coiled up ready to strike. That's not funny.

"Who are you texting?"

Her brother's voice made Dani look up with a start. She hadn't noticed him there in the doorway. "A friend from the States." Not exactly a lie. Not exactly the truth, either.

"Cool. I could end up at school there, too. Dad thinks I might be able to get into MIT."

"Really?" She was surprised their father would even consider it after the way she'd gone off track. "That's great. It's one of the best schools in the world."

"I know. They have an aerospace engineering program."

"I didn't know you were interested in rockets." She could feel her phone vibrating, but she resisted the urge to look at it.

"I'm more interested in satellites. You'd be surprised how important they are these days. All our information is bouncing around in space. It's the new frontier in information technology." He glanced at her phone, which was vibrating. "I think you're getting another message."

"Oh." She pretended to glance casually at it.

I'm still crazy about you even though you're ignoring me.

"I can't get used to people being able to contact me wherever I go. I'm not sure I'm ready for all these new frontiers."

"I think it's awesome. Tell your friend I said hi." He smiled and headed off to do his homework. Dani blinked and felt another vibration.

I'm on your doorstep.

Her blood ran cold. He wouldn't, would he? Did he have that little respect for her wishes and her reputation? Her heart squeezed.

Just kidding.

She narrowed her eyes. You're really starting to tick me off.

You still miss me, though, don't you?

She hesitated for a minute, and pursed her lips. Yes. But don't come here. We need somewhere very discreet to meet. I'll text you in the morning. What if someone saw this conversation on her phone? She deleted the thread, shoved the phone into the pocket of her pants and pulled out the sugar and cardamom and rosewater to start her preparations for *halwa*.

* * *

The next morning Dani donned a conservative blue ensemble and headed for the university campus. She'd printed her resumé and intended to drop in on the administrative offices and ask about available openings. Her interview with the human resources coordinator was humbling. Although she had a Ph.D. and had published several papers, didn't know any of the new database software and had no office or management experience. She'd been so successful, or lucky, at finding great mentors and work in her field that she'd never had to develop the peripheral "fall-back" skills most people her age had.

Although they had three administrative openings, none of them was "quite right for her." Friends in college had teased her that a degree in art history was preparation for would-you-like-fries-with-that? jobs. Maybe they were right.

Keeping her chin in the air, she went to the history department, thinking that perhaps she could get her foot in the door by volunteering her time here. The older building was barely air-conditioned and looked neglected and run-down compared to the rest of the state-of-the-art campus. Apparently the school put more stock in the future than in rehashing the past—and could she really blame them for that? When it came to the modern world, her academic expertise was of limited use.

An older man in a rumpled dishdasha was pinning something to the cluttered notice board inside the door when she entered. "Excuse me, does this department have an art collection?"

He looked up slowly. "Art collection?" He snorted. "I think not. There used to be a collection of swords but I think it was sold off when the roof needed fixing." He looked her up and down with some distaste and she got the distinct feeling he didn't approve of her. "This department focuses exclusively on military history. Unless you're looking for a collection of ancient battle maps, you're in the wrong place."

"Oh. Thank you." Deflated by his hostile gaze, she turned and left. As far as she'd been able to discover, the other universities nearby were entirely science- and technology-oriented.

She stopped into a boutique selling pretty traditional dresses and asked about a job there. The owner, a rather glamorous middle-aged woman, was kind, but said that currently she didn't need help.

As she walked through an unfamiliar souk in a neighborhood more than twenty minutes from her own, she realized it was a good place to meet Quasar. He answered his phone immediately and eagerly agreed to meet her there right away.

Feeling better already, and trying to hide her smile, she walked among the stalls, and tasted a sugary date. She even bought a bag of almonds so she wouldn't look as if she were only there to meet her lover. She still couldn't believe they'd made love in her bedroom. It was so wrong, and yet so exciting and exhilarating.

"Hello, gorgeous." Quasar's low voice in her ear made her spin around and her grin probably announced their relationship to anyone who was paying attention.

"Hi." Her skin prickled with awareness in his presence. Something about him lit her on fire, even out here in the everyday atmosphere of the market. She noticed a lime seller eyeing them curiously. "We should probably go somewhere else."

"I've been thinking about nothing but seeing you since yesterday." His eyes glittered with a desire that echoed her own.

"Me, too." It was hard to think straight with him around. Colors grew brighter and the sounds of the street seemed to blur into white noise. "I missed you."

She knew she was admitting too much, letting him know the power he had over her. He knew already, though. How could he not? She melted like butter in the hot sun whenever he was near.

"Let's walk." He gestured along the road that led south, toward the ocean. His hand twitched slightly and she could swear he wanted to put it around her waist, but was resisting.

They rounded the corner out of sight of the market stalls, and were now alone on a dusty street of modest houses. Quasar took her in his arms with a swiftness that almost pushed the breath from her lungs, and kissed her with intensity.

When their lips finally parted she was shocked for a moment at how bold he'd been to kiss her in public. "We shouldn't do this. Someone might see."

"Let them." His blue eyes flashed defiance. "I don't care who knows how crazy I am about you."

"You're not the one whose reputation is already in tatters."

He laughed. "That's where you're wrong. You should see what the media says about me."

She'd forgotten about that. "I did. I looked you up on the internet after I learned your full name, remember? All the more reason I shouldn't be seen smooching you in public. If I had any sense I'd stay far away from you."

"Don't believe everything you read." He had the decency to look somewhat concerned. "They make most of that stuff up to sell magazines."

"Where there's smoke there's usually at least a spark of fire." She raised a brow. "The most recent stories were about you and Laura Larson. Apparently one minute you were planning your wedding, the next she was telling everyone she prefers to be single. Did you dump her?"

His mouth quirked into a wistful smile. "She dumped me."

"Were you heartbroken?"

He looked at her for a moment, then shook his head gently. "No. I enjoyed her company but I didn't feel the same kind of…intensity I feel with you."

"She's very beautiful."

"You're more lovely than she is."

"Okay, now I know you're toying with me."

"You are. She gets this weird wrinkle between her eyebrows when she's thinking. And she always glances to the left when she's telling a fib. She's almost always acting and I realized over time that she's not as interesting as most people think."

"Really?"

"Really. She's nice, but pretty kooky. Far too much drama on a daily basis."

"More than, say, my father calling your family sons of dogs?"

He laughed. "I asked for that by going to see him when you told me not to."

"Or maybe you actually like drama, and seek it out."

He was silent for a moment, contemplating what she'd said. A little frisson of alarm crept through her when she realized there might be more than a grain of truth in her words.

"I am something of a thrill seeker, but in sports, not in romance."

"Or so you'd like to believe." Were things getting too dull and predictable with their romance, making him want to stir the pot by approaching her father? "I told you to leave my house and promised I wouldn't see you again. Next thing I know, you're making love to me in my own bedroom. You're a bad influence." She was kidding, but only just.

She glanced up and down the street. A white car drove by. "We shouldn't hang around here. Let's walk like we have somewhere to go."

Quasar put his arm through hers and started walking. She wanted to tug her arm back, but he resisted when she tried. His powerful muscles were hard to argue with.

"I'm a good influence. I'm here to help you out of your cloister before you spend your life locked away in it."

"I'd probably be a lot safer locked away in a cloister."

"Safety is overrated." He shot a teasing glance at her. "Adventure is a lot more fun."

"Until you end up in the jaws of a lion."

He squeezed her gently. "I'll protect you."

"Unless you are the lion."

"Even then." He pressed a warm kiss to her cheek. Then he stopped and spun her to face him. "Come back to the United States with me."

"What?" She let his words echo inside her brain. His arms were now around her waist, possessive, holding her steady so she couldn't move. Couldn't leave.

"I mean it. I'm planning a move to the East Coast. Most likely Boston. There's some top technical talent there that I want to leverage for one or other of my newest business ideas."

"MIT is there."

"Exactly. And Harvard. Harvard must have an art program or museum of some kind where you could find a job."

"Oh, I'm sure I can walk right into a curatorial position at Harvard." She chuckled. His idea was so outrageous that it was funny rather than scary.

"You think I'm kidding? If you worked at Princeton, you can work at Harvard."

"I was very lucky to get the position at Princeton. I was an idiot to give it up."

"Have you ever been to Boston?"

"Sure. I've attended a couple of conferences there. I even lectured at one. I talked about Mesopotamian metalworking techniques."

"Did you like the city?"

"Uh, sure."

He was serious. At least the look in his eyes said so. "It's not as big and bustling as New York or L.A., but I like that about it. And there are some lovely neighborhoods in the older parts of the city."

She blinked, still not really sure this was happening. "So, in your vision, we'd live together in Boston?"

"Yes." He squeezed her. "I can see us in a pretty brick house with a garden."

No mention of marriage, of course. Did he anticipate that she'd be happy shacking up with him, no commitment in sight? On the other hand she was not at all keen to venture into marriage again. It was probably safer to keep the exit door open at all times by keeping any partnerships free of legally binding obligations to stay together until death did them part.

"What about when you get tired of me?" She tried to inject a note of humor but it fell rather flat. Because she truly wanted to know the answer.

"Tired of you? Impossible." He squeezed her again, and her heart leapt. The kiss he pressed to her lips flushed her with heat and passion that made it impossible to think straight.

"How can you say that when you barely know me?" It was hard to remember that they'd only known each other a few days. Things had happened so fast between them.

"Instinct. And I've learned to trust my instincts. They rarely fail me."

She sighed. This was all a bit much to take in. "Outrageous as your idea sounds, I like it." Warning bells and alarms flashed in her mind. Was she really going to place her trust in a man and venture off into unknown territory with him, away from friends and family?

Possibly. She'd have to carefully consider all the pros and cons.

Quasar was already grinning. "Sensible woman. Salalah is lovely, but it's no place for a woman with a great career in art history ahead of her. And we'd come back regularly to visit."

We'd come back regularly. The *we* got her attention. He was thinking of them as a couple. Which shouldn't sound so odd since they were a couple.

She took in a deep steadying breath. It was really too perfect. Too good to be true. Surely she was missing something?

"What if it takes me a long time to find a job? I have very little left in my savings. Probably the plane flight alone would finish them off, and then…" She didn't relish the prospect of being financially dependent on a man again. It was probably the most effective way her ex-husband had exerted control over her—cutting off her income source and preventing her from finding another.

He looked thoughtful for a moment. "I'll offer you a fifty-thousand-dollar grant to research the frankincense trade in Salalah. How does that sound?"

"Like you're trying to buy my consent."

"Nonsense. It's purely academic curiosity that prompts me."

She tried to look like she was thinking it over. "There's some excellent scholarship in that field already."

"But I'd imagine that advances in technology allow satellite analysis that could reveal more lost settlements like Saliyah."

She frowned. "You might have a point."

"Think it over." He pressed another soft, warm kiss to her lips, then pulled his arms from around her waist and continued down the street. She hurried to catch up. Her mind spun so fast it was hard to walk at the same time. Her father would be sure to protest but if she could reassure him that she had "grant" money and he didn't have to support her, she might mollify at least some of his objections. And if she decided to go—if she really thought it was for the best—he could hardly stop her.

Quasar's wild scheme was entirely doable. It could transform her life instantly.

Or be the biggest mistake she'd ever made.

"I will think about it."

"Good. And if your thoughts aren't heading in the right direction, then call me and I'll set them back on the right course." His effortless confidence was both inspiring and a little infuriating. Oh, to possess some of that herself.

And the truth was, the more time she spent with Quasar, the more confident and optimistic she felt. Just the fact that she'd gone to look for a job today was a big step forward from lounging around her bedroom feeling like a loser. She'd once had big dreams—and the prestigious job she'd dreamed of—and maybe it wasn't too late to pursue them again.

She was starting to feel like her old self: the college

student who thought anything was possible. "I think I should go home now."

"Already? We only just met. I need to stare into your beautiful eyes for at least another half hour before I go live on memories for the rest of the day and night."

She giggled. "I can't think straight. What you suggested is so huge that it's taking over my brain. I have to make up a list of pros and cons."

"Cons? There aren't any."

"It's certainly hard to think of them when I'm standing here with you. That's why I need to go home."

He smiled, then shrugged. "Okay. I'll drive you home to dream up some cons. And maybe we can make love in your bedroom again."

"No way! I can't believe my brother almost caught us together in there. Never again. Really, I mean it!" She was talking too loud and looked about quickly to see if anyone had heard.

Quasar pretended to pout. "So cruel. But okay, I'll be good and drop you off if you promise to come to an event at the hotel this evening. It's Kira's fifth birthday party but it's for the grown-ups as much as the kids. Salim's hired a bunch of carnival acts to walk around the hotel and entertain people, and practically everyone in Salalah is invited."

"That alone is a good reason for me not to come. I don't want to become the subject of gossip."

"We'll tell people we're old friends." He grinned. "They'll just assume that since we were both in the U.S. that we bonded over there."

"What will I tell my father?" She frowned and shook her head. "Geez, I feel like a teenager. I can't believe I even have to think about this. I'll just tell him I'm going to visit a friend."

"Invite him to come, too." Quasar grinned.

"I'm sure he'd love that. Into the den of the Al Mansurs."

"You never know. People pull out all the stops to get invited to some of Salim's exclusive parties. He might surprise you."

"I don't think so. He's depressingly predictable." What would he say if she announced she was moving away with Quasar? She couldn't even imagine. If he were angry enough he could cast her out of the family and refuse to ever speak to her again. She hoped he'd never do that but there was no way to know for sure. She certainly wasn't going to breathe a word about it until she'd made up her own mind that moving to Boston with Quasar was a good idea. "I'll try to come, though. What time?"

"Five. It's early because of the kids."

"Okay. I'll come for a while and then go home for dinner."

"I could come pick you up."

"No! It's barely a twenty-minute walk. I'll see you there."

They walked to where his car was parked a couple of blocks away, and he took her home. Once again he drove around the back. There would have been plenty of time for her to invite him in but she was glad he didn't suggest it again.

She kissed him for a solid minute before climbing warily out of the car. She was reluctant to leave him. To wake up and find this was all a figment of her imagination. A dream that crept over her during an afternoon nap.

She could hardly believe he'd asked her to move back to the U.S. with him.

That meant this wasn't a fling but the start of something real.

Once inside the back door, she waved and watched him drive away.

With a sigh, she walked from the back of the house to the front and went to put her keys on the hall table, as if she'd come in the front door like a normal person with nothing to hide.

And that's when she saw her father and her brothers standing in the kitchen, right next to the window that looked out onto the street.

Nine

"What is the meaning of this, Daniyah?" Her father's lips grew white as he stared at her.

She could tell he'd seen Quasar. She didn't know what to say.

"Of what?"

"Don't treat me like a fool. Apparently you forgot I took your brothers to the engineering symposium at the university today. It was over by two and we returned to find you gone. You've been out with that…man."

"Only to the market. I bought some almonds." She held up the bag she'd almost forgotten about. "We didn't do anything else." For once, it was the truth.

His eyes started to bulge as his face reddened. "No? What else have you done with him on other occasions? You told me you weren't going to see him again. Clearly you lied to me so now I'm wondering what else is untrue. If your mother were alive today…!" He shook his head and exhaled as if he were going to breathe fire. "Perhaps I should forbid you to leave the house. I literally cannot believe that you were out walking around Salalah in broad daylight with one of those accursed Al Mansurs."

The mention of her mother chastened Dani. Who knew where they'd all be if her mother were alive. Dani would likely never have moved to the United States, or met Gordon. She'd probably have been fixed up by her mom and aunts with a nice, quiet Omani man, who didn't have flashing blue eyes or a reputation as an international playboy.

"I'm thinking of moving to America with him."

She said the words entirely without premeditation. They slipped out of her mouth as she was testing them in her mind.

Her father stared at her, speechless. Then his eyebrows started to twitch. "Have you taken leave of your senses?"

"You said yourself that I won't be able to find a job here. My skills may seem useless in Salalah, but I have a prestigious academic background and I was a curator at Princeton. In America my skills are far more marketable, especially in a university town like Boston."

"Boston? You've actually discussed this with him?" Her father's voice was hoarse with incredulity.

"Yes. Just today, in fact. I told him I'd think about it." She sounded surprisingly calm. Much calmer than she felt. She hadn't even had a chance to think this plan through properly and already she was announcing it almost as a done deal.

Her youngest brother stared, openmouthed. The other one stared at her through slightly narrowed eyes as if afraid he'd be blinded by what he was witnessing.

"Has he proposed marriage?"

"No." There wasn't really anything she could add to make this sound better. By Omani standards he probably should have proposed before they even kissed, certainly before they moved in together. She could say they were "just friends," but that would be a lie and she didn't want to make things worse by lying.

"How will you support yourself over there? Are you to be a kept woman?"

She wanted to mention the grant, but on reflection that probably would make her a kept woman. "I have enough savings left to get there. Then I'll find a job. Maybe not my ideal one, at first, but I'll find something."

"While living with this man?"

"I'm not a virgin, dad. I was married before."

"To your discredit." His bushy eyebrows lowered. "And now your own opinion of yourself is so low that you plan to willingly live in sin?"

"It's not like that in the States. It's quite normal for adults to live together for a while before they marry. To test each other out, really. If I'd done that before I married Gordon I probably could have saved myself a world of grief."

"I don't know you. I don't know who you are." He stood there, panting slightly. "You are not the daughter I raised."

His words cut her to the quick and she felt tears rise in her throat. "I'm just trying to do what's best for me. I don't even know if I should move to Boston. I'm thinking it through."

"You should move to Boston." His voice was calm and firm. "There is no place for you here. You are a bad influence on your brothers."

She glanced at them. Mute and horrified, they didn't even meet her gaze. Was she really a bad influence on them? With one failed marriage behind her and an illicit affair going on under their noses, she could hardly recommend herself as an example to follow. Her hands were starting to tremble. She wasn't ready for this. She'd meant to ponder her options, to plan and prepare and gear herself up for any inevitable showdown.

Right now she felt as if her life were exploding in her face and she needed to get out of here. She turned back to the door and slipped out, before the conversation could spiral any further downhill. There was no sense talking to her father when his temper was running so high he couldn't think straight. If she stayed he might do something drastic, like lock her in her room and take away her phone. It was better to escape while she still could.

Moving to Boston wasn't such a crazy idea. Her father had given her almost no choice. Although she realized there were risks inherent in going with Quasar—he readily admitted that he got bored easily, and he had a playboy reputation—if she could get her career going again she'd be fine by herself if the relationship fell apart.

Not sure where to go, she headed first for the familiar bookshop where she'd met Quasar. Thumbing through the soft pages of an old history book soothed her nerves. It was now late afternoon and since her father was already mad at her she had no reason not to go to the party.

She walked along the quiet streets with a growing sense of resolve. Her time of rest and recuperation was nearing its end and she was ready to get back in the swim of life.

The walk to the hotel took almost half an hour and it was odd walking through the grand hotel gates on foot, rather than arriving in a luxury car, but the staff welcomed her almost as if they recognized her—maybe they acted like that with all the guests?—and she soon found herself in the large, music-filled central courtyard surrounded by at least three hundred people, including jugglers, sword swallowers, even a snake charmer. Excited children darted about in their smartest party clothes, and their parents laughed and talked and watched them fondly.

The festive atmosphere further boosted Dani's mood and she looked eagerly about for Quasar. He'd be thrilled that she'd decided to come to Boston with him. Maybe they could even talk about booking the tickets and some of the logistics of the move?

She scanned the area around the fountain—which bubbled right now in a rainbow of LED colors—looking for his face in the crowd. At last she spotted Sara walking with Elan, who carried a sleepy little Hannah in his arms.

Dani greeted them with relief. "I'm looking for Quasar. I can't seem to find him."

Sara glanced at Elan. He cleared his throat. "Hmm. I'm not exactly sure where he is." He looked around the sea of partygoers. "Would you like me to go find him for you?"

"Oh, no. I'll find him myself, eventually. I can always call him on my phone as a last resort." She patted the phone in her pocket. Elan glanced at Sarah again before they smiled and moved away. Dani got an odd feeling from the way they looked at each other. Almost as if they were trying to communicate without her figuring something out. Suddenly the music seemed louder and the bustle and thrust of people rather disorienting.

She drew in a breath and headed for the other side of the courtyard, where tables were set up to serve drinks. She accepted a glass of pinkish lemonade from a waiter and was about to turn back to the crowd when she spotted Quasar under a colonnade off to the side of the courtyard. He appeared to be talking to someone who was hidden by a carved stone column.

A smile spread across her face as she headed toward him. But her enthusiasm cooled when she noticed the serious expression on his face. His gaze was intently focused on the person in front of him. Dani's pace slowed when she realized that he was talking to a woman who gripped both his hands in hers. She could see gold bangles on her wrists, and gold rings on long, elegant fingers.

Her gut crawled with unease. She paused and sipped her lemonade. Maybe she shouldn't intrude. She could just wait until he was done with this conversation. She tried to tug her attention away from him and back to the festivities, but her eyes kept swiveling back to the shadowed arches of the colonnade where he stood with the strange woman. It was odd that he hadn't glanced up and seen her yet, considering all the nervous energy she must be sending in his direction. His attention was riveted on this woman, who still clutched him like a life raft.

Keeping her eyes on a nearby knot of children watching a magician pull a string of colored scarves from his mouth, she moved a few steps closer, ears straining to catch some of Quasar's conversation.

"Oh, darling, you always kill me with that mysterious Arabian charm of yours." The woman's voice was rich and full, confident, too.

"I'm not Arabian. I'm Omani." He said it with a smile.

"I know that, silly. I'm here in Oman, aren't I? Crazy long flight, too. You know how that airplane air dries out my skin, but I did it all for you."

Dani glanced at them in time to see one of the ringed hands rove up his forearm, reaching over the cuff of his elegant shirt. She froze. Now she could see the familiar profile, topped with expensively coiffed blond hair. This was Laura Larson, screen goddess, and one of the many glamorous women Dani had seen pictured on his arm when she did her internet search.

She wondered if she should turn and disappear back into the crowd. But wasn't this the man she'd just resolved to move across the world with? Curiosity and a growing sense of alarm propelled her forward, even while her instincts cued her to flee. Even when she was only fifteen feet away, he still hadn't looked up and noticed her. His famous companion was keeping him fully occupied with a giggly account of her appearance two nights ago at an awards ceremony, where she'd had too much to drink.

"Hello, Quasar." Dani said it quietly during a momentary break in the conversation. She didn't want to get any closer without announcing herself. She already felt like an intruder.

He glanced up and smiled. Relief swept over her. For a moment she'd wondered if he'd even acknowledge her. "I came to the party," she said, pointlessly. "The kids are really enjoying it."

Quasar ignored her blathering. "Dani, this is Laura. Laura, Dani."

Laura thrust out a hand with sharp-looking nails and Dani managed to produce a reasonably firm handshake and a smile. "Nice to meet you," she said, though it wasn't nice at all. She'd come here excited to tell Quasar that she'd decided to move to Boston with him. And the presence of Laura Larson made that impossible.

"What brings you to Oman?" Dani couldn't resist asking.

"Quasar, of course. Is there any other reason for visiting such a tiny and faraway country?" Laura tossed her luxurious gold hair and shone an adoring glance on Quasar.

"You flatter me, but Dani knows that Oman's charms far outshine mine."

Laura gave Dani the once-over, then looked back at Quasar. Dani became self-conscious of her Omani attire. Laura herself had on a slinky cream dress with a plunging neckline that revealed her spray-tanned boobs, gold high-heeled sandals and a necklace of what looked like gold nuggets.

"Do people here not drink alcohol?" Laura surveyed the crowd.

"Not really." Quasar winked at Dani, which gave her a pleasant conspiratorial feeling. "It's a Muslim country. It's served to guests at the hotel who want it, though. Would you like a drink?"

"Absolutely, darling. I'm parched and this Shirley Temple they gave me isn't doing anything for my jet lag. A whisky sour would be a dream."

"Dani, would you like anything?"

"I'm fine, thanks."

"I'll be right back."

Quasar headed for the bar, leaving Dani with Laura. Awkward! "Do you work at the hotel?" Laura inquired while looking over her shoulder at the crowds.

"No. I'm a friend of Quasar's." She lifted her chin as she said it. Now would be the perfect time to announce she was about to move in with him, but prudence prevented her. She knew this woman was one of his ex-lovers. And she'd come all the way to Oman to see him. They were obviously still on friendly terms.

Maybe their relationship wasn't even over.

"Are you one of the girls whose hearts he broke when he was a ridiculously dashing teen heartthrob?"

"No. We met recently." She could see Laura's curiosity growing, and decided that being mysterious was the best policy. No need to even let on that she recognized her. Which was petty, since she quite liked her movies. Oh, well, she was jealous of Laura right now and that was making her petty. At least she could acknowledge it.

But it was rather scary to see herself grow green claws over Quasar. How was she going to feel in Boston when he had business meetings with women, or even social gatherings and networking? He was an outgoing, friendly and popular guy, so she'd better get used to sharing him if their relationship was going anywhere. "How do you know him?"

"Oh, Quasar and I go way back." Laura inhaled her pink mocktail like it was a shot of rum. "He's like the brother I never had." The platonic reference was strangely reassuring. "But who I sleep with!" Laura let out a giggle. "He's irresistible. What can I say?"

Dani swallowed. What could she say? Hopefully Laura didn't intend to sleep with Quasar tonight. But if she did, what exactly could Dani do about it if Quasar were ready, willing and able?

Where was Quasar? She turned and saw him returning with three tall glasses. "Whiskey sours for everyone." He handed Laura hers, then gave one to Dani.

She looked at it suspiciously. She didn't really drink. Apart from any religious objections, she was a total lightweight.

Quasar took a sip of his and Laura took a few refreshing gulps of hers. "Quasar, darling, you should come down under for my next shoot." She grabbed Quasar's shoulder. "It's near Melbourne, which is such a fantastic city. Beaches, nightlife, fun people."

"Sounds like Salalah." Quasar winked again at Dani. The gesture warmed and relaxed her.

"Have you been to Australia, darling?" She squeezed his shoulder.

"Never have."

"Come then, you'll love it. I promise."

This is where Quasar should have protested that he couldn't because he was about to move to Boston with Dani. But he didn't.

"Maybe I will. There's an interesting biotech firm in Sydney I've been keeping tabs on. I might come down and eyeball the place."

"Wonderful." Her hand rose up to cup his cheek. Dani tried not to squirm and spill her whiskey sour. "When shooting wraps, we can take a Jeep across the outback. I've always wanted to do that!"

How could Quasar let this strange woman fondle him right in front of her after all they'd shared over the last few days? He was acting as if Laura was his girlfriend and she, Dani, was his old and platonic friend. Which is of course what he'd said he would do to protect her reputation. Was he just trying to deflect attention from her by pretending Laura was still his lover?

"Laura surprised me today," he said to Dani. "She showed up unannounced with about forty pieces of luggage."

"Oh." Dani nodded. That was not at all reassuring. He obviously wouldn't have invited her to come here tonight if he'd known Laura was arriving.

This situation was uncomfortable. Not only was he trying to convince everyone else they were "just friends," he apparently wanted Laura to think that too. Dani decided to take the hint and make her exit at the first available opportunity.

"Forty pieces of luggage! There aren't even eight. And I had no idea what the climate would be like here. Deserts can be quite freezing at night. I wonder if the outback gets cold at night. I could bring a light fox fur." She giggled again.

Dani's drink was sweating in her hand and she was tempted to drink it just for something to do, but she worried that she might cough and splutter at the disgusting taste of whiskey. She had no idea what to say and was beginning to wish that the shining marble tiles of the floor would slide apart and allow her to sink gracefully into oblivion.

Mercifully, Salim announced over the mike that it was time to sing "Happy Birthday," and the crowd moved in toward where a giant, multilayer cake, iced with rainbow-colored unicorns, stood in the middle of the courtyard.

Dani made a dive for the exit and didn't look back to see if Quasar had noticed. This was possibly the most embarrassing experience of her life. Luckily only she knew that. Laura—even Quasar himself—had no idea she'd come here to tell Quasar of her plans to go back to the States with him. To live with him and accept his generous offer to support her, which basically would have made her a kept woman.

Kept by a man for whom she was just one of many women whose company he enjoyed.

Thank goodness she'd seen Quasar's true colors and come to her senses. She put her drink down on a table as she passed out of the large courtyard, unnoticed amongst the joyous crowd singing "Happy Birthday" in several languages at the same time. She felt like a killjoy that she couldn't at least celebrate his niece's birthday, but tears were dangerously close to the surface and she needed to get out of here before they erupted.

It was over. Her exhilarating romance with Quasar. Her bold plans for starting over again in Boston. All of it. Now she was right back where she'd started except that now her father thought she was a loose woman as well as a foolish one.

She managed to keep a straight face as she hurried past the army of valets and bellhops and maintenance staff, striding along the wide driveway that led out the hotel gates. Out on the main road she kept going, walking as fast as she could. The chiffon fabric of her clothing kept catching on itself, and she cursed the fact that traditional Omani women's wear consisted of both a dress and pants. Maybe it was planned that way to make it harder for a woman to escape from her lover in a moment of crisis.

She should be glad, really. Her brain raced and her breathing got faster as she strode down the dusty sidewalk. She'd been saved from the humiliation of embarking on yet another disastrous live-in relationship with a totally unsuitable man. She'd just have to accept the truth that she had awful taste in men. She needed to find some kind of job where she could support herself, move out and get a cat for companionship.

She'd hoped the walk home would clear her head and settle her emotions; instead the first tears fell as she rounded the corner into her neighborhood. She wiped them hurriedly away with her scarf. Would her father even let her back in the house or would she be ordered to leave the way Quasar had been when he showed up?

She bit her lip and fought back the tears. The walk had flown by so quickly on her way to the party when she was filled with excitement and hope for the future. Now she prayed she wouldn't run into her neighbors out for an evening stroll. She couldn't bear to see anyone right now.

Why hadn't Quasar kissed her? If he had she'd probably have been shocked, and worried about her reputation, and scolded him. But now the fact that he hadn't made her feel like a castoff. His conspiratorial winks had suggested that they were still a team in some sense. Just not in any public sense where he'd claim her as his actual girlfriend.

Had she really thought Quasar was going to take her to America as his sweetheart? The idea seemed ridicu-

lous. She'd been swept away on a tide of lust and anticipation and started thinking that anything was possible.

Just the way she had in her marriage. If she'd thought
it all through, as her friends suggested, she'd have realized from the start that Gordon was already insecure and
controlling. Warning signs were flashing almost from
their first date. His obsessive questions about where she'd
been and who she'd seen. His preference for her to wear
modest clothing and avoid makeup. His enthusiasm for
spending every spare minute with her. She'd taken them
as signs that he was crazy about her, had traditional val-
ues and was going to be a wonderful and doting husband.

She'd been right about one part—he was crazy.

She turned onto her block and cringed at the sight of
three of her male neighbors talking in the street. They'd
probably mutter under their breath about this wayward
woman out and about without a male escort. She lifted
her head and smiled, though, and they greeted her. She'd
better be polite to everyone, as currently staying here was
her best-case scenario, and if she had any sense she'd be
grateful to have a roof over her head.

She'd have to apologize to her father. Tell him he was
right.

Tears still pricked at her eyeballs and she wanted nothing more than to let them flow down her cheeks again.
Her heart clenched at the thought that her lovely romance
with Quasar was nothing but a brief fling. Even though
she'd been telling herself that all along, trying to protect
her heart from this kind of pain.

"Back so soon?" Her father opened the door before
she even had a chance to try her key. He must have seen
her coming down the street. "Your lover didn't even have
the decency to drive you home?"

"He's not my lover." Her voice wore a heavy tone of resignation.

"No? I thought that you intended to live in sin with him in America."

"Not anymore." The confession seemed to sap her last ounce of energy.

"He's turned you away already?" The gleam of triumph in her father's eye made her heart sink further.

The question was so cold and mean that she decided not to answer it. She couldn't even bring herself to apologize. She simply walked toward him, where he stood blocking the hallway to her room, and prayed he'd let her go there in peace. "May I go to my room?" she asked softly.

"Don't disgrace the family." She'd expected a cold retort, but the sad look in her father's eyes cut her even deeper. Then he moved aside to let her pass.

He was trying to do the right thing, from his perspective. She had to remember that. He was afraid that she'd ruin her reputation and be a burden to him for the rest of his life. Maybe he was right to worry. All her exciting prospects for the future had dried up within the last hour.

Quasar hadn't officially dumped her. Not yet, anyway. He probably had his hands full with Laura Larson and wouldn't get to that for the next few days. And maybe not even then. He'd be busy planning his trip to Australia and the sex-filled romp across the outback with Laura wearing her fox fur over nothing but lacy lingerie.

Jealous! She cursed herself for her hateful feelings. Laura Larson hadn't done anything to her except be gorgeous and charming and bubbly and wildly successful. She had no idea she was stealing someone else's man, since she obviously saw Quasar as hers. The proprietary way she'd touched and fondled him left no doubt.

And he'd hardly slapped her hand away like it was an irritant.

In her room, Dani locked the door and carried her laptop to her bed where she sat and opened it with shaking fingers. She needed information. She wanted to see if she could find out how long Quasar and Laura had been together and if there was any further information about their relationship.

She entered their names, quietly hoping for news of a dramatic and tear-filled breakup. Instead she was confronted with picture after picture of them, dressed in stylish clothing at red carpet affairs, dancing together at hot L.A. nightclubs, on Rollerblades at Venice Beach, even shopping together at Whole Foods like a married couple.

Her heart descended further into her chest cavity. She wasn't in the least bit cheered to learn that Laura was twelve years older than Quasar and almost twenty years older than her. Who cared? She looked fabulous and was clearly living life to the fullest. Laura Larson was a woman in control of her own destiny, not one sitting around as an unwelcome guest in her father's house, wondering if she'd ever earn a single penny again, let alone fulfill all her dreams of romance and riches.

Laura Larson Dumps Young Lover, blared one headline. It didn't mention Quasar by name but it was recent and the description—"sexy entrepreneurial sheikh"—fit him to a T. In the article, Laura explained, and Dani could almost hear her giggling as she read it, that she needed to focus on her new role in an upcoming space opera blockbuster. In another article a week later there was speculation that she was dating George Clooney. Then rumors of an affair with Leonardo DiCaprio swirled. Dani began to wonder if Laura's publicist was just sending out press releases to boost her profile, while she was still quietly enjoying the many pleasures of Quasar's company.

He probably didn't care what the tabloids said. He was too busy buying and selling billion-dollar companies and drinking thousand-dollar bottles of champagne.

And making passionate love to Laura Larson.

A tear dripped down onto her keyboard and she cursed her self-pity. She should be congratulating herself on a narrow escape. She could have uprooted herself and gone to Boston with him, only to find herself abandoned while he headed off to enjoy Laura, or any of the other beauties he'd dated before. Or someone new.

He'd flirted with Dani so readily and seduced her so quickly that it was almost ridiculous. Especially as she had good reason to be wary of men! He must possess almost hypnotic powers over women, and they'd certainly worked on her. It was hard to believe that she of all people had allowed him not only to kiss her, but also to seduce her into bed.

Had she lost her mind?

Her phone chimed and made her jump. Was it him? She couldn't resist checking.

Where are you?

She frowned. Had he just noticed that she'd gone missing from the party? It must be nearly an hour since she'd left. He'd probably been so busy with Laura running her hands all over him that he hadn't realized Dani wasn't there for the cake cutting.

She put the phone facedown on the comforter and went back to her laptop screen. Looking at more pictures of him and Laura would save her from weakening. He was all wrong for her. He'd break her heart.

She bit her lip when she realized it was probably already too late to avoid getting her heart broken. She'd become attached to him so quickly, that it was already hard to imagine her life without him

Her phone chimed again. She tried to summon the strength to leave it facedown on her bed. She failed and picked it up, heart racing.

Dani, I've been looking for you everywhere.

I left the party. She'd typed a reply before she could stop herself. And why shouldn't she tell him? It was the truth. She'd have to tell him that she wasn't moving to Boston with him, and why, as well, so there was no point in totally avoiding him.

Though it was essential to keep enough distance that he couldn't work his hypnotic charms on her as usual.

I can see that.

She bit her lip. She wanted to type *I miss you, too*, but that was some foolish part of her that got swept up in a romantic fantasy that had little to do with what was really going on between them. She put the phone down again and stood staring at it, with her arms crossed, as if daring it to try something.

How did you slip away?

She watched the words appear on the screen, from her safe vantage point a few feet away. Her brain supplied an answer: *It wasn't hard. You didn't even notice me leave.*
She didn't type that, either.

I need to see you.

Had he decided he preferred her to Laura? Did he now want to apologize for acting as if Laura and he were an item at the party? Or did he just want to keep Dani warm on the back burner in case he wanted some steamy sex later that week.

It was sad how quickly her optimistic, romantic glow had turned cynical.

Will you meet me?

She drew in a deep breath and approached the phone as if it were a snake that might bite her if handled wrong. No.

Did he really think she'd want to see him after he let Laura paw him at the party? He must live in a world of illusion. Then again, of course he did. He'd grown up as one of the storied Al Mansurs, with their millions in oil wealth and everything handed to them on a platter. He was used to women bowing at his feet and doing whatever he wanted.

She'd certainly done it easily enough, and she hadn't even known who he was at first.

Dani half waited for him to text again, explaining that Laura meant nothing to him, and she—Dani—was the only woman he cared about. That was probably beneath his dignity, though. He'd certainly never mentioned his other woman friends to her. Likely he thought them none of her business.

Are you at home?

She hesitated for a moment, holding the phone in her hand. If she told him she was at home he'd probably come over, and embarrass her even further in front of her father and brothers.

Her fingers twitched to reply. She could vividly picture Quasar typing on his phone and being confused and possibly hurt by her brusque responses. She didn't want to hurt him. She cared about him. Her feelings for him were confusing and intense and she'd almost begun to think they might be that elusive and dangerous thing she'd once called love.

She wasn't falling down that rabbit hole again, though. Her heart wanted to text Quasar back. To make plans to meet with him. To fall into his arms, to believe whatever he promised and float along on a rose-scented cloud of bliss for as long as she could.

But she'd tried that approach to life once. Ignoring warning signs. Being nice. Hoping for the best. Smoothing things over when they got rocky. Trying to save everyone's feelings but her own. And she wasn't doing that again.

Ever.

Then she heard a knock on her window.

<u>Ten</u>

The sound of knuckles rapping on the glass made Dani jump and drop her phone. She spun around and a barrage of confusing emotions assaulted her as she saw Quasar's face emerge from the evening gloom outside her window: relief that he cared enough to come; horror that once again he'd ignored etiquette to pursue her; and fear that she'd fall immediately under his seductive spell.

He knocked again, more softly this time, to draw her from her frozen indecision. She realized she had to open the window. After yesterday's experience of being stuck in her room with the bars locked from the outside, she'd found the key and snuck it into her desk drawer. She drew it out, pulled up the window sash—pressing her finger to his lips to warn him into silence—and handed it to him.

He slid the key into the lock at the bottom of the barred grating. She watched his moonlight-dusted profile, sharp cheekbones, proud nose, characteristically tousled hair. Looking at him made a girl forget about common sense and what was right.

The lock clicked open and he lifted the large, heavy iron grid that hinged from the top, eased himself under it and opened the window. In a few brief seconds, he was inside her room and standing on her carpet.

"You can't stay," she whispered. "My father and brothers are home."

"I know. Come with me." He gestured at the window with his chin.

She shook her head silently. She could hear the TV from down the hall. Al Jazeera news on full volume. It was unlikely that anyone would hear them if they kept their voices down. "We can talk here," she said softly. "It's time to end this madness and go back to our separate lives."

"You can't be serious." He stepped toward her and seized hold of her hands. "A few hours ago you liked the idea of coming with me."

"That was before I saw you with Laura." The confession was an instant weight off her mind. That was the true reason she'd changed her mind—totally and irrevocably—about moving to Boston with him. She'd caught a glimpse of the real Quasar, in his own element, and felt like the outsider she would be if she were foolish enough to try living with him.

He squeezed her hands and she felt an echoing squeeze in her heart. "Dani. Laura was important to me. That's all over. Now she's simply an old friend."

"I think she wants to be a lot more than friends."

"She's very touchy-feely, but she's really like that with everyone. Besides, it doesn't really matter what she wants. I know what I want and that's you."

Dani swallowed. She wished he wasn't holding her hands so tightly so she could pull away and put some space between them.

"Maybe you can't admit to yourself that you really want her back."

She saw the familiar twinkle of humor in his eyes. She wasn't sure whether to be reassured that he found her worries amusing, or appalled that he could find humor even when she was trying to dump him.

"I don't want her back. I don't like to talk about past relationships, as I think it's more respectful to both parties to keep everything private, but I was relieved when our relationship ended. I don't want a woman who lives to see and be seen, and who gets restless if she stays in one city for more than two weeks. I want someone calming and steady, whose resources come from within and who prefers peace and intimacy to a glittering crowd." He squeezed her hands again and took another step closer until his chest was almost touching hers. "I want you."

Her heart leaped and she cursed it. The sincerity in his voice clawed at her. Now that they were alone together again, all her doubts and fears seemed to shrivel away and the grand hopes and dreams he inspired reinflated and threatened to warp her perspective. "I know you think that now. That you really believe it. But I felt like the outsider at that party, like she claimed you and owned you and I was an intruder. I know she's only one of many women you've dated, and I just can't compete with them. I don't want to. I'll be jealous and resentful and hate myself. Why didn't you tell her to take her hands off you?"

He frowned. "I should have. I was thoughtless and assumed too readily that you knew I was yours and only yours. From now on, no woman shall touch me but you." He lifted her hands to his mouth and kissed them.

A strange sensation shivered through her belly. "You can't promise that. What are you going to do? Beat them off with a stick?"

"If necessary." The look in his eyes suggested that he was entirely serious. "Or perhaps I can carry a *khanjar* at my belt and slice at them if they try."

She giggled. It was impossible not to. She could totally picture Quasar with the traditional dagger tucked into his Armani suit.

Then she stopped laughing. "I'm scared. Everyone who knows me will think it's wrong, that I've lost my mind."

"Do you listen to them, or to your heart?" His eyes narrowed, and he peered into hers with what looked like the wisdom of a thousand years.

"I listened to my heart before, and it was wrong. I thought I'd met my life partner and I tried to make it work but he was cruel and destructive to me. I don't trust my judgment anymore."

"I love you, Dani. I want you by my side. What will it take?"

She blinked, staring at him. Cool resolve crept over her. "If I'm not happy, you'll let me go, no questions asked?"

He frowned again. He seemed to be considering her words. "Though it would pain me to let you go, I'll agree."

"Even if I ask you to let me go right now?" This was the ultimate test. He'd refused once. Did he respect her enough to do what he promised?

He gave her a confused look. "You want me to leave right now?"

"And never come back."

His mouth moved, as if he were at a loss for words. "I can't promise that." His regal brow furrowed. "I can't."

"See? You can't promise you'll let me go. You want me to be yours, no matter what the cost to me. I've played by those terms once and I won't do it again." Her own determination strengthened as she stood up to him.

She watched his chest rise as he drew in a steadying breath. "You want me to leave you—forever—to prove how much I love you?"

What she asked didn't make any sense, but she was going to lose him either way. She couldn't go with him and plunge herself into a life of uncertainty. She nodded, her lips pressed together.

Quasar raised her hands to his lips again. His blue eyes were shadowed with darkness as he kissed them one more time—so softly—sending tremors of sensation and emotion to her toes. Then he bowed, turned to the window, climbed out and walked off into the night. Her heart breaking, she watched his white shirt disappear into the darkness.

He did it. He promised he'd let her go, and he did. And the worst part was that now she loved him more than ever.

Quasar's heart pounded so hard it could break a rib. He was glad of the brisk walk to where he'd parked his car a couple of blocks away. He understood where Dani was coming from. She'd been pushed around, told what to do, what not to do, and she had to be sure she was in charge of her own destiny.

As a man used to being in control of his life and that of many people around him, it didn't sit well at all to just walk away. It was hard enough to leave when he knew he'd see her the next day. Now she expected him to go back to his life and forget all about her?

No way.

He'd go back to his life—what there was of it without her in it—and breathe through each day until she came to her senses and claimed him. That was the only reason he'd been able to leave. He knew it was a test. It was easy to fail, very hard to pass.

And who knew how long the test would last?

He'd ached to wrap his arms around her and draw her into his embrace. His skin had crawled when Laura kept touching him earlier, but he'd never needed a strategy for keeping a woman at arm's length so he'd never developed one. From now on he'd wear invisible armor—projected in his bearing—that kept anyone but Dani from even touching him.

He wouldn't text her. He wouldn't call her. He wouldn't show up at her usual haunts, or hover outside her window like a ghost.

But he would win her back.

"You've taken leave of your senses," Salim growled. He rose to his feet and towered over his desk. "You've lost all perspective on reality."

"I love her."

Light blasted through the window of Salim's austere, white-walled office with its view out over the glittering ocean. Quasar had come to tackle an important hurdle on the road to winning Dani over.

"You love her so much that I need to take a piece of land worth millions—billions in future revenue—and simply give it away to a man I detest who's wasted untold hours of my time and thousands of rials with his meritless lawsuits."

"I'll buy the land from you at market value."

"The market value is in no way commensurate with the value that land has to me as the site of my future flagship hotel."

"Then I'll pay whatever value you set."

"Even if it's fifty million dollars?" Salim arched a brow. "That, in fact, is an approximate figure for my construction costs alone. I have big plans for this property."

"I won't be able to simply write a check for that amount. I'll have to free up some assets, but I can have the money for you by the end of next week. Tell me which account you'd like it transferred into." He pulled out his phone to type in the information.

"You really have taken leave of your senses."

"Quite the opposite, brother. I've finally come to my senses." He smiled.

"But she hasn't even agreed to marry you."

"I haven't asked."

"Why not?"

"Because she'd say no."

"If she doesn't want you, why would you risk fifty million dollars trying to win her favor?"

"She does want me." He cocked his head. "She's afraid of herself, though. She's afraid of making a poor choice. I have to prove to her than I'm an excellent choice, and I won't stop until I've done that."

Salim sighed, and sat back in his big leather chair. "I know how you feel, brother. I've been there myself. There's no pain more acute than the loss of a woman your happiness depends on."

"Elan told me that Sara would only come live with him if he agreed not to marry her. She didn't want to be trapped or tied down by convention. It seems that sometimes we Al Mansur men have to learn to let our women fly free before we can convince them to come nest with us."

Salim laughed. "And Celia made me sign a contract promising that she and Kira could leave whenever they wanted. But neither myself nor Elan had to pay fifty million dollars for the privilege of being with our wives."

"Daniyah Hassan is a very special woman. I've never felt the kind of peace and happiness I know in her arms. I had no idea it was even possible."

"That's sweet and romantic, brother, but I'm extremely attached to that piece of land. Why don't you give your princely sum to her father in exchange for it? I'm sure one million would buy him off with a smile, never mind fifty."

"Dani says her father won't take money for the land. The whole affair has dragged on so long that it's personal. He won't stop until he gets the land back."

"The courts would never side with him."

"Are you willing to wait twenty years for that outcome? Surely you can buy another piece of property. Maybe one of those big houses along the shore? Or perhaps Hassan will gladly sell it back to you for money once he's had the satisfaction of walking on it. I doubt he has any plans for it other than a quick sale."

"True. You can buy it from me for fifty million and give it to Hassan for nothing, then I'll buy it back from him for five. I'm suddenly seeing this as a very profitable venture." Salim grinned. "If you're really madly in love enough to go through with this, then may your sweetheart come running to you before you come back to your senses and realize how nuts this all is."

"Great." Quasar grinned back. "I'll need the SWIFT and IBAN numbers for the transfer."

"No need for all that fuss." Salim reached across the table and shook Quasar's hand firmly. "I'll take a check."

Dani returned from a trip to the local American school in an upbeat mood. She'd applied for an advertised position as a teacher's aide, and been told that she had a good shot at getting it. While assisting in a classroom wasn't the position she'd studied and trained for, it was a job and would provide income and independence to get her back on her feet. She was almost whistling with joy as the taxi dropped her off at the house.

"Dani!" Her heart sank when she saw her father in the

doorway with an anxious expression on his face. Uh-oh. He'd be angry that she'd gone out, yet again, without a male family member to escort her. She couldn't possibly expect to find a job, let alone keep one, if she had to wait until he or one of her brothers had the free time to take her somewhere.

"Something extraordinary has happened." His eyebrows were jumping all over the place. He didn't look angry, though. If anything he looked stunned.

"What is it?"

He waved a big brown envelope in the air. "A courier just delivered this package. It contains a deed to the property on Beach Road. And a contract that conveys the title back to me. All that I have to do is sign it and send a token ten rials to seal the deal."

"Ten rials? Is this a joke?"

"The token amount makes it legal. Quasar Al Mansur says he wants to gift the property to me outright and return it to our family."

Her mouth hung open. That property was worth millions. And she'd seen how passionate his brother Salim was about it. Had he persuaded his brother to part with it just because of her?

It didn't seem possible. "Let me see."

Her father handed her the envelope and she pulled out an old deed typed on yellowed paper. There was also a contract for the change of ownership, signed by Quasar and requiring her father's signature. The part that made her heart thud, however, was a letter from Quasar insisting that he wanted to return the land as a gesture of goodwill between their families.

He'd been true to his word and not contacted her since she sent him back out through her window three days earlier. She was impressed that he'd managed to obey her wishes, when he was clearly a man used to demanding—and taking—what he wanted.

She was even more impressed that she'd managed to stay strong enough not to call him herself. Her mind and body ached with missing him. At night she craved the feel of his arms around her—even though she'd never felt them around her at night, only during snatched sojourns in the heat of the day.

Taking time apart from him allowed her to breathe. To think. Now that she had time to ponder, she was glad she hadn't run away with him. They barely knew each other and what she knew about him was alarming. If she'd accepted his "grant," she would have basically been an expensive mistress, which wasn't how she wanted to start out her new life. She thought he'd soon get over their whirlwind affair and move on. She'd be just another in a long line of women he'd earnestly adored and left behind.

But discovering that he wanted to give her father a piece of land worth millions put an entirely different spin on the situation. It proved he was serious. Even if money was virtually no object for him personally, he'd had to persuade his brother to shelve his hotel plans—which couldn't have been easy—and he'd gone to the trouble of having the legal paperwork drawn up.

She looked up at her father. "Are you going to sign it?"

"Do you think it's a trick?"

"I don't know." She tried to focus but all the small print on the contract blurred in front of her eyes. "It certainly seems real. You should have a lawyer look over it."

"I don't trust those Al Mansurs. It could be some kind of trap. If I sign this paper allowing them to transfer the land to me, it will be like admitting that I never owned it in the first place. I'd be giving up my claim that I currently own the land."

"But if the contract is genuine you'd be giving it up in return for outright ownership of the land. Ten rials is a lot cheaper than the thousands of rials you'd have to pay to your lawyer to take your claim all the way through the courts."

"That is certainly true." Her dad rubbed his mustache with a finger.

"What would you do with the land?" Now that ownership of the property was within reach, her father seemed oddly lackadaisical about it. Which was strange, since he'd been gnashing his teeth over being "robbed" for as long as she could remember.

"Sell it, of course." His brows lifted, probably as he contemplated how much he could get for it.

"Maybe you could sell it back to Salim Al Mansur."

Her father's brows lowered. "Why would he give it to me for free only to buy it back? Maybe there's something I don't know. Maybe he's contaminated the land. He could have buried toxic waste on it. It seems too good to be true."

Like her relationship with Quasar. Too sudden, too easy, too fabulous, too far, too fast. She sighed. "I'm not sure we can ever truly understand other people's motivations. You just need to decide if you still really want it, and if you do, then get in touch with a lawyer and make sure all the documents say what they are supposed to say. If they do, then sign them, take your fishing rod to the land and catch some fish." She attempted a half smile. It couldn't really be that easy, could it?

No way. Nothing ever was.

Quasar didn't want to go back to the United States. His visit to Oman was stretching into its third week, but now that Dani wasn't coming with him, the prospect of moving to Boston and exploring the intriguing business opportunities there had palled. For one thing he'd miss these jovial breakfasts on the hotel veranda, where the whole family gathered together to start the day. Elan and Sara still showed no signs of returning to their home in Nevada, and he felt the same way about leaving.

He watched Celia's long fingers deftly wind a hair tie around the bottom of Kira's fishtail braid while the little girl munched on a blueberry muffin. Would he ever have children of his own to take care of? Since he'd met Dani, he'd thought about the prospect more than once.

Celia glanced up. "Salim told me about the land deal. When are you going back to propose marriage?"

Quasar ripped a croissant in half. "It's not a done deal yet. Dani's father has had the contract for two days and I haven't heard a word. Maybe he's so difficult he'll refuse to take the land back as a gift because he'd rather win it in court." His chest tightened as he thought about it. Could he lose his chance of a lifetime with Dani due to her own father's stubbornness?

So many pieces had to fall into place for this to work.

"It may well be a done deal, brother. A courier left a big envelope at the front desk for you this morning," Salim said.

"What?" Quasar leapt from his chair. "Why didn't you tell me?"

"I just did." Salim smiled enigmatically.

Quasar felt like punching him. Salim still hadn't cashed the damn check, either, which made the whole deal feel rather illusory since the contract gifting the land was between Quasar and Mohammed Hassan. He dialed the front desk and asked them to bring any mail to him. He glared at Salim. "You're enjoying this, aren't you?"

"Enormously. Who'd have thought that my baby

brother would be so madly in love with a woman that he'd part with fifty million dollars for the chance to win her favor."

"It is adorable." Sara smiled and smoothed a cowlick in Ben's hair. "But then you Al Mansurs are the biggest romantics once you finally fall in love."

One of the front-desk staff brought the envelope to the table and Quasar ripped into it with his heart pounding. There was the contract—signed and notarized—and a letter from Mohammed Hassan thanking him for recognizing his long-held claim to the land and returning it to its rightful owner. Quasar smiled. "It's all signed, sealed and delivered."

Salim shook his head. "I've never seen anyone so happy about parting with fifty million dollars *and* a prime piece of oceanfront real estate."

Quasar winked. "Thanks for making it possible."

"So now you can go back and propose." Celia looked at him down the length of her elegant nose.

"Not so fast!" Sara exclaimed. "Dani just extracted herself from a miserable marriage. It might be quite some time before she can be persuaded to go down that road again. If ever. Why does marriage have to be such an important part of every relationship? It's as if you can't enjoy being a couple until there's some legal paperwork saying you own the rights to each other in perpetuity."

Elan laughed. "See what I have to deal with? I did finally persuade her to marry me, though."

"How?" Quasar couldn't hide his curiosity.

Sara leaned forward. "By proving to me, day after day, that he really wanted to be with me, and enjoy my company, and share a family with me, not own me and control me and run me. You Al Mansurs may be successful but you've been raised with some bad habits that can need breaking."

"I don't want to own Dani or run her life."

"You don't think you do, but you do expect her to fall neatly into your plans. What if she wants to stay in Salalah rather than moving to Boston?"

He frowned. "I'm pretty sure she wants to move back to America."

"But if she didn't you'd be willing to stay here with her even if it means giving up on that biotech company you're all excited about acquiring?"

He thought for a moment about the considerable sacrifice required, then answered with conviction. "Yes. I have a strong feeling about it. Call it intuition, or a hunch, or maybe even destiny, but I truly believe Dani and I are meant to be together."

Elan leaned forward and clapped him on the back. "Then take your time and make sure you don't screw it up like I nearly did. Sara scared me so good I waited through her entire pregnancy with our son, and half of our first year as parents, before I even dared ask her again."

Sara looked at him lovingly. "Luckily by then I was ready to say yes."

"How soon before I can try to buy the land back?" Salim cocked his head. "I have plans drawn up and was waiting to resolve the title issues before submitting them for approval."

"If I can hold my horses, brother, you can, too." Quasar let out a sigh. "Patience may not be our strong suit but it builds character for us to apply it."

"Finding the right woman is what builds character most of all," Salim said quietly. "I was bulldozing my way through life trying to get everything so perfect that I almost destroyed my one chance at happiness. I consider myself the luckiest man alive that Celia was able to find it in her heart to forgive me for being such an utter ass."

Celia laughed. "The whole situation was character-building for me, too. I kept your daughter secret from you because I was too afraid you'd tried to seize control of her." She squeezed Quasar's arm. "But as you can see he managed to win me over, so hang in there and keep your goal in sight."

Elan leaned back in his chair. "It certainly sounds as if you've found a woman strong and steady enough to handle you, so take her needs seriously, and don't blow it. What do you plan to do next?"

"Propose to her."

Quasar guided his silver Mercedes through the now-familiar streets of Dani's quiet neighborhood, past the silent houses with their shuttered windows. Unfamiliar trepidation quickened his heartbeat. The next step was a big one, and he wasn't entirely sure how to handle it. Since he wasn't used to such uncertainty, the effect was decidedly unsettling.

Despite his brothers' experiences, he'd decided that Dani was obviously uncomfortable with the idea of accompanying him to America with her status in his life uncertain. So it was important to clarify that status. Which meant proposing marriage.

And since this was Oman, he also needed her father's permission. Right now he had no idea how either of them would respond to his proposal.

He parked his car directly in front of the house, announcing his arrival to anyone who happened to glance out a window. He half hoped someone would open the door and say something, so he could avoid the suspense of climbing the doorstep and knocking. He still remembered how badly his last visit had gone.

The difficult part was that he had to ask Dani to marry him first. He'd deliberately chosen to come here in the early evening, when her father and brothers were home, so everything would be proper and aboveboard and he couldn't be accused of sneaking around or trying to seduce her into bed. The snag was that if her father answered the door, how did he explain his purpose and ask to see Dani without either giving the game away or getting thrown out on his ear or...both?

It would take some cunning.

Dani had been at her computer since lunchtime, typing letters. Buoyed by her positive experience at the American school—from which a job offer seemed almost certain—she'd decided to broaden her horizons. She'd polished her resumé and written letters of introduction to five different universities with art history or history programs that featured a strong interest in Near Eastern art. She was putting the final touches on them and intended to sleep on them and, if she were still feeling bold enough, to email them out tomorrow morning. One of them was to a department at Harvard. Unlikely as it seemed, she was opening the door to going to Boston all by herself.

And all the activity kept her from thinking about Quasar, who had somehow engineered the return of her father's land.

She missed him so much that her belly ached. The urge to text him, just to say hi, was almost irresistible. She yearned to hear his deep, rich voice in her ear, even if it were only through her phone speaker. She wanted to speak with him about her plans and get his opinion of her letters. She craved his encouragement and support even as she told herself she could get along fine without it.

He'd been true to his word and let her go. And right now she felt like a complete idiot for letting him.

"Dani!" Her brother's voice accompanied his sharp knock on her door. "Dad's calling you."

She frowned. Why didn't he just come get her? Why send her brother? "Coming."

She saved her document and closed it. She'd been so busy and wrapped up in her plans she hadn't noticed it was nearly dinnertime. She washed her hands and smoothed her hair and tried not to laugh—or cry—at her lovelorn expression in the mirror. Two tiny dark smudges had formed under her eyes, making her look like a mournful maiden from an ancient miniature. Or a zombie. She sighed. Sooner or later she'd get over Quasar and the dark rings would go away again. She probably just needed more exercise.

"Dani, what's keeping you?" Her father's gruff voice startled her out of rubbing her fingers on her face and pinching color into her cheeks.

"I'm on my way. What's the rush?"

"We have a visitor."

"Who?"

"Come here." Maybe her aunt Riya had stopped by to say hello.

She turned into the hallway, and saw a tall silhouette just inside the door. Her heart started to pound. It was Quasar.

"Hello, Dani." That familiar, rough yet smooth voice sent excitement coursing through her.

"Hello, Quasar." She tried to sound cool and non-committal as her blood heated several degrees. Why was he here? Should she be mad at him for breaking his promise to stay away, or thrilled that he cared enough to come back?

A broad smile widened her dad's mouth and his body language suggested that Quasar was an old friend rather than a sworn enemy with undesirable designs against his daughter. Apparently the priceless gift of oceanfront property had earned him a place in her father's heart. Had he done that for her?

"Come, Khalid and Jalil. Let's leave them in peace." Dani stared as her father ushered her brothers out into the garden, leaving her and Quasar alone in the house.

"What's going on?" She blinked, suddenly confused. She'd forgotten how tall he was, and how broad his shoulders were. The sight of him, blue eyes flashing, was enough to dazzle her completely.

"Dani." He took her hands, enveloping them in his. As usual, this action had a disturbing effect on her entire body. "I know you told me to stay away from you, and I did for as long as I could possibly stand. Now I'm going to ask you something very important and I want you to think carefully about your answer. What you say now will affect both of our lives, one way or the other, so take your time."

She stared at him. He must be about to propose marriage. What else would come with such dramatic foreshadowing? She'd have to say no, of course. They didn't know each other well enough.

And she was far too deeply in love to make any kind of rational decision about it.

"Why did you give my father the land?" The question had burned in her brain since she'd seen the contract.

"I wanted to solve a problem."

"But it wasn't your problem. It was between your brother Salim and my father." There was something so chivalrous about his attempt to bridge the divide between their two families. His efforts touched her deeply.

"It's important to me that both of them are happy. I sincerely hope I'll be able to make that happen."

"I can't believe you just gave it to him as a gift. It's worth…I have no idea what it's worth." More than a million, for sure. She tried to rein in her enthusiasm. Quasar had done all this behind her back, without her knowledge or consent.

"It's worth whatever someone is willing to pay for it."

"I really don't want to know what you were willing to pay for it." A chill slithered down her spine. "Why did you give it to him?"

"Why do you think?" As usual he looked calm and rather pleased with himself. Which under the circumstances could be adorable or infuriating, or both.

"To buy his approval of you having a relationship with me." No point in beating about the bush.

"I like the way you don't mince words." He squeezed her hands, which were either ice-cold, or boiling hot; she couldn't really tell anymore.

"But what if I don't want a relationship with you?" She tried to keep her voice steady while emotion threatened to close her throat. She wanted a relationship with him desperately. But not desperately enough to risk her independence, her self-esteem, her heart. "What if I feel a whole lot safer by myself?"

He frowned. "Dani, I won't ever force you to do anything you don't want to. I won't ever boss you around or treat you with anything less than the utmost respect. We can have it written into the marriage contract, if you like."

"Marriage?" Her voice emerged as a squeak. She'd seen this coming yet she still felt herself grow dizzy.

"I don't want you to be my girlfriend, or to reluctantly

accept a research grant from me. I love you. I want you to be my wife, my partner in life, my soul mate and the person I turn to every day to give and receive love and support." He inhaled a shaky breath. "Say you will, Dani. Please say you will."

She swallowed as conflicting emotions battled in her heart. "You just commanded me to say yes."

Confusion darkened his eyes. "I didn't mean it as a command. I was imploring you."

"Beseeching me." She giggled. Probably nerves. Quasar Al Mansur had just begged her to be his wife, and parted with millions to gain the privilege of asking her, and she had no idea what to say.

Of course her brain and body were screaming at her to agree.

Even though moments ago she'd been sure that she should calmly say no.

A weird shiver of excitement was rising from her toes, creeping up her limbs and torso and along her arms. Exciting possibilities unfolded before her—visions of a new life filled with love and hope and joy.

She *was* going to accept.

If this man loved her enough to do all this for her, it was worth the risk to take a leap of faith with him. "What was the question again? I'm not sure if you even asked me."

"Dani Hassan, will you be my wife?"

"Yes." She said it so fast it came out like a gasp. The sense of relief she felt afterward almost made her collapse in his arms. She'd made her decision and she knew in her heart that it was the right one.

He didn't say anything at all. His gaze softened and he inhaled a slow and steady breath. "Thank you. I promise I'll make you glad you married me." His wide, confident mouth broadened back into a smile, then she lost sight of it as he leaned in and kissed her with more passion than she'd ever dared to dream of.

Epilogue

Dani opened the front door, then stepped aside as the men burst into the house laughing and singing. Quasar led the way, followed by Dani's brothers, Khalid and Jalil, and Quasar's brothers, Elan and Salim. Her father brought up the rear in a rather dignified manner. "It's not easy to follow Omani wedding customs here in Boston," Quasar explained to her with a kiss. "We're really supposed to play drums, fire shots into the air and drive from my house to yours flashing our lights and honking horns the whole way, but I don't want us all to get arrested for disturbing the peace."

They'd decided to drive into Cambridge and cruise around MIT in a limo blasting the stereo instead.

"You should see the campus. It's awesome." Khalid's eyes shone with excitement.

"I have seen it." She grinned. "And if you don't want

to stay in one of the MIT dorms you could come live with us while you're studying there."

"Now, now." Her dad smiled sheepishly. "Khalid has to get in first. An application to MIT is no laughing matter."

"We all know Khalid is a genius." Quasar ruffled Khalid's hair. "And MIT will be lucky to get him."

White flowers ornamented almost every surface in the elegant brownstone. It was wonderful to see the place filled with life, even with noise and too many people trying to use the bathrooms at the same time. What a difference from the hushed and somber atmosphere at her first wedding, which her friends had warned her against and her cousins were forbidden to attend.

All the ladies had their hands hennaed the night before, another Omani tradition she'd skipped over last time. She expressed her admiration for the women, and Quasar came up behind her and gave her a kiss. "You look stunning."

It was the first time he'd seen her long white gown— even Omani brides usually wore white these days—with pearl beads sewn into swirling patterns on the skirt. Strapless and cut low in the back, it made her feel daring and sexy as well as beautiful.

She'd been so sure she'd never feel that way again, until she found Quasar reading the one book she wanted in her favorite bookstore. "It's so strange that I had to go back to Oman to find you."

"And that I had to go back to Oman to find you." He kissed her softly on the lips, then led her through the house and out into the decorated garden. The leafy canopy of old oak and maple trees filtered the bright afternoon sunshine. A white pavilion, decked with flowers, was set up for the imam to perform the brief marriage ceremony.

She couldn't believe how involved Quasar had been in planning the wedding. He really seemed to want to discuss every detail, even though he was in the middle of a deal big enough to make the front page of the *Financial Times*.

Salim, always one to take charge, moved through the gathered crowd, ushering them out into the garden. Celia and Sara organized the children around the pavilion with baskets of flower petals to toss at the moment the marriage became official.

"Where's my shawl? I don't think the imam wants to see my bare shoulders." Dani bit her lip and grinned mischievously.

"I put it under the pavilion so you'd have it when you needed it," answered Quasar. "Let me get it for you."

"What have you done to my brother?" asked Salim. "I don't remember him being thoughtful."

"He seems determined to prove to me that I'm making the right choice by marrying him."

"Determination is a core Al Mansur trait." Elan walked up, carrying little Hannah, whose eyes glittered with freshly dried tears. Fortunately her face also glowed with a dazzling smile. "It's particularly exasperating during the toddler years. But it's one of the things that makes us so loveable."

Quasar returned and draped the silky white chiffon carefully over her shoulders and hair. "See, you can be both traditional and modern at the same time."

"And American and Omani." She winked. They'd found a live band composed of Harvard students who swore they could play both traditional Omani music and classic rock. Just watching them try promised to be fun.

"The Al Mansur family is officially global," Sara chimed in.

"Speaking of the Al Mansur family, when do you plan to add to the lineage?" Celia moved next to Dani. "I think it's quite miraculous that Dani managed to get all the way to her wedding vows without getting pregnant."

"Or did she?" Sara raised a brow.

Dani laughed. "No plus signs on the pregnancy test for me. I've just started my job at the Harvard Art Museum Research Center and I'm hoping to travel to their ongoing excavation in Sardis next year. Besides, Quasar and I intend to enjoy each other for a while before we add to our family." She loved that he hadn't put any pressure on her at all to have children yet. They had plenty of time for that.

Quasar took her hand and they walked together along the stone path toward the pavilion where they'd be joined in marriage. Tears welled inside her, but this time they were tears of happiness.

* * * * *

"I'll see you at eight," Monroe said, breaking the standoff.

The sensation of his warm breath on her face gave Kim a ridiculously flushed and tingly feeling. The look in his eyes doubled that. What kind of boss was he? The kind who wouldn't mind breaking a few laws in order to get his way? The kind with a casting couch?

She broke eye contact. Her lashes fluttered. She stood there, helpless to get out of this, speechless for once, before backing up and turning abruptly.

She left Chaz Monroe, knowing that he stared after her, feeling his heated gaze. That scrutiny was so hot, she had an absurd longing to run back to him and press her mouth to his in a brief goodbye kiss, then laugh manically as she headed back to her cubicle to clear out her things.

The strangest bit of intuition told her he wanted that, too. In those insane moments of confrontation and unacceptable closeness, her senses screamed that Chaz Monroe had wanted to kiss her.

THE BOSS'S
MISTLETOE
MANOEUVRES

BY
LINDA THOMAS-SUNDSTROM

Published in Great Britain 2014
by Mills & Boon, an imprint of Harlequin (UK) Limited,
Eton House, 18-24 Paradise Road, Richmond, Surrey, TW9 1SR

© 2014 Linda Thomas-Sundstrom

ISBN: 978-0-263-91484-9

51-1114

Harlequin (UK) Limited's policy is to use papers that are natural, renewable and recyclable products and made from wood grown in sustainable forests. The logging and manufacturing processes conform to the legal environmental regulations of the country of origin.

Printed and bound in Spain
by CPI, Barcelona

Linda Thomas-Sundstrom writes contemporary romance and paranormal romance novels for the Mills & Boon® Nocturne™ and Desire™ lines. A teacher by day and a writer by night, Linda lives in the West, juggling teaching, writing, family and caring for a big stretch of land. She swears she has a resident Muse who sings so loudly, she often wears earplugs in order to get anything else done, but has big plans to eventually get to all those ideas.

Visit Linda's website: www.LindaThomas-Sundstrom.com.

Connect on Facebook: www.facebook.com/LindaThomasSundstrom

One

Chaz Monroe knew a great female backside when he saw one. And the blonde with the swinging ponytail walking down the hallway in front of him was damn near a ten.

Lean, rounded, firm and feminine, her admirable backside swayed from side to side as she moved, above the short hemline of a tight black skirt that did little to hide a great pair of legs. Long, shapely legs, encased in paperthin black tights and ending in a pair of perfectly sensible black leather pumps.

The sensible pumps were a disappointment and a slight hiccup in his rating overall, given the sexiness of the rest of her. She was red stilettos all the way, Chaz decided. Satin shoes maybe, or suede. Still, though the woman was a visual sensory delight, now wasn't the time or place for an indulgence of that kind. Not with an employee. Never with an employee.

She wore a blue fuzzy sweater that molded to her slender torso and was on the tall side of small. Her stride was purposeful, businesslike and almost arrogant in the way she maneuvered through the narrow hallway, skillfully avoiding chairs, unused consoles and the watercooler. Her heels made soft clicking sounds that didn't echo much.

Chaz followed her until she turned right, heading for Cubicle City. At that junction, as he hooked a left toward his new office, he caught a whiff of scent that lingered in her wake. Not a typical floral fragrance, either. Something subtle, almost sweet, that would have decided her fate right then and there if he'd been another kind of guy, with a different sort of agenda.

This guy had to think and behave like the new owner of an advertising agency in the heart of Manhattan.

Taking over a new business required the kind of time that ruled out relationships, including dates and dalliances. In the past two months he'd become a freaking monk, since there wasn't one extra hour in his schedule for distractions if he was to turn this company around in a decent amount of time. That was the priority. All of his money was riding on this company making it. He'd spent every cent he had to buy this advertising firm.

Whistling, Chaz strolled past Alice Brody, his newly inherited pert, big-eyed, middle-aged, fluffy-haired executive secretary. He entered his office through a set of glass doors still bearing the name of the vice president he'd already had to let go for allowing the company to slowly slide from the top of the heap to the mediocre middle. Lackluster management was unacceptable in a company where nothing seemed to be wrong with the work of the rest of the staff.

"There is one more person to see today," Alice called after him.

"Need a few minutes to go over some things first," Chaz said over his shoulder. "Can you bring in the file I asked for?"

"I'll get on it right away."

Something in Alice's tone made him wonder what she might be thinking. He could feel her eyes on him. When he glanced back at her, she smiled.

Chaz shrugged off the thought, used to women liking his looks. But his older brother Rory was the real catch. As the first self-made millionaire in the family, his brother made headlines and left trails of women in his wake.

Chaz had a lot of catching up to do to match his brother's magic with a floundering company. So there were, at the moment, bigger fish to fry.

First up, he had to finish dealing with old contract issues

and get everyone up to speed with the new company plan. He had to decide how to speak to one person in particular. Kim McKinley, the woman highly recommended by everyone here for an immediate promotion. The woman in line for the VP job before he had temporarily taken over that office, going undercover in this new business as an employee.

More to the point, he had to find out why Kim McKinley had a clause in her contract that excluded her from working on the biggest advertising campaign of the year. *Christmas.*

He couldn't see how an employee headed for upper management could be exempt from dealing with Christmas campaigns, when it was obvious she was a player, otherwise.

He'd done his homework and had made it a priority to find out about Kim, who spearheaded four of the company's largest accounts. Her clients seemed to love her. They threw money at her, and this was a good thing.

He could use someone like this by his side, and was confident that he could make her see reason about the Christmas campaigns. Intelligent people had to be flexible. It would be a shame to issue an ultimatum, if it came to that, for Kim to lose what she had worked so hard for because of his new rules on management and contracts.

Chaz picked up a pencil and tucked it behind his ear, knowing by the way it stuck there easily that he needed a haircut, and that haircuts were a luxury when business came first.

He was sure that his upcoming appointment with Kim McKinley would turn out well. Handling people was what he usually did best when he took over a new company in his family's name. Juggling this agency's problems and getting more revenue moving in the right direction was the reason he had bought this particular firm for himself. That, and the greedy little need to show his big brother what he could do on his own.

The agency's bottom line wasn't bad; it just needed some TLC. Which was why he had gone undercover as the new VP. He figured it would be easier for other employees to deal with a fellow employee, rather than an owner. Even an employee in management. Pretending to be one of them for a while would give him a leg up on the internal workings of the business.

He would be good to Kim McKinley and all of the others who wanted to work and liked it here, if they played ball.

Did they have to love him? *No.*

But he'd hopefully earn their respect.

Chaz turned when the door opened, and Alice breezed in without knocking. She handed over a manila file folder held together with a thick rubber band. Thanking her, he waited until she left before sitting down. Centering the file on his desk, he read the name on it.

Kimberly McKinley.

He removed the rubber band, opened the folder and read the top page. She was twenty-four years old, had graduated from NYU with honors.

He already knew most of that.

He skimmed through the accolades. She was described as a hard worker. An honest, inventive, intelligent, creative self-starter with a good client base. An excellent earner recommended for advancement to a position in upper management.

A handwritten scribble in the margins added, *Lots of bang for the buck.*

There was one more thing he wished he could check in the file, for no other reason than a passing interest. Her marital status. Single people were known for their work ethics and the extra hours they could put in. McKinley's quick rise in the company was probably due not only to her ability to reel in business and keep it, but also to her availability.

What could be better than that?

He stole a glance at the empty seat across from him then looked again at the overstuffed folder. He tapped his fingers on the desk. "How badly do you want a promotion, Kim?" he might ask her. The truth was that if she were to get that promotion, she'd be one of the youngest female vice presidents in the history of advertising.

And that was fine with him. Young minds were good minds, and McKinley truly sounded like the embodiment of the name her coworkers had given her. *Wonder Woman*.

Although he was already familiar with her tally of clients, he checked over the list.

Those four clients that he'd classify as the Big Four, refused to work with anyone else, and it was a sure bet McKinley knew this, too, and would possibly use it as leverage if push came to shove about her taking on holiday-themed campaigns that didn't suit her. Would those clients turn away if he accidentally pushed McKinley too hard, and she walked? Rumor had it that three of them had been hoping she'd add Christmas to her list and stop farming those holiday accounts out.

He looked up to find Alice again in the doorway, as if the woman had psychically picked up on his need to ask questions.

"What will Kim have to say about believing she has been passed over in favor of me in this office?" was his first one.

Alice, through highly glossed ruby lips, said, "Kim had been promised the job by the last guy behind that desk. She'll be disappointed."

"How disappointed?"

"Very. She's an asset to this company. It would be a shame to lose her."

Chaz nodded thoughtfully. "You think she might leave?"

Alice shrugged. "It's a possibility. I can name a few other agencies in the city that would like to have her onboard."

Chaz glanced at the file, supposing he was going to have

to wear kid gloves when he met McKinley. If everyone else in town wanted her, how would pressure tactics work in getting her to stay put and take on more work?

He nodded to Alice, the only staff member who knew what his real agenda was for playing at being the new VP, and that he now owned everything from the twelfth to the fourteenth floor.

"Why doesn't she do Christmas campaigns?" he asked.

"I have no idea. It must be something personal," Alice replied. "She'll attend meetings when necessary, but doesn't handle the actual work."

"Why do you think it might be personal?" Chaz pressed.

"Take a look at her cubicle."

"Is something wrong with it?"

"There's nothing Christmasy about it. It's fifteen days until the big holiday, and she doesn't possess so much as a red and green pen," Alice said.

An image of the blonde in the hallway crowded his mind as if tattooed there. He wondered if Kim McKinley would be anything like that. He tended to picture McKinley as a stern, no-nonsense kind of a gal. Glasses, maybe, and a tweed suit to make her seem older than her actual age and give her some street cred.

"Thanks, Alice."

"My pleasure," Alice said, closing the door as she exited.

Chaz leaned back in his chair and scanned the office, thinking he'd like to be anywhere but there, undercover. Pretending wasn't his forte. To his credit, he had been a pretty decent young advertising exec himself a few years back, before entering the family business of buying up companies. In the time since then, he'd made more than one flustered employee cry.

He was responsible for the decisions regarding the upper echelon of this agency. But once he revealed he was the new owner, the future occupant of the VP's office would require more than a rave review on paper and a few happy clients. He found it inconceivable that anyone considered for such a promotion would avoid working on campaigns that brought in big revenue for the company. What was Kim McKinley thinking?

Chaz swiveled toward the window, where he had a bird's-eye view of the street below. Though it was already dark outside, he got to his feet and peered out, counting four Santas on street corners collecting for charity in a city that was draped in holiday trappings.

When the knock came on his door, Chaz looked around. He wasn't expecting anyone for another hour, and Alice never bothered to announce her own entrance. The thought that someone could bypass Alice seemed ludicrous.

The knock came again. After one more sharp rap, the doorknob moved. It seemed that his visitor wasn't going to wait for permission to come in.

The door swung open. A woman, her outline exaggerated by the lights behind her, straddled the threshold in a slightly imperious stance.

"You wanted to see me?" the woman said.

Chaz figured this could only be the notorious McKinley, since she was the only person left on his list to see that day.

After realizing she wasn't actually going to take a single step into the room, he blew out a long, low breath without realizing he'd been holding it, and squelched the urge to laugh out loud.

Had he wished too hard for this, maybe, and someone had been listening?

The woman in his doorway was none other than the delicious blonde.

Yep, *that* one.

"The Kim McKinley?" the man by the window said.

Kim was so angry, she could barely control herself. Her hand on the doorknob shook with irritation.

"You wanted to see me?" she repeated.

"Yes. Please come in," he said from behind the desk that should have been hers. "Have a seat."

She shook her head. "I doubt if I'll be here long enough to get comfortable."

This was an unfortunate double entendre. Chaz Monroe was either going to praise her or hand her a pink slip for being his closest competition.

With a familiar dread knotting her stomach, she added, "I have a pressing appointment that might last for some time."

"I won't keep you long. Please, Miss McKinley, come in."

She stood her ground. "I have a tight schedule to maintain today, Mr. Monroe, and I came here to ask if we can have our sit-down appointment at a later time?"

She had been expecting this talk from the new guy, but truly hadn't expected *this*. His looks. The shock of seeing the usurper in the flesh held her in place, and kept her at a slight disadvantage. At the moment, she couldn't have moved from the doorway if she'd tried.

For once, rumors hadn't lied. Chaz Monroe was a hunk. Not only was he younger than she had imagined, he was also incredibly handsome…though he was, she reminded herself, in *her* office.

This newcomer had been handed the job she had been promised, and he'd summoned her as if she were a minion. He stood behind the mahogany desk like a king, impeccably dressed, perfectly gorgeous and not at all as rigid as she had anticipated he would be.

In fact, he looked downright at home. Already.

She stared openly at him.

Shaggy dark hair, deep brown, almost black, surrounded an angular face. Light eyes—blue maybe, she couldn't be sure—complemented his long-sleeved, light blue shirt. He flashed a sensual smile full of enviable white teeth, but the smile had to be phony. They both knew he was going to gloss over the fact that he'd gotten this job, in her place, if he'd done any research at all. He no doubt would also ask about the Christmas clause in her contract, first thing, without knowing anything about her. He'd try to put her in her place, and on the defensive. She felt this in her bones.

A shiver of annoyance passed through her.

She was willing to bet that this guy was good at lording over people. He had that kind of air. Monroe was a devil in a dashing disguise, and if she didn't behave, if she said what was really on her mind, she'd be jobless in less than ten minutes.

"Did you want something in particular?" she asked.

"I wanted to get acquainted. I've heard a lot about you, and I have a few questions about your file," Monroe said, his eyes moving over her intently as he spoke. He was studying her, too. Maybe he searched for a chink in her armor.

She'd be damned if she'd let him find it.

A trickle of perspiration dripped between Kim's shoulder blades, caused by the dichotomy of weighing Monroe's looks against what he was going to do to her when she refused to play nice with him. Maybe it wasn't his fault that she'd been passed over for the promotion, but did he have to look so damn content?

And if he were to push her about her contract?

Monroe had only been in this building for two days, while her guilt about Christmas was years-old and remained depressingly fresh. Her mother had died only six months ago; it hadn't been long enough for Kim to get over the years of darkness about the Christmas holidays that had prevailed in the McKinley household.

Kim shut her eyes briefly to regroup and felt awkward seconds ticking by.

"Please come in. If you're in a hurry, let's talk briefly about the Christmas stuff," he said, verifying her worst fears.

"If it's the Christmas files you want, you'll need to see Brenda Chang," she said coolly. "Brenda's the one down the hall with the decorated cubicle. Red paper, garlands, tinsel, and holiday carols on CD. You can't miss it. Brenda oversees some of the December holiday ads."

She watched Monroe circle to the front of the desk, where he sat on the edge and indicated the vacant chair beside him with a wave of his hand. *Just a friendly little chat...*

Refusing to oblige his regal fantasies, Kim stubbornly remained in the doorway, anxiously screwing the heel of one shoe into the costly beige Berber carpet.

He maintained eye contact in a way that made her slightly dizzy from the intensity of his stare. "And you don't have any Christmas accounts, why, exactly? If you're one of the best we've got, shouldn't you be overseeing our biggest source of revenue?"

"Thanks for the compliment, but I don't do this particular holiday. I'm sure it's all there in my file. I can help Alice locate my contract before I go, if you'd like."

Monroe's calm, professional expression didn't falter. "Perhaps you can explain why you don't *do* Christmas? I'd honestly like to know."

"It's personal. Plus, I'm very busy doing other work here." Kim held up a hand. "Look, I'd love to have this get-acquainted chat." The words squeezed through tight lips. "But I'll have to beg off right now. I'm sorry. I really am expected somewhere."

"It's almost five. Do you have a work-related appointment?" Monroe asked.

Kim started to ask what business it was of his, then thought better of voicing such a thing because like it or not, he was her boss, and it was his business. She had agreed to meet some friends for a quick drink in the bar downstairs, and it was important that she got home right after that, before the beautiful holiday lights made her think again and more seriously about dishonoring her mother's memory.

Lately, she'd been having second thoughts about what she'd experienced growing up, and what she'd been taught, both about the insensitivity of men and the pain of the holidays.

Her mother hadn't approved of anything to do with Christmas. For the McKinleys, Christmas meant sorrow and the extremes of loss. It meant sad memories of a husband and father who had deserted his wife and five-year-old daughter on Christmas Eve to be with another family.

Kim looked at Monroe levelly. No way she was going to tell him any of that, and she shouldn't have to dredge up the details of something that had already been hammered out a year ago when she negotiated her contract with somebody else on this floor.

"Sure, meeting later would be fine," Monroe said. "Maybe around eight?"

"I'm usually in by seven, so yes, I can return first thing in the morning if that's what you'd like," Kim said.

"Actually, I meant tonight. 8:00 p.m.," he clarified, enunciating clearly. "If it wouldn't be too terribly inconvenient, that is, and you're still around. We can keep it casual and meet in the bar downstairs. That's not too much out of the way, right?"

"The bar?" Kim heard the slip in her tone.

"In the bar, yes," he said, without losing the charming, almost boyish smile.

Damn him. It was a really nice smile.

"I'm told it's a regular meeting place after hours for employees," he continued. "Maybe we can snag a quiet table?"

So they could do what? Have a friendly drink before the ax fell? Before the arguments began?

Don't think so.

"Will you be finished with your appointment by then?" Monroe pressed.

Realizing that she couldn't lie, and since others from the agency were going to be in that same bar, and still might be hanging around at eight, she said, "Yes," adding in another job-related double entendre, "I'll be finished."

With those last three words dangling between them, Chaz Monroe got to his feet and walked right up to her.

She had to wince to keep from backing up.

He came very close. Obviously, he had no intention of preserving her tiny circle of personal space.

Then he invaded it.

And hell…

Up close, he was even better.

"Your appointment isn't a date?" he asked in a husky tone that wasn't at all businesslike.

Kim felt breathless so close to this incredibly gorgeous guy who was her new boss, and chastised herself for being affected by him in such a physical way. Monroe was a time bomb comprised of every woman's sexual addictions, from his shaggy hair to his loafered feet. In order to become de-sensitized to this kind of personal frontal attack, she'd have had to experience quite a few near misses in the past with men of Monroe's caliber.

No such thing was in her dating history.

Her feet inched forward to close the distance to him before she could stop them. Her breasts strained at her sweater with a reaction so unacceptable, she wanted to scream. But she heard herself say, "Not tonight. No date."

The words *wrong* and *harassment* sailed through her mind. He was close enough to touch. Why?

He was also near enough to punch, but she didn't take a swing.

Chaz Monroe was a head taller than she was and smelled like *man,* in a really good way. He radiated sex appeal and an easy, unattended elegance. He didn't wear a coat or a tie, yet what he did wear was confidence, in an unintimidating manner. His casualness was reflected in the fact that his shirt was open at the neck, revealing a triangle of bare, lightly tanned skin. That taut, masculine flesh captured her attention for what seemed like several long minutes before she glanced up....

To meet his blue eyes.

That's when she heard music.

She shook her head, not quite believing it, but the music didn't go away. It was Christmas music, she finally realized, coming from the lobby and signaling the nearness of closing time for most of the staff. She had to get out of there and was caught between a rock and...a hard body.

"Good. I'll see you at eight," Monroe said, breaking the standoff.

The sensation of his warm breath on her face gave Kim a ridiculously flushed and tingly few seconds. The look in his eyes doubled that. What kind of boss was he? The kind that wouldn't mind breaking a few laws in order to get his way? The kind with a casting couch?

Had her mother been right about overly attractive men being saps, after all?

She broke eye contact. Her lashes fluttered.

"Eight o'clock. In the bar," he said in a tone that gave her an electrical jolt and made her clothing feel completely inadequate as a barrier against the sleek, seductive hoodoo he had going on.

Excuses for her reaction beat at her from the inside. The air around her visibly trembled with the need to shout "Go to hell!" Yet she stood there, helpless to get out of this, speechless for once, before backing up and turning abruptly.

She left Chaz Monroe, knowing that he stared after her, feeling his heated gaze. That scrutiny was so hot, she had an absurd longing to run back to him and get it over with. Just press her mouth to his in a brief goodbye kiss, then laugh maniacally as she headed back to her cubicle to clear out her things.

The strangest bit of intuition told her that he wanted that same thing. In those insane moments of confrontation and unacceptable closeness, her senses screamed that Chaz Monroe had wanted to kiss her.

She knew something else, as well. Because of the fire in her nerve endings and the way her heart thundered, meeting Chaz Monroe at the bar tonight was a very...bad...idea.

Two

Chaz faced the distinct possibility of being in serious trouble before Kim McKinley had left him standing in the open doorway. He had very nearly just breached every rule of decorum in the book. Well, he had thought about it, anyway.

She hadn't helped any.

Resisting the urge to loosen his collar, which was already loosened, he cleared his throat and looked to Alice, who was watching him with a raised eyebrow. Only practice allowed him to keep his expression neutral when he felt an annoying shudder in the abs he had worked so hard on in the gym before his takeover of this company shot down his regular routine.

Nodding to Alice, he stepped back into his office.

"Damn."

He had gotten up close and personal with an employee. His idea to dish some of that haughty attitude of McKinley's right back at her had backfired, big-time.

Not only were her body and her sexy scent tantalizing as hell, Kim's face and voice were undeniably appetizing. She had an accent, a slight Southern drawl that resulted in a slow drawing out of syllables. Her voice was deep, sultry and a lot like whispered vibrations passing through overheated air.

As for her face…

It was the face of an angel. The pale, silky-smooth, slightly babyish oval wasn't in any way indicative of her crisp attitude.

He could feel the residual intensity of her expressive hazel eyes, and didn't even want to think about her lips.

Pink lips, moist, slick and slightly parted, as if just waiting to be kissed.

Chaz touched his forehead absently. Hell, if he didn't have a bone to pick with her over the Christmas stuff, and if he actually relied on first impressions of a physical nature, he'd have been tempted to throw in the towel and give her the office right then and there—anything to get closer to her.

Anything to taste those lips.

Man. His mind had taken an inconvenient slip, a sudden, unexpected detour, and he wanted to laugh at the situation and at himself. However, there was more to be considered here. If he was going to be around Kim McKinley on a regular basis, he'd have to be able to keep his mind on business; a real feat, given the outline of the world-class breasts he'd seen through the thin layer of cloud-blue cashmere.

Damn it, why hadn't anyone told him about *that*?

Returning to the desk, pulling the pencil from behind his ear, Chaz scratched *Personnel files should contain all pertinent information in the future* on a yellow notepad.

Tapping the pencil on McKinley's file, he vowed not to debate with himself about what a pouty mouth like hers might do, other than kissing, while realizing that X-rated thoughts had no place in contract negotiations or the boardroom.

He shook his head. In spite of the untimely, if temporary, dilemma, Chaz didn't lose the smile when he looked again to the doorway where Kim had just stood, cute as a bug from the neck up and devilishly delicious from the neck down, while she made a decent attempt at blowing him off.

Can we talk later?

I have a schedule to keep to.

Kim McKinley, it seemed, wasn't going to take losing this office well. She was angry and trying to deal. It was possible that as long as she remained on his payroll, thinking he had the job she coveted, she might do everything in her power to either avoid him or bust his chops.

True, he had pushed her a little, and hadn't explained what he was doing here, undercover—which would have defeated the purpose of being undercover.

Could she really be so good at her job? She might be decent at what she did for this agency and damn nice to look at, but no one was so indispensable that they could afford to anger the new man in charge within the first sixty seconds of meeting him.

Yet that's just what she had done. Sort of.

Reopening her file, Chaz pondered the question of whether she had actually just offered up a challenge. Had McKinley meant to wave a flag in front of the bull, a flag bearing the legend *Leave me alone, or lose me?*

The back of Chaz's neck prickled the way it usually did when the anticipation of a good challenge set in. This particular tickle was similar to the feelings he'd had when he had handed over ten million dollars for a company he had every intention of making more successful than it was before he stepped in. The tickle was also similar to the one brought about by thoughts of the self-imposed challenge of tackling his brother's track record of successful takeovers, and proving his own business acumen.

Testy employees had no place in either of those particular goals, except for doing the jobs assigned to them. He really could not afford to be distracted right now.

Chaz stared at the door, where Kim McKinley had drawn an invisible battle line on several levels. His mind buzzed with possibilities. Maybe she used her looks to get what she wanted, and that was part of her success. It could be that she believed herself to be so valuable that he wouldn't mess with her if she resisted his logical suggestions.

Or if she resisted his advances.

What? Damn. He hadn't just thought that. *Advances* were totally out of the question.

Sitting down in his chair, Chaz placed both hands on the desk, disgusted that he'd been waylaid by this surprise. Kim McKinley just wasn't what he had expected, that's all. And the firm could always find someone to replace her if her attitude got out of hand.

Was that a fair assessment of the situation?

As he tapped his pencil on her file, he mulled over the fact that she had avoided their first sit-down appointment. Did she consider that a point for her side? Would she believe she had racked up another point for failing to give him any of the information he had been seeking, or meeting his demands on that Christmas clause head-on?

Was she the type to keep score?

Chaz rubbed the back of his neck where the darn prickle of interest just wouldn't ease up. Buttoning the collar of his shirt, he firmed up his resolve to get to the bottom of the McKinley mystery. Wonder Woman would be wrong if she thought him a fool. He was a master at compartmentalizing when he had to. He hadn't gotten to where he was in business by tossing employees on the carpet according to whim, or dumping their sorry backsides in the street without real cause. He was bigger than that, and he always played fair.

He would meet Kim McKinley tonight and set things straight. He'd give her the benefit of the doubt about adhering to his company plan, and get her onboard, whatever it took to do so.

"Your contract. No question marks. Not up for negotiation."

He practiced those words aloud, repeated them less forcefully and set his mental agenda.

The bar, in three hours.

They'd have a friendly chat and get to the specifics of the deal. McKinley might turn out to be a good ally.

As for the bedroom dreams...

He let out a bark of self-deprecating laughter over the time he was spending on this one issue, a sure sign that truly, and admittedly, he hadn't been prepared for the likes of this woman.

He really would have to be more cautious in the future, because, man-oh-man, what he needed right that minute, in Kim McKinley's saucy Southern wake, and in preparation for meeting her again was...

...a very long, very cold shower.

Kim tumbled into her chair and laid her head down on her desk. She turned just far enough to eye the golden plaque perched next to her pencil sharpener that had been a gift from her friend Brenda.

Kim McKinley, VP of Advertising.

"Some joke." She backhanded the plaque, sending it sailing. Who had she been kidding, anyway? Vice president? A twenty-four-year-old *woman?*

There would be no big office with floor-to-ceiling windows in her immediate future. No maple shelving for potted plants, and no opportunity to implement her plans and ideas for the company. So didn't she feel exactly like that jettisoned plaque—shot into space, only to land with a dismal thud right back in her own six-by-six cubicle?

Could the moisture welling up in her eyes be *tears?* As in about to *cry* tears?

Unacceptable.

Twenty-four-year-old professionals didn't blubber away when they were royally disappointed, or when they were overlooked and underappreciated at the office.

No tears. No way. No how.

She was mad, that's all, with no way to express how sad she was going to be if she had to leave this building and everything she had built here in the past five years.

"Why does everyone want to push me about the damn contract?" she grumbled, figuring that Brenda, in the next cubicle, would be listening. "Haven't I worked extremely hard on every other blasted campaign all year long? I've all but slept in this cubicle. I keep clothes in my desk drawers. Would it be fair to dock me over one single previously negotiated item?"

Inhaling damp desk blotter and the odor of evergreen that now pervaded the building, Kim reviewed the proverbial question on the table.

Was there another person on earth who could say that Christmas had been their downfall?

Plunking her head again on the desk, she muttered a weak "ouch." Rustling up some anger didn't seem to be working at the moment. It was obvious that she needed more work on self-defense.

"You okay?" a voice queried from somewhere behind her. "I heard a squeak."

Kim blinked.

"Kim? Are you, or are you not okay?"

"Nope. Not okay." She didn't bother to sit up.

"Are you in need of medical attention?"

Moving her mouth with difficulty because it was stuck to some paper, Kim said, "Intravenous Success Serum would be helpful. Got any?"

"No, but I've got something even better."

"Valium? Hemlock? A place with cheap rent?"

"An invitation to have drinks with the new boss tonight in the bar just arrived by email."

Kim muffled a scream. What had Brenda just said? They were both to have drinks with *Monroe?* The bastard had invited a crowd to witness her third degree and possible dismissal?

"Now's not a good time, Bren," she said. Having a co-worker for her best friend sometimes had its drawbacks.

Like their close proximity when she wanted to pout by herself.

"I think now would be a good time, actually," Brenda countered. "We can find out what the new guy is like, en masse."

"I'll tell you what he's like in one word. *Brutus!*"

Brenda stuck her head over the partition separating their cubicles. "I'm guessing your meeting didn't go well?"

Kim pried her cheek from the desk, narrowed her eyes and turned to face Brenda.

"So not afraid of that look," Brenda said.

"That's the problem. Neither was he."

"Yes, well, didn't you just know that the damn Christmas clause was going to jump up and bite you again someday? I mean how could they understand when they don't know…."

Kim held up a hand that suggested if Brenda said one more word along those lines, she might regret it.

"I've probably just lost my dream job, Bren. For all intents and purposes, this agency considers me an ancestor of old mister Scrooge. And by the way, aren't best friends supposed to offer sympathy in times of crisis, without lengthy lectures tacked on?"

Not much taller than the five foot partition in her bare feet, Brenda, who went shoeless in her space, was barely visible. All that showed was a perfectly straight center part halving a swath of shiny black hair, and a pair of kohl-lined, almond-shaped eyes. The eyes were shining merrily. There might have been a piece of tinsel entwined in a few ebony strands near Brenda's forehead.

What Brenda lacked in stature, however, she made up for in persistence. "I might suggest that nobody will believe that anyone actually hates Christmas, Kim. Not for real."

Brenda didn't stop there. "That's what the new guy will be thinking. So maybe you can come up with an alternate reason for holding back on the holiday stuff that he will buy into. Like…religious reasons."

"Seriously?" Sarcasm returned to Kim's tone as she offered Brenda what she thought was a decent rendition of a go-away-and-leave-me-alone-or-else look.

Brenda performed a glossy hair flip. "Still not afraid," she said. "Or discouraged."

Kim got to her feet and smoothed her skirt over her hips. "I think it's already too late for help of any kind."

"Tell me about it," Brenda said. "But first you have to dish about whether Monroe really does have a nice ass."

Kim kneaded the space between her eyes with shaky fingers, trying to pinpoint the ache building there.

"You didn't think he was hot?" Brenda continued. "That's the word going around. H-o-t, as in *fan yourself.*"

"Yeah? Did you hear anything about the man being an arrogant idiot?" Kim asked.

"No. My sources might have left that part out."

"I don't actually care about the nice ass part, Bren. I prefer not to notice an area that I won't be kissing."

"Don't be absurd, Kim. No one expects you to kiss anyone's backside. It isn't professional. What happened?"

"I'll have to start over somewhere else, that's what. Monroe won't let me off the hook. He expects me to explain everything. He'll expect me to cave." She waved both hands in the air. "I can't tell him about my background. I can barely talk about it to myself."

"You told me."

"That's different. Best friends are best friends. How I grew up isn't any of his business."

"What about the fact that you've been wanting to forget about this issue with your family for some time now, anyway?" Brenda asked. "Maybe it's the right time to take that next step."

Kim couldn't find the words to address Brenda's remark. She wondered if anyone really knew how bad guilt trips felt and how deep some family issues went, if they hadn't experienced it.

She had a hole inside her that hadn't completely closed over and was filled with heartaches that had had plenty of time to fester at a cellular level. Her mother had constantly reminded her of how they'd been wronged by a man, and about the dishonest things all men do for utterly selfish reasons.

Her mom wouldn't listen to advice about getting help in order to emerge from under the dark clouds surrounding her traumatic marital disappointment. Instead, she had spread those dark clouds over Kim.

The guilt about wanting to be rid of the deep-seated feelings of abandonment was sharp-edged, and nearly as painful now as the old heartaches. The warnings her mother had given her had calloused several times over.

Kim had thought long and hard about this since her mother's death. What she had needed was a little more leeway to get used to the fact that with her mother gone, she could embrace change without angering or hurting anyone else. Still, did that entail capitulating on the Christmas issue so soon? Was she ready for that, when this particular holiday had played such a negative role in her life?

Brenda hurried on. "If you don't want to tell Monroe the truth, you have about an hour to formulate a reason he'll accept in lieu of the truth. Fabricating illusions is what we do on a daily basis, right? We make people want to buy things."

After letting a beat of time go by for that to sink in, Brenda spoke again. "Call me selfish, Kim, but I'd like to keep you here and happy, and so would a whole host of other people. I doubt if the new guy would actually fire you, anyway. He'd have no real reason to. You can work this out. Also, you could try the truth. Talking about it might be cathartic."

Kim shook her head. Brenda hadn't witnessed Monroe's show of personalized aggression in his office doorway. Monroe had used the physical card to get her to back down, intending to intimidate her with his stockpile of charisma. And it had worked. There was no way she'd talk to a complete stranger about complicated and painful personal details and have him laugh them off as childish. Or worse, have him wave them away as being inconsequential.

"If the truth is still too painful, maybe you can spin the issue another way." Brenda snorted delicately. "You could tell Monroe that you have a Santa fetish."

Kim gave her a look.

"You can tell him a therapist explained that your Santa fetish means that you're looking for a father figure to replace yours, and you've attached yourself to a fantasy ideal. So much so, that it's embarrassing to discuss or work with."

Kim knew a ploy to lighten the mood when she heard one.

"Bren, you are usually so much better than that."

"The source of the idea wouldn't matter, Kim. Mention the word *therapist,* and Monroe would be afraid of a lawsuit if he were to ever fire you for mental health reasons."

Brenda had the audacity to giggle, despite the seriousness of the subject matter, because she was on a ludicrous roll. "You secretly long for the person who is supposed to possess magical powers that he uses for good, and this longing makes you crazy at this time of year."

"Bren, listen to yourself. You're suggesting that I tell my boss I have a secret hard-on for the guy whose belly shakes like a bowlful of jelly, and reindeer with dorky names."

"Humor aside, isn't that what you're actually waiting for? Haven't you been searching for a man with the ability to override your background issues by making dull things seem shiny and bright? You'd like to find an honest man who could disprove your mother's ideas about relation-ships."

Kim rubbed her forehead harder. Brenda was right. She did want a man with those quasi-magical qualities. Some-one caring, understanding, strong and above all, loyal. She got breathless just thinking about it, and about separating herself from the dark spell her mother had woven.

The problem was, she seemed to only date men who had none of those things to offer. Every one of her companions so far had come up short of ideal. Maybe she'd made her poor choices to subconsciously confirm her mother's phi-losophy of relationship instability and injustice. She could see this. It made sense. Honestly though, she did not want to end up alone, and like her mother.

She sagged against the wall. "There's a fatal flaw in your reasoning, Bren. If I had a desire for Santa Claus and his magic, why would I be opposed to working on Christmas? I'd love Christmas. But you are partly right."

Kim pressed the hair back from her face and contin-ued. "Secretly, I've always wanted to dump the darkness and embrace the holiday celebrations. I've wanted that for as long as I can remember. It's been my secret heartache."

More to the point, she couldn't stand anger and blame and insidious hatred, and had missed a good portion of her childhood fantasies because of her mother's take on those things. The idea of a real Santa Claus had been her one on-going illicit passion from early on. A dream. A ray of light in the dark world she'd grown up in.

She had never disclosed this secret longing to anyone. What good would it do? What child didn't want to lighten the load and share celebrations with her friends, in spite of the fact that some things were forbidden?

Guilt was a desperate emotion. Its tentacles ran deep and clung hard. Nevertheless, contrary to her mother's feel-ings, she had never wanted to commit her father to the fires of Hades for making her mother's life miserable. For Kim, there had only been sadness, emptiness. Little girls needed their fathers.

She had grown up desiring the ability to absorb pain, table it and move on. She wished to fill the emptiness inside her with something better than loss. Creativity had done that for her. This job had done it. She made other peoples' fantasies come true on a regular basis. Just not hers.

Not that one specific fantasy, anyway.

"I want to participate in the holiday festivities and be really truly happy," she confessed. "I just don't know how to go about it, or where to start. I'm afraid my mother might roll over in her grave if I did."

As for the theory of cheating men, wrong men…that image seemed to fit the new boss, Chaz Monroe. Although she'd had tingly feelings in his presence, and her heart rate had skyrocketed, all that proved was that her pattern of choosing inappropriate males hadn't ended. She was attracted to flighty men caught up in their own needs. If she went down that particular path, led by Chaz Monroe, she'd regret it.

"I'm considering shock treatment," she said. "I don't rule it out."

"To my way of thinking, a little therapy now might save you a load of trouble in the long run," Brenda agreed. "Please don't be mad that I'm telling you this. Friends have obligations."

Way too much time had been spent on this. Kim could hear her watch ticking.

Brenda sighed. "There is always plan B. If you don't want to discuss this tonight, you could distract him. Throw Monroe a curveball. A sexy new outfit and some killer shoes worn as a talisman against unwanted negativity might work. At least it might give you another day or two to decide what to do."

"I didn't know shoes could repel negativity."

"They can if they're the red stilettos in the window of the shop next door."

"Those shoes cost more than my rent."

"Won't they be worth it if they work?" Brenda pointed out.

"If they don't, will you pay my bills?"

"I have a little cash saved up," Brenda admitted.

Kim tried not to choke on the Tree In A Can spray coming from Brenda's cubicle. She didn't want to bring Brenda down with her. The fact was that this new boss was likely going to create some havoc, and she'd have to wiggle her way out of the situation in order to prolong her employment. Chaz Monroe hadn't seemed like the kind of guy who was used to compromises.

Was Monroe a jerk? Maybe. He'd wanted to make her uncomfortable with all that forbidden closeness, and his method had scored. Worse yet, he had seen her squirm. If he got close to her again, though, she'd cry foul, in public, where she'd have witnesses to his behavior.

Oh yes, Chaz Monroe, playboy, would be trouble, all right.

"He has big blue eyes," she said wistfully, then looked to Brenda, hoping she hadn't just announced that out loud.

"Then there's nothing to worry about," Brenda concluded. "Because real demons have red eyes. And tails."

A chill trickled down Kim's spine, messing with the heat left over from her meeting with Monroe. Misplaced heat waves aside, the real question was whether she wanted to keep this job, and the answer was yes. No one wanted to find out how long the unemployment lines would be in December. Plus, she truly liked most of the people she worked with.

So…could she afford to allow Christmas to be a deal breaker, or was she willing to fight for what she wanted?

"A sexy dress and some shoes, huh?" she said.

Brenda nodded. "It's a bit aggressive, but it's been done for ages. Think Mata Hari."

Kim tilted her head in thought.

"Uh-oh," Brenda said, disappearing from behind the partition and appearing in the entrance to Kim's cubicle. "I don't think I like what I see in your eyes."

"I don't know what you mean."

"You wouldn't do anything stupid, right, like trying to seduce Monroe out of his title?" Brenda advanced. "You wouldn't play the harassment card, if it came to that? Seduce him and then blow the whistle to get him out of the way? That would be a terrible plan, Kim. It would be desperate, and unlike you."

Kim nodded. "In any case, I'm thinking I might have to get plastered before that meeting in the bar."

"You don't drink. You never drink."

"Exactly."

"Fine," Brenda said doubtfully. "But if it goes all haywire, please leave me the red shoes in your will for when this is all over, and the comfy chair by the window in your apartment."

Kim grabbed her purse and headed for the door. Brenda was right. Revenge wasn't like her. Not even remotely. However, if Chaz Monroe continued to play the intimidation card, and if he proved himself to be another unreliable male adversary, she'd have to find the strength to enact Plan C. Char his ass.

"Cover for me, Bren," she called over her shoulder. "I'm going shopping."

"May the force of Mata Hari be with you," Brenda called out conspiratorially as Kim headed for the door.

Three

Chaz had pegged the bar scene perfectly. Young people were expensively turned out. Women in chic attire carried neon martinis and threw air kisses. At thirty-two and in a sports coat, he felt like their slightly out-of-it older brother, though women eyed him up and down with avid interest and unspoken invitations in their eyes.

Half of these people probably worked for him in some capacity or another and didn't yet recognize him by sight. By the end of the month, he would know each and every name on his payroll, and all ten of the building's janitors. Just now, however, he needed to remain incognito and observe the scene while he waited. For her.

He chose a table in a dark corner and sat on a stool with his back to the wall and his eyes on the door.

"Big Brother is watching you," he said beneath his breath.

He didn't really like chic bars where the young and the restless gathered to prance and preen. He preferred quiet corners in coffee shops where actual conversation could take place. The bar would likely be neutral territory for Kim, though. There'd be no battle lines here, away from official turf. Nor would there be any one-on-one private time that might get him into trouble.

He ordered a draft beer from an auburn-haired server in a tight black dress, who had a small tattoo on one sleek upper arm. He kept his attention on the doorway Kim would soon walk through, wanting to witness her entrance and observe her for a minute before she saw him.

He had spent the last hour trying not to imagine what she would be like in action, and he now wondered which of the guys surrounding him might have dated her and known her intimately. The thought made him uncomfortable, as did the image of some other guy tasting the heat of her hot pink mouth.

He did know one thing for sure. He had put way too much emphasis on their brief meeting, and had given McKinley far too much credit as a femme fatale. Not long now, and he'd find out how ridiculous his fantasies had been, because nobody liked a diva who ruled from within the confines of a short, tight skirt, and a lot of people in this building liked Kim.

His beer arrived, along with a phone number scribbled on a napkin. Chaz looked around. A pretty brunette at another table raised her glass and smiled at him.

He smiled back.

Pocketing the napkin, he took a swig from his long-necked bottle and refocused on the door.

Business first.

Several people entered in a group, but Kim wasn't among them. The noise decibel was rising quickly as the crowd swelled and empty glasses piled up. Chaz could barely hear himself think—which might have been a good thing in this instance, since thoughts turned to *her* again.

Would she work this crowd or ignore it?

Had someone else been waiting for her before this meeting? That *appointment?*

His stomach tightened when he thought about it. He was beginning to feel damp around the collar in spite of the cold shower.

With the bottle hoisted halfway to his mouth, Chaz suddenly paused, feeling Kim's presence before he actually saw her.

Then there she was, at last, the sight of her like a drop-kick to his underutilized libido.

Again.

For the third time that day, he absolutely could not take his eyes off her. Tonight, the reason was downright blatant. Kim McKinley was a carnal vision in an eye-popping red dress. Tight, short and silky, that dress pulsed with the word *sex*. Cut low enough at the neckline for a far too revealing peek at bare, glistening, ivory flesh, it caressed her body, hugging each curve.

Diva with a red dress on...

He stifled a chuckle as she moved through the crowd by the door like a tawny-haired hurricane. He wasn't the only person who stared.

She had let down her hair. Golden strands gleamed in the darkened room, floating an inch or two below her chin and giving the impression that she possessed a halo. But it was a fact that no angel would dare to dress like that.

Chaz's stomach twisted at the sight. But Kim wasn't alone. Another woman accompanied her, as dark as Kim was fair. Points went to him for inviting Brenda Chang, who hopefully might already have knocked some sense into Kim about her future job description.

Another good gulp of his draft seemed to settle him as Chaz waited to see if McKinley would come over, or if she would expect him to bend in her direction. Her beautiful features were set. She didn't smile.

When Kim finally sighted him with a gaze like a search-light, Chaz did a quick head-shake and slapped his bottle down on the table. He stood up.

As she approached, his gaze traveled down her length, stopping at her ankles. She looked taller tonight because she was perched on dangerously high heels, the kind he'd imagined her wearing the first time he'd seen her. Shiny crimson stilettos.

Chaz whistled to himself. He couldn't help it.

Had she read his mind that afternoon?

So you really do know how to make an entrance. Well, okay. You have my full attention.

He raised his bottle in acknowledgment of her presence, and ditched the urge to clap his hands at the show she was providing, sure the sexy clothes were meant for some lucky bastard's sensory pleasure in taking them off. It was possible she had lied about not having a date.

"Mr. Monroe," she said in greeting.

"Ms. McKinley." Chaz gave her a nod.

The electrical current whizzing through the air between them from the distance of two feet felt strong enough to have burned the bar to the ground. He didn't imagine that. Their chemistry was undeniable, at least on his end.

Fine hairs at the nape of his neck were stirring. Fire roared through his muscles, causing a twitch. These reactions were a further indication of their instantaneous attraction, and also a hint about being so close to a sin-coated challenge.

"I've brought someone you should meet," she said in that seductive drawl. "This is Brenda Chang."

Chaz held out a hand to Brenda, who took it, though her eyes avoided his.

"I'm happy to meet you in person, Brenda," he said.

"Thanks for the invitation to join you," Brenda returned.

"I heard that you two work closely together, and that you're a good team," he said.

"Yes, that's true," Brenda agreed.

She was an attractive young woman with porcelain skin, dark eyes and a slender body encased in a tasteful blue suit.

Gesturing to the table, Chaz said, "Care to sit down?"

Would Wonder Woman act on any suggestion he made? Quite surprisingly, she did. She slid sideways onto a stool and crossed her legs, placing the heel of one dagger-sharp stiletto just inches from his right calf and making Chaz ponder the idea of what those heels would feel like if they were in bed together. It was a thought he had vowed not to have tonight.

"So," he began, once they all were in place around the little table. He avoided staring at the spot where Kim's shapely knee disappeared beneath the colorful silk. "Thanks for coming."

"Shall we get right to it?" she asked.

This, too, was unexpected. Chaz rallied with another nod.

"I believe you wanted to speak about the Christmas campaigns?" she said.

Brenda passed her pal a silent glance of interest.

"Yes," Chaz replied. "I've read the contract from front to back. But first, would you like something to drink?"

"I could use some Chardonnay," Brenda announced in a breathy outburst, smiling at him.

"Martini," Kim said.

"Oh, boy," Brenda muttered after hearing her friend's drink order. She flashed Chaz another pretty smile.

Of course Kim wanted a martini, the drink of choice for the young, pretty people these days. Still, Chaz, for reasons he didn't quite understand, had expected her order to be bottled water with a lemon wedge. He was a little disappointed to have been wrong about that as he flagged down the server.

"What kind of martini would you like?" he asked.

Oddly enough, the simple query seemed to stump her. She glanced to Brenda.

"You always like the appletinis here," Brenda prompted.

"Yes. That's what I'll have," Kim said. Turning to Chaz, she added, "Now, where were we?"

Was he wrong in his impression that she didn't know what an appletini was, and that there was something going on between Kim and Brenda that caused Brenda to show concern? He was pretty sure that Brenda had just fed Kim a line about the drink order.

"I'm aware of your rather unusual contract," he said. "What I'd like to do is ask politely that you ink it out. I'm hoping you can see this as a special favor to the agency and to our clients."

"Do you mean the clients who would like to continue working with me?" she asked, stressing her point of being well liked by those accounts.

Chaz shrugged. Kim's scarlet dress and her chilly vibe were at odds with each other, a dichotomy that did nothing to lessen the warmth searing through him each time she moved.

"A vice president has to oversee all accounts," he said.

"Yes, you do," she tossed back, emphasis on *you*.

"Being new, I'd like your help," he said. "Maybe we can start small on the help, and see how it goes?"

"I'm all ears, Mr. Monroe, as to what you might require." She did not glance at her watch, but added, "For the next ten minutes."

"It's Chaz. Please call me Chaz."

He was peripherally aware of how Kim's chest rose and fell laboriously with each new breath she took. Was that a sign of anger or anxiety? Outwardly, she looked calm enough. Cool, calm and collected. Yet she was electrically charged. He felt that charge pass through him. His heart beat a little faster.

"We've been asked to attend a special party for a potential new client, and I have volunteered to help make this an event. It's a very last-minute request, so with Ms. Chang already inundated, I'd need your help," he said.

He looked to Brenda, who passed the look on to Kim.

"Sorry." Kim carefully folded her hands around the stem of her glass when it arrived. "If you mean helping with something right now, that's impossible. I have the next two weeks off, starting tomorrow at noon."

"I'd be willing to double your holiday bonus for the extra time and effort," he said, applying a bit of preplanned pressure to see if money floated her boat. "We can talk about the clause afterward if you like."

Brenda took a sip of her wine and continued to gaze at Kim over the rim of her glass. Brenda appeared to be nervous about being in the middle of this conversation, and had started inching her glass sideways on the table as if she and the glass might make a quick getaway the first chance she got.

Good for her, for noticing where she wasn't needed. And to hell with the crowd. Chaz now wanted Kim all to himself. He wanted nothing more. They could hash this out, once and for all. If she remained stubborn, maybe they could arm wrestle a deal.

"I'm really sorry I can't help," Kim said, lush strands of gold brushing her face when she shook her head. "I've already made plans for my time off."

Chaz was actually starting to enjoy this game. He had always been good at chess. He did wonder, though, how far she'd go...and how far he'd go to stop her.

"Any way you might break those plans?" he asked.

"I'm pretty sure I can't at this late date."

"If I say please?"

She sat motionless for a minute, and then began to turn her glass in circles on the table without taking a drink. Chaz didn't fail to notice that she hadn't so much as placed her lips on the glass since it had arrived.

"As a favor to a potential client, then," Chaz said. "Not to me personally."

Another beat of time passed while he awaited her response.

"Didn't you just say that you read my contract?" she finally said with a subtle tone of disappointment underscoring her reply.

Chaz found himself fascinated with thoughts about how this would play out. He had said *please,* right? Surely she had to realize that this one decision could make or break the upward mobility of her career, at least with this agency.

He downed some beer and waited to see if she would explain herself.

"I truly am sorry," she said seconds later. "I'd be happy to help out any other time, with any other holiday. Really, I would help now if my situation were different."

"Different?" Chaz couldn't wait to hear this. If she was seriously involved in a relationship with some guy, and had *that* kind of plans for the next week, he'd have heard it from the people feeding him office gossip that afternoon. According to Alice, his agency bloodhound, Kim was pretty much a free agent in the serious relationship department.

"I'm..." she began.

"It's against her religion," Brenda said for her, and immediately flushed pink for having spoken out of turn.

Kim squirmed. He saw it. In the process, her left arm brushed his. Chaz's body responded with a jerk. The aftereffects of the surprise ignited a new and relatively irritating blaze of heat in his chest that robbed him of his next decent breath.

"Oh," he said. "That's what prevents you from working on all this holiday stuff?"

She recrossed her legs and blinked slowly. "Well..."

She didn't finish her excuse. A lovely flush crept up her neck, presenting a very seductive picture, for sure. The best he'd seen in a long time. But right then he wanted badly to throw her over his knee and give her a good spanking. *Bad little princess,* he'd say. *Why the white lies and the avoidance? Let's get right to the truth. You could do this if you wanted to.*

Or maybe he should just kiss her pouty mouth for all it was worth and see if that got a rise out of her. Maybe if they got that kiss out of the way, Kim might confess the real reasoning behind her ridiculous holiday reluctance.

On the other hand, she might slap his face and call it a night, and he'd be back to square one. Taking it further, she might take that walk, and take her clients with her.

Well, okay, there was a fine line between pushing her away and getting what he wanted, but he did owe her a shot at the title she coveted.

His inner musings on how this might go ceased abruptly when she leaned forward over the edge of the table. His eyes dipped to the sight of the dewy top of her rounded breasts and the fact that she wore nothing beneath the red dress. Nothing visible, anyway.

Although the sight doubled his heart rate, a thought occurred about this sudden closeness potentially being a purposeful move on her part to distract him, an enactment of the power of her all-too-obvious feminine wiles. Of which she had plenty.

Hell, maybe he just got turned on by the promise of a good fight. In his family, close as they were, fighting had become a sport.

The truth, though, was that he had grown tired of women who assumed they were owed something because of their looks. That aside, he had a short span of time to get this agency working better, and a Wonder Woman could help him do that.

Working this out would be the decent thing to do. The best outcome for everyone.

"Anyway, as I was saying, it's a special event," he continued. "If you'll hear me out, I'll explain."

She had no immediate reply to that, and continued to absently fondle the fragile stem of her glass in a way that he found extremely appealing.

At the same time, he was nearing his limit on patience. He noticed Brenda looking at him intently, and that look served to clear his mind.

"I'll find someone to help you," Kim finally offered. "I can find someone who will do a good job and is an ace at spur-of-the-moment stuff."

"Who would that person be?"

"Will you excuse me a minute?" Brenda broke in. "I have to, well, you know." Her exit was abrupt.

Kim didn't seem to notice her friend's departure. She didn't lean back or try to make her own escape.

"All right," she said. "I'll hear you out since I don't seem to have much choice in the matter, and then suggest somebody to help you. What is this special project?"

Chaz tried really hard not to grin. Kim had just given in, and an inch was better than nothing.

"It's a party. A Christmas party, and as much of an extravaganza as we can pull together this late. Nothing huge, really, and more indicative of a big family celebration. We'll need decorated trees, live music and a couple elves."

"Elves?" she repeated with a touch of sarcasm in her tone.

Chaz nodded. "Can't have Christmas without elves. Then we'll need packages. Large boxes, small boxes, all with big red bows. And snow."

"Snow?" Kim offered up an expression of surprise that overrode her former skepticism about elves.

"Sure. We can bring some snow inside a building, can't we? Aren't there snow machines? We can bring in some of the real stuff on trays and carts for the buffet table, as well as ice sculptures."

She winced, probably unwilling to tell him what an idiot he was for suggesting real snow inside a building. It likely cost her plenty to hold that chastisement in.

"We're not party planners," she said calmly. "You do know that we're a respected advertising agency?"

Chaz couldn't address that. He didn't dare. This was a test. A silly one, true, but he had to make it sound as if he needed her help. He couldn't say that it was his family's party he'd invade with all those Christmasy things if Kim actually agreed. In the meantime, he'd try to find out what irked her about the holiday stuff. He'd use all the holiday terms to push her buttons.

"Candy canes," he continued. "Mounds of them. Also anything and everything else that could make an indoor fantasy come true for the company and its top tier of stockholders."

McKinley's lush lashes closed over her eyes. Her hand stopped caressing the glass. She seemed to have stopped breathing.

"This must be a big deal," she said at length.

"Indeed, it's very big. For you."

McKinley's expression changed lightning fast. She sat upright on her stool, taking most of her deliciously woodsy scent with her.

Chaz's grin dissolved. Had he accidentally put the wrong spin on that last remark, making it sound sexual? Hell, he hadn't even thought about it, and sure as heck hadn't meant it that way.

"It's a potentially huge contract," he rushed to say, thinking that if she would merely agree, this would be over. One little "yes" and she'd be on her way to the metaphorical Oval Office. She just had to be willing to circumvent that stubborn mind-set and get down to business.

She didn't have to set one red-hot foot in his apartment. She didn't have to breathe in his goddamned ear. Those were daydreams. Man stuff. Wishful thinking. Most men were wired with those kinds of thoughts. All she had to do was cave on one little point, encapsulated by a single paragraph on paper.

But again, and to her credit, Kim didn't run away.

"Who is offering the contract?" she asked politely.

"I'm not at liberty to say. Not until you agree to help out."

"I did mention that I'm on vacation next week?"

"I'll give you a longer vacation at another time."

"I can't help you," she declared. But contrary to sounding smug about this persistent refusal, Chaz heard in her voice something else. Sorrow? Wishfulness? A silent desire that she didn't have to be so stubborn and inflexible?

He looked at her thoughtfully. "Are you really of a religion that shuns this holiday?"

She shook her head. "Irish. Completely. Three generations back."

"Ah." Chaz's breath caught in his throat as one of her hands rested lightly on top of his hand on the table, flesh to naked flesh, and cool from her grip on the martini glass.

The urge to tug at his collar returned.

"I'd like to be honest with you." As her eyes met his, Chaz couldn't help but feel as if he were drowning. The look in her eyes made the crowd around them disappear.

"I'd appreciate it if you would," he said, slightly shaken by the intimacy of her touch and her sudden change of expression. Truly, it wasn't a normal occurrence for him to be affected by the antics of a woman. He wasn't sex starved. He didn't need to count on Kim for those fantasies when the pretty brunette at the next table continuously looked his way.

"It would be better for me if you didn't pressure me into this," she told him in a carefully modulated tone that deepened her accent.

"Explain, and maybe I won't. I am human, you know."

When she frowned, the delicate skin around her eyes creased.

"I have a problem," she said.

Her fingers moved on his as if trying to stress a point he didn't see. Chaz found himself listening especially diligently for whatever excuse she'd come up with next. He could hardly wait to hear what she had to say.

She moistened her lips with the tip of her tongue, a provocative, erotic action.

"It's embarrassing to speak of, so I don't," she began. "If you were to fire me because of sharing this very personal confidence, I don't know what I'd do."

She hadn't removed her hand from his. His gaze lingered on her mouth.

"I have a problem with Christmas." As she spoke, earrings buried somewhere in her fair blond hair tinkled with a sound like stardust falling.

"It's not the holiday itself that bothers me," she went on. "An objection to the commercialism of Christmas would be funny in our line of business, wouldn't it?"

Kim's wan smile lifted the edges of her lips. "That's not the source of my problems."

"I'd sincerely like to know what is," Chaz said.

In another surprising move, she slid closer to him, inching her stool sideways and leaning in so that she didn't have to shout. With her mouth all but touching his right ear, she said, "Santa is my problem."

When Chaz turned his head, their lips almost met. He felt the soft exhalation of her breath. "Santa?" he echoed, his abs shuddering annoyingly beneath his shirt. "As in Santa Claus? You have a problem with Santa Claus?"

"Yes." Her reply was devastatingly breathy.

Was she making fun of him?

"How can Santa Claus be a problem?" he asked.

"I want him," she whispered.

He waited for the meaning of this to hit. Then he began to laugh. She wanted Santa? This was so much better than her shunning the holiday for religious reasons, or thinking Christmas too commercial as an advertising executive, that it came off as completely unique. Kim McKinley deserved a crown for this excuse.

She had put him on, of course, and she'd had him going for a minute. Her acting skills were applause-worthy. This was another point for her, well played.

But she didn't look so well, all of a sudden. Her smile had faded. Her face paled. The hazel eyes gazing into his were glazed and moist, very much as if she had just disclosed a terrible secret and was awaiting a dreaded response. As if she'd been serious.

And he had laughed.

Sobering, rallying quickly, he said, "I'm sorry. Please forgive me. I must have misunderstood your meaning. In what way do you want Santa Claus, exactly?"

"I..."

"Yes?"

"Well, you see, I..."

Her eyes held a pleading, haunted cast. She didn't want to explain herself, couldn't find the words. As he watched her, she began to look less like a mistress of fire, and more like a young, lost waif.

Chaz was moved by the change. Without thinking, he reached up to cup her face with his hands in an automatic reaction of empathy, sensing real trouble in her past. She stared into his eyes, and he stared back, groping for what was going on here, and what she might mean.

When her lips parted, they trembled enough that he could see the quakes. She wasn't acting or kidding around. Kim had been deadly serious about needing to shun what was going on with this holiday.

Wanting to ease the pain reflected in her eyes, and needing to fix what he had set in motion, Chaz pressed his mouth to hers before even knowing what had happened. When realization hit, he kept very still with his mouth resting lightly on hers as he sized up what he had just done.

Her lips were soft, slick and completely, heartbreakingly tender. Way better than anything he could have imagined. Light-years beyond better. But the biggest surprise of all was that he hadn't gotten close to her out of lust or the lingering effects of the dress and the shoes. It had been an unconscious need to comfort her, protect her.

He had just glimpsed something sad curled up in McKinley's core beneath the glamour and efficiency. He had wanted a confession, and instead had stifled that confession with a kiss.

He didn't move, draw back or try to explain. Neither did she. His pressure on her lips remained slight but steady, in a connection he had desired from the first time he'd seen her. He supposed she might scream when he let her go, and he completely deserved the slap he'd receive, though in this circumstance, his intentions had been honorable.

Her lips, her breath, her taste, fascinated him and moved him further, stirring emotions tucked inside. Strands of her blond hair tickled his cheek in a way that suddenly seemed right and completely natural. And since it was too late, anyway, and the damage had already been done, he added more pressure.

As the illicit kiss deepened, Kim's lips parted beneath his. She let a sigh escape and didn't pull away. The slap Chaz expected never came. Their bodies remained motionless, inches apart, as their breath and mouths explored the parameters of this very public forbidden kiss.

Her breath was enticingly hot, deliciously scented and as seductive as anything imaginable. Reeling from the sensations and spurred on by those seductions, Chaz dared to draw his tongue slowly along the corners of her mouth.

As he breathed her in, tasted her lipstick, felt the moistness of her tongue meeting his, she joined him in this unexpected faux pas.

For a minute, for Chaz, they were no longer employer and employee, or adversaries; only a man and a woman acting on a primal attraction that they had tried unsuccessfully to ignore. Giving in, ruled by feeling, Chaz tossed away all thoughts about the possible consequences of such a public display, and went for broke.

Four

Kim gripped the table with both hands. She heard the sound of her glass tipping, rolling, and couldn't reach out to stop it from crashing to the floor. She was locked to her new boss in a battle of bodies and mouths and wills. In a bad way. A physical way.

And it was sublime.

It was…beyond words.

With her eyes closed, she could sense Chaz Monroe's body in relation to hers and knew it was too far away for the flames to be so hot and all-encompassing. After several seconds with her lips plastered to his, her hands left the table as if they had a mind of their own. She was only vaguely aware of curling her fingers into the front of his beautiful blue shirt.

He tasted like beer, desire and of plans gone south. They weren't supposed to be doing this, like this. They were enemies of a sort, which made their actions run contrary to everything she had planned. How could she actually like the kiss she was supposed to hold against him if the harassment case idea became necessary? And was that plan necessary now?

Then why didn't she run away?

She hardly thought of anything but Monroe's mouth, and the result had her floating in a sensory fog. The kiss seemed to go on forever. Some distant part of her mind warned that she had to get out of this situation. She had to get away right that instant. This kiss could prove her downfall as well as his.

Yet her breasts strained against the red silk, her nipples hard and aching. The dress seemed much too tight and restrictive. Between her legs, she quaked with a new awakening.

She wanted more than a kiss. Her body demanded more. Damn. She really hated this guy!

As his tongue teased and taunted and his lips became more demanding, Kim struggled to think. She had to keep it together. Plans A and B had failed miserably in the very fact that they were a success, but she could still turn this around. She could use this. *Would* use this…as soon as he stopped doing whatever the hell he was doing that felt so good.

His tongue swept over her teeth and across her lower lip, urging more participation. She tore at his shirt, tugging him closer with treacherous fingers, seeking a way inside his clothes.

His warm hands remained on her face, holding her while she drowned in his essence, his heat and the intensity of what they were doing. Chaz Monroe really was the epitome of everything masculine and powerful, right down to his kissing talent. He didn't ravage her or threaten to overpower. The kiss had started off tender and exploratory, without being tentative, then quickly escalated.

These feelings were a first, and they were outrageous. She wanted Monroe to throw her on the table and slide his heated palms over her thighs. She had never felt this out of control, had never been attracted to a man in such a fierce, feral manner.

But other than his warm hands on her cheeks, he made no further move to touch her. No illicit fondling, nothing that would have earned him a shove and a sharp reprimand if she had been thinking properly.

Kissing was supposed to be like this, yet for her, never was. No man had ever moved her in this way, making her want to surrender her hard-won hold on control.

And just when she had started to weaken further, he

tugged lightly on her lower lip and withdrew. The pressure on her lips eased. He removed his hands from her face slowly, as if reluctant to do so, leaving chills in their wake.

He remained close. His eyes bored into hers questioningly, offering a hint of a new kind of understanding that was so foreign to Kim, she misread it as sympathy. He spoke from inches away.

"What about Santa? Exactly?"

She expected to see a flicker of amusement in his eyes. Her stomach seized up as she waited for it, wondering if Monroe had merely been proving a point about being an experienced playboy able to get whatever he wanted from his latest acquisition.

Bastard!

Her heart tanked. Her mouth formed a steely line. She had almost fallen for that kiss, and for him. She hadn't been the one to put a stop to it.

"Kim?" Monroe's tone was a silky caress with a startlingly direct link to her trembling lower regions.

"I'm sorry," she replied breathlessly. "I just can't."

The words were forced, pitched low, angry. Kim got to her feet. Her knees felt absurdly weak and unsupportive.

"Kim," Monroe said again, standing with her, using her first name as if the kiss had earned him the right to be familiar. "Help me here. Give me something."

"That's funny," she said. "I thought I just did."

It was too late for confessions and explanations. There would be no laughing this off as a simple mistake. Dread filled Kim, so heavy it made her stomach hurt. Following that came a round of embarrassment.

She had worn the dress and the shoes, and those things had worked their magic, just as Brenda had predicted they would. Going beyond distraction, they had seduced Monroe into unwarranted intimacy. And though she had liked that moment of intimacy, in the end, Monroe had successfully manipulated her. As her boss, he would continue to push for answers.

She steadied herself with a hand on the edge of the table. Telling the truth was out of the picture now for sure, as was remaining in Monroe's presence for one second longer.

The ridiculous harassment case idea wavered in front of her as if it were written in the air. They had made out in the bar, surrounded by people, some of which were her fellow employees. Hopefully, none of them had noticed that she hadn't shoved Monroe away, and also the fact that she could no longer breathe properly.

After a kiss like that, so completely mind-numbing and seductive, she saw no other way out of this mess but to play the damsel in distress in order to save her traitorous ruby-covered ass. She hated that; despised the thought. But Monroe was a master at games.

With the hazy lingering imprint of his mouth on hers, Kim lifted a hand. She slapped Monroe across the face, hard, and said loudly enough for others to hear, "What were you thinking, Mr. Monroe? That I'd jump at the chance to bed my boss?"

Pivoting gracefully on her absurdly expensive shoes, she headed for the door, feeling the burn of Monroe's inquisitive gaze on her back and thinking that if she'd wanted to cry in frustration before, she had just taken it to a whole new level.

Shell-shocked, and beginning to get a bad feeling about what had just happened, Chaz smiled at the people at the next table and shrugged his shoulders. He couldn't quite believe this, though. He'd been completely helpless in resisting Kim McKinley. Once again, his plan had backfired.

He had locked lips with her. In public.

And he knew what that meant.

Waiting out several agonizing seconds before throwing

down cash for the drinks, he started after her, deciding that he wouldn't apologize if he caught up with her, since she had provoked that damn lip-lock.

That dress…

Those shoes…

The sudden waifish expression in her eyes.

There was no time like the present to get to the bottom of this charade and find out what Kim had up her sleeve. Certainly she had something up there.

He had taken the bait in what might have been a ploy to catch him off guard. Possibly a public seduction had been her goal all along. If so, this made McKinley a real master at manipulation.

He had believed, with his mouth on hers, and with her throaty moan of encouragement, that she wanted closeness as much as he did. That she enjoyed the kiss as much as he had.

Bottom line—he had believed her. He'd fallen victim to the flash of pain in her eyes and the acceptance of her lush mouth. He thought those things were real, as was the sorrow that had overtaken her saucy demeanor. He'd been sure the real Kim McKinley was facing him for the first time.

And she had played him?

What a sucker he'd been. Only one reason came to mind for an objective like hers—either the threat of a harassment case against him, or out-and-out blackmail. *A kiss for a clause.*

He didn't like his new title, which was Chaz Monroe, fool. People in the bar were looking at him. The brunette who had handed over her phone number winked knowingly.

Did Kim have any earthly idea what he'd like to do to her, now that he knew the score?

How could he have been so completely wrong? Because he would have sworn, testifying with one hand in the air and another on the Bible, that she had kissed him back and meant it.

Oh yes, she was good. Damn good. It had been a great performance. Perfect, actually.

"But it isn't over," Chaz said through gritted teeth as he moved through the crowd.

Kim strode past the bar's doorway and into the corridor beyond that led to the building's marble lobby. When she reached the bank of elevators, she punched a button with her palm and stamped her feet a couple of times in disgust. The wrong plan had worked. She felt terrible, sick.

All that evocative talk had done her in. Snow. Elves. Presents and candy canes. She hated the slinky red dress and the shoes she couldn't return.

The fact that she'd almost blurted out the truth about her family simply added fuel to the fire of an already demented situation. Now there was no going back. She'd have to nail Monroe to the wall by using that very public mistake if he continued to bug her about the contract.

To hell with Chaz Monroe for making her feel guilty about having to force her to use bribery and revenge to get him off her back. She cursed him for bringing up her dark past and causing her to become someone else, someone who would do such a thing for their own personal gain.

Darkness bubbled up inside her, coating her insides.

Once upon a time, she had wanted to trust a man for his good and magical qualities. She had wished hard for Santa Claus to bring her father back. On each anniversary of her father's exit, she had prayed for something to stop her mother's crying jags and all those days when her mom couldn't get out of bed.

She had secretly written to Santa once, and mailed the letter. But Santa hadn't bothered to respond or grant her that wish. Her father never returned, and her mother's depression got progressively worse until relatives had threatened to take Kim away.

The emptiness in her past was riddled with fear and loneliness and a young girl's angst. Her mother's rants and monologues had followed Kim everywhere, and guilt had made her stay close. Her mother didn't need another disappointment; couldn't have withstood her daughter leaving, too.

There had been no escape until college, and even there, while testing her wings, guilt had been part of Kim's existence. She had fled some of that darkness, while her mother had not. She was okay, and her mother stayed sick.

Tonight that sickness had become hers. She had become a player, against her will, as if her mother had risen from the grave to goad her on. She had been willing to hurt someone, a man, so that her secrets could go on being secrets, and her hurt stayed tucked inside. She had wanted to trust, and had been shot down.

"Kim?"

The voice was close, deep and too familiar for comfort. A wave of chills pierced Kim's red dress. The elevator was too damn slow, and she hadn't expected Monroe to follow her.

Now what?

Wobbling on her weakened knees, Kim whirled to face Monroe in all his gorgeous male beauty. The persistent bastard wasn't going to let her off the hook, but he wouldn't touch her again if he knew what was good for him.

He leaned toward her before she could voice a protest, and placed both hands on the wall beside her. It took him several seconds to speak.

"There's no need to run away." His tone seemed too calm for the expression on his face. He pinned her in place, within the cage of his arms, as if knowing she'd bolt at the first opportunity. The front of his shirt showed creases from where she had greedily tugged at it in a moment of blissful mindlessness.

Kim didn't reply. She could not think of one appropriate word to say.

"I really don't see the need for an all-out war, or whatever you imagine this is," he said. "I asked to meet in good faith to discuss the problems facing us. I was trying to find a way out of this mess."

Kim tried to hit the elevator button with her elbow. Though there'd likely be a hint of snow on the ground outside tonight, the corridor felt stiflingly warm. Part of that heat came from Monroe, who acted as if he knew exactly what she had done, and what the outcome had to be. *Clever man.*

"I believed we could work something out," he said. "For a minute back there, I thought you might honestly want to."

She had to fight for a breath. Monroe's closeness was a reminder of how far she had strayed. That kiss, in public, would be career doom for her if rumor of it got around. She wasn't the one with the VP spot. He was.

She tried to touch her lips, to wipe away the feeling of him, but couldn't raise her arms. Monroe's inferno pummeled at her, overheating her from the inside out, rendering her excuses for her behavior useless.

"I tried to explain," she managed to say.

Maybe he hadn't gotten the picture, after all, about the blackmail. His mouth lurked a few millimeters away from hers. Dangerously close.

"But you didn't explain. Not really," he said. "None of that was the truth, right?"

"More than you know."

"There's still time to explain, Kim."

She shook her head.

"I wasn't the only one who wanted that kiss," Monroe remarked. "And it wasn't planned."

"How dare you presume to know what I want?"

"Well, at least one of us is honest. I'll admit that it wasn't the goal of tonight's discussion, but I will also confess that I liked it. I liked it a lot."

"It was business suicide for me, and you know it."

"So, you'll use the kiss against me?"

"Do I have a choice?"

"Well, if it's a lawsuit you want, we might as well make the best of it. There's no need to slap me this time. What good would it do if no one is watching?"

Each time Kim inhaled, his shirt rubbed against the red silk of her dress, sending pangs of longing through places she hadn't focused on in a long time. The closer he got, the more of his disarming scent she breathed in.

She wanted that kiss his lips were promising. Another kiss. A better one, if there was such a thing, especially given that no one, as he said, was there to witness it.

With that thought, Kim knew she was screwed. Chaz Monroe wasn't merely an intelligent bastard, his actions were highly suspicious. Was he a man ruled by what was in his pants, or did he have some nebulous plan of his own to humble her with?

When his mouth brushed across her right temple, Kim squirmed and glanced up to meet the directness of his gaze. She absorbed a jarring jolt of longing for the closeness she had to repel. Monroe was her boss. No one in the company could condone a relationship with him that might eventually lead to the promotion she already deserved. Rumors were a plague in business. If she were to get a promotion in the near future, some would now say she had slept her way to the top.

Several coworkers had witnessed what happened in the bar. Whereas it might have gone unnoticed if she'd kept quiet, in a moment of panic she had idiotically made sure it hadn't gone unnoticed. Plan C had been set in motion.

Damn him. Damn you, Monroe.

"Why can't you leave me alone?" she demanded.

His breath stirred her hair. "Obviously, that contract involves personal issues for you that I hadn't anticipated."

"Bravo for concluding that."

"I have no way of knowing what those issues are unless you tell me about them."

"They aren't your business. Not something so personal. Leave it, Monroe. I'm asking you to let it go."

"Or what? A bit of blackmail will back your request up?" He sighed. "I'm concerned, that's all. Neither of us has to be those people in the bar. We can be friends if you'd prefer that. I'm actually a good listener. We could go someplace quiet and talk things over."

"Like your apartment?"

He shook his head.

"But you'd like to take me to your apartment," she said.

"What fool wouldn't? But that's not the point here."

"I've asked you to back off."

He touched the cheek she had slapped. "Right. I got that."

"And you refuse to listen," Kim said.

"I don't tend to take no for an answer when a moment like the one in the bar told me otherwise."

"Then we can finish this tomorrow," Kim said. "After we've thought it over and had some distance."

"I'm fairly certain we should finish this now," Monroe countered. "I'd really like to know what upsets you. I thought you were going to cry."

His gaze was volcanic. He had nice eyes. Great eyes. Light blue, with flecks of gold. Those eyes wouldn't miss much, if anything. He would see her cave. Right then, his gaze sparkled with a need to understand what she had been thinking, beyond the possibility of blackmail. Or else maybe he just wanted to know more about the terms of their deal.

Letting Monroe strike a nerve is what had gotten her into this mess. He was too handsome, and too willing to get to know her better. Men like him often used women, her mother had preached. If you gave them your secrets, they'd betray those secrets at the drop of a hat. If you gave them your love, they'd easily destroy it.

Kim wanted desperately to stop hearing her mother's voice. She would have covered her ears if Monroe had let her.

"If you're going to fire me for slapping you, go ahead," she said a bit too breathlessly for the sternness she had been aiming for. "There's no need for us to further humiliate each other."

"Fire you? Humiliate you? I wanted to meet with you to avoid those things."

"Well, you didn't do a decent job of reaching that objective. Now you do want to fire me, right? You'll have to, unless I protect myself?"

"That was never the idea, Kim. You'll have to believe me."

"Then why can't you leave me alone? We were doing fine here until you arrived."

"Fine? This company was sliding, whether or not you knew about the bottom line. It was in serious decline. I came here to help the agency out of that decline. The company's success means a lot to me because I have a stake in it. I need everyone to work, including you. If you're one of the best people here, your help is needed in all areas."

"I've been doing more than my share."

"I know that, and yet I need more. I'd ask you to do things you don't necessarily want to do because the company requires it right now, and for no other reason."

"Not because you want to kiss me again?"

"Yes, damn it. I want to kiss you. But believe it or not, I do have some control."

He leaned closer as he spoke, so that Kim felt every muscle in his body from his shoulders to his thighs, and everywhere in between. Yet his mouth drew her focus: the sensuous, talented mouth that had nearly done her in.

"It's going to be yes or no," Monroe said. "You have it within your power to upgrade, maybe even to upper management someday. All you have to do is what I ask, or explain why you can't."

Kim shut her eyes.

"Look, Kim. Do this one thing for me, and we'll reevaluate your position here."

Kim stopped shaking just as she realized she was shaking. Like the last VP, Monroe was promising her the moon when he had no real capacity for giving it to her. He was the vice president. The only way for her to take over that job was for him to leave it.

"I'd like you to leave me alone," she repeated.

"The company needs you."

"Yes. With your body pressed against mine in a public hallway, I can feel how badly you need me."

That did it. Enough was enough. No more squirming. No more playing around. Chaz Monroe had finally done it. He had just buried himself.

Smiling grimly, Kim reached into the purse hanging at her side. She pushed Monroe away and drew out the small tape recorder she kept there. With a precise movement of her finger, she clicked the gadget off.

He glanced at her in surprise, then looked down at what she held in her hand as if not quite believing what he was seeing.

"My lawyer will be talking to your lawyer in the morning if there is any further mention of my contract," Kim said, slipping out from beneath his arm. "You have heard of sexual harassment, being number-one boss man and all?"

He was staring at her as though he'd just felt the arrow of doom pierce his heart dead-on, and also as if he had been betrayed. His arms dropped to his sides. His expression smoothed into something unreadable.

The elevator pinged as the door rolled open. Kim walked inside and turned, wearing a smile she had to struggle to maintain. Her insides were in knots. Both hands were shaking. She hid her sadness and the urge to throw the recorder at Monroe. She felt like sinking to the ground.

He just stood there. He didn't look angry, only disappointed. He had been bushwhacked, broadsided. Did he fear what would happen to him if this conversation were to fall into the wrong hands? Did he now fear for his job?

Monroe had a casting couch, pure and simple, and she'd nearly been flat out on top of it. So what if she had liked the kiss and his hard body pressed to hers? It was best not to think about those things now. The guy, gorgeous as he was, charming as he could be, shouldn't have taken such liberties. The vice president should have known better.

With a stern bite to her lower lip, Kim used her purse to snap the button inside the elevator that would close this case once and for all. Was she proud of how she'd accomplished this? *No.* Happy about it? *Absolutely not.* She felt dirty. Yet she had remembered the recorder at the last minute and done what had to be done.

Monroe wouldn't fight her. Nothing good ever came of a lawsuit. So, the hope she maintained right that minute was that he would realize this and stop bothering her to change the terms of her contract. Life as usual would be the result.

The dark clouds she had been trying so hard to shake off drifted over her. She pictured her mother smiling. In reaction, Kim felt her face blanch. She swayed on her feet, truly hating what she had done and the memories that wouldn't stop invading her mind, all because of her mother's far-reaching influence.

This night was over, and it was too late to take anything back. She had made her bed, but at least Monroe wasn't in it.

"Good night," she said to him with a catch in her throat.

He stood in the corridor, motionless, his eyes on her as the elevator doors finally closed.

Five

Well, well...

Kim had called his bluff. She thought she'd done pretty well in this game, and he had to hand it to her. She'd hung in there and had been fairly creative about it. Still, the result was a disappointment. He hadn't figured she would go so far in the wrong direction.

As the elevator doors closed between them, Chaz shrugged his shoulders. He knew that Kim had to be feeling a little guilty after hearing him state his case. She wasn't dense. The telling detail about her current state of mind was that aside from the tape recorder, she hadn't slapped him again.

Hearing the clink of rapidly approaching heels on the marble floor, Chaz turned and said, "That wasn't remotely close to what we had discussed."

Brenda Chang strode up to him wearing a frown. "I don't feel very well. I feel like I've just stabbed my best friend in the back because—oh wait—*I have.*"

"You left us alone out of the goodness of your heart," he pointed out.

"Yes, but you didn't pay me enough to betray her."

"I didn't pay you anything at all."

"That's what I mean."

"I had to try to reach her. I did try." Chaz shook his head, eyeing the elevator.

"You have no idea how much she'd like to capitulate. She's just not ready," Brenda said.

"There's no way to help with that? You won't tell me what her problem is?"

"Not for love or money. Wild horses couldn't drag Kim's secrets from me without her permission."

Chaz ventured another lingering look at the elevator.

Brenda's voice sounded small. "What next?"

"My hands are tied. She wants to be left alone."

"You already knew that."

Chaz shot her a look that indicated quite clearly that he wasn't in the mood to prolong this discussion.

"All right," Brenda said. "But you'd better turn out to be a good guy, that's all I can say, or you'll have problems added onto problems. That's a promise."

Chaz leaned back to read the numbers on the elevator panel above the door. "If she's going back to the office, will she stay up there long?"

Brenda shrugged.

"Does she need your shoulder to lean on?" he asked.

"I doubt it. Besides, she'll probably get out one floor up and use the stairs to leave the building, knowing she'd get past you that way."

Brenda's eyes widened when she realized she'd said too much.

"That shrewd, eh?" he asked.

She blew out a sigh. "Every woman knows how to do this, Monroe. Avoidance is coded into in our genes."

"So what will she do after that?"

"Simmer awhile, most likely, and then start thinking."

"She doesn't really have a case you know," he said. "There's no one to remove me or waggle a finger over a kiss."

Brenda nodded. "I know that, and who you really are. You might have changed your name if being undercover here is your game, because I just looked your family up online. Kim doesn't know yet because I didn't get to it until now."

"You looked me up?"

"The internet is a marvelous thing," Brenda said. "Your family's business dealings are plastered all over it."

"Then you know why I'm here?"

"Yep."

"You'll tell her?"

"I would have already, if you hadn't followed her to this hallway. Just so you know, friends don't usually allow each other to do anything they might regret."

"When she knows about me, and without her little blackmail scheme getting her the office she wants, will she leave the company?"

"I wouldn't put it past her. What would you do, in her place, if you found out that the man you were going to resort to blackmailing was in fact the owner of the agency?"

"I'd take the damn Christmas gig and get on with it," Chaz said.

"Yes, well you have millions of dollars to fall back on, and no female hormones. Kim has a tiny apartment she can barely afford as it is, close by because she's here working most of the time."

Chaz gave her a sober sideways glance. "Point taken."

"Is it?" Brenda countered.

"Quite."

"She's not putting you on, you know. She has been dealing with holiday stuff for years. Very real issues. Serious setbacks."

Chaz looked again to the elevator, which had indeed stopped two floors up. He then glanced to the revolving doors leading to the street. "I don't suppose you'll tell me where her apartment is?"

"The name is Chang, not Judas."

"I want to keep her, but I'm running out of options, Brenda. I'd like to tell her about my real position here, myself, before she does anything stupid."

"So you'll show up on her doorstep?"

"Do you have a better idea?"

"I think that might be going beyond the call of duty. Unless there's another reason you want to keep her here, other than her ability to work her tail off."

Chaz thought that over, deciding that Brenda was right. He was letting an employee dictate his actions, actions that might appear as desperate. As for a reason for wanting to keep Kim, beyond chaining her to her desk…his body had made it pretty clear that he was interested in more than her work ethic. The intensity of their attraction that had led to the kiss couldn't be ignored, and hadn't lessened one bit.

It was a double-edged sword. If he went out of his way to keep her at the agency, his actions tonight might hurt her reputation. If she walked out, taking those big clients with her, the agency might tank.

This was an impossible situation that he had to try to put right.

"You're right," he said to Brenda. "She has to decide for herself, without further interference, what she will do next. Feelings have no place here."

Brenda thought that over with her head tilted to the side. She searched his face. "Feelings, huh?"

He shrugged.

She sighed loudly and opened her purse. Removing a piece of paper and a pen, she scribbled something and handed the paper over.

"If you tell her I gave this to you, I'll tell her you lied. Three guesses as to whom she will believe."

After a hesitation, she handed him something else. It was a tiny tape recorder just like the one Kim had used to record their conversation.

Chaz glanced at her questioningly.

"I taped something in case Kim and I needed a laugh later," Brenda said. "You might want to listen to the tape before finding her. It might help with that lawsuit business and save everyone some serious damage."

Chaz pocketed the recorder. "Does this mean you'll trust me to set things straight?"

"Hell, no. It's bribery for you to leave me out of whatever happens from this point on."

Chaz decided right then that he really did like Brenda Chang.

"Will she shoot me if I show up at her place?" he asked.

"I would."

He smiled. "I suppose following her seems desperate."

"Completely."

"Okay then, wish me luck."

"Boss, you are so going to need it," Brenda declared as Chaz headed for the street.

Kim's feet were killing her. Stilettos required a lot of downtime and motionless posing, not trotting down New York sidewalks, contrary to what TV shows might have everyone think. The shoes were impossible, especially on the icy sidewalk.

She waved down an oncoming taxi, waited until it stopped, then ran in front of it to cross the road, assured of not getting hit when the taxi blocked traffic. The driver grumbled, and might have extended one finger in a rude gesture. She didn't wait to see.

Thankfully, her apartment was around the corner from the agency, at the end of the block. Though close in terms of actual distance, she'd still have to soak her feet when she got there, and also work with her fractured ego.

The heels made sharp pecking sounds on the sidewalk as she threaded her way between other pedestrians. She'd left the office without her coat, and the red dress garnered a few stares and catcalls from men she passed.

"Imbeciles." What kind of man gave a woman a whistle on the street that she could hear?

She was shivering, but she'd had to get out of the agency building. Since Monroe had followed her into the hallway, he might have continued to the office. If he had pushed his way into the elevator with her, filling the tiny, confined space with his musky, masculine maleness, there was no way to predict what might have happened. Plus, there were cameras.

Any more time spent in Chaz Monroe's sight would be bad, and how much worse could she feel?

She walked with her gaze lowered, having set up her mental block against the windows in the stores she passed that were decorated with December finery. Some of them presented animated holiday scenes. Others showcased giant trees decorated with everything under the sun that could fit on a branch. It was especially important she didn't view these things in entirety; not after dealing with Monroe.

She was already on edge.

With great relief, she made it down the block without seeing a single Santa suit on a street corner—a sight that would not only have filled her with the old regrets, but also reminded her of what she had told Monroe.

She wanted Santa....

Yes, she had told him that.

Well, okay. So she had been impulsive enough to use Brenda's ridiculous excuse in a moment of panic and extreme need. Therefore, could she really blame Monroe for thinking her an idiot?

She wanted Santa. *Jeez*...

Feeling sicker, Kim rushed on. She nodded to the doorman of her building and whisked by without the usual benign chitchat. Six floors up and down one long hallway, and she was home free. No one had followed her. No pink slip waited on the floor by her door.

Kim stood with her back to the wood as the door closed behind her, only then allowing herself a lungful of air. She really did feel sick. Tonight she had been possessed by her mother's teachings. She'd been set back a few years with the flick of a tape recorder switch.

"There's no going back. No taking it back," she muttered.

The guilt tripled with her second breath of air. Even from the small front room, not much larger than her cubicle at work, she smelled the cookies she had dared to bake the night before.

Christmas cookies.

Her first disloyal batch.

The damn cookies might have been some kind of terrible omen. She had looked up the recipe in secret, and baked them as her first baby step toward freedom. Now her new boss had whispered fantastical things in her ear without realizing how much she'd love to participate in Christmas festivities, and how much it hurt to think of actually doing so.

Elves. Snow. Packages in red ribbons. She might have given her right index fingernail to join in everything going on around her, and had been slowly inching in that direction.

Then she kissed Chaz Monroe.

She hung her head. Her apartment smelled like a sugar factory. Worse yet, she wanted her place to smell like *him*. Like Monroe, companionship, sex, holiday glitter and all the other things her mother had shunned so harshly. You'd think she'd know better. Someone looking in on her life might expect her to just wipe the slate clean and start over, now that her mother was no longer in the picture. Who from the outside would understand?

If she tossed the cookies, would things change? If she marched into the kitchen and got rid of the little doughy stars and trees, would time reset itself backward so that she'd have another chance to get things right?

Monroe was a jerk. He had to be. Because if he wasn't, then she was.

Tossing her purse to the floor, Kim staggered to the couch and threw herself onto it, face-first, listening to the side seam in her tight red dress tear.

Chaz glanced at the paper, then up at the tall brick building. This was it. McKinley lived here, and he was going to trespass on her space and privacy because tonight he felt greedy. He wanted a showdown to get this over with once and for all.

She lived in a place that was a lot like his on the outside. He didn't know her well enough to gauge her decorating skills, but figured martini glasses wouldn't be one of her prominent fixtures.

In truth, he didn't really know Kim at all and was relying on the concept of animal attraction to nudge him into doing what he'd never done before—plead his case a second time.

He offered a curt but friendly nod to the doorman and went inside. The doorman picked up the lobby phone and dialed apartment 612.

"Yes?" she answered after a couple of rings.

The doorman spoke briefly, then handed the phone over.

Hearing Kim's voice left him temporarily tongue-tied, something so unlike him that he almost hung up. He thought about the napkin with the brunette's number on it crumpled up in his pocket. Calling that number might have taken his mind off Kim McKinley for a few hours.

So, the fact that he was standing here meant he was either acting like a madman, or a man possessed. Maybe even like a sore loser refusing to give up on the outcome he wanted. Those flaws made him see red. And in the center of that puddle of red was Miss Kim McKinley, the cause of all this.

"Delivery for Kim McKinley, advertising queen," Chaz said to her over the line, managing to keep his voice neutral. "I can't be sure, but from the feel of the package, I think it contains an apology."

A short span of silence followed his remark. His heart beat faster. What was he doing here, anyway? Had he just uttered the word *apology?*

"This only adds to the harassment, you know," she eventually said. "I believe stalking might be a felony."

"Yes, well, what's one more year behind bars when there's so much at stake?"

"None of this is funny, Monroe."

"No, it isn't. At least we agree on something."

"You can't come up."

"Then maybe you'll come down."

"Sorry."

"Are you sorry?"

After another hesitation, she said, "No."

"Not very convincing," Chaz remarked. "It's that gap between what you say and what you don't say that keeps me wondering what you might really be thinking."

More silence. A full twenty seconds, by his calculation. Chaz lowered the phone to keep her from hearing his growl of disappointment, then thought better of it. With the phone so close to his heart, she might be able to hear how fast it raced. She'd know something was up.

"You just don't get the picture," she accused. "I don't know you at all."

"You know me well enough to want to prosecute me for minor indiscretions. Also, I did say I'm willing to take on an added year in the slammer if you think I need it after we hash this out."

"Can I have that in writing? About the slammer?"

"I'm fresh out of pens."

"How convenient."

"You do have a tape recorder, though," he reminded her. "It's possible you're using it now."

Silence.

"You don't know how persistent I can be, Kim. Lawsuit or not, blackmail or whatever, I still have to take care of business while the fate of that business rests in my hands. Don't you have a sympathetic bone in your body? Can't you put yourself in my place?"

"I was supposed to be in your place."

"Water under the bridge, Kim. How long can you hold that against me?"

Another silence ensued. Chaz held his breath.

"Let me speak to Sam," she said.

"Sam?"

"The doorman. He'll come if you call."

Chaz called out to the man, and he ambled over and took the phone.

"Yep," Sam said to the receiver, nodding. "Yep. I certainly will, Miss McKinley." Then Sam hung up the phone.

"What did she say?" Chaz asked.

"I'm to take something as collateral, then send you up."

"Excuse me?"

"Miss McKinley wants me to hold something as ransom, in order for you to visit her apartment. You can pick that item up again when you come back downstairs. I have instructions to call the police if you don't pick it up within the hour."

"Like what?" Chaz said. "My wallet?"

"The value of that as collateral depends on what's in it," Sam said without missing a beat.

"Who do I call if I come back and you're not here with my wallet?" Chaz asked.

Sam looked dramatically aghast at the suggestion. "I

have a drawer right here, and I'll lock it up, minus whatever you see fit to give me for keeping it safe. If you prefer, I can give the wallet to a neutral third party."

"What kind of doorman are you?"

Sam held out his hand, palm up. "The kind that cares about his wards."

Chaz fished for his wallet, took out a wad of cash and his credit cards, then handed a twenty-dollar bill and the wallet to McKinley's private watchdog.

He held up the rest of the cash. "Just in case I have to buy off anyone else between here and her apartment."

Sam grinned and pressed the elevator button for him. "Apartment 612. Have a nice night."

The elevator was slow and bumpy, but Chaz stepped out on the sixth floor. He found number 612 a few doors down, its oiled wood glowing in the light from the wall sconce beside it.

As he waited to knock, he pondered further what Kim's home would be like, half dreading finding out. Personalities were reflected in a person's surroundings. If she preferred chintz chairs, mounds of pillows and draperies with fringe, he wasn't sure what he'd do. Run away, maybe. After all, he didn't want to marry McKinley. He just wanted to...

Well, he wanted to...

God, would she have a cat?

He'd be a dog guy, himself, if he had any time or space for pets.

And it was perfectly clear that what he was doing with all this ridiculous speculation was trying to talk himself out of this next meeting with her after getting this far.

Fingering the tape recorder in his pocket, he knocked softly.

"Yes?" she called out.

"Monroe. Not completely broke, I might add, because

Sam showed a little mercy. I think he recognized your real intention, which was to put me in my place."

"Say what you wanted to say and then go away."

"From here, with the door between us? What would the neighbors think?"

The door opened a crack. Kim's face appeared behind a stretched brass chain. "Go away, Monroe. We have nothing further to say to each other tonight."

"Then why did you let me come up?"

"To tell you that to your face."

He noticed right away that she looked smaller. She had ditched the red shoes, but still wore the red dress that glowed like liquefied lava in the light from the sconce.

"If I let you in," she added, "it might ruin my lawsuit. So why are you here?"

"You're a challenge I have to take up."

"Is that supposed to be a compliment, or are you merely the type of person that needs to win at all cost?"

"Winning isn't everything," he countered. "The need to understand you is why I'm here."

"What part of *none of your business* don't you get?"

"You kissed me," he said, wondering why he'd brought that up again. He'd kissed other women, for heaven's sake.

"So?" she said.

"Was it me or the game you might be playing that made you do it?"

She closed the door. He heard it seal tight.

"Would you prefer I spoke about holiday clauses here? How about if I mention Santa, and how you made that sound in the bar?"

The door opened again, not quite as widely, showing off Kim's exquisitely creased expression. "That's not funny."

Chaz shrugged. "What more have I got to lose?"

"How about your job?"

"Okay, Kim. But remember, you forced me to do this."

From his pocket, Chaz pulled out the tape recorder Brenda had handed him. He had listened to it on the way over, and bookmarked a starting point in case of just such an instance as this, figuring Brenda wouldn't have handed the tape over if it wasn't something useful to his cause.

He hit Play. Brenda's voice came from the tiny speaker.

Tell me about it. But first you have to dish about whether Monroe really does have a nice ass. You didn't think he was hot? That's the word going around. H-o-t, as in fan yourself.

Yeah? Did you hear anything about the man being an arrogant idiot?

No. My sources might have left that part out.

I don't actually care about the nice ass part, Bren, preferring not to notice an area that I won't be kissing.

Don't be absurd, Kim. No one expects you to kiss anyone's backside. It isn't professional. What happened?

I'll have to start over somewhere else, that's what. Monroe won't let me off the hook. He expects me to explain everything. He'll expect me to cave.

As Chaz fast-forwarded slightly, he said, "I don't think Brenda knew she was recording that. She had been making notes for herself on a project."

He held the recorder up and pressed Play again.

If you don't want to tell Monroe the truth, you have about an hour to formulate a reason he'll accept in lieu of the truth. Fabricating illusions is what we do on a daily basis, right? We make people want to buy things.

Chaz pocketed the recorder. "Then there was something about shoes and therapy and a Santa fetish."

Kim stared at him through the crack.

"Also, I believe that seducing me was mentioned, which might tend to negate that harassment suit and the blackmail you might have planned on using to get me to back down."

Kim looked very pale, in stark contrast to her red dress.

"So, there is no Santa fetish?" he asked. "You made that up?"

Now she looked sick, and he felt bad. But he wanted her to let him in. He needed to get that far for reasons he did not want to contemplate.

"Why are you here?" she asked. "What do you want?"

"You and I tending to that Christmas party by working together."

"You have no idea what you're asking."

"That's the point. I want to understand. Until you can help me do that, we're back to square one."

"No. We're back to you filling my place at the agency, because I'm out of there as of right now."

Chaz shook his head. "Now you're being stubborn. No one wants you to go, myself included. I've come here personally to tell you so, at much risk to my ego, I might add. Can't that constitute a win on your part if you're keeping score?"

She paled further. Possibly she wasn't used to direct confrontations.

He held up the recorder. "How about if you get yours and we toss them both out the window?"

"We're six floors up."

"There's little chance of them surviving the fall, right?"

"They might hit somebody. Maybe Sam."

Chaz nodded thoughtfully. "Okay. You're right. It would probably be simpler if we exchanged tapes. Then no one would have the goods on anyone else."

"This is ridiculous," she said. "What do you want?"

"Talk and a holiday party," he said. "That's all I ask."

"Okay."

"Okay?" he repeated, surprised by her reply.

"When is this damn party?" she asked.

"In a week or so."

"That's only a few days before…"

"Christmas," Chaz supplied.

She looked hesitant. "I can make some calls."

"You will do this personally, Kim?"

"Yes."

"Thank you." Chaz wasn't sure about feeling relieved, because winning this round wasn't as satisfying as it should have been. Kim was going to pass the test after being shoved into it, but he might have pushed her too far. Her sudden acceptance reflected that. He had, he supposed, lost by winning, and he experienced an immediate pang of regret.

"It's the last thing I'll do for you," she said, confirming his diagnosis of the situation.

Chaz wanted to let it go at that. At the same time, he desired to tell her she really didn't have to work on the ridiculous and imaginary project, and that he was sorry for putting her through this. Breaking her would have hurt both of them, and that realization came as a further surprise, because he found that he liked Kim exactly the way she was.

"I know it might be true that you'll decide to leave, but I'm counting on convincing you otherwise. I am sorry we had to meet like this," he said.

How serious he had grown in saying what he truly meant. Chaz fought a strange impulse to break the little chain keeping them apart and wrap his arms around the pale version of McKinley facing him. Again, his instinct was to protect her, comfort her, though he had no idea why. She was Wonder Woman, after all.

Okay. Backtracking, maybe he did know why he wanted to hold her. He had started to like her more than was appropriate, in spite of her stunt in the bar.

"Where is the party?" Her voice sounded dry. Her accent was pronounced, and no less sultry than the first time he'd heard it.

"I'll give you the details tomorrow. Unless you'll let me in right now," he said.

"Good night, Monroe. I think we've said all there is to say for one night, don't you?"

He supposed they had. Besides, Brenda would tell Kim about him any minute now, and that would be that. Cat out of the bag.

"Tomorrow, then."

She closed the door.

Wishing he had another beer to chase away the thrill of being so close to the woman he didn't want to feel anything for, Chaz instead considered calling his brother for a stern reprimand about pleading with any woman for any reason, and for putting himself in such an awkward position.

Big bro Rory, his elder by four years, wouldn't beat around the bush. He'd just reach out and take what he wanted, perfectly willing to suffer the consequences. Then again, Rory at times seemed a little insane.

McKinley had agreed to help out. Soon she'd know that he wasn't only her boss, but the new owner of the agency. His actual title shouldn't make any difference, in theory. Still, she might take the undercover boss business badly.

He could knock again and tell her the truth about this being a test of her willingness to work with him, before Brenda called to tell her the truth of the situation.

What about when he sold the agency, flipping it for a profit, as he'd planned to do? What would happen to her then, if she didn't back down first?

By helping Kim now, he'd be doing a good deed. So how the hell did he turn this situation around? Seriously, was that impossible?

As Chaz headed for the elevator, he had to concede that he'd at least given this a shot. But he didn't make it to the elevator before hearing a door open. He turned to see Kim standing with her hands on her hips in the hallway, her pallor ghostly white, her lips parted for a speech she didn't make.

In that moment, he thought how magnificent she looked, even in anger.

Six

Fighting off a round of pure, livid anger, Kim faced Chaz Monroe with a distance of thirty feet separating them. Her pulse thudded annoyingly in her neck and wrists.

"You're a bastard," she said. "Is this a game for you? Tell me that much."

"It wasn't a game until you kissed me back and then pulled out that recorder," he replied.

The door to the apartment next to Kim's opened, and her neighbor looked out. Kim smiled wanly at the man. "Having a difference of opinion," she said, explaining the noise.

"A lover's spat," Monroe clarified.

"Please do it elsewhere," the old guy said, retreating back inside. "You're spoiling my dinner."

She pointed a finger at Monroe. "How did you get that tape recording? Did you plant bugs all over the building to keep an eye on things?"

"I did nothing of the sort," he said. "It just happened to fall into my possession."

"Like hell it did."

"Maybe I should come in," he suggested. "We're beyond lawsuits, don't you think? Unless…"

"Unless what?" she snapped.

"Unless you're afraid you'll do what you said on that recording."

"What are you talking about?"

"Seducing me."

"Get over yourself, Monroe. That wasn't a plan, it was girl talk."

"Yet you accomplished it," he pointed out, shaking his way-too-handsome head and dislodging a strand of shaggy hair that fell becomingly across his forehead. It didn't help her cause that he in no way looked like a monster.

Nor did Monroe look as smug as she had expected him to. Frankly, he didn't appear to be pleased with his behavior any more than she was. He didn't grin or let on what he might be thinking, though she did see something in his expression that left her short of breath.

"You didn't think—" Her voice faltered. She started over. "You didn't come here to—"

"As a matter of fact, I think I must have," he replied.

"Dream on." Kim placed a hand over her heart in disbelief as her body produced a quake of longing so intense for that very thing they were both thinking, she nearly gasped aloud.

Was it possible to despise a guy and want to bed him at the same time? Monroe had this ultrasexy thing going on that affected her as if it were magical. But he was clouding her judgment and preying on her attraction to him. Obviously, he knew about that weakness. He had heard her conversation with Brenda, where she had wistfully mentioned his looks.

And then again, there had been the kiss.

Kim widened her stance with a crisp show of authority she didn't actually feel. The red dress strained at the seams.

"Letting me in would be a fitting end to this stalemate," Monroe suggested.

Kim glanced down the hallway. Anytime now her nosy neighbor would be back in his doorway. She had to move this conversation out of the open, yet was afraid to get closer to the gorgeous guy who had mesmerized her into facing him again. This meeting went against every principle she had erected to protect herself.

"Letting you in would also be business blasphemy," she said.

"Fortunately, I'm no longer talking about the business, Kim. Neither are you, I'm thinking."

Monroe closed the distance between them with long strides. He was terribly seductive, even when he pleaded his case so crassly. His features and his body were damn near perfect. She hadn't found a single physical flaw in the entire package, except for the shirt, visible beneath his open jacket, which still bore the creases from when she'd grabbed him earlier.

He possessed a damnable, pit-bullish persistence. She wasn't at all sure about the state of his mind.

Or hers.

"Look, Kim," Monroe said, "I can hardly explain how much I want to put business aside for just this one night, call a truce and get to know you better. That's the truth."

Kim's mind sluggishly tripped through rules of negotiation. Should she toss caution to the wind and maul Monroe in the hallway? In the midst of thanking her lucky stars that he hadn't yet reached her, her traitorous body had started to sag. She leaned a shoulder against the doorjamb and considered the ramifications of taking Monroe up on his offer. What could it hurt to speak to him further if she was going to leave the agency, anyway?

It wasn't as if she *cared* for Monroe, beyond her acute physical craving for him. Allowing him inside might be a fitting end to all this infuriating heat and drama.

He stood before her wearing a questioning expression, one eyebrow raised.

"Monroe," she began. "I'm not sure what's going on."

Her neighbor's door opened. Kim tossed him a friendly wave. Sighing heavily in resignation, she wrapped her hands in Monroe's coat and hauled him inside her apartment, hoping she hadn't gone completely insane.

The first thing Chaz noticed was the sweet smell of her apartment. The second was how his body had ended up pressed tightly to Kim's against the wall beside the front door that slammed shut behind them.

They were body to body, without an inch of space between, and below his waist, pertinent body parts were already thankful. Tight against her like that, he couldn't think about business, what her home looked like or about mistrusting her. In fact, he'd just discovered that he was no longer able to trust himself. His body had the lead on this one, and his mind seemed curiously foggy about the future.

Kim's long-lashed hazel eyes, mostly green, remained fixed on him. Her expression was hard to read. Her soft lips finally parted, and sensing another excuse coming that might end the highly sensual, highly addictive position he found himself in, Chaz didn't let her voice a protest. He pressed his index finger to her mouth and shook his head. "Now's not the time," he whispered. "Backward is never the right direction."

She offered him an expression that fell precariously close to being a grimace, and at the same time eyed him warily. But Kim's mind, it seemed to him, had to be in the gutter, next to his.

Wonder Woman was in his grasp, and had welcomed it. Her lips weren't pouty, exactly, but close to it, and relatively ruby-tinted, though he had kissed some of the color away in the bar. Her chest, against his, strained at the confines of the red dress. She breathed shallowly, in shudders.

"What do you propose we do about this?" she asked, biting down on her lower lip hard enough to leave an imprint of teeth marks.

"Are any tape recorders running?" he said.

She glared at him in a way that did nothing to ruin the glorious beauty of her pert oval face. Her ivory neck pulsed with a racing heartbeat. Feeling the firmness of her breasts pressed to his chest, Chaz knew the time for talk was over.

In a smooth motion, he slid one arm around her waist.

The other arm followed. He stroked her slender back with his open palm in a gradual downward glide over the red silk that had been such an inspiration, and now seemed like an unnecessary barrier between them and their crazy, wayward desires.

He found the silk warm and fragrant, the texture exotic. Around them, the room felt cool, dim and distant. Between them, the fires of lustful attraction beat at the air.

Kim shivered as his fingers trailed down her spine. This time when her lips parted, a sigh of resignation emerged. Chaz watched her intently, holding on to his control with every ounce of willpower he possessed.

Just a little longer...

All he needed was one more little sign that she actually agreed to what was going to happen next.

He felt downright greedy now that he'd gotten this far. He wanted more of Kim McKinley, and getting closer than this wasn't possible unless it became acceptable for two objects to actually occupy the same space at the same time. He yearned to be inside her, and to enjoy all of her. He hoped they'd settle for nothing less.

She closed her eyes in a flutter of long lashes. Her body swayed as if, parallel to his reactions, she had moved beyond the point of no return. She placed her hands on his hips, but didn't push him away. She gave a slight tug, as though she shared his desire to relish the physicality of the moment.

This was the sign he had been waiting for.

He kissed her.

Not a soft, tender kiss, but a hungry devouring one. There was no hesitancy in McKinley's response. She allowed this mouth-to-mouth exploration and joined in, meeting him in a white-hot dance of lips and tongues and fire, giving as much as receiving.

The McKinley he had wished for in his wildest dreams

kissed him with a fury backed by her own level of greed. As his hands moved over her fine, sleek body, she rubbed up against him, fanning the flames of his raging desires.

Chaz could not recall ever feeling this way. Never this greedy, this needy, or this consumed.

The woman was driving him crazy....

And the damn dress was in the way.

Wanting to feel the smoothness of her skin beneath the slinky fabric, Chaz slowly began to raise the hem upward, over her thighs, toward her hips, listening to the rustle of the expensive silk. He couldn't see the lace he hoped would be underneath, though he located its delicate pattern with his fingers.

Lace...

Narrow strips of elastic crossed her hips, holding the dainty lingerie in place. His fingers slipped under, sliding down the cleft that led to her feminine heat from the back.

She groaned. Their mingling breath was volcanic. He breathed hard and fast, ready to explode, and hadn't even seen her naked. Kim was like catnip, with her mouth, her flawless skin and her inferno-like heat.

He desperately wanted all of her, and knew he couldn't take the time. His pulsating body wouldn't allow for the slowness of a proper bedding. Plus, no bedroom was in sight.

He shifted his hands to find the zipper at her back. The zipper made no sound as he eased it downward.

Dragging his mouth from hers, he took seconds to study her face, wondering if Kim was truly going to allow this, not quite believing his luck. He felt compelled to speak. "It will be worth it," he said. "All the best things are."

Her wide-eyed gaze unflinchingly met his. "Then why are you dallying?" Her voice was low-pitched and sensuously breathy.

"Is that what I'm doing?" he asked.

"Don't you know?"

"I'm afraid you'll change your mind. Should I give you that option?"

"Why, when you're so barbaric about everything else?"

Chaz's physical urges escalated with the flirty tone of their repartee. It was to be a fight to the very end between them if their minds got in the way.

One of his hands remained on the zipper. He tilted her head back with his other one, with his fingers under her chin. "Maybe we can pretend we're just two people enjoying each other."

"Maybe I should have chugged that martini."

"Was that your first?"

"Kiss?"

"Martini."

"It couldn't actually be the first if I didn't drink it."

Chaz tilted her head back farther, wanting to see deep into Kim's soul through the pools of green in her eyes.

"And the kiss?" he said.

"Are you now asking for an accounting of other things in my personal life?"

"I'm jealous just thinking about your personal life."

He eased the zipper the rest of the way down. Kim's hands, on his hips, hadn't moved again. Each turn of her head sent her lush scent scattering. Chaz inhaled her woodsy fragrance and felt it mix with the rising heat waves inside his chest. Talk couldn't really spoil this for him. Nothing could. The deepness of her voice was a vibration that made him want her more than ever.

He feathered his lips over her forehead and placed a series of kisses on her cheek in a trail that led back to her mouth—not entirely sure why she allowed this kind of liberty.

She had a small waist and delicate bones. Touching her gave him a thrill equal to being caught in a lightning storm.

This wasn't love, it was lust, he reminded himself. Love didn't leave a man breathless and overheated. He'd always figured love as a lukewarm emotional state that developed slowly over time between long-standing acquaintances. He and Kim didn't know each other. They had barely spoken a few hundred words, total, and were acting on instinct.

"This is a truce," he said, brushing her mouth with his. "A white flag."

In a replay of the kiss in the bar, he rested his lips on hers lightly before drawing back far enough to note her response. Her eyes were half-closed now. Her lashes were blackened by eye makeup she didn't need to enhance her appearance. Her skin gleamed as though their steamy encounter had moistened it. Up close, she really did look younger. She looked...delicious.

The red dress, he decided in a whirlwind of thought, probably wouldn't hold a candle to Kim in a baggy T-shirt and nothing else. Kim with her hair mussed, getting out of bed on a weekend morning, or emerging from a shower, wet and soapy.

Those thoughts turned him on.

He wedged his thigh between her legs and pressed her roughly to the wall. Her mouth molded to his, and her mouth was a marvel. She nipped at his lips, breathing sultry streams of air into him.

Her hands found their way underneath his coat, and tugged at his shirt. Finding bare skin, her fingers splayed, hot as pokers, and sent streaks of pleasure soaring through him.

Who needed control when faced with *this?*

What man wouldn't consider giving up a future for a night like this one?

Liking how light she felt in his arms, he lifted her up. Her legs encircled his thighs. The spot he achingly wanted to reach settled over his erection as he held her close, though there were still too many clothes in the way.

Backing up a step made things worse. Part of him wanted to hold her like this forever, culmination be damned. But he was also aware of how close they had come to losing the chance of working anything out after this ferocious sexual escapade.

His mind's chatter stopped abruptly when her mouth separated from his and moved to his ear. Her lips flitted over his lobe teasingly before she came back for more, her mouth hungrier this time, their kiss resembling the furor of anger in its intensity.

She was giving in, meeting him halfway as an aggressor. He had never desired anything so badly as to be inside her. Surely there was a place to finish this—a sofa or a rug?

He caressed her, devoured her, his elation escalating. Her fingers dipped under his waistband, searching, scorching, ensuring his hardness, driving him mad. The only sound in the room was the rasp of their breathing. The only sensation left to him was Kim McKinley in his arms.

And then the air shook with the shrill sound of a phone ringing. The sound echoed loudly throughout the room.

Chaz's heart missed a beat. His lips stalled. It was Kim's phone, and a bad omen, he just knew.

The click of an answering machine turning on followed the second ring.

"Kim?" a voice said, loud enough for Brenda Chang to have been in the room with them.

"Kim, are you there? Pick up the damn phone! Listen. Monroe isn't who we think he is. He isn't the VP. He's the new owner of the agency, and is occupying that office in order to spy on the masses. He owns the agency and us, lock, stock and barrel. Kim, please pick up! Monroe might be on his way over there. I wanted to catch you before he arrives and pass on that news. Kim? Oh, hell. Tell Sam. Don't answer the door. Where are you? Call me back."

By the time the machine turned off, Kim's tight hold on him had gone slack. She stiffened so fast, her actions didn't register until her legs loosened, and he had to press her against the wall to support her.

Some of her glorious heat slipped from his grasp. Her eyes were averted, her lids lowered. Once she had regained her feet, she got her hands up between them.

She couldn't seem to catch a breath. Her chest still strained against his. When she finally looked up, her big eyes met his as if searching for something. Her pallor brought a whole new meaning to the word pale, despite the splashes of pink in her cheeks.

"Kim," he said, addressing her accusatory gaze. "It's okay. I knew Brenda was going to tell you. My role at the agency is supposed to be a secret for now. I wanted to get to know the workings of the place and play catch up."

"You own the agency?" The words tumbled out between harsh breaths.

"Yes."

"You're not the vice president?"

"No."

Her eyes projected an expression of betrayal. She blinked slowly. When she spoke, her voice shook. "Get out. I think you'd better get out right now."

"Kim—"

"You can see the door. Use it," she directed. "Please."

He held up both hands in a placating gesture, and tried to find the right words to ease the tension. No words came. Kim didn't look angry about this, she looked ill.

"Now," she repeated.

He had to explain, had to make her see. "I bought the company to make it better, more successful. The position you want is still on the table. I'll make a decision once I get a grip on the rest of the agency's personnel needs and can move things forward. We already have a truce, you and I, so we're in the clear about the situation. Nothing has changed."

"Oh, we're far from clear about anything," she countered. "And everything has changed."

"That doesn't have to be the case."

"Doesn't it? You were going to sleep with me, withholding a secret like that. You let me think you took my job, and you were willing to let me hang myself and my profession by directing me toward a bed."

"A date with a bed has nothing to do with work or the issues there," he protested.

She sucked in a big breath of air and lowered her voice. "What was this all about then, for you? A test of my character? You wanted to see if I'd actually sleep my way up the ladder? Maybe you wondered if I'd done it before, and that's why I had been promised your office?"

Chaz stared at her, sensing she wasn't finished.

"Are you so naïve that you'd actually believe I could remain at the agency after sleeping with you? That being here with you, like this, wouldn't affect my reputation, or reach the ears of the other employees, and eventually my clients? Or that it would all go away if you were to promote me now?"

"Kim, listen—"

She shook her head. "Tell me this, Monroe—is there actually a holiday party to cater?"

"There could be," he said, hating the way that sounded.

She turned her face. "Please leave."

Chaz's stomach tightened with pangs of regret over the way he had approached this, understanding how it must look to Kim. In his defense, he'd been smitten, for lack of a better word to describe the immediacy of his attraction to her. Had certain parts of his anatomy made him come here, under the premise of testing her work ethic? Could he have slipped that far?

She had told him to get out. What other option did he have after a command like that, except to do as she asked? His explanation hadn't swayed her. She was angry. Her eyes blazed. Kim was hurt, half-naked and feeling the need to protect herself from further harm…and he'd been less than stellar in his approach to this whole situation.

It was obvious she took into consideration things he hadn't thought over before showing up here and placing his hands on her. Also clear now, after what she'd said, was the idea that she might have opened herself to him because she truly hadn't planned on returning to her job. In that case, a liaison to explore the sparks between them would have been okay for her.

That had been ruined by one simple withheld truth.

Damn it.

"I'm attracted to you." Chaz retreated a step. "I'll confess that here and mean it. I wanted to get to know you, and still do. But what you're thinking wasn't what brought me here. I wasn't going to use you for some sordid purpose."

Her eyes met his. "Here's the thing, Monroe. Some women probably do sleep their way to the top, and I'm telling you now that I'm not one of them. In fact, it looks as though I've just kissed my way to the bottom."

His hands remained suspended in the air. Chaz had prided himself on being decent at handling people, yet had botched the hell out of this situation. He supposed that's what came of mixing lust with work.

He had known better and ignored the signs, but he wasn't an idiot or completely ruled by what was in his pants. He did comprehend her take on this predicament, and it was a damn shame, because in her mind the damage had been done, and he wasn't going to allow himself to beg her to change her mind.

A man could only go so far.

"Okay," he conceded, reaching for the doorknob. "Though you might not believe this, I am sorry the news has upset you. My purpose was never to hurt or demean you. And from everything I've heard about your job performance, you've proven your talent and superior work ethic to justify being in line for the promotion."

He really did not want to leave, especially like this. He gave her one last lingering look before opening the door, hoping she might soften. "No one needs to know about this. I'm not a kiss-and-tell kind of guy, and you can trust me on that. I've apologized. I've confessed to liking you. I guess what you do with that is up to you."

With a frown of disappointment etched on his brow, Chaz closed the door on what might have turned out to be the hottest night in history.

In the hallway, he slapped the wall and uttered a choice four-letter oath. This night had not gone well. In fact, it couldn't have been worse.

McKinley wanted him. Of that there was no doubt. She had been willing to take him in and take him on. Perhaps, now that she knew the score, she would come around. They could pretend this never happened and start over.

Or maybe not.

Seeing her at work might bring on his feelings of lust for her all over again. He wouldn't be able to touch her, talk to her privately or smell her rich fragrance up close, if she returned to the job.

Things were truly messed up, yet he couldn't go back and demand to be let back in. It was too late for that.

Sighing in frustration, he walked to the waiting elevator and stepped inside. Kim didn't open her door and call after him this time. It was like a slap in the face—the second in two hours. He didn't have to take that lying down. He shouldn't have to. He would move on and forget her.

Staring blankly at her door, Chaz rolled his shoulders. Something was definitely wrong with him. Despite arguments to the contrary, he'd already started imagining a strategy for getting Kim back, if not at the office, where she ultimately belonged, then into that baggy T-shirt he'd envisioned—and the naughty red shoes.

At the very least, he had to know what this was about, what her dislike of the holiday work meant. Research would be the key to unlocking Kim McKinley's secrets, and he had plenty of know-how at his fingertips.

"Nobody hates Christmas," he muttered as the elevator descended. "Not even you, Kim. I'll just have to prove that to you."

Kim slid down the wall, staring at the door the devil had just used to make his exit. Chaz Monroe was a monster, and she had been foolish to believe anything else.

He had almost succeeded in making her forget the hovering darkness of the season, and about men being liars when given the chance. She had been willing to share tonight with him under the waving flag of truce and the lure of the laws of man-woman attraction. And look where that had landed her.

Monroe had spoiled things, in essence tromping over her mother's grave in motorcycle boots and kicking up clods of freshly turned earth. She could hear her mother shouting *I told you so*.

Head in her hands, knees drawn to her chest, Kim sat without moving for a long time before finding the strength to get up. She had wanted so badly to believe that her mother didn't have to be right.

She walked to the kitchen and removed aluminum foil from the top of a pan on the counter. Turning slowly, she hit a lever with her bare foot and dumped the entire batch of frosted Christmas cookies into the trash.

"Lesson learned the hard way," she said, slipping out of the red dress and leaving the puddle of silk discarded on the hardwood floor.

Seven

She was supposed to be on vacation starting at noon the next day, and debated whether to show up at the office at all. After spending a sleepless night thinking about it, she had decided to go in.

If she was lucky, she'd beat Monroe to the office and be able to pick up a few things. She also needed to put the finishing touch on a project before heading out to take the vacation time due to her. At least she'd get something in terms of a paycheck before finding out if she'd have to terminate her employment.

But she was angry enough at the moment to keep the job and drive Monroe crazy, just to spite him.

Entering the building quickly, Kim hustled into the first open elevator. She got off on her floor and sighed with relief to find the hallway empty that led to the little cubicle that had been her home away from home for the last few years.

Monroe had said the next step was hers, so she'd ignore him and get on with things more or less as usual, for as long as she could. Time away would be necessary, and would allow her to set up a barrier between herself and the agency's new owner until they both cooled off. If more bad news was to come her way, it would have to find her someplace else.

In order to get unemployment money, she needed to be fired.

At the entrance to her cubicle, she stopped short. Brenda sat in her chair with her arms and legs crossed.

"You did not, in fact, call me back," Brenda said. "I worried all night."

Kim leaned a hip against what couldn't really be called

a doorjamb. It seemed there was no escaping some of what she'd hoped to avoid.

"Did you get my message?" Brenda asked.

"I got it."

"Did he show up?"

Kim nodded.

"Did you let him in?"

Kim nodded.

"Is that why you don't look so good?" Brenda asked frankly.

"Trust me, I feel even worse."

"So, you aren't going to speak to me ever again?"

The question got Kim's attention. So did the tone. "Is there a reason I shouldn't?"

"No. Well, maybe. But he swore all he wanted to do was keep you here, like I do, so I was with him on that one."

Brenda had done something bad and felt regretful—and that was the reason for her early arrival—though Brenda wouldn't have done anything to hurt her on purpose.

Kim's thoughts returned to the dress, the shoes...and then to the tape recorder Monroe had in his possession last night and her idea that he might have bugged her office in order to have captured conversations on tape.

"He got the tape from you, Bren," she said.

"Oh, crap." Brenda covered her face with her hands. "Yes, he did."

"Because?"

"I believed him. He seemed sincere when he said he wants to keep you here. I know he likes you. The way he looked at you in the bar was..."

"Inappropriate?"

"No. I don't think so," Brenda said. "Not exactly. More like he was awed."

Kim's heart shuddered with the memory of how blind-sided by Monroe's sexual magnetism she had been as she stood against that wall in her apartment with Monroe's hands and mouth all over her. After anger, embarrassment sat high on her list of emotions to avoid at night when attempting to count sheep.

She nailed Brenda with her gaze. "Cough it up, Bren. What else don't I know?"

"In his email yesterday he asked if I'd attend the meeting in the bar, then let you two work things out if the meeting went well. That's why I left. Well, that and I was trying to avoid watching you two going for the other person's jugular. Honestly, though, I wasn't sure you noticed I had gone."

"Moot point. It didn't work out, anyway," Kim said. "Monroe's a barbarian when it comes to negotiation."

And also a sexual barbarian, Kim inwardly added. The moniker probably fit, due to all those Celtic genes behind a name like *Monroe* that conjured images of men with blue faces. Marauding Vikings. People with wooden clubs.

Brenda looked up. "You're not going to do that party?"

"There was no party, Bren. I think that was a sham to see if I'd bend over backward."

Brenda's eyes went wide with surprise. She echoed Kim's word for Monroe. "Barbarian!"

"I suppose you didn't know for sure if there actually was a spur-of-the-moment holiday project?" Kim pressed.

Brenda crossed her heart with her index finger. "I most certainly don't know anything about that. I'm so sorry for having anything to do with last night. Really sorry."

Kim sighed. "It's okay. I almost fell for his line, too."

That was the hard part, the unacceptable part of this mess. She had sort of fallen for Monroe, despite his antics. She liked the angles of his handsome, slightly rugged face, and the shaggy hair surrounding it that often fell across his forehead. She liked the way his wide shoulders stretched his shirt, and the warmth of his hands on the exposed skin of her lower back.

She liked his voice and the easy way it affected her.

Heck, she might have fallen far enough to have assumed she'd be working on a project dealing with the North Pole today. If Brenda hadn't left that warning message in time, she might have ended up naked on the floor next to the new owner of this place, with nothing to show for it but a bruised backside.

The thought of that...

"What happened after you let him in?" Brenda's voice seemed distant, drowned out by the sound of Kim's heart-beat, which suddenly seemed uncharacteristically loud. It had been a mistake to think about Monroe.

"I got your message, Bren," she said, "and he left."

Brenda looked relieved. "You're still here, then? You didn't quit?"

"Not for the next several days. I'm going to take my vacation."

"This would be the first time you did."

"It's time."

Her heartbeat refused to settle down. Why?

She inhaled a breath of—not Christmas In A Can, but something else. A masculine scent. One she recognized.

Oh.

She saw her fear confirmed in the look on Brenda's face.

"There's someone behind me, isn't there?" Kim said.

"Yep."

Turning slowly, Kim's gaze met with the top button of Chaz Monroe's perfectly pressed blue- and white-striped shirt.

"Miss McKinley," Chaz said, reverting to formality to get over the shock of seeing her in the building after last night's anticlimactic rebuff.

Here she was, and he felt slightly taken aback.

"Mr. Monroe," she said, refusing to glance up at him as she took a step back.

She was perfectly tidy, dressed in a knee-length black skirt and a lavender sweater that covered her hips and other notable curves. Her fair hair fell softly toward her shoulders in a sheet of gold. The lips that had mesmerized him were freshly stained pink.

She looked ravishing. No evidence of a sleepless night showed on her face. There were no dark circles under her eyes. Not one eyelash seemed out of place. Had she dismissed him and what had nearly transpired between them so quickly, when he hadn't slept a wink? When his thoughts never strayed from her, and what he might say if she showed her pretty face on this floor?

Chaz cleared his throat. "You're working today?"

She still hadn't glanced up, though Chaz sensed she wanted to meet his eyes as much as he wanted her to. The electricity crackling between them hadn't diminished because of what had happened the night before. If anything, it was worse.

His wish list hadn't changed, he realized. His lust for this woman was now the size of a bloated balloon. Office or no office, and decorum be damned, he desired Kim McKinley more than ever. He'd start to work on that mouth of hers if given the opportunity, and torture it into a grin. He would offer half his earnings to be able to earn her smile, her trust, and to hear her laugh.

"I'm only in for an hour, then I'm off on that vacation I mentioned," she said, her voice unreasonably calm.

"Are you going someplace nice?"

"I'm going home," she said.

Brenda got to her feet, as if that were her cue to jump in. "I'll help with those last-minute details, Kim, so that you can get out of here."

They were presenting a united front against him. For

a minute, he actually envied Brenda her closeness to the woman he had come near to bedding. Again, though, it was a new day, and he'd deal.

"Okay. Have a good time." His tone was commendably casual, reflecting professional interest and nothing more. "By the way, have you decided on whether you'll be returning after that vacation?"

"I'm thinking on it. I'll be sure to let you know."

Kim's tone suggested to him that she wasn't going to let him ruin a good thing if she could help it, and also that she expected him to mind his manners if she did decide to keep her job.

Checkmate.

"Great. I'm sorry the party didn't work out for you," he said. "Maybe next time."

Kim raised her chin defiantly. Their gazes connected. Chaz rode out the next jolt that came with the blaze of inquiry he saw in those greenish eyes. He didn't want to push her buttons. Not now. Research awaited him. He had been able to access a few things about her background in those sleepless hours of the night, though nothing personal enough to give him a leg up on her issues.

"Yes. Maybe next time," she said.

He inclined his head and muttered in parting, "Ladies."

When he turned, he felt Kim's eyes on him in a gaze intense enough to burn a hole in his back. She was angrier than ever, though she looked to be in control of her emotions this morning. They were continuing to play this strange game with each other, with the outcome unclear.

This wasn't over. Not by a long shot. If she returned after that vacation, he would probably desire her more. When she left, he'd miss the spark of whatever existed between them.

Did this make him a lust-sick idiot?

He shrugged.

Back in his office, Chaz picked up the phone and hit a

number on speed dial. He hated to make this call, since he'd been trying to beat big brother Rory at his own game for more than a year…and maybe all his life. Other than his own personal need to be successful, Rory was always in the background setting the gold standard as far as the family business was concerned. Those business dealings weren't actually supposed to achieve the status of a competitive sport, but things between the brothers had turned out that way.

However, this wasn't *all* about business.

A male voice on the line answered in a brisk tone. "It's early, bro."

"I need some help, Rory. As my elder, I'm sure you're obliged to listen, in spite of the hour."

"I've been at work for three hours already, Chaz. It's not like I just got up. I call this early-rising routine CEO Stamina. It does my heart good to see that you're getting with the program."

Chaz sat back in his chair. "I need some intel."

"On a company?"

"On a woman."

Rory chuckled without bothering to hide it. "Well, that's a first. But you do know how to use the internet?"

"Tried that, and nothing pertinent turned up. I'd like to use your information source."

"Must be an interesting woman," Rory remarked.

"She's an employee."

"Do you suspect agency espionage?"

"I suspect she might have an interesting background that forces the issue of a contractual dispute."

"Is this employee attractive?" Rory asked.

"Would that matter to your source?"

"Nope. Does it matter to you?" Rory countered.

"Nope. So do I have your permission to contact Sarah?"

"With my blessing. And bro?"

"Yeah?"

"What's your ETA for getting that agency ready to flip? I have another business you might be interested in when you get the money out of your first big acquisition."

Hell, he had only owned this agency for a week.

"Still working on it," he said. "It's too early to tell how long it might take."

"Well, it doesn't pay to hang on for too long. You might become vested and actually see yourself as the head of a firm. Buy, fix and sell is the key."

"The family mantra," Chaz agreed, unwilling to think about the ramifications of Kim finding out he had planned all along to sell the company once it was on its feet.

"Want some more unasked-for advice?" Rory said.

"I'm all ears."

"Mom would appreciate a call now and then. She says it's been two weeks."

"Wherever does time go?" Chaz muttered before disconnecting.

That hadn't gone too badly.

As for Kim, he didn't really owe her anything. He just wanted to play fair. In pursuit of fairness, he'd get the intel on her lined up. Sarah Summers was Rory's secret weapon for finding things out. A grad student at M.I.T., Sarah specialized in what amounted to cloak-and-dagger information trading. She might be considered a hacker for her rogue-like pursuits, but no one was quite sure how she did what she did, and the results were more than satisfying. Over the last couple years, her reports had added a lot of bucks to the Monroe family business coffers.

If Kim had anything in her background to find, Sarah would be the one to find it. Chaz didn't need any more office intrigue or rumors spreading about that casting couch Kim mentioned. The situation would be out of his hands until Sarah got back to him. In the meantime, Kim would be gone, and he'd be able to keep his mind where it belonged…on business. Definitely not on McKinley's ultra-hot body, or the look in her eyes when Brenda's call had come in last night—the look showcasing betrayal and pain.

Other than Kim and Brenda, not one person at the agency knew he had bought this company in order to turn a quick profit, and that he hadn't planned on remaining here for long. He sure as hell didn't plan on becoming too comfortable, or being overly involved with employees' personalities. He had just inadvertently gotten stuck on the issue of a very tempting blonde.

After the sale, and after he departed, Kim might gain access to the job she coveted. Win-win? He'd move on, and she'd move up. If she got her promotion with somebody else in charge, he'd be off the hook, and this would work in his favor in terms of the possibility of getting to know her better.

That scenario might, in fact, solve everything.

But, his annoying inner chatter reminded him, Kim would probably still have to capitulate on the holiday clause in her contract, or risk being overlooked for the promotion by the next owner. She'd be hurt all over again. She'd be crushed.

Interestingly enough, he couldn't stand the thought of Kim suffering.

He had gone soft.

It looked a lot like Chaz Monroe cared too much about his employees already. Some of them, anyway.

One of them.

Chaz rubbed his temple as he stared at the phone. Certainly it appeared as though big brother Rory didn't linger for long on those kinds of things. If he did, he never spoke about it, or let on. Then again, it was entirely possible that Rory wasn't human. Did Chaz actually want to emulate the successful business profile of an alien?

He absently tapped on the desk with his fingers. He had not lied to anyone here. Owners went undercover all the time to ferret out business details. With the agency running smoothly and well in the black, the next owner would be crazy not to keep things the way they were.

As for Kim, the best thing for her and his conscience both would be to help her in any way he could, and then back away. He'd have to shelve his feelings for her in order to make sure she got what she deserved. And okay, so he was way too addicted to her. He could hide that, get over that.

At least he could try.

Leaning forward, he punched another number into the phone and waited until someone picked up. "Mom," he said, "about that party..."

Eight

"**S**he's gone," Brenda said when Chaz appeared in her cubicle an hour later. It was probably just as well, he decided, because he hadn't actually thought out what he'd say to her now that he was here.

In spite of the arguments and his sense of fairness where Kim was concerned, he wasn't ready to just let her go away, maybe for good, without dealing with her future at the agency. Until he heard back from his intel source, he was willing to try to change her mind on this holiday issue one more time. The Monroes never backed away from a good fight, especially if there was a reward at the end.

"Fine," he said to Brenda, reordering his thoughts on the new challenge and how he'd have to play it. "It's you I came to see, anyway. Can you help me in Kim's place with the party event?"

Brenda raised an eyebrow. "The party that is no party?"

"Oh, there's a party, all right. Did she tell you there wasn't?"

Brenda swiveled in her chair. "Now I'm confused. But just so you know, I won't do anything else that involves my best friend's feelings for you or her job."

Chaz withheld a grin. "She has feelings for me?"

"You don't want to know about the name-calling," Brenda replied. "From both of us."

"I suppose I deserved that for my behavior at her apartment, but there is a party, and I do need help. Can I count on you?"

Brenda blinked slowly. "Depends. Are you offering the same deal you gave Kim? Time off after the holidays and a nice bonus?"

"Yes. Okay. Same deal."

"You'll sign that in blood? Your blood?"

"Brenda, I might remind you that I'm the owner of this place and have something better than blood."

"Power?"

He smiled.

"And we're not supposed to know about you owning the agency, or let that get around, right?" Brenda said sheepishly. "Though a couple of us do know that?"

"You're a heartbreaker, Chang. I had no idea blackmail made the world go around."

"I believe I said *nice* bonus."

"To which I agreed."

"So, will you appear at my apartment if I refuse, and…?"

"Never. That's a promise."

"Darn." Brenda smiled back. "Oh well, with an offer like that, how can I refuse? I may have to use the bonus to help support my friend if she leaves the job."

"I'm not sure Kim would like our deal," he said.

"I'm positive she won't," Brenda agreed. And the really good part, Chaz knew, was that Brenda wouldn't be able to resist running to Kim with this bit of news. He only hoped that Kim might react the way he hoped she would, and face him down. Again. At least he'd get more time with her if that happened.

Fighting with her was better than not seeing her at all, he had just that minute decided. *At least in theory.*

Kim hustled to the floor beneath her office, where the art department had their space. Just one more detail to take care of, and Monroe would be out of her hair for at least seven days. She wouldn't have to think about him, dream about him or convince herself to despise him.

Going home to her mother's meant dealing with things she had been avoiding since her mother's death. She hadn't set foot in that house since, and had dreaded going there for ages before that.

Because Kim was an only child, the house and all of her mother's belongings were now hers. She should have relished combing through her mother's things for remembered treasures. The fact that she didn't look forward to it piled on more guilt.

She read somewhere that emotions can attach to objects, and she wanted nothing that might remind her of the problems they had shared. Had she loved her mother? Absolutely, and maybe too much. Witnessing the level of her mom's nearly constant self-inflicted pain and suffering had become too much for one daughter to bear. She hadn't been able to keep up with the treatments and the arguments and the ups and downs of her mother's diagnosis of clinical depression.

This was the season that had kicked off the whole thing in the first place. December. Christmas. Betrayal. Would those things be contagious with her mother gone? Did houses retain the sorrow and joys of the people who had lived in them, or would her mother's house be just a house, empty and waiting to be dealt with?

She had given that house six months to let loose of its old memories and feelings. It was high time she dealt with this.

The art department had been waiting for her, and took less time than she had anticipated to finish up what she needed. On her way out, someone stopped her with a painting on a piece of white cardboard and a question.

"Do you like this rendering?" Mark Ogilvie asked, showing her the board. "It was done super quickly, but I thought I'd run it by you before you left on vacation."

"Sorry, Mark?" Kim took the board.

"The special Christmas party you and Brenda are doing as a favor to Monroe."

"I'm not sure what you're talking about." Kim flipped

the board upright. It took her a minute to understand what she was seeing. Then it dawned. On that board was a watercolor rendering of the party Monroe had asked her to do. The party that she believed wasn't really a party, and a complete sham.

Decorated tables, wrapped packages, ice sculptures, servers dressed up like elves—all of this had been painted in sparkling detail from Mark's artistic point of view, and it was a beautiful, magical wonderland.

Her heart stuttered. She sucked in a breath. Closing her eyes briefly, Kim handed the painting back to Mark. "This has nothing to do with me. Sorry."

He looked perplexed. "Can you get it to Brenda then, if you're on your way back up? She requested it about twenty minutes ago as a top priority."

"I don't think Brenda…" Kim didn't finish the protest. "Twenty minutes ago, you said?"

"She told me to show it to you on your way out. She made me promise to catch you before you reached the elevator."

Kim forced a smile. "Okay. Thanks. This looks terrific, Mark. I'll take it right up to her. I'm sure Brenda will tell you the same thing."

It took every ounce of strength she possessed to walk toward the elevator with the painting in hand. Brenda had given her a heads-up on some new turn in the tide, and this painting said it all. Monroe was at it again, with Brenda this time.

Had Brenda somehow fallen for his line? After not getting his way with her, had Monroe moved on to her friend with hopes of luring Brenda into bed?

"Monster!"

When the elevator arrived, Kim got on, punched the floor button with the edge of the painting and clenched her teeth. Monroe's antics were so unacceptable they were the definition of ludicrous. She wasn't going to take this lying down. Neither would Brenda.

She wasn't going back to Cubicle City. She'd ram this painting down Chaz Monroe's throat for causing yet another hitch in her exit strategy.

"Monster," she repeated, causing two other employees occupying the elevator with her to glance her way. "Brute."

Surely Brenda wouldn't fall for his nonsense after their conversation on the matter of Monroe's lack of integrity and business ethics. Brenda wouldn't have provided this heads-up if Brenda hadn't known the score.

She stormed out of the elevator, strode briskly to the offices and past Monroe's secretary, Alice.

"Kim?" Alice said, standing up.

"Personal matter," Kim tossed back as she reached for the door handle of the office that should have been hers, but now kept the king of jerks tucked inside.

Monroe was there. He stood with his back to the window, watching her as she entered. He was looking more attractive than she had allowed herself to remember from only an hour ago.

Propelled by the thrashing heartbeat in her chest and an uncontrollable wish to see Monroe squirm, Kim crossed to the desk and tossed the painting on top of it.

"What do you think you're doing?" she demanded, sounding winded. "One partial conquest isn't enough for you? You'd suck my best friend into your web, too? What I want to know is if you're doing this to get back at me, or if you're some kind of fiend? Sex fiend, maybe? I'd truly like to understand your actions. I'd like to know how far your lies usually get you."

She saw her mistake as soon as she'd said those words. Monroe wasn't alone. A woman sat in the leather chair beside the desk.

A chill ran down the back of her neck as Kim looked at

the woman, who without standing up said, "You must be Kim McKinley. I'm Dana Monroe. Chaz's mother."

"I…" Words failed Kim. "Excuse me."

She was really damn glad that the door was still open when she turned to rush through.

Chaz steeled his determination not to go after Kim, though he very badly wanted to. The blonde whirlwind had made his heart double up on beats.

"Feisty," his mother said, eyeing him instead of the doorway Kim had fled through. "Witnessing that little tantrum was part of the reason you asked me to rush over here, I suppose?"

"No. Not exactly. But thanks for coming, Mom. Lucky for me you were headed across the street when I called."

"Sex fiend, Chaz?"

"It's a long story."

"You've known her for how long, and she already knows your secrets?"

Chaz grinned. "Those kinds of things might be Rory's secrets, but not mine."

She waved a hand. "That's the woman you'd like to keep?"

"She is good enough at what she does to occupy this office someday."

"Yes, well, I hope she doesn't talk to everyone like that, or I fear there won't be any clients left."

He shrugged. "She's mad at me for being here, in this office, on this floor."

"That's all she's angry about?"

"Possibly not. Again, long story. So, the party is still on?"

"Everyone loves a good party, Chaz, including me. Hand me that picture, and I'll make some calls. I won't be stepping on anyone's toes by putting this together myself?"

"No toes."

"This is all for her? For McKinley?"

Chaz lowered his voice. "I have a feeling it might be the first Christmas party she has ever attended. If I can get her there, that is. She has a sad spot that surfaces when the holiday is mentioned."

"This is a goodwill effort on your part, then?"

"You could say that, yes."

"All right." His mother stood up and waited for Chaz to give her a peck on the cheek. "My sons know I'd do anything for them, and if it's a goodwill mission, so much the better."

On her way out, she paused to get in a longer last word. "You should probably spend less time with Rory. Whatever he has might be starting to rub off on you."

Dressed as well as any woman of substance in New York, diamond earrings, fur-trimmed suit and all, his mother said her farewells and left. Alice filled the doorway soon afterward.

"I suppose you were eavesdropping?" Chaz said.

Alice made a zipping motion across her lips and tossed away an invisible key.

"I suppose you'll be expecting a nice bonus, too, to keep that zipper zipped?" Chaz asked.

Despite the drama of the mouth-closing routine, Alice was able to speak. "Not necessary, since I'm only doing my job."

"Well, that's a relief," Chaz muttered as the door closed, sealing him off from some of the most enigmatic women to ever cross an office threshold.

As a matter of fact, he was starting to feel a little funny about that.

Now, he thought, turning back to his desk, if Sarah would call with that intel report on Kim, he might actually have a leg to stand on.

Big reminder here: he had only been in this office for a few days, and his mind had been hijacked for the last two by a woman he wanted to help as much as he wanted to...

Well, until Sarah called, maybe he could get some official work done, and be of use.

Glancing out the window, he smiled. "Hopefully, it will be a merry Christmas, Kim," he whispered as the phone beside him rang and Sarah Summers's number lit up the screen.

Brenda was waiting for Kim in the elevator and pulled the red Stop button once she had entered.

"I've been riding these things up and down for the last twenty minutes, changing elevators every five," Brenda said.

"Thanks for the warning," Kim managed to say before resting her head against the gray metallic wall. "Shall I warn you about him in more detail, Bren?"

"You're kidding, right?"

"Actually, no."

"You imagine I was born yesterday, or that I can't read between the lines? I'm hurt that you'd think I could be a traitor to our friendship, which means more to me than this job."

Kim smiled weakly, thinking about the tape recorder Brenda had given to Monroe.

"So, you're going home?" Brenda asked. "To your mother's house? Would you like me to come with you?"

"Thanks, but no thanks. You said yourself that it's time I face my demons."

"It's the season for joy, Kim," Brenda said. "You could wait until next month to confront those buggers."

"I don't think I have an option. It's now or never, or this might never be behind me. I can see that now."

They were silent as the remark soaked in.

"I won't help him," Brenda said. "I had Mark do the work, and promised that he would get the bonus."

Kim nodded.

"They're not all scoundrels, no matter what you tend to believe," Brenda continued. "The fact that Monroe is attracted to you doesn't mean he's a creep or that he can help it."

"You're taking his side?"

"I'm presenting both sides of what's going on without addressing what's at the core of all this."

"Which is me facing or not facing this damn holiday."

"Yes, and it's good that you know it."

Brenda was right. She had gone along with this fear of Christmas for the past few years, always rallying for Kim and helping to protect her—until now, when the time for frankness and real concern had finally arrived.

"Possibly going home will help," Kim said.

"If you need me, call."

Kim pressed the button. Instead of the elevator moving, the door opened. Chaz Monroe stood there, a serious expression on his devastatingly fine, chiseled face.

Nine

"Jeez. You'd think there were only three of us in the entire building," Brenda quipped, looking back and forth from Kim to Monroe.

"Will you please excuse us for a minute, Brenda?" Monroe said.

Kim stood very still, afraid to say more of what was on her mind after doing so in his office, in front of one of his family members. In all honesty, she didn't feel angry anymore, anyway; she felt drained. Dealing with Monroe had already taken its toll, and it seemed that toll kept on climbing.

"Kim?" Brenda awaited word on what to do.

"It's okay, Bren. I've got this."

Without further protest, Brenda left the elevator.

The door closed.

Monroe faced her from a distance of two feet; close enough for her to reach out and touch if she dared to confront the feelings she had tamped down in an effort to retain her dignity and sense of self. If she lost that sense of self, she feared what might happen. Would the past bring up trouble or be left behind in favor of something worse?

"I'm sorry," Monroe said, out of the blue.

The apology surprised her. She hadn't expected him to be so frank and straightforward, and had to distrust him, still.

More questions surfaced, like bubbles rising to the top of water, all of them concerning the man across from her.

If she were to start over, to leave the darkness in the distance, would she be setting herself up for a fall?

If she confessed to liking Monroe more than she should

after knowing him for a mere two days—the same man that had teased her, kept things from her and then made her overheat with pleasure on more than one occasion—he might act upon that weakness and take further advantage.

If he realized how difficult it was for her to keep her hands off him, he might throw her against the wall and kiss everything from her lips to her berry-colored toes. Too much kissing, fondling and overheating sexually would mean that their relationship, however temporary, might fizzle equally as fast as it began. Flames this hot tended to burn out quickly. If that happened, her secret dread of ending up like her mother, holed up in a house and simmering in defeat, year after year, alone, would reappear as a possibility.

Tendencies for depression and mental instability sometimes ran in families, she had read. Though she had successfully avoided the symptoms, fear of them had more or less made her an emotional hermit.

The good thing—if there was a good thing to be found here—was that she knew how flawed she was.

"Sorry?" she echoed, wondering if Monroe was sorry for the pressure he was putting on her over her contract or the seductive heat he caused.

Did he regret last night?

"I know I have a problem," she admitted, though the confession was difficult. "I've been trying to work it out, but it hurts me to do so. You'll have to take my word that this isn't some game I'm playing, and that I've protested the change in my contract in earnest."

"Can we forget the blasted contract for a minute?" he said.

Kim glanced up at him from beneath her lashes.

"I'm not using you," he went on. "I didn't comprehend how serious this holiday thing was for you, and had to push for what the company needed. So I tested you, yes, but with good intentions, as I said last night."

His expression confirmed his seriousness. The angles of his face were shadowed. He looked as if he hadn't slept, as if he also had tossed and turned, going over the events that had transpired and regretting not being honest earlier.

Was the elevator to become a confessional booth for issues that could be addressed right then in the secluded space, with no one else present? Personal confessions?

"I need time to process problems in my past," she said. "You've helped to make that clear, though I've known it all along. But because I might be vulnerable in my personal life doesn't equate to weakness in my professional ethics. It's just one thing that I need to deal with. Don't you have something you'd like to leave behind, even though it might be tough?"

"Yes," he said then added, "I'm sure everyone has something like that to face."

"It's easier when you have a family to back you up, though," she said. "As well as enough money to buy a company where you can set your own rules."

He took his time before responding. "There is a lot of risk involved with these investments. Not to mention stress," he said. "This has been an extraordinary few days, and I'll say one more time that I don't want the company to lose you. Will you agree to stay after all is said and done? Will knowing you have your job help with whatever it is you're going to do this week?"

Kim shook her head to hide the fact that the rest of her shook, as well. She felt something for this man, but wasn't sure what. The sensations had come on too quickly, were too intense and all-consuming. Their relationship had started with anger and ended with heat.

Last night had been over the top, for as long as it lasted. Monroe's body, his attention and his talents had caught her up, making her forget everything else that stood between them. But those moments of free fall had been ruined, and now she felt unsettled. The simplicity of an emotion like anger no longer fit or covered the situation. She wasn't sure what did.

She lifted her gaze to the level of his chin. "I'm sorry I said those things in front of your mother. That was inexcusable."

"I think my mother liked you. She called you feisty."

Kim blinked slowly to block out the scene.

"We don't have to talk now," he said. "Do whatever you need to do to fix what you have going on. Just don't count me as another problem to face, okay?"

"Are you offering to forget about the contract?"

"I can't forget it in a potential vice president. I know you understand that, and that I have to do what's best for the agency."

"What is it you want, then? Friendship?"

"Yes, if that's what it takes to keep you here. And no if I'm being completely truthful."

Kim's gaze rose higher. She didn't want to be his friend, either, though that might not have been possible anyway, given the intensity of their connection. Despite trying to repress her feelings, she imagined what his hands would again feel like on her bare back, and how his lips might again sweep her away if she and Monroe dared to allow the sparks between them to dictate their future actions.

Kissing him last night had seemed right. In his arms nothing else had existed for a while, beyond two flames merging.

Now...

Now they were embarrassed and taken aback by their behavior, and he wanted to mend the situation.

"We are having the party," he said. "It's my family's holiday celebration. I thought you should know that we're going to utilize all the ideas you and I talked about in the bar, and more. You don't have to be a part of planning, Kim, but I'd like you to attend."

"As your disgruntled employee whose covert nickname is Scrooge?"

"As my guest."

"I can't commit to that right now."

"Then you can give me your answer later. Maybe after a couple days off, you'll accept."

"Besides, I couldn't possibly be welcome after your mother witnessed the drama in your office," Kim said.

"On the contrary, my family thrives on drama. Trust me, you'd fit right in."

Kim fisted her hands, ready to get away from him and the things still left unsaid. Confusion reigned. She wanted to take a step forward, yet she couldn't allow it. She wanted to forget the past, but that past remained tied to her by a few tenacious threads. Relationship avoidance was one of them.

People got hurt if they fell hard and heaped love on one another, only to eventually have that love lost. Depression sometimes took over a lovesick soul. She had seen it happen firsthand.

She might like Monroe if she allowed herself to. She might have been able to love him someday, had the situation been different and she met him elsewhere.

"I'll send you the details," he said, bringing her out of her thoughts.

"You have a habit of refusing to take no for an answer," she said softly.

"Only where it concerns me personally, and I feel as though I have a stake in the outcome."

Of course, by personal, he was talking about his business, not about her. She had to keep that in mind. Monroe had to do what was best for the agency. His agency. Inviting her to the party was a final parting shot before sending her back to her cubicle.

He added, "If keeping you means hands-off, then that's the way it will be. However, I'm not lying to you when I say that I'd like to kiss you right now. Hell, I'd like to do much more than that, and take up where we left off last night. I will also tell you this, Kim. I have never invited a woman to my parents' home. You'd be the first. My guest. Night of fun. Truce in place."

She didn't have time to reply, and wasn't sure how to, anyway. The door opened with a whooshing sound. A wave of cooler air swirled around them. Kim didn't move until the doors started to close again and Monroe stepped in the way, a move that brought him closer to her and ensured that she had to touch him when she left the elevator.

Kim's motionless body brimmed with longing for the man she should be wary of. He was the boss, and she fully comprehended his problem with her. If getting the most out of the agency meant having management that oversaw every aspect of it, she was not that candidate.

Because she understood that, she also realized that Chaz Monroe wasn't the bad guy here, after all. She was disappointed about the job, but her anger with him had been misplaced.

The doors started to close, pushing at Monroe's wide shoulders. As she brushed past him, her left arm touched his. The charge that careened through her was powerful enough to bring on a gasp. The urge to turn to him, get close to him, walk right into the circle of his arms, was so strong, she stiffened. And in her peripheral vision, she watched his hands mirror hers, fisting so that he wouldn't catch her, change his mind and throw her against the gleaming metal.

And how she wanted him to do that, in spite of everything.

She paused close enough to him to feel his breath on her

forehead. Close enough that all she had to do was look up, and her lips would be within reach of his. The sensations running through her were blatant reminders that she really did feel something for this man.

"It should be easy to agree." Her voice caught. She sought his eyes, her pulse thudding hard. "When doing so might solve everything for a while."

"Maybe you will come to the party as a start toward a mutually beneficial future," he said. "I'm rooting for that."

He didn't grab her or kiss her, though Kim felt the pressure of that imaginary kiss as if he had overpowered her completely. She nearly backpedaled into the tiny space to make sure he did; almost asked him for a repeat of the mindless hunger that every cell in her body craved.

But Monroe moved out of the way, holding the door with one hand so that she could leave the elevator without further contact that would have spoken volumes about what they wanted to do to each other.

She had no alternative but to go.

Once she had passed him, Monroe stepped back inside and smiled at her earnestly, devastatingly, tiredly, as the elevator doors closed and the contraption took him from her, leaving her standing in the hallway.

Dozens of employees went about their business all around her, doing their jobs, unaware of the turmoil roiling through Kim that for one more brief moment made her need a wall for support.

Ten

Kim stood on the sidewalk, staring at the house. In the late-afternoon sun, the two-story brick structure had a forlorn appearance. Not shabby, exactly, but uncared for, unkempt.

Dark windows punctuated the 1940s brick cottage. On the front porch sat a collection of empty clay pots that had once contained pink geraniums to brighten the place. The small lawn was neatly trimmed, and a concrete walkway had been swept clear of debris. She'd seen to that by hiring a neighbor kid, who had taken the job seriously, though not once in the past six months had she thought to check.

"Welcome home, Kim," she said to herself.

She picked up her small suitcase. Though the house in New Jersey was merely a half an hour's train ride from her apartment, she planned to stay during her vacation.

It was several minutes before she took the first step up that walkway. Kim had to consciously remember that times here hadn't always been dark, and that angst hadn't always ruled the space between those walls. There had been good times. Fun times. Lighter moments. She had loved her mother, doted on her mother, until very near to the end when others took over the daily routine. Her mother had loved her back, to the best of her ability. It was just that her mother must have loved the husband that had long ago disappeared, more.

The windows, devoid of holiday trappings, were not welcoming. The blinds were drawn to keep out the world, and possibly to keep the old darkness contained.

Kim set her shoulders. This trip home was about coming to terms with those moments of darkness and banishing them for good. Harboring guilt about the past was unreasonable, unhealthy and getting in the way of living her life the way she wanted to.

It wasn't Monroe's fault that this confrontation had come up. She had meant to take care of this ages ago.

She wished now that she'd taken Brenda up on her offer of company. Having a friend along would have been preferable to facing some ghosts solo. But she was a woman now, no longer an impressionable child. She'd inform this house and its ghosts of her plans to let in the light and dust away cobwebs. Her presence might reinforce the good times.

If Monroe wanted a hassle-free associate, he'll soon have one, she thought as she blinked slowly and gritted her teeth. Then she headed up the walkway, determined to see this housewarming through, trying hard to keep her thoughts from turning to charming Chaz Monroe, and finding that task way too difficult.

Chaz could not sit down. He paced his office, stopping now and then to gaze out the window. Each time he did, he noted as many holiday details on the street below as he could from this height, and also took stock of the clouds rolling in to ease the transition from evening to night.

Each detail brought Kim to mind with the heft of a full mental takeover.

He had picked up the phone twice in the past fifteen minutes to call her, or Brenda Chang, or damn it, anyone else who knew Kim. Deep down inside him was a feeling of emptiness, of being lost and cast adrift.

He had rudely passed Alice without a word on his way to the water cooler not half an hour ago, and that had not gone down well with Alice. She had ignored him ever since.

He knew all too well the word Rory would have used for this current agitated state. *Whipped.*

Did that describe him, at this point, and the sensation of being helpless to fix things in light of Kim's fast exit?

He was acting as if she had become an obsession, when there were plenty of other women in New York, and plenty of years to find them. McKinley, with her obstinate refusal to meet his terms, was a pain in his backside.

He kept telling himself that, over and over.

In all fairness, though, she had confessed to having problems and had spoken honestly about the possibility of facing them. So, what did that make him for wishing she'd hurry up and do so, when he now knew a few of the reasons that might have contributed to how messed up she felt this time of year? Sarah Summers had been thorough with the few details she dug up for him.

Kim was alone. He sympathized with her lack of family. The Monroes were a tight clan. His mother and father were together after forty years of marriage, with a loving relationship still going strong. His sister, Shannon, had found her guy after her first year at Harvard and settled down with a ring on her finger by the time of her graduation last year. Rory was…Rory.

His family life wasn't perfect. Whose was? Yet they were supportive in the fierceness of their loyalty to each other. Their time together, though rare these days, was always a welcome delight.

What if, like Kim, he had no family? No brothers or sisters. No mother and father to use for backup. Taking that further, what if after working hard to gain traction in his career, some newcomer suddenly threatened to derail that career?

He leaned against the windowsill, deep in thought. Kim's father was probably alive, but lost to her. The man had filed for divorce when she was a kid. Intel said that Kim's mother had gone in and out of hospitals after the divorce, until Deborah McKinley passed away earlier this year. Had

those things—the divorce and being left by her husband—
been the cause of Kim's mother's prolonged illness?

That would have been hard enough to take, but nothing he had found explained why this holiday in particular
got to Kim, and how it got her down. He needed to know
about this. He had to understand what lay at the root of her
dislike for the season. If as an only child, things had been
bad with her mother, had some of her mother's depression
rubbed off on Kim in ways that continued to show up?

With a quick glance at his watch, Chaz hustled out of
the office, grabbing his jacket from the chair by the door.
There was only one person who could help him out by
filling in a few more blanks. He had to persuade Brenda
to talk, knowing her to be Kim's best friend, and that it
wouldn't be easy.

Kim climbed the stairs to her old bedroom and dropped
her bag on the floor. The room smelled stale. Dust covered
every available surface. The really scary thing was how
nothing else had changed. Her bedroom remained exactly
the same after all this time, yet another example of her late
mother's need for pattern and constancy.

"I refuse to feel bad about the state of the place. I do not
live here anymore."

She heard no answering voice in the empty house, only
silence. The place felt cold. Outside temperatures had plum-
meted, and the inside of the house matched.

"Next stop, the furnace." She spoke out loud to ward
off the silence.

On her way downstairs, she passed her mother's room.
The door was closed, and she left it that way, preferring
comfort to memory at the moment, and believing her recent mental adjustments to be good signs of being on the
road to recovery.

"Thermostat up. Check."

To her relief, the furnace kicked on. She took this as another good omen, and headed for the kitchen, which would have been in pristine condition, except for the layer of dust.

Glad now that she hadn't turned off the electricity or gas, Kim took one good glance at the room where she and her mother had cooked and then dined at the small square table against the wall, preferring the warm kitchen to the formal dining room.

She opened a few cupboards and the refrigerator then headed upstairs for her purse. Kitchens needed to be stocked, and her stomach hadn't stopped growling. She couldn't recall the last time she'd eaten, or sat down for a meal. The hours spent in her apartment always seemed rushed, with lots of takeout Chinese.

She used to like to cook. Her mother, during her good spells, had taught her. Baking became her favorite, though those cookies she dumped last night had been her first foray into trying out those skills in years. *Christmas cookies...*

Well, she had plenty of time now to explore her talents. With a few days off, she'd get back in the groove and whip up something good. A roast, maybe, with vegetables. She'd clean up the house and make it sparkle before putting it up for sale with the hope that some family might be happier here than she and her mother were. Like most people, she supposed houses needed love and attention in order to feel homey. She'd see to that.

But first, groceries.

She'd change her clothes, walk to the market a block over, and be back before dark if she hustled. There'd be time to thoroughly clean the kitchen after she got something in the oven. She would have to learn to slow down in measured increments. She felt all riled up. She wasn't used to off-time from work, though her plan to fix up the house would occupy her for a while.

Plus, she was happy to note, she hadn't thought about

Monroe much in the last ten minutes. That also meant headway.

Damn his handsome hide. She'd see to it that running away from Chaz Monroe would turn out to be productive....

"Brenda?"

She did a slow rotation in her chair and looked at Chaz warily.

"You're working late," he said.

"If this job was nine to five, Mr. Monroe, maybe I'd have time for a date."

Alice had been right about Brenda, who obviously shared none of Kim's abhorrence of the season. A miniature Christmas tree sat on her desk, wrapped with blinking lights and tiny ornaments. Tinsel garlands hung between two bookshelves. The cubicle retained a faint smell of evergreen.

Chaz waved a hand at the tree. "Does she come in here?"

"Not this time of year." Brenda did not pretend to misunderstand whom he was talking about.

"You don't push your ideas on her?"

"She's my friend and has a right to her own opinions."

Chaz sat on the edge of her desk, looking at the wall separating Kim's cubicle from this one.

"You seem to be worried about her," Brenda said.

"Aren't you?"

She eyed him as if sizing him up. "She's a big girl and will get on with her life as she sees fit."

"She's sad, I think."

Brenda did not respond to his diagnosis of Kim's state of mind.

"Do you know what problems she has with the holiday, Brenda?" he asked.

"Sorry, can't talk about that. I promised."

"Yet I get the impression you'd like to help her somehow."

Brenda sighed. "Of course I'd like to help her out of the current mess she's in. I'm not insensitive to what's going on."

"But you believe that nothing, other than her job here, is my business?"

"That's right. I'm sorry."

Chaz stood up. "Fair enough. Can you tell me something, though, that might help? Anything?"

"I doubt it. So will you fire me for protecting my friend's privacy?"

"Only if I was the monster everyone seems to think I am."

"Are you saying you're not?"

He smiled. "I'm pretty hopeful that Kim might be the only one who thinks so."

"Yet you want more information from me so that you can do what?"

"Whittle away at her resolve," he replied.

"Which part of that resolve? The contract, or staying away from you?"

"I like her," Chaz said. "More than I should."

Brenda took a beat to think that over. "What makes you think whittling can work?"

"Because of something I just recalled about her apartment last night that I can't forget."

"What?"

"Last night her apartment smelled like cookies."

Brenda waved a hand in the air to dismiss the remark. "That tells you something, how?"

"Sugar cookies hold a fragrance unique to this holiday in particular," he said. "I grew up with that smell. It's unmistakable and always makes my mouth water. Sugar cookies are a Christmas staple. Even old Claus himself can't resist them."

Brenda took another minute to reply. Chaz watched her mull that information over. "Could have been something else, and you are mistaken," she suggested. "Could have been chocolate chip."

"I'm not wrong about that one thing," he said. "She had baked those cookies pretty near to Christmas. My question for you is if that's usual, and if Kim bakes all the time?"

Brenda's brow creased. Chaz noted how much she hated answering that question.

"I've never known her to bake anything," she admitted.

He nodded and asked the other question plaguing him. "Then how is it that a person who shuns the season and all of its trappings would bake Christmas cookies, especially after having it out with her boss about a holiday clause in her contract?"

Brenda, Chaz realized, was not at a loss. Rebounding from the cookie inquisition, she said, "If you're right about the cookies, it means she's trying."

"Trying to what?"

"Move on."

"Regarding the holiday?"

"In regard to everything."

Chaz glanced again at the wall between the cubicles. "Thank you, Brenda. That's all I needed to know."

She stopped him with a hand on his arm. "It's not all you need to know, and I can't tell you the rest."

"I know about her mother," he said. "And also about her father leaving early on."

"Maybe you do, but the story goes much deeper than that for Kim."

"Yet you won't help me to understand what that story is."

"My lips are necessarily sealed."

"Nevertheless, it's possible that she might be attempting

to deal with change. In the elevator, she told me she wants to. You do think she is seriously open to trying?"

Brenda nodded tentatively. "I do. But you're pushing her, you know. There's a chance you'll push too far."

"I feel as though I need to get to the bottom of this. I'm not completely insensitive. I have feelings, too. I like her. I've admitted that. And I know how to sell a project."

"Kim's not a project. She's a person."

"Yes," he agreed. "A special one."

Brenda looked to the hallway. "I get that you like her, yet I'm not sure you should be poking around where you don't belong, or that your interest can speed things up."

"I can only try to make things better. I won't purposefully hurt her. That much I'll swear to you right now. Any time you want to jump in and help my cause, you'd be more than welcome."

Brenda dropped her hand.

"I suppose," Chaz said, "it might not be a good idea to tell Kim about this conversation. Knowing where your loyalty lies, I'm asking for your trust in the matter."

Brenda looked terribly conflicted when he left her. He heard her say behind him, "You have feelings, huh? I certainly hope you prove that."

Eleven

An hour and a half after getting back from the market, the kitchen had filled with the delicious smell of a roast cooking. Pile a few carrots on, a cut-up potato and some broth, and the atmosphere of the house had already changed for the better. The place had started to feel lived in.

Kim wore an apron, which she figured officially earned her the title of Miss Homebody for the next few days. She had already scrubbed away at the layer of dust piled everywhere in the kitchen and dining room, and mopped the floors. Keeping busy was the key to kicking off this hiatus from her daily routine. She was used to being busy all the time. In advertising, there was little if any downtime because the mind had to constantly be on the move.

Wasn't there an old saying about idle hands?

She set the table for one and opened a bottle of wine to let it breathe, as the woman in the market had recommended. With no wineglasses in the house, she washed out a teacup and tried to recall when she had last dated. Thanksgiving week? Maybe nearer to Halloween? Could it have been as far back as Valentine's Day? She never went out after Thanksgiving, and tended not to look at men at all until after the New Year had rung in. Being anti-holiday had always been difficult to explain.

Clearly though, meeting Chaz Monroe brought home the fact that she'd been alone for too long. Being so very physically connected to him likely was the result of having saved herself from any kind of personal contact for a while. That's why her body and her raging hormones had been perfectly willing to allow Monroe's talented hands and mouth to take her over.

She might be flawed, but she was a woman, with a woman's needs. Monroe had made that all too obvious.

The cup rattled on the table when she set it down. *Monroe*. There he was again, in her thoughts, seeping through the cracks of her determination not to think about him.

Merely the idea of him set off physical alarms. Her neck began to tingle as if his lips touched her there in a soft, seductive nuzzle. Her back muscles tightened with the memory of the red dress's zipper inching down slowly to grant him access to her naked, heated skin.

There was something so damn sexy about a zipper.

She took hold of the back of the chair and tossed her head to negate those memories, tired of feeling torn by them and believing she was a freak. She refused to let all the pent-up emotion she'd withheld for so long come to a head before she'd spent one night in her mother's home.

"Facing this house has to be the first step," she said aloud to set that objective in stone. "If I can do this, I can tackle anything."

She got to work. When she had finished cleaning the dining room, she moved to the living room. Dusting, vacuuming, plumping pillows, she worked up a sweat. Finally satisfied that she'd done all she could for the moment to make the place habitable, she saw to her dinner.

Seated at the small table in the kitchen, she poured the wine. Without the talent to discern if it was good wine or not, she took a sip. "Not too bad, I guess, if alcohol is your thing."

Hell, if there was no one to talk to, she'd continue to talk to herself.

Dishing up the roast took seconds. Digging in took a little longer. Without anyone real to talk to, the kitchen seemed way too quiet. The clock on the wall no longer worked. There had never been a radio in the kitchen for comforting background noise—which might have set a good atmosphere for dinnertime conversation, and had never really turned out that way.

In contrast to the busy hallways and thin walls of her apartment building, the two-story house felt like a fortress of solitude, exemplified by the empty chair next to her. As Kim sat there with her uneaten dinner a pang of loneliness hit, accompanied by a wave of deep-seated sadness.

She had the power to fix this. She had to fix it by looking back logically. Her mother's decline was a lesson in how not to behave. Kim might have tossed some good guys with potential to the wayside because of a few deeply ingrained and very silly ideas about relationships.

If she didn't face her problems head-on, she'd never have anyone in her life. Being good at her job was one thing, and satisfying, but coming home to an empty house or an empty apartment night after night forever was a nightmare she had feared to confront.

She pictured her mother here, cooking dinner for one and eating in the quiet. The image broke her heart. The guilt she'd harbored for growing up and being away, for leaving her mother for school and work, plagued her all over again. She just hadn't been able to cope year after year with her mother's mental illness.

Kim lifted her chin. Raising her cup to the empty chair, she spoke with more confidence than she felt. "If things are going to change, we're going to have to break the spell."

The cup was halfway to her lips when a bell rang. Startled by the sound, Kim jumped to her feet.

Doorbell?

Her city sensibilities kicked in. Single women didn't answer the door unless they knew who stood on the other side. Buildings had doormen for that reason.

Other than Brenda, no one knew she was here. But, she reminded herself, this wasn't the city. This was a family neighborhood. Things were different here. Maybe the kid down the street had seen the lights and wanted payment in person for mowing the lawn.

With a glance through the small glass panel in the front door, Kim flipped on the porch light. She saw no one on the steps. Cautiously, she opened the door. Nobody was there. Her gaze dropped to the large cardboard box on the doorstep.

There had been a delivery, but it had to have been a mistake.

Stepping outside, looking around, she again glanced at the box. Her name was written on it, but there was no return address.

She took the box inside and carefully tore it open, then drew back after viewing the contents. The box contained several smaller boxes with see-through lids and big red bows. All of the boxes contained cookies. By the looks of things, every kind of cookie under the sun, including decorated Christmas trees.

It took her a moment to remember to breathe. Forgetting her mother was no longer there, Kim waited for the rant against the holidays to begin. A Christmas gift had been delivered to a house that didn't take kindly to such things. *Who would dare to deliver such a thing?* her mother would have shouted. *Who would allow items like that in their house?*

Of course, no rants came. Her mother's tirades were over. The walls hadn't fallen down because of the box on the living room floor. Her mother hadn't been raised from the grave by the pretty sugar-coated shapes.

Kim let out a breath and went back to the door for a second look outside. Cars went by. Two kids rode skateboards down the middle of the road. There was no one else in sight.

"Okay, then. It's an anonymous gift. A surprise."

Leaving the box on the floor, she headed to the kitchen. At the table, she sat down and picked up her fork, though jumbled thoughts prevented her from taking a bite of the roast, which was getting cold. Brenda wouldn't have delivered a package like that, thinking to help Kim's vow along. Brenda probably would have presented the box in person if it was to be an offering to the House of Christmas Doom. Besides, Bren didn't know about the secretly baked sugar cookies she'd dumped the night before.

If not Brenda, who had sent them?

She felt a chill on the back of her neck. Kim sat up straighter, not liking the idea that sprang to mind.

Monroe?

No. It couldn't be him.

She wasn't sure why his name had come up with regard to this box. He had no idea where she'd gone. However, Monroe might do such a thing if he knew where she was. She wouldn't put it past him to send his own version of a peace offering.

The tingle at the base of her neck returned, along with a fair amount of heat that wasn't in any way reasonable. The telltale flush creeping up her throat wasn't reasonable, either.

She couldn't allow herself to go there, to think about him, when already her forehead felt damp, and her hands were shaking. But accepting his gift would amount to another step in the right direction in her plan to tackle each problem that came up, and deal.

There wasn't any reason to close the box back up and put it outside. Letting it remain there, on the floor, was okay, but it did press home the fact that she was no longer bothered by one objective, but by two: how to face the holiday positively, and what to do about her boss.

Her stomach tightened, but not in a bad way.

Leaving her dinner untouched in the kitchen, Kim stood up. There was only one way Monroe could have found her, if in fact he had.

"I'll get you for this, Bren," she muttered, heading up-stairs for her cell phone.

But she didn't call Brenda. Instead, she dialed the num-ber of the VP's office, wondering if she'd hang up if some-one answered this late, and what she planned to say if *he* picked up the phone.

He did.

"Monroe," he said in the way he had of making the sim-plest words sound provocative.

Kim didn't speak. She hadn't been prepared for her re-action to the deep richness of his voice. Her finger hovered over the button that would disconnect her from him even as her mind registered this kind of reaction as being silly. All she had to do was ask him if he'd sent the box, and the mystery would be over.

"You got the package?" he asked, somehow knowing she was on the line, obviously confident she'd respond posi-tively to his gift.

For the first time in her life, Kim felt at a loss.

Hang up now, she told herself. *I don't need this.*

"I found your mother's address and wanted to send you something," he said, as if they weren't having a one-sided conversation. "Everybody likes cookies. And I'm still hop-ing that you'll be staying on at the agency."

"So you sent a bribe?" she managed to say, realizing only then that he'd have access to her files and her old address, and that Brenda might not have been a traitor.

"You do know they're Christmas cookies?" she added.

"I had them delivered to you by courier because I thought returning to your former home with your mother gone might make you sad, and that you might need cheer-ing up."

That made Kim hesitate. He might or might not have known about the depth of her aversion to this holiday, but he did know about her mother's passing. He hadn't sent this package to distress her further, but with hopes of making her happy. The gift was kind of personal. He had chosen it himself.

Kim wasn't sure how to take that. She did feel a ridiculous amount of anxiety—or maybe it was excitement—over the thought of Monroe taking the time to buy her a gift and get that gift to her not long after their conversation in the elevator.

Uncertain, she said, slightly breathlessly, "Thank you."

It was his turn to hesitate. She heard him breathing, and she also fought for each breath taken. The electricity in their connection felt like tiny jabs of lightning piercing her skin. Their chemistry was palpable, even this far apart.

"Are you okay?" he asked, sounding concerned.

"I'm fine," she lied.

"The gift didn't offend you, I hope? I swear that wasn't my intention."

"Not anymore."

"Good." Relief lowered his voice. "The red bows made me think of you in the red dress. You caused quite a stir in that dress, you know."

"Are you going to talk dirty to me on the phone?" she asked, at a loss for keeping the conversation on a serious track.

He laughed, and the sound rippled through her like a warm, sunny breeze. She loved that laugh. It made her feel lighter and not so alone. It made her want to laugh with him, and at herself for being so serious.

Maybe Monroe wasn't so full of himself after all.

Maybe she was.

Chances were that they could at least be friends if she allowed it.

"Actually," he said, "it's not late, and I wondered if you'd invite me over to eat some of the cookies."

"I'm pretty sure that wouldn't be a good idea."

She was positive that having him over wouldn't be a good idea. With a connection this strong, being in the same room with Monroe might lead to another situation she'd regret. This was her mother's home. A man of interest had no place here until she got her act together and banished the multiple years of gloom.

"I can bring dinner," he said. "No strings, just dinner."

"Thanks, but I've made dinner."

"Made dinner?" he repeated. "You cook?"

The astonishment in his sexy voice ruffled her ego.

"As a matter of fact, I do a lot of things you don't know about, and rather well, I might add," she said.

"I don't get much home cooking these days. Of course, you've probably already eaten, and you're busy getting a start on that vacation. So, all right. I didn't mean to pry any further into your affairs."

"Of course you did," she said.

"Well, yes, I guess I did…though I respect your right to turn my company down."

"Not your company, necessarily. Just you."

"Ouch. Well then, enjoy your time off. I hope those cookies bring you some happiness, too. I'd like to think they could, anyway."

Not knowing how to respond to the attention, Kim muttered "Thank you" again, and let it go at that. After reluctantly disconnecting, she immediately wished she hadn't. Monroe's voice and the interruption caused by the arrival of his gift had made the empty house almost seem livable for a change.

She felt excited—for no reason at all.

The phone remained in her hand for several more seconds before she made an SOS call to Brenda.

"Help," she said when her friend answered. "He's at it again, and I'm afraid I might be weakening."

Twelve

"Just to be clear," Brenda said, "when you say you're weakening, are we talking about the jolly guy in the red suit, or our gorgeous, if rather nosy, new boss?"

"Both," Kim said, her skin prickling with a new kind of anxiousness.

"Shall I come over?"

"No."

"You know, it isn't always a bad thing to have temporary insanity, and for you that might mean letting go of preconceived notions about liking a man."

"He sent me a gift."

"Who did?"

"Monroe sent a package. Here. Tonight."

Brenda's pause amounted to a dead line. "Please tell me there were diamonds involved, as in a bracelet or necklace, because otherwise what would constitute a proper apology for behaving like a cad in your apartment last night, and leading you astray about the job?"

"Cookies. He sent a box of cookies," Kim said.

"Doesn't work for me, Kim. That's much too benign for a sincere apology. Do you want me to come over there and help you break those cookies into tiny pieces?"

"I'd like your idea on what to do about *him*."

"I'm honored by your confidence in my advice, Kim, but honestly, I'm not sure about this."

"Brenda!"

"Well, okay. In this case, I'd probably note that Monroe sent you his version of an earnest apology."

"He said he hoped they made me happy."

"You talked to him?"

"I thanked him on the phone."

"I see. Well, it's probably okay, I'm thinking. Cookies, though delicious, aren't truly personal. They're not like lingerie, so you can probably ignore this and move on if you choose to."

"Thing is…" Kim didn't finish the sentence. She really felt confused.

"Thing is, a box from Monroe might actually help you in this self-imposed crisis?" Brenda observed, picking up on Kim's thought pattern.

"Yes." Kim silently applauded Brenda for understanding the pros and pitfalls of the situation.

"Then it's a win-win, Kim," Brenda concluded. "He was being nice, and you've thanked him. Now you can eat those things and make more progress on your objective behind going home. Did you actually open the box?"

"I did."

"How did that make you feel?"

"Scared."

"I do kind of get that, but will ask this question, anyway. Why? Why were you scared?"

"It's my mother's house, Bren. Feeling good here seems strange. Holiday gifts were taboo, sacrilege."

"Were taboo, but not anymore. That stuff happened when your mom was alive, but she's gone, and you've gone home to change and rearrange your attitude about things. There's not one person on the planet to stop you from accomplishing that goal, except yourself."

"Right." Kim sighed. "Except for me."

After an audible breath, Brenda asked, "Are they from a decent bakery?"

"Becons, by the park."

"Well, you can be thankful he has good taste. Take them out of the box. Have some for dinner. Sweets always make us feel good, right?"

This was good advice and another necessary push along a new path. She wasn't a child in need of a lesson, though Kim felt like one every time she entered this house. In her own world, she took charge. In her own world, she was successful and happy enough…if there was such a thing as being happy *enough*.

"I'm flawed, Bren, and I don't want other people to find out. One in particular."

"Because you care what he thinks?"

"I think I do."

"So what's stopping you from dropping the *I think* part of that?"

Brenda spoke again over Kim's thoughtful pause. "I was heading to the bar with the art guys to catch up on gossip, but I can grab the next train if you need me. Say the word and I'll be on that train."

"No. I'm okay. Thanks for the pep talk."

"No problem. Sending you hugs over the ether. Good luck with the caloric fallout, Kimmy."

"Have an appletini for me, Bren."

"Heck, it has been a very long day, so I might have two."

Disconnecting, Kim glanced around, inwardly reciting the words Brenda had offered. There was no one to stop her from attaining her objective for coming here, but herself.

Time to get on with things.

The old bathroom in the hallway seemed big and drafty after the tiny one in her apartment, but the shower still worked, and she had brought along clean towels. She took her time under the spray of water, trying not to think about how Monroe had nearly succeeded in getting her naked.

She scrubbed her back hard, sloughing off the sensation of his hands on her skin, erasing the memory of his fingers exploring with a blistering heat…but not quite ridding herself of those sensations.

In her determination not to think of him, she was doing a

lousy job. In fact, she failed miserably. In Monroe's strong arms, and for a few brief, sizzling moments, she had been someone else. She had let him in. For the first time, she hadn't allowed her past to influence her actions.

She did like Chaz Monroe.

She'd been hot and bothered since that first glimpse of him in his office. Her body responded favorably each time he neared, as if her nervous system needed to bypass her damaged, overworked brain, and get to the good part.

Fact was, she had the hots for her boss and wished he was in the shower with her, working his magic right that minute. Heck, if she was that far gone, was she so severely damaged that she'd refuse to accept his offer of a truce?

Yes. Because liking him and pursuing a liaison would surely mean professional suicide eventually, as she had told him. And she had nothing without her job.

In her bedroom, she removed clothes from her bag and shook them out. She pulled on a pair of well-worn sweatpants and fingered a silky blue camisole as she drew it over her head, knowing Monroe would also have liked its texture and color. Covering that with a loose wool cardigan sweater, gathering her hair into a ponytail, she headed downstairs in her bare feet.

The house had warmed up considerably now that the old heater hummed. She turned on all the lights, hesitating at each switch to think about how Monroe seemed to like her, too. Not all had to be lost in this situation, if she looked on the bright side. He was willing to overlook the clause in her contract if she stayed in her cubicle. He just couldn't promote her or send her any more gifts if she remained an employee.

She might or might not be able to deal with that.

Circling back to the living room, she stared at the floor. *Step one: take the cookies out of the box. Eat one, or ten. It will be a good thing, a helpful thing.*

Kneeling next to the box, she lifted out the first smaller box, noting again that lightning did not strike. The walls did not fall down.

She lifted out another container and went back in memory to the times as a child when she had wished for a gift like this.

"It's okay. Therapy."

After she had unpacked all four-dozen cookies, she got to her feet. The first step was working. Some of her guilt had already fled, chased away by things that weren't really magical at all, but at the moment seemed magical to her.

She was smiling.

"What if I had invited him to dinner?" she said aloud. "Wouldn't that hurry things along?"

No reply came. No argument or lament from the house's ghosts. She was free now to make her own choices, and had been for some time. Suddenly, she understood that fully.

When her phone rang, Kim took the stairs two at a time, figuring that Brenda would be checking in. She plopped down on the bed. "Bren, guess what?"

A low-pitched masculine voice said, "Are you sure you won't change your mind and invite me over if I say please and categorically deny being a stalker, providing references upon request?"

Monroe. Her heart began to thud inside her chest. Her throat tightened. How persistent was he going to be? And why wasn't she displeased?

"I'm nowhere near where you are, as you already know, having sent the package," Kim said.

"You'd see me otherwise?"

"No," she lied again, ill-equipped to handle what he was suggesting. Admittedly, the house might have been brighter already, though it remained too quiet. More cleaning would only get her so far in terms of occupying her time. A whole night stretched in front of her, with far too many hours to fill.

She missed her cozy apartment.

Clearly, Monroe's gift had shocked her into some kind of middle ground where she might consider seeing him.

If she did, she'd find out what he really wanted from her. She could stand her ground and face him; she'd show him that she was taking charge of her life in all situations, and that she would make up her own mind about her future. In that light, seeing Monroe might be a good idea.

"Kim? You there?"

It was rotten how her pulse jumped after hearing his voice, and how the hand holding the phone trembled, especially when only five minutes before she'd made up her mind to stand firm against the potency of his allure.

"Well, maybe. If you were closer," she said, not really having to worry about that remark since she was no longer in the city.

There was a knock on the front door.

"You'll have to excuse me. Someone is at the door," Kim said. "I have to go."

"Take me with you, in case it's someone you don't want to see," Monroe said. "Be on the safe side."

Kim ran back downstairs, turned on the porch light and looked through the glass. She whirled with her back to the door and leaned against it, raising the phone.

"What is it?" he whispered in her ear.

But she could not speak.

Outside, on her porch, was a Christmas tree, its shape unmistakable.

"Did you send a tree?" she demanded, her voice faint, her heart hammering.

"I did not, in fact, send the tree," Monroe replied.

Do not open the door, Kim's inner lecturer told her.

It's too much, too soon.

Placing a hand on the knob, she waited out several racing heartbeats. An idea came to her, along with a sudden waft of familiar heat. She said into the phone, "I suppose if I open this door, someone will be holding that tree?"

"Someone who could possibly contract pneumonia from standing in the cold," Monroe said. "Plus, I did get an invitation, sort of. I am in the area, as it turns out."

Kim lowered the phone and opened the door. Monroe stood there, all right, holding the tree. The sight registered as surreal.

"Semantics," he clarified. "I didn't send the tree, I *brought* it."

Before Kim knew what was happening, she was up tight against him, listening to the muffled crash of the tree falling to the porch floorboards as she pressed her mouth to his.

Thirteen

Kim McKinley was a frigging enigma. But who had the time or inclination to put on the brakes?

The woman who occupied every waking thought was in his arms, at least for the next minute or two, until her sanity returned. And though he had planned on talking to her and keeping a discreet distance, his hunger came raging back from where logic had stored it, overpowering his struggle to comprehend the situation.

What else could he do except let himself go?

The meeting of their mouths was intense, and like food for the starving. She welcomed his touch, his tongue, his strength, seemingly determined to have a replay of the night before, and to see this through. Whatever *this* was to her.

She did not want the kiss to stop, and made that quite clear. But she was tense. When his arms tightened around her, she breathed out a sound of distress.

He loosened his grip, moving his hands to her rib cage, waiting to see if she'd repeat the sound. She didn't. Through the sweater, he caught a feel of something slick, like a silky second skin. The thought of Kim's body again sheathed in the filmy material was a deal breaker in terms of his vow to keep his distance.

A big-time vow breaker.

Deepening the feverish kiss, then easing up, he stroked her softly, almost tenderly, with a desire to discover every part of the body he had dreamed about. Her hips molded to his. Her back arched each time his hands moved. She clung to his shoulders. Her breasts pressed against his chest. She was going for this. There was nothing to impede the forward momentum of this reunion.

Well, okay.

Chaz backed her up, through the open doorway. As he turned her to the wall, the impact of their moving bodies slammed the door. The sound seemed to reverberate through Kim, as though she'd felt a chill wind. A shiver ran through her. Her mouth slackened. Her hands were suddenly motionless.

Hot and cold...

Seriously?

The dichotomy of those temperatures ran through his mind with the fury of a wildfire. Chaz drew back far enough to see Kim's face in the dim light of an overhead entryway lamp. As before, when Brenda Chang's voice had driven a wedge between them, her face paled. Did she regret her reaction to him already? Was she nothing but a tease? Damn it, what just happened? He was all fired up.

"What is it?" he asked. "What's going on?"

Her eyes were wide and unseeing. He cradled her face with both hands and spoke again. "Kim? Look at me."

The hazel eyes, more green than brown, refocused.

"It's okay," he said. "I didn't come here to do that. We don't have to do anything but talk. See?"

He dropped his hands and stepped back. "You sounded lonely on the phone. I'll go if you ask me to, though I'd like to stay."

She shook her head. "It's just that... It's just that there hasn't been any company in this house for as long as I can remember. Certainly never a man. I felt..."

"I can be good company when I put my mind to it," he said when she didn't finish. "So what do you say we make up for lost time?"

"Yes." She smiled, though she looked wary. "Okay."

He glanced past her at the living room and withheld a frown. This wasn't like any room he had imagined her in, and nothing like what he'd seen of her apartment. This room didn't reflect her personality at all…unless of course she actually had a split down the middle.

The place wasn't drab, really, but very close to it. There were faded floral curtains, a beige cushioned sofa, and hardwood floors covered by rugs. The musty smell hinted at the house having been closed up for some time, though he also caught a whiff of a cleaning product.

On the floor sat the box he had sent. Kim had looked at the contents, at least. She'd had her hands on that box.

He wanted her hands back on him, but had to play nice and see how far he got with that idea. His plan was to break the news no one else yet knew—about his intention to turn over the agency to a new owner in the near future. Once the finances were settled in the black zone, he'd be gone. If he told Kim about this, and she realized she would still have a shot at the job she coveted, they might have a chance to explore the heat building up each time they came into contact with each other.

It wasn't the first time he'd thought about that. He just had to wait for the right time to spring it on her.

"Shall we start by bringing in the tree?" he asked. "I feel sort of sorry for it out there."

He took her silence for a no. Maybe she wasn't ready for another surprise gift.

"Conversation would also be nice," he suggested. "How about if I start, and clear the air?"

Her eyes remained on him in such a way that he wanted to kiss her again and bypass the rest of what kept them apart. Even her serious expression was sexy. As for her killer body…well, that was the icing on the cake he couldn't yet have a bite of.

"I'm here because I didn't want to leave things the way they were," he said. "Our confessions in the elevator only whetted my appetite for truthfulness. I thought by coming here, we could patch things up and move forward at a faster pace. If you're game, that is."

"Is there a rush?" she asked, tilting her head, showing off more of her long, bare, graceful neck.

"I thought so," he replied, stunned at how that stretch of pale skin affected him. "And now that I see you here, in this place, I'm not so sure this is a good location for you to spend your vacation time."

She didn't argue with his assessment. "This is a sad house."

"Does that mean you have to be sad in it?"

"It's hard to change the past, but I'm here to try."

"Yes, I suppose change is difficult. You might start by inviting me in. We could liven up the place for an hour or two."

She raised an eyebrow. "Do you recognize the word *pushy?*"

Chaz raised his hands. "How about if we start over and I go outside and knock, and you don't accost me wickedly this time when you open the door?"

She made a face. He had to wonder how deep her inner pressures went for her to embrace so many different emotions in the span of a few minutes.

This was indeed a sad house, but houses were built of wood and plaster, and possessed no souls. Though the temperature was warm inside, the room had an empty, cool feel. Already, after a few hours here, Kim looked like a different person, a sadder version, and his protective hackles had gone up.

Was he back to being a fool for wanting what he might never have? Why would he desire her when she was so confusing most of the time?

"Or you could ask me to take off my coat and sit down." He gestured to the sofa. "And we could try to behave like civilized people."

"Be my guest," she said, stepping aside.

Chaz tossed his coat on a chair and sat down on the couch, relieved to have gotten this far and wondering how she could look as good in sweats as she did all dolled up for work. He liked the fact that Kim seemed less formidable in this kind of casual wear, and in her bare feet. He liked her hair swept back in a ponytail, and felt an urge to pull strands loose to run between his fingers.

"Would you like something to drink?" She remained by the door. "I've got wine in teacups. I'm thinking of starting a new fad at wine bars. Merlot in chipped china. Very snazzy."

Chaz smiled. "All right. I'll try that. Can I help?"

"Let's confine you to one room at a time," she replied with a slight smile.

Kim seemed to have thawed again, though he had a feeling she might run out the back door and leave him there. Relief came when he heard her closing cupboard doors in the next room.

He didn't bother to check out more of his surroundings, noting only that there were no pictures, either on the walls or in frames set on the end tables. Not one photo of Kim existed in this room, whereas in his parents' home, every surface held a snapshot or two chronicling the family through the years.

The lack of personal touches here bothered him. After seeing a small portion of her apartment in the city, albeit in the dark, Kim's taste ran to modern. No clutter. Sleek lines, with lots of leather. That kind of decor suited her much better. This was old stuff, and quite depressing.

Clinking sounds brought his gaze to the kitchen doorway. Kim hadn't been kidding about the cups. She appeared carrying two, and handed him one without allowing her fingers to touch his in the transfer. She moved his coat and sat in the chair opposite him with her legs curled under her.

Very much like a kid. Also like a seductive siren with no idea of how hot she really was.

Several deep breaths were necessary before Chaz's first sip of wine. He eyed her over the rim. "Hate to tell you this, Kim, but even our agency couldn't sell your new wine in china fad to the public."

She smiled earnestly, he thought, and the smile lit up her face. "Something about the textures being wrong," she agreed. "Porcelain adds a taste of its own."

"What's the wine?"

"I've no idea. It was recommended by the local grocer."

Chaz chuckled and took another sip before setting the cup on the coffee table. He folded his hands in his lap to keep himself from reaching for the woman who had the ability to drive him mad with desire.

"How long has it been since you lived here?" he asked.

"A couple years. I stayed as long as I could and until…" She let whatever she had been about to say go, and started over. "Nothing has changed in here since I was a kid. I'm going to fix it up to sell. There will be a lot of work to get it ready."

"That's why you're here?"

"Partially."

"The other part?"

"Confronting ghosts."

It was a reply Chaz hadn't anticipated. His smile faltered as he watched Kim slip a silky aqua-blue strap back over her shoulder, beneath the sweater, where it stayed for a few seconds before falling back down. *Treacherous little strap.* His eyes strayed to her breasts, their contour visible through the slinky blue-green silk. She wasn't dressed for ghost hunting, but for cuddling.

And he had to stop thinking about that.

Whether or not she noticed his appreciative gaze, Kim pulled the soft sweater around her, which was a good move, and helped him to avoid more thoughts about how smooth her skin was, and where touching it might lead.

Still, as he saw it now, they were faced with a quandary. He was, anyway. Perfume wafted in the air he had to breathe. Kim's body taunted him from behind its cloth barrier. His reaction to these things were proof positive that he couldn't work in the same building with her after this. Maybe not even in the same city.

But he had started this by asking for a night of sharing confidences, and by showing up on her doorstep. Confidences and sex didn't necessarily go together.

He wanted her, but so what?

"Are we past the tape recorder duel?" he asked.

"Are we still negotiating?" she countered. "Is that the reason for the gifts?"

He shook his head. "No. Since we're being honest, I'll admit again to feeling uneasy about the way things have gone down between us. As I mentioned, our chat in the elevator didn't ease my mind much as to what to do."

"Why?"

"I don't honestly know. I wish I did."

"Are you sorry about the kiss in my doorway?" she asked.

"No." He zeroed in on her eyes. "Are you?"

"Not really."

Chaz swiped at the prickle on the back of his neck that was a warning signal to either get out of there with his masculinity intact, or get on with things. Talking about emotions wasn't listed in his personal portfolio of things he liked to do best. He was pretty sure no guy excelled at this kind of thing.

"I do hope you don't welcome everybody like that, though," he said in a teasing tone.

Kim shrugged. "How do you suppose I've kept my clients so happy?"

Chaz grinned before remembering her comments about sleeping her way to the top.

"Shall we move on to something else?" he suggested.

"I don't think so. Part of my healing process is to deal. So I'm going to tell you what you've wanted to know, and fulfill your objective for showing up here tonight."

When she took a breath, the damn sweater fell open. He did not look there. Her serious expression held him, and also made him uncomfortable. All of a sudden, he felt like the bad guy, when he'd never, as far as he knew, hurt anyone on purpose.

"I kissed you because I wanted to," she said. "I find you extremely attractive and hard to resist on a physical level."

"Only physical?"

She waved his question away and let her gaze roam the room.

"My mother basically died of depression, as a direct result of a disappointment too terrible for her mind to accept."

Her gaze lingered on the door. "She had stopped eating, and wouldn't get out of bed. She didn't die here, at home. My mother isn't the ghost I came here to confront. Her ideas are what I need to address, ideas that were pounded into me since the time of the event that kicked her decline into gear."

Chaz swallowed. Should he stop her from digging deep into her secrets, when he had been pushing her for this explanation? Though it wasn't entirely what he had expected, it was also much more than he could have imagined.

"My father left us on Christmas Eve when I was very young," she went on. "He left presents under the tree, as if that would make up for the loss to follow. He walked out without explanation and never looked back, leaving his uneaten dinner on the table. We heard sometime later that he had chosen another family to spend that Christmas morning with, and the rest of his life with after that, which meant that he had cheated on us for some time."

Uncomfortable with her disclosure, Chaz carefully watched Kim readjust her position in the chair and take another long, slow breath.

"I don't do Christmas because my mother hated it, and hated the memory of the night my father left. She never got over the betrayal, and didn't speak to my father again. Neither of us did."

"I see," he said to fill the following pause.

"I've honored my mother's wishes about avoiding this holiday for a long time. So long, I can't remember what life was like before that promise. My mother died six months ago, and since then I've kept up the routine by refusing to celebrate Christmas either in my work or my personal life."

Chaz ran a hand through his hair, feeling like an idiot for pressuring her into admitting a thing like that, and for having almost convinced himself on the way over here that her issues might have derived from something as simple as never getting the gift she asked Santa Claus for. In retrospect, he had failed to give her full credit for having real and serious causes that required the special clause in her contract.

He felt like a heel, and deserved every name she might have called him. The cookies he sent were in a pile of boxes on the floor by his feet. He had brought a tree, planned a party and insisted she go—which made him no better than a goddamn bully.

It was too late for his lame excuses, though as her boss, this was something he had needed to understand. The question now was how much damage he had done to a potential relationship by applying all that pressure?

He kicked a box with his foot and sent it skidding in McKinley's direction. Her gaze moved from the box to him, where her focus stayed.

Chaz was certain the hunger he felt for her was mirrored in her eyes.

* * *

"Will you excuse me a minute?"

Kim got to her feet, fending off two urges at once. The first was to throw herself at Monroe again, no matter the consequences. He stared at her seriously, as if seeing her inner workings for the first time. Kissing him would break the tension in the room and release some of her pent-up emotions after a confession like that.

The second urge was to sprint for the kitchen, close the door and lock herself in.

The latter seemed the best option now that he knew her secrets. If he equated her frank announcement with her recent mental state, it might someday undermine their business relationship. He'd keep an eye out for signs of the same tendency for depression exhibited by her mother, or her threats to pack up and leave. But if that were the case, and he held this against her, Chaz Monroe wasn't worth the shirt on his back.

Laugh maniacally or cry? Run or break down?

She wavered among all of those options, having disclosed what haunted her. Her life had been laid bare, the darkness had taken wing, but elation didn't come right away. Some ghosts were clingy.

The way Monroe studied her was sensuously sober, and produced another flicker of heat deep inside her. She had all but begged for him to leave her alone, though she desired the exact opposite. She craved closeness and sharing and mind-bending sex. With Chaz Monroe.

She had bought into her mother's beliefs about men long after they had stopped making sense.

"Suffering isn't supposed to be prolonged, especially this time of year," she said. "Christmas is about joy and light, ideas that might have made a difference to my family if my mother had gritted her teeth and moved on."

Did things have to be so complex? Light…company…

happy times…cookies and a tree. A man beside her to love, and who would love her back unconditionally, loyally and forever. These were what she wanted so badly.

Sex with Monroe wasn't going to get her those things, and yet it somehow seemed a fitting end to the evening. He would hold her. He would be here and make her happy, if only temporarily and for tonight. The main result would be that with his ultramasculine presence in this house, her mother's dark spell over her daughter would be lost, once and for all. She felt that spell already beginning to crack.

To hell with work, her job and how she'd feel tomorrow.

"I'm sorry you had to go through that," he said, getting to his feet, moving to stand beside her.

He didn't touch her and didn't need to. His voice and his tone created a vibration that worked its way down her spine and keep on sliding, finding its way beneath the waistband of her sweatpants and along the curve of her hips to end in a place a vibration had no right to be.

Monroe was no longer the enemy, and she didn't want him to go away. Arguments aside, she felt good around him. She felt completely awake and alive, every nerve tingling, each neuron she possessed calling for her to get closer to him.

"I'm not sure what you'll do with all that," she said, feeling unsteady, unnaturally warm and slightly queasy with him beside her.

The touch came. Only a light one. He tilted her head back with a finger so that she had to look into his eyes. "I'd like to move on to another confidence, one of mine, putting yours aside for now, if you don't mind."

Kim tried to turn her head. He brought her back.

"You do like me, in spite of all this, and all that we've been through so far," he said. "I can feel this. Am I right?"

He went on when she didn't answer. "I want to be near

you. As a matter of fact, I can't seem to stay away. I believe we can make this work. You and me. We can try."

"How? It's already going to be bad when rumor of the scene in the bar spreads. I love my job, and it looks like I'll have to leave it."

"No. Trust me, Kim. Ride this out, and you'll see what can happen. Stick out your tongue at those rumors. I'll take the heat. While I'm in that building, I'll spread my own story about everything being my fault, and we'll make the other employees believe nothing bad happened."

"Nothing did happen."

"It's about to now, I think. Don't you?"

His mouth came close. Kim worked desperately to keep from closing her eyes, needing to see him before feeling the truth of his statement.

"There are more things to disclose in the future about the business that might positively impact your position in the agency. We will get to that, I promise. For now, for to-night, let's enjoy what this is."

His arms encircled her possessively, his warmth per-suading her to give in to the rush of need coursing through her body.

She had spoken the magic words to free herself from her mother's tyranny, and she had let a man in. The dif-ference here, between this situation and what happened to her mother, was that she didn't expect any future with Chaz Monroe. If he left that minute, she'd be no worse off because she wasn't fully invested in this liaison producing any kind of relationship and neither was he.

That's what she told herself, anyway, knowing it to be a lie and afraid to admit otherwise. Each minute in Monroe's presence was like one of those holiday gifts she had never received. Being with him brought her some long-awaited anticipation and joy.

"Bedroom," he whispered to her, a world of meaning in that one word.

"No. Not there." Her heart continued to pound. Adrenaline rushed through her to whip up the flames.

They were going to do this.

"Then it will have to be here," he said, swinging her into his arms, kneeling on the floor and placing her there, beside the pile of boxes and bows.

Kim looked up at him, realizing she'd really done it this time. She would soon see all of Chaz Monroe, test her theory on one-night stands being okay for the truly needy, besides being one hell of a spellbreaker...and trust him to take her mind off the rest of the world.

Just for tonight.

No one could stop what was about to take place. She craved heat and closeness and for the pain of her family's story to end here, now, completely.

"There's only one problem," she said, pulling him closer.

"What's that?" The mouth hovering over hers held promise in the way it curved up at the corners.

"We have too many clothes in the way," Kim replied with her hands on his chest.

Fourteen

The kiss was new and intense. Open mouths, damp, darting tongues, breathlessness. There was nothing patient about their need. This wasn't going to be a night of foreplay and tender exploration. They were too excited.

Kim savored the burn of Monroe's closeness, drank him in with each kiss, bite and scratch of her fingernails across the fabric of his shirt. The lid was off the pressure cooker, and she was savage, desirous, anxious for everything he had to give, anxious to find out if it would be enough to permanently keep the ghosts of Christmas past at bay.

In between deep kisses, he gave her time to breathe and searched her face. Their bodies were pressed tightly together, his stretched out on top of hers. His hands were in her hair, on her cheeks, feathering over her neck. Trails of kisses followed each touch of his fingers.

Kim thought she might go mad with her need for him. Her body molded to his, their hips meeting in all the right places as if their bodies were a perfect match. His lips inflicted a torture of the highest caliber, offering promises of what was to come.

When he pulled back, it was only to head south with his incendiary mouth—over her collarbones and over the blue silk covering her breasts. He kissed her there, and she moaned.

She tore at his buttons with impatience. The next sound was of fabric tearing. He had ripped apart the thin ribbon straps of her camisole, exposing her shoulders. Hungrily, he pulled her forward, kissed her again then eased the sweater off and away.

He paused to look at her, his gaze incredibly intimate.

Upright, and without the straps, the silk slid downward over her breasts in a sensuous rustle.

He pressed the palm of one hand against her right breast then cupped her. Kim shut her eyes and began to rock, first backward, then forward. He quickly replaced his hands with his mouth and drew on the pink exposed tip of her breast so deftly, she fought back a cry.

It was too much, and too little. She had never felt anything remotely like this, or wanted so much.

Finding the strength to withstand the pleasure Monroe's mouth gave her, she shoved him back, and with her hands on his buttons, looked at him pleadingly. *No more time. No distractions.*

He understood.

His shirt came off with a twitch and a shrug, baring a muscular chest with a slight dusting of brown hair. As if his magnificent nakedness were a magnet, Kim couldn't keep herself from touching him, running her fingers over him, getting to know every inch from his shoulders to his stomach. He was taut, in perfect shape, the epitome of masculine perfection. But then, she had guessed that from the start.

Aware of her silent approval, Monroe eased her back to the floor and removed her sweatpants in a graceful move that left her shuddering in anticipation. He didn't have time to get to his own pants. She had his belt off and was at his zipper with shaky fingers.

That sexy sound of a zipper opening filled the room. Kim saw only Monroe's face—his expression of lust, his own version of need. Mixed in with those things lay something else: something that she didn't dare put a name to, but knew was reflected in her own expression, and somewhere deep in her body. Deep in her soul.

Chaz Monroe hadn't been kidding. He liked her. He wanted her. His expression said he cared, and that he needed her, at least tonight, as much as she needed him. Knowing this changed things for her, and upped the ante.

He scooped her hips up in both hands and settled himself against her, still looking at her with his eyes wide open. She felt how his muscles tensed. He dipped into her gently at first, easing inside, eyeing her all the while for her reaction.

She had to close her eyes again. Had to. The pleasure of having him inside her was extreme. Suddenly, she wasn't sure if she could handle this, handle him. Already, she felt the rise of a distant rumbling deep inside her body.

He must have felt that rumbling. He used more force after that, entering her with a slick plunge that rocked her to her core. The cry she had withheld escaped.

"I know," he whispered in her ear. "I know."

With strong thighs, he urged her legs to open wider. This time when he entered her moist depths, it was with real purpose. The plunge went deep, forcing another cry to emerge from her swollen mouth.

The internal rumbling gained momentum quickly, hurtling toward where he lay buried inside her, threatening to end what she refused to have finished.

"Can't…" she gasped.

"Yes," he told her. "You can."

His hips began to move, building a rhythm that drove him into her again and again. Her hips matched his, thrust for thrust. Her hands grasped at his bare back, tearing at his flexing muscles with no intent to control his talented ministrations, but to encourage him to proceed, lock him to her, ensure that he wouldn't get away until this was finalized. Until it was over.

The claiming was mutual, necessary and too hot for either of them to prolong. Finally, as time became suspended and the world seemed about to crash down, he drove himself into her one last time…and their startled cries mingled loudly, shockingly, in the room's musty air.

They lay on the floor, quiet and trembling while they caught their breath. Moments later, they started the whole process over again.

Fifteen

Chaz spiraled in and out of dreams. He wasn't cold, exactly, yet he felt a distant discomfort that forced his eyes open.

He was on his back, on a hard surface. His shoulders ached. So did his knees. Something soft covered him. A blanket?

It took a minute to remember where he was. The room was dark, which meant that not much time had passed since he and Kim had gone at each other.

She wasn't beside him. He sat up, noticing right away that he was buck naked. Their clothes had been discarded completely after round two, in preparation for round three. The edge of a shaggy rug scratched at his thighs.

Kim was gone, but had covered him with a blanket, which was a nice touch. Maybe she preferred a soft mattress to cushion her spent body after a couple hours of sexual gymnastics, and had trotted off to find one. He couldn't really blame her. Then again, she hadn't offered to take him to bed with her, and this threatened to bring on a bout of concern.

Using the coffee table for leverage, Chaz got to his feet. He felt for a lamp on a table next to the sofa and clicked it on. Their clothes were there, strewn across the floor and the chair. Seeing those clothes, Chaz felt slightly better. Kim hadn't tidied up, gotten dressed or removed the outward evidence of their union.

He blew out a breath, unable to recall having spent a night like this in…well, ever. And, he reminded himself, this didn't have to mean love was involved. Great sex amounted to great sex, that's all. Problem was, he wanted her again right that minute. Stranger yet, he desired to hold her, nestle against her, sleep beside her, with Kim curled up in his arms.

This realization came as a shock. Usually the one to grab his clothes and hit the road to terminate a one-night stand, he had stayed, drifting off into a blissful slumber.

And Kim had left him on the floor.

Her absence didn't have to mean she had left him altogether, though. After all, this was her house. So, what did this incredible impulse to nuzzle her imply?

More trouble ahead.

The intensity of the sex they'd shared was rare, sure, but did the rest of his urges have to have anything to do with *love?*

Surely not. He was merely feeling satisfied and empathetic.

He looked around. The floor was a mess. Piles of cookies had been scattered. Crumbs were everywhere. They had left the tree on the porch. Nothing in this room reflected comfort, really. Kim needed to get out of here. She no longer belonged in this place, and how she felt mattered to him.

She mattered.

His gut tightened. "Kim?" he called out, daring to wake her, needing to disturb her to confirm the new sensations rippling through him.

Finding the stairs, he took them two at a time. Although the hallway at the top lay in darkness, light from below made it possible to see four closed doors and one open doorway. Chaz made for the latter with his heart in his throat.

The blinds in the room were partway open, and the curtains drawn back. By the light from a streetlight, he made out the outline of a bed, a dresser and a light switch, which he flipped on.

Though the bed looked rumpled, Kim wasn't in it.

"Kim?"

No reply came.

He found the bathroom in the hall filled with Kim's scent, but she wasn't there. Back in the hallway, he stopped to listen. The house lay in complete silence.

Bedroom number two was empty, as were the rest of the rooms on that floor. Kim McKinley simply wasn't there.

He'd been jilted. Left. Abandoned in somebody else's house.

And that left him with a very bad feeling about what this meant.

Kim waited by the curb after calling for a cab. Nearly out of breath from hustling to get her act together, she was sloppily dressed in a pair of old jeans, a turtleneck sweater and boots she had found in the closet.

Sore, tired and anxious, she limped back and forth along the sidewalk. The man of her dreams lay on the floor of her mother's living room, surrounded by the cookies he'd brought her. There should have been a law against leaving a man like that, but her first waking instinct had been to flee.

They had broken the house's spell, smashed it to smithereens. And she wanted to run right back inside and do it again, have Monroe again, feel his breath on her face and his naked body against hers.

Breaking old rules had never been so glorious, and at the same time confusing. She hadn't made love to him in order to plan for a future of bedrooms and kitchens. She looked for companionship and warmth on a chilly night, a temporary relationship worthy of blasting away the past. Well, she had found those things. Too much of those things.

She was doing the walking-away routine. As hard as that was and as bad as she felt about it, she had to leave. Monroe might be one hell of a guy, but leaving him now meant he wouldn't have the chance to leave her later or be afforded the opportunity to break her heart. Monroe would cause trouble in her future if she stuck around, because she really, really liked him. She wanted him badly. More than ever. She needed iron willpower in order to remain on the street.

What would he do when he woke up in a strange house, alone? Curse? Get angry?

She wasn't going to see that reaction now or in the future. In the aftermath of shared confidences, confessions and a night of raw animal sex, being in the same business, in the same building, would be out of the question. No way would she be able to hide her hunger for Chaz Monroe after tonight. If she caved on this point, she'd be setting herself up for a fall.

She felt as though she'd had a taste of the fall already. Her chest hurt. The inner fires still raged.

When the cab pulled up, Kim took one more glance at the dark house before giving the driver her destination and some special instructions. Then she climbed into the backseat. With Monroe off-limits from now on, she'd at least have a keepsake. A trophy to remember this night by…as if she could ever forget it.

It's okay. I'll be all right.

The hurt of leaving Monroe would stop eventually. With her mother's hold broken, she was free to sell this house and enjoy the things she had shunned. Acknowledgment of that gave her a sense of freedom.

Having made the decision to part company with Monroe and get on with her life, she'd be embracing the phrase *starting over*. Monroe had helped with that. "Thank you," Kim whispered as the cab headed for the city.

Halfway there, her tears began to pool.

Damn if she didn't miss him already.

Chaz didn't want to focus on the phrase that came to mind as he sat down on a step in Kim's mother's house.

The little vixen used me?

After years of dating, he'd been jilted after the best night of his life. By the only woman he wanted in his life.

How did that happen?

Could he have been wrong about her? Wrong about how fully she'd enjoyed the sex and his company? No one had that kind of ability to fake the pleasure of round after round of mind-blowing physical connection. No, Kim had thoroughly enjoyed what they'd done. She'd participated, wanting that union as much as he had. Tears had stained her cheeks once or twice, and that had damn near broken his heart.

What about the blanket she'd covered him with? Was that the action of someone who had faked her way through an entire evening, possibly with an ulterior motive or secret agenda?

Can't see that.

So, if she had gotten as much pleasure out of their evening together as he did, why had she gone, and where?

Chaz glanced at his watch. *Two o'clock in the morning.*

In a few hours, he had a meeting with some bankers to discuss the possibilities of a future sale, a meeting that had been set up before he stepped foot inside the agency, and before he'd first caught sight of Kim's enviable backside in the corridor. Her disappearance sidelined the opportunity to tell her about his plans for the future sale of the company. Likely she had left him believing it imperative for one of them to go. The way she left, without a word, presented only one scenario. Kim was saying goodbye to all of it—the job and him.

"Well, that sucks," he muttered, looking around the room where they had *merged*. An appropriate term for what they had done, as many times as they'd done it, since they hadn't taken the time or the precision necessary for it to have been called *making love*.

Making love would have meant something more than casual sex. The thing that came after all the lust had been explored, involving slow exploration and much softer kisses.

Tonight had been about casual sex between consenting adults. Right?

All of a sudden, he wasn't so sure.

His spirit took a dive.

He wanted her back.

Kim McKinley had one-upped him again in a game he had no longer planned to play. Regretting that, Chaz looked to the front door, then to his clothes on the floor.

So, okay, he had tried and lost. He had lost *her*. He'd live. Monroes were champion survivors. Buying and selling businesses hardened his anti-relationship stamina, and he had every intention of learning to deal with the consequences.

In need of air, he picked up his pants and dressed. Opening the front door, hoping Kim might be on the porch, his stomach took a tumble when she wasn't.

But he paused in the doorway, heat shooting up the back of his neck. He grinned. Something about that porch seemed different, and that difference told him this wasn't over.

The silky-skinned little siren might have fled, yes. But she'd taken the Christmas tree with her.

Kim woke exhausted and achingly sore in every muscle after two full days of recuperation time from her evening with Monroe. The sense of being perpetually on the edge of a state of anxiousness refused to leave her. Her heart continued to race. Her ears rang.

Not her ears. The cell phone on her table by the bed made the racket.

After rolling onto her side, she checked the caller ID, holding the phone aloft while it continued to screech. The screen said the call came from a private number. Letting it go to voice mail, she tossed the phone to the foot of the bed and stretched out on her back. She had nowhere special to be on day three of her plan to not only eradicate the sadness of the past, but to obliterate it, too.

Her fingers slid sideways to the empty spot next to her on the mattress, then recoiled. *He* wasn't there. No one was. Funny how real dreams could be.

Her project for today was to make another attempt at forgetting Chaz Monroe, which had so far proved difficult. She'd spent another mostly sleepless night thinking about what to do next and trying to erase all thoughts of him. Each time she closed her eyes, he was there, strong, handsome and tenacious. Last night, six cups of strong black tea had been necessary to keep her eyes open and the memory of him controlled.

Her body now paid for the lack of sleep, as well as the antics of her hours spent with Monroe on a hardwood floor, by offering up protests, bruises and stiffness whenever she moved. Monroe had deliciously involved every part of her body, over and over, until she thought she might perish in a state of pure, blissful pleasure. Being manhandled by him had been outrageously satisfying.

But that was in the past.

Today was all about new beginnings that didn't include Monroe or his advertising agency. This was about her, moving on.

And what was the best way to take a break from reality? *Shop.*

She planned to pile on new sensations, spend some of her savings and revel in the freedom of a new mind-set.

Today was the first day of the rest of her...

She sat straight up.

Somebody knocked at the door.

Scrambling out of bed, wincing with each movement of her tender thighs, Kim limped to the door. The visitor had to be a neighbor, or Sam would have let her know. Maybe it was Brenda, who had her own key, and therefore didn't really have to knock, except out of politeness and to prevent Kim from having a heart attack.

Through the peephole she saw Brenda, chic and festive in a dark green suit.

Kim opened the door. "I don't actually want a gossip hour today, Bren, unless you've heard of a decent job opportunity through the grapevine *and* brought breakfast along. I'm starved."

Brenda gave her a pained look, pursed her mouth and stepped aside.

Traitorous Brenda wasn't alone.

Surprised, Kim stepped back with her heart hammering.

"I have a line of gossip I think will interest you," Monroe said in the husky voice that always made her knees weak and made them weak now.

Kim blinked, and looked to Brenda.

"It's news you truly might like," Brenda seconded. "You can kick me later for delivering it this way."

Though she tried hard not to look at Monroe, the strength of his presence drew her like a suicidal moth to an impenetrable flame.

Sixteen

Monroe stood on her doorstep, looking like every woman's idea of a prebreakfast treat.

Dressed to impress in soft gray pants, black leather jacket and another blue shirt that matched his eyes to perfection, he stared back, his expression a mixture of stoicism and worry.

After denying herself the luxury of purposefully giving in to her thoughts about him for the last couple days, Kim's first instinct was to jump his bones. From a distance of three feet, he smelled like heaven.

Her inner alarm system went to full alert. She said firmly, "You understand the meaning of the term *vacation?*"

"I'll explain if given the chance," he said.

"Do I actually have to be here?" Brenda interjected. "I have a meeting in twenty minutes. You two can work this out without me."

"You brought him here," Kim reminded her friend. "This one's on you."

"Wrong," Brenda argued with a shake of her head. "It's quite possibly all about *you,* and I'm merely the middleman *again.*"

"I'm in my pajamas, Bren."

"I didn't notice," Monroe said lightly, lying through his teeth. His eyes continued to roam over every inch of her anatomy, from her head to her bare feet.

She crossed her arms to cover herself, hoping to delay the quick-rising crave factor from reaching her breasts.

"I've been calling you for the past fifteen minutes, to warn you that we were on our way," Brenda said.

Kim glanced over her shoulder as if she could see her cell phone through the wall. "From another cell?"

Brenda nodded. "Mine's at the office. We left in a hurry."

"How was I supposed to know you were calling?"

Brenda threw up her hands. "I don't know. Psychically?"

Brenda was usually connected to her phone at the hip, so for her not to have it meant that Monroe had dragged her here. As what, a buffer or a mediator?

Kim confronted Monroe with narrowed eyes. "You can't come in."

"I'm having a déjà-vu moment in this hallway," he remarked, "when I thought we were beyond that."

His meaning wasn't lost on her. Yes, they were beyond it, if their recent nakedness and exchange of body fluids meant he had a free pass to bother her anytime he wanted to.

Kim felt the flush spread up her neck and into her cheeks. Her sore thighs were heating up, as if she were more than willing to go another round on any surface with the man across from her.

Managing to tear her gaze from him, Kim looked to her friend. "Go on. You wanted to tell me something important enough to bring him along?"

Brenda nodded. "His plans were to sell the agency after getting it up and running and more profitable. That's what his family does. They buy and sell businesses, and they've made a fortune doing so."

Brenda tossed a glance Monroe's way before continuing. He remained mute.

"If he sells the agency, you'll still have the opportunity to be promoted, and he will be gone, so no worries there about pesky rumors or anything else. It looks like all this is in your favor," Brenda said. "I trespassed on your vacation time to tell you this so you won't plan on leaving the agency, or town. You don't have to. Not now. Plus, I wasn't supposed to tell anyone, so the boss decided to come along when I did."

Kim's gaze bounced back to Monroe. "Is this true?"

He nodded. "Yes, it is."

"You never planned on owning the agency for long, or being there long-term?"

"That was the initial plan," he replied. "I was going to tell you about this the other night, but we got distracted."

Distracted? Seriously? That's what he called it?

"This is the news you said you'd postpone until later?" Kim asked.

"Yes," he said.

"You didn't think it was important enough to bring up right away?"

"There were other issues to deal with first."

Admittedly, the news should have made her feel better. She should have jumped for joy. She didn't have to leave the job she loved. She just had to make it work, or prolong the vacation until Monroe sold the place. Instead of feeling relief, though, her stomach churned.

Chaz Monroe would be gone.

The last few days of her life passed before her eyes. Monroe hadn't really taken the VP spot but had simply gone undercover in his own business to help it along on the road to full financial recovery. She didn't have to worry about him in the future, as far as work went, because he wasn't going to be there to give her hot flashes each time they passed in the corridors.

And the part of this situation that had bitten her in the backside—the contractual issue—was ebbing away due to having confronted her mother's ghosts.

She was nothing like her mother. Not even a bit. She had a lot to look forward to.

Monroe's news was good, all right, though it also left them both on uneven ground. If he left the agency and wanted to see her, there'd be no more excuses to stay away from him. In truly shedding her mother's fears, there'd be no need to stay away from him. If he left the agency, she might *want* to see him, often, and would be free to do so, if that one small fear didn't remain about being left behind after giving her love to a man.

"Kim?" Brenda said.

Does that meet with your approval?" he asked. "I'll soon be out of your hair, and you can pursue the promotion any way you'd like to."

Out of her hair?

Her stomach constricted. The words were like a blow.

His comment didn't sound as though it came from a man ready to pursue a relationship with her.

She'd been fantasizing about him for nothing?

Kim closed her eyes. *Fool.*

Maybe he'd already gotten what he wanted from her, with no plans for furthering their connection. A male victory. A conquest.

His expression had become guarded. He hadn't made the slightest move in her direction, or agreed with Brenda's suggestion that she leave them alone to work this out.

Because there was nothing to work out?

Kim staggered back a few inches, struck by the pathetic degree of her own vulnerability. *I haven't learned anything.*

"Fine," she said softly. "Good."

Then she closed the door in Monroe's face.

She leaned against the frame, gathering her wits, bolstering her courage to be the new Kim McKinley she had only three days ago set out to be, while sensing Monroe's presence through the closed door.

"I take it she wasn't happy with the news," he said in the hallway.

"She was in her pajamas," Brenda remarked, as if that fact explained everything.

"Well, I'm done here. I've given up trying to determine what might make her happy," Monroe said. "I went out of my way to reconcile, with every intention of helping her out, but I'm no idiot. She's on her own. Come on. I'll walk back to the office with you. Sorry you came along without a coat. It's cold outside, so you can use mine."

"Hell, Monroe," Brenda said. "You can be downright chivalrous when you want to. If you weren't in love with my best friend, I might want to date you."

"Love?" Monroe said. "I think you must be a true romantic, Brenda."

"Your eyes lingered."

"I'm a man, and she was in her pajamas."

"You can't fool anybody, Monroe, except maybe yourself."

Their voices faded, but the comments rang in Kim's ears like an echo. *Love?* How little Brenda knew about what had happened, and about Monroe's subsequent victory.

He had given up, thrown in the towel. Why did his proclamation send icy chills through her overheated system?

The other night, everything she dared to want had been within her grasp, yet she hadn't reached for it, needing to be strong on her own terms. Now some of those happy endings were no longer viable, and only the stuff of dreams.

She was sick to death of what-ifs and games and hypothetical problem solving. Monroe had given up without a word to her about their night together and how he felt about it, personally. He'd needed to accompany Brenda here; there was a chance he wouldn't have come on his own.

He hadn't agreed with Brenda about loving her, or mentioned anything other than wanting to help her to get the promotion she deserved.

A professional visit, then.

Not personal at all.

Nothing remotely resembling love.

All right. She'd have to make that work, and for now occupy her time elsewhere. Keep busy, and on the right path. Back to shopping. She'd indulge every other whim to its maximum potential. This would make her feel better and blur the emptiness deep inside that Chaz Monroe had temporarily filled.

Pondering how many times in the last seventy-two hours she'd arrived at the same conclusion, Kim headed for her closet to dump the pajamas. There was some serious *forget-him* therapy to do, and no time to waste.

"Who am I kidding?" she whispered, dropping to her bed with her head in her hands. "What we had felt like love to me."

It was insane. Possibly the worst idea she'd ever come up with. Nevertheless, it was what a mature grown-up would do.

Her dress was black, short, sleeveless, with a moderately cut neckline and a perfectly fitted waist. She covered it with a fur-trimmed sweater and added a string of crystal beads at her throat. Her shoes were black Louboutin knockoffs with tall, gold heels that significantly increased her height and lent her an air of confidence that came with overspending.

She sat in the cab, eyeing the big house with determination, and took a few deep breaths before emerging on a cobbled driveway bordered by a knee-high hedge. The mansion was aglow with bright golden light. Windows and doors glittered handsomely, welcomingly. Garlands of evergreen and holly swooped in perfect loops, tied with red velvet bows and dripping with colored glass balls. Rows of cars lined the driveway, as well as part of the street.

What would growing up in a house like this have been like? She hadn't thought to ask Monroe where he lived now, and it no longer mattered, anyway. Ten days had passed since he last stood in her hallway, declaring his decision to give up on helping her further. Ten miserable days. She hadn't been back to the office yet, since her projects had been completed before she'd taken a break. Time and distance away from Monroe had been necessary in order to contemplate her future.

So, here she was, at Monroe's parents' home, about to attend a Christmas party she was supposed to have helped design. It was Christmas Eve, and she was here as she'd promised Monroe she would be, before the rift with him widened. Coming here was a big step, but doable, now that she was getting used to the idea of going it alone.

She would smile at Monroe, and maybe shake hands. They'd share a laugh over how silly they both had been. She'd wish him well with the sale of the agency.

The front door of the house stood wide open, manned by a greeter in a black suit holding a silver tray of sparkling champagne flutes. Kim took a glass as she entered the expansive foyer with its warmly aged wood floors, mirrors and framed oil paintings of lush landscapes.

People of all ages were everywhere. Children raced through the foyer, and back and forth into adjoining rooms, laughing, teasing, having a good time. She envied them. Christmas was magical for children, and this party exemplified that magic to perfection.

If the exterior radiated glow and welcome, the interior of the Monroe house magnified that. Kim knew what the living room would look like before entering, and found it exactly like the rendering she'd seen. Ice sculptures towered over plates of food on center tables. Foam snow whitened windowsills. There was gilt tableware and crystal. Best of all, the largest tree she'd ever seen took up one full corner, at least ten feet of greenery loaded with decorations, twinkling lights and dangling candy canes.

Though she expected this kind of sensory wonderland, the sight stopped her. Her eyes filled, and she choked back a sob. The room was unbearably beautiful. For a holiday-starved woman only now overcoming the past, the magic seemed overwhelming.

Her hands began to tremble. Champagne sloshed from her glass. Would Monroe find her? Welcome her? Save her from all this beauty by snapping her back to reality?

A subtle movement, singled out from the comings and goings of the people around her, caught her eye. A man stood in the opposite doorway, leaning casually against the jamb. He was dressed in a tasteful black sweater and pants and wore a look of casual unconcern. Kim's heart skidded inside her rib cage. She almost spilled more of her drink.

But it wasn't Monroe who raised his glass at her. It wasn't Monroe who smiled, or Monroe's eyes that took her in. Similar in height and weight, and nearly as handsome, with the same dark hair and fair face, whoever this was pushed off the wall and headed in her direction when their gazes connected.

The lights suddenly seemed too bright, too real, too magical. In the middle of the wonderful holiday glitter she'd only began to wrap her mind around, dealing with another man who looked like Monroe, but wasn't, became too much for Kim to handle.

She should not have come. She wasn't ready.

Setting her glass on the table, she turned. Before the man could reach her, she'd reached the foyer, and with just one more look over her shoulder at the luxurious wonderland that was Monroe's life, she exited quickly, and as silently as she had arrived.

"Rory?" Chaz said, finding his brother in the foyer looking perplexed.

"You missed it, bro," Rory said, staring at the door.

"What did I miss?"

"Only the most gorgeous creature on the planet."

Chaz grinned. "There are a lot of beautiful women here tonight."

"Not like this one."

"By the way, how much champagne have you chugged? Have we run out yet?"

"I'm serious," Rory said. "She was a vision."

Chaz looked past his brother. "So, where is this goddess?"

"She left."

"The party just started," Chaz pointed out.

"That's what makes her exit so dramatic."

"Sorry you lost her so soon, bro."

"I didn't imagine her, Chaz."

"Sorry," Chaz repeated, ready to get another drink in order to catch up with Rory, and intending to drown his sorrows.

Rory's laugh was self-deprecating. "Well, I suppose there is another blonde here somewhere with an alluring hazel-eyed gaze and a body like sin. If so, I plan to find her."

Chaz experienced a slight bump in his drinking plan, but couldn't have explained why. "Hazel eyes?" he echoed.

"Yeah. Aren't we all suckers for eyes like that?"

Chaz had to ask, knowing the question to be ridiculous, but unable to beat off the strange feeling in his gut. "Did she wear a red dress?"

Rory shook his head. "A little black number that fit like a glove. But hey, this isn't all about women. Tonight's for celebrating. You've found potential buyers for the agency, I hear, and they'll wait six months to decide to move forward on a sale if you get the place running smoothly."

"Yes. I suppose that's good news."

"Suppose? Chaz, it's your first big deal. Shall we have a toast?"

That bit of odd intuition returned and clung. Chaz couldn't seem to shake it off.

"Did she have hair about to here?" He touched his shoulder. "And long legs?"

"You did see her, then?" Rory replied teasingly. "I didn't imagine her in some Christmas-related state of hopefulness?"

"Was she alone?" Chaz pressed.

"I wouldn't be pining if she'd had a guy by her side."

Chaz barely heard Rory. He was already out the front door and thinking that if it could have been McKinley...

If there was any way it might have been Kim, and she had made the effort to show up here after all...

Did that mean she was interested? Had she hoped to find him?

He didn't see her on the portico or in the yard.

Hell... Wasn't there an old fairy tale about finding a shoe on the steps that would fit only one person on the planet? Which would help to narrow things down a bit for a poor, lovesick guy tired of pretending he didn't give a fig about the woman who owned that shoe, when he cared a whole frigging lot?

When he, Chaz Monroe, cared about Kim McKinley so much, he felt empty without her?

His keys were in his pocket. His car was parked in front of the garage. Waving people out of the way, uttering quick words of greeting and something vague about an emergency, he got in, started the engine and stepped on the gas.

Seventeen

Chaz couldn't get past Sam, no matter how hard he tried.

"No, sir. Not tonight. Strict orders to let no one in, on the threat of ending my life as I know it."

Kim wouldn't answer her phone. At first Chaz thought that she might not have come home, but at last, Sam, sensing a desperate man's weakness and caught up in the holiday spirit, confirmed she was indeed up there.

"Hate to see her alone on a fine night like this," Sam said.

All Chaz thought about was seeing her. She had come to the party, showed up on his parents' doorstep, and he'd somehow missed her. Rotten luck. But she hadn't stayed long enough for him to find her. According to Rory, she'd dashed out the door. So here he was, with his heart thundering way above the norm, determined to see Kim tonight. And as he paced in front of her building, looking up, there seemed only one way to accomplish that…if he didn't get arrested first.

The fire escape.

Floor six. Several windows down ought to be hers, but it was possible he'd gotten turned around. That window virtually beamed with flashes of red and green light emulating the wattage of an alien spaceship trapped in a tunnel.

Could that be her window?

The only thing left now was to scoot over, ledge by ledge, until he reached that one. Briefly, he wondered if Santa had a fear of heights.

He slipped twice, caught himself and began to sweat, despite the chill factor. Glancing down, he swore beneath his breath and continued, placing one foot on the ledge outside where he thought he needed to go.

The light in that window was blinding, so it couldn't be hers. If it was, she'd had a major turnaround, and he was going to need sunglasses.

He got his second foot on the ledge and reached the window unscathed. Maintaining a fairly tight hold on the brick, he craned his neck and peeked around the corner.

The light came from a tree, lit up and glowing. There had to be twenty strings of lights on that tree. Tinsel dangled like silver icicles. Gold and silver baubles gleamed.

But that wasn't all.

Candles lit other surfaces, one of them on the sill not twelve inches away from where he clung. The wonderful scent of cinnamon wafted to him through the closed window.

This can't be hers.

All this?

Yet somehow he knew it was, and that if she had progressed to this degree on the serious issues, where did that leave him?

The truth hit him like a blow to the gut as he looked inside that window. He loved Kim McKinley for this.

He loved her for showing up at the party, and for that room full of lights. He loved her beautiful face, the graceful slope of her shoulders, her bare feet, berry-colored toenails, and her slightly haughty attitude when she got angry. He loved the big eyes that held the power to make a grown man, a confirmed bachelor, climb a fire escape in the middle of winter.

Come to think of it, he didn't need a tally of all the things he loved about her. There were just too many things to list.

His heart ached to be inside of that apartment with her, and to know everything else about her, down to the smallest detail—all the stuff, bad and good, sickness and health.

He put a hand to his head to make sure it was still screwed on tight, sure he'd never felt like this, or considered the *M* word before. Yet he was seeing a future with Kim McKinley that included a ring.

He grinned. Rory was going to have a heart attack.

The only thing now was to convince Kim to take him back, and to remain by his side. *Forever* seemed like a good place to start.

Though elated over this decision, Chaz did not raise a victory fist to the moon, which would have been a dangerous move for a man stuck to a ledge six floors above pavement, wearing entirely unacceptable clothes for the weather. And it was time to go before someone called the cops. He'd bribe Sam to plead on his behalf for Kim to let him in. He would take Sam with him to her front door if necessary. Just one more look in this window, then, he swore to God, he'd go.

He pressed his face close to the pane…

And nearly fell backward when Kim peered back.

Kim stepped away, stifling the urge to scream. There was a man outside her window, and she had to call the cops.

But the face looking in was familiar.

"Monroe?" she said in disbelief.

He grinned. "Just trying this fire escape out to see if it will hold Santa, and wondering why cops never go after him."

The sight of Monroe on the other side of her window made her blink slowly. "What do you want?"

"You left the party without saying hello."

"I made a mistake thinking I could handle the party."

"The mistake was to flee before I could stop you."

Kim shook her head. "Why are you out there?"

"Why did you give Sam orders to shoot me on sight?"

"I wanted to suffer alone."

He took a beat to reply to that. "Suffer?"

"Go away, Chaz."

"I have a better idea. Why don't you let me in?"

"For one thing, I haven't been able to open this window since I moved in."

He stared at her thoughtfully. "How about if I knock on your door?"

"You haven't answered my first question about what you want," Kim said. Her heart was leaping frantically. Monroe was on the fire escape. He had left the party and come here to see her. This had to mean he wanted to see her pretty badly.

When he didn't answer, she repeated the question. "What do you want, Chaz?"

He shrugged without losing his balance and said, "You. I want you. And you just called me Chaz."

And then he was gone, and Kim didn't think she could move from the spot. He hadn't given up. If this was some particularly nasty joke, and the business needed her for something…

Would he do that?

She couldn't have read his expression incorrectly—that look of longing in his eyes that probably looked exactly like her own.

She'd been halfway out of her dress, and yanked it back over her shoulders. She pressed the hair back from her face and looked at the tree and the trimmings that had set her bank account back more than the dress and shoes combined.

What would Chaz do now that he had seen how she embraced Christmas? That the tree he brought her had made her happy, despite the thought of losing him.

The call came. Her hand shook when she told Sam to let Chaz come up. She waited by the door, planning what to say first. Maybe she'd start by asking him to repeat what he said about wanting her, just to be sure he meant it.

She opened the door before he knocked, unable to wait or keep calm. Chaz stood there with his hand raised. He reached for her instead.

He held her tightly for several seconds before pushing her back through the door. The momentum carried them to her kitchen, where he paused long enough to look at her and smile.

"This isn't what you think it is," he said.

"Damn." Heat flooded Kim's face as she smiled back.

"You want it to be what you think it is?" he asked.

"Yes," she answered breathlessly.

He closed his eyes briefly. Then he kissed her, long, deep and thoroughly, with his body tight to hers. After that, he kissed her again and again, as if he had saved up longing and had to get it out.

When he drew back to allow her a breath, he said, "You have a tree."

"Yes."

"You came to the party."

"I did."

"You were looking for me?"

"Yes."

"Because you wanted to be with me? Had to be with me? Could no longer picture a life without me in it?"

"Yes. Yes. And yes."

When Chaz smiled again, his eyes lit up with emotion. She saw relief, joy and the finality of having found something he was sure he'd lost. Genuine feelings. Very personal stuff.

"What do you think of the word *love?*" he asked quietly.

"Highly overrated," she said with a voice that quavered.

"Unless it covers us?" he suggested.

"Does it cover us?"

"I believe so."

"When will you know for sure?"

"As soon as you take me to that bedroom. The one all lit up like the North Pole."

"That's sex, not love."

"To my way of thinking, the two are mutually beneficial. Am I wrong?"

She shook her head. "Isn't there some kind of law against naked bodies under a Christmas tree?"

"Oh, I don't think so. Definitely not. So let's make love, Kim, beside that tree and under the lights. Let's slow down and create a path to the future that will suit us both."

It was the defining moment, and Kim knew it. The future Chaz spoke of had to be built on trust and understanding. She must believe he would make good on those things. In return, she'd have to do the same. She'd have to believe him, and believe in a future with him.

He pressed a kiss on her forehead and another on her cheek. His hands wrapped around her, warm through her dress, as he pulled her to him possessively.

Her world spun off into blissful chaos. Goose bumps trickled down her spine. A rush of delight closed her eyes tight.

Each glorious inch his lips traveled over hers left a trail of fire, the same raging flames she'd felt before, though this time, he also ran a hand down her bare arm, to her wrist. He clasped her fingers in his and held her hand.

Something so simple. So defining and rich. Better than anything. Two promises in one. She wasn't alone. Together, they would get through this, and be better for it.

Kim's shoulders twitched. Her hips ground to his hips as she kissed him back, matching his hunger with hers and forgetting everything else but the desire to have this man inside her, and with her always.

She was going to take this chance. She was going to trust Chaz Monroe because she loved him.

She moaned into his waiting mouth. With a tight hold on her hand, he turned and led her toward the lights.

"The best Christmas ever," he said over his shoulder.

Eighteen

"Kim?" Brenda called out from her cubicle, standing up quickly. "What happened? I haven't seen you for days. I haven't heard from you."

"I didn't get fired," Kim said with a straight face.

"He left a message on your desk about wanting to see you the minute you came in."

"Yes. I have to sign a new contract."

"He convinced you?"

"He's one hell of a negotiator, Bren."

"You'll fill me in, won't you? There's something strange in your expression. Not at all like a woman having lost a battle of wills. It's going to be okay, isn't it? You're going to stay?"

Kim nodded. "I'm staying."

"I knew you could work it out," Brenda said, showing major relief.

Kim took the longest strides her tight skirt allowed, stopping in her cubicle just long enough to open a drawer and retrieve something she had stored there, before heading down the corridor to Chaz's office.

Alice didn't stop her or offer up a protest. Instead, Alice smiled, and nodded her head.

Kim didn't bother to make a pretense of knocking or waiting to be asked to come in. This was her déjà-vu moment, and she intended to experience it to the fullest. Things had changed. She had changed, and felt downright hopeful about the future.

Her heart beat thunderously, tellingly, as she opened the door. The anticipation of seeing Chaz was always like that, and had grown worse over the last few days of spending nearly every waking minute with him. She'd been wearing a smile since his daring use of her fire escape.

He wasn't at his desk. She waited, pulse soaring, body anticipating the onslaught of sensation.

She didn't have to wait long.

All of a sudden he grabbed her by the wrist and swung her around. The door closed. The lock clicked.

His warm mouth covered hers immediately, and her lips opened in a ravenous response. Warm tongues danced. His hands explored possessively, already knowing what they would find. She had lost count of the number of times they had made love lately, but the vast number was a dizzying indication of shared feelings. They had talked, too, and laughed. Together, they had banished the dark and let in the light.

His incredibly steamy kiss was indicative of his new need for her. She wanted to protest when the treacherous bastard peeled his lips from hers way too soon and began to hum a tune that turned out to be a slightly off-key rendition of "Jingle Bells."

Several seconds passed before Kim said, "See? I'm cured. And that's behind us now." Then she began to laugh. All the emotion of the past had just melted away. They had made Christmas wonderful; a time never to forget.

Chaz laughed with her as he began to raise her skirt. She loved that he never had enough of her. That's the way she liked it. She loved everything about him, too. This was love at its most exhilarating.

But she placed her hands on his hands to stop his progress.

"We won't do this kind of thing in my future office," she said.

"Luckily, it's still mine," he countered. "And I have no such rules."

"We already did it this morning."

"Are you tired of me already?"

"What if they still say I slept my way to the top?"

"I'll agree."

Kim cuffed his shoulder then ran her hand along the seam of his perfectly ironed shirt, looking for a way inside. There was something hard in his shirt pocket. A tiny box.

She glanced up at him.

"I'm pretty sure I can't show this to you yet," he said, his grin firmly in place. "Seems too pushy. Too desperate. And after all, as the owner of this agency, I have a reputation to maintain."

Kim waited this out, anticipating a punch line.

"But I have another present for you today, one that you might not have noticed."

She raised an eyebrow, nervous and excited about the contents of the box in his pocket.

"To see the other surprise, you'll have to open that door again," Chaz said. "The one you just waltzed through."

"I'm kind of content right here," she protested.

"Well, then… Have you ever made love on a desk?" he asked teasingly.

Faking a fluster, Kim smoothed her skirt down and turned to open the door. She saw right away what she had missed on her way in, and her heart again began to thump. In black paint, outlined in gold, was her name, printed on the glass. *Kim McKinley, Vice President.*

It took her a full minute to realize this was going to be true.

"I've decided to hang on to the place for a while," Chaz said. "So I'll need someone I can trust in this office while I pursue other interests."

Kim stared at the name on the door. After that, she looked to Alice, who was smiling. She looked to Chaz, also smiling. Heat began to drift over her. Way down deep in her body, in a place reserved for his touch, a drum beat started up.

Chaz Monroe was going to trust her with this promotion in a company he had decided to keep, at least for now, and hopefully long enough for her to prove herself. Waves of happiness washed over her. She squeezed her eyes shut to contain her joy.

"I won't be around much, so rumors about us won't matter," he said.

Kim didn't open her eyes. This Christmas, her wishes had come true. She had the job, and a relationship with the man beside her. That was all she needed. She could do this. Mutual trust was a beautiful thing.

"Will you say yes?" Chaz asked.

Her eyes again met his.

"About the office," he clarified, his voice dropping to a whisper that told her he meant something else entirely.

She nodded.

He smiled.

"You're an asset to the company, Kim Monroe," he said. "Come on, let's take a good look at your future desk, and see if there might be anything else you'll need to put on it."

It wasn't until he pressed her across that desk with his arms around her that Kim dropped her stranglehold on the golden plaque she'd fished from her drawer. She'd soon be able to use the plaque that announced her new position in the agency.

Vice President.

She didn't have to toss it away or wave it in his face.

Only then did she realize what he'd said. The name he had spoken. *Kim Monroe?*

He placed a finger over her lips to stop her from commenting. His eyes shone a merry, vivid blue. "Good. Great. Terrific," he said. "More on that later, and plenty of time for that conversation. Just now, I find that I can't let you waste another good, overheated breath."

The kiss, probably the hundredth like it since she had met Chaz, each of them better than the first, told her all she needed to know. He was not only going to trust her with the business, he was going to trust that she'd stay with him forever, too.

And the desk she had coveted for so long was as fitting a place as any to seal that new bargain.

"Happy New Year, my love," Chaz said in a scintillating whisper before he proceeded to make good on the meaning of the sentiment.

* * * * *

MILLS & BOON®

Want to get more from Mills & Boon?

Here's what's available to you if you join the exclusive **Mills & Boon eBook Club** today:

✦ *Convenience – choose your books each month*
✦ *Exclusive – receive your books a month before anywhere else*
✦ *Flexibility – change your subscription at any time*
✦ *Variety – gain access to eBook-only series*
✦ *Value – subscriptions from just £1.99 a month*

So visit **www.millsandboon.co.uk/esubs** today to be a part of this exclusive eBook Club!

X